MURDER ON TOUR

The Francis Meadowes Mysteries

Book 4

MARK MCCRUM

BLOODHOUND
— BOOKS —

First published in 2024 by Bloodhound Books.

www.bloodhoundbooks.com

Print ISBN: 978-1-916978-52-2

Jonni K
The Ungendered Tour of Europe
Calendar

Monday 05 Feb — Travel day, crew only — London
Tuesday 06 — Travel day — London
Wednesday 07 — ISSTADION — Stockholm
Thursday 08 — Day off — Copenhagen
Friday 09 — FORUM — Copenhagen
Saturday 10 — SPORTHALLE — Hamburg
Sunday 11 — Day off — Hamburg
Monday 12 — SEIDENSTICKER HALLE — Bielefeld
Tuesday 13 — Day off — Berlin
Wednesday 14 — VELODROM — Berlin
Thursday 15 — MITSUBISHI ELECTRIC HALLE
—Dusseldorf
Friday 16 — Day off — Amsterdam/Rotterdam
Saturday 17 — AHOY — Rotterdam
Sunday 18 — FOREST NATIONAL — Brussels
Monday 19 — Day off — Brussels/Frankfurt
Tuesday 20 — FESTHALLE — Frankfurt
Wednesday 21 — ARENA — Nuremberg
Thursday 22 — Day off — Stuttgart
Friday 23 — MARTINSHLEYERHALLE — Stuttgart
Saturday 24 — OLYMPIAHALLE — Munich
Sunday 25 — Travel day — Vienna
Monday 26 — Day off — Vienna
Tuesday 27 — STADTHALLE — Vienna
Wednesday 28 — Travel day — Paris
Thursday 29 — ZENITH — Paris
Friday 01 Mar — Travel day — Home

Official tour lists of the Band and the Crew are at the back of the book.

Thursday 8th February. Copenhagen.

'Ricky!' cried Garry, pushing and pulling at the keyboard tech as he lay comatose in his upper bunk. 'Wake up, mate! We're here. Copenha-a-a-a-gen.' The Gaffer manhandled his friend some more. 'Mate!' he shouted. 'We've crossed the bridge. We're in the land of the Danes. It's ten thirty on a beautiful morning and there's breakfast to be had. Smo-o-o-o-rgasbord. Strong coffee. Beer. Lively young Danish ladies who speak perfect E-e-english. Come on, mate. It's a day *orf!*'

With each push, Garry's satirical enthusiasm waned. OK, so it had been a heavy night and he and his team of lampies had broken the solemn rules of touring in a number of bad and illicit ways, including inviting three crazy party women onto the bus, only to kick them off in some one-horse town just off the E4 at three in the morning. But they had made it to Copenhagen, thanks to the sober driving of the saintly Ray 'Jolly' Rogerson, the man who always kept his eyes to himself.

Normally Ricky was quick to revive, on even the worst morning after – at least enough for a protesting grunt or groan. Today he seemed dead to the world.

With that awful thought, Garry stopped pushing and leant

in to scrutinise, in the orange-curtained gloom of the first-floor sleeping area, his old mucker's face. It was, he realised, motionless – and, he saw, a faint blue.

'Jesus,' he muttered, dashing to pull back a curtain and let in some daylight. 'Christ,' he added, as he got close again and felt, with the backs of his fingers, the awful cold-meat chill of Ricky's cheeks. A debauched charm still lingered – on those snaky thin lips, those dimples, that handsome Roman nose. Terrified, Garry pushed at one of Ricky's closed eyelids, half expecting to be met with a wicked wink from his knowing brown eyes. 'Gotcha, mate! Ha ha ha!' But his lid slid back to reveal the glassy death stare of a fish on ice.

'Oh my God,' Garry said quietly. 'He's OD'd.'

It was a phrase that Garry knew all too well; though he had, in his thirty-five years, which had included many wild nights on some legendary rock and roll tours, never personally encountered the reality.

The others had all upped and left some time before. Unless Jolly was still downstairs, he and Ricky were alone on the bus. Correct that. He was alone on the bus. With a corpse.

'Jolly!' Garry shouted in desperation. Tears pricking his eyes, he clattered blindly down the narrow winding stairs. But Jolly wasn't in his console. The bus was empty. 'Don't shit on the bus' was the crew's mantra, but Garry couldn't help what he was doing now: leaning over the filthy, urine-splashed toilet bowl, vomiting. Vomiting and sobbing. Could it really be true? Ricky was no angel, but he was his mate. They had been touring together for nigh on fifteen years.

Finally wiping his lips on the last scrap of toilet tissue, Garry pulled himself up and stumbled back to Ricky's bunk, to give him one last awful confirmatory poke. He wasn't stiff yet – and how long did that take? – but Ricky was a goner all right.

The bus was parked in a wide street of four-storey, cream-painted buildings, with tall, eight-paned windows in the Danish style. There were bicycles chained up everywhere: a couple with old-fashioned wicker baskets, one with a child seat. Garry tried the internal handle of the coach door, but it wouldn't budge. Why hadn't Jolly checked the bus before he'd locked up, the bloody idiot? Garry reached for his phone, still in the pocket of his baggy combats. But it was, like Ricky, dead. For fuck's sake! All those stupid selfies they'd taken last night – videos too, quite apart from the other dicking around they'd done. Now where was his charger? Upstairs in his case? Or down with the gear in the flight cases at the venue? It was in the flight cases. Oh for double fuck's sake. What was he going to do now?

Outside, a young woman was strolling past. She was a pale Danish beauty, with her brown hair in a crimson headscarf and a tiny baby slung to her midriff.

Garry hammered at the window to attract her attention.

Chapter One

'Teeyahyee hey hey hey hey ya. Ya ya ya hey hey. Ya one one one one hey yeah yeah hey yeah yeah.'

Strange noises emanated from the mouth of the squat roadie with the wild straw-like hair as he stood level with the central microphone. Next to him, a female stage technician rubbed her hands and grinned. Like all the other workers in this huge arena, they were dressed entirely in black: shapeless black T-shirts and jeans, black trainers or boots.

'Jonni's vocal, check, one, two,' the crew member continued as he moved across the stage, giving each microphone a little twist as he sorted it. 'Vanko's vocal, Vanko's vocal, Vanko's vocal…'

'He certainly is,' came a disembodied voice over the speaker system, followed by an amplified cackle. Female, Kiwi. It looked as if it emanated from one of two tiny silhouetted figures standing behind the big control desks a third of the way back down the empty, echoing floor.

'And horny,' the roadie replied, to laughter from his companion.

'Now, now,' came the voice. 'No dissing the overlords. They'll be here in a minute.'

Halfway up the low-banked ring of seats, Francis Meadowes was quietly enjoying himself, eavesdropping on this strange new world in which he had so suddenly found himself. Just two days ago he had been sitting quietly at home in London, his laptop and coffee thermos in front of him, writing the latest in his Braithwaite series of crime novels. Then his mobile had rung and his adventure had begun.

A female voice with a quivering upspeak inflection had asked him if she was speaking to Francis Meadowes. On being informed that she was, she told him – rather rudely, really, considering it was she who had phoned him – to wait. After a minute her boss came on: his accent rolling, deep, with the definite flat *tweng* of South Africa.

Within an hour Francis was studying the face that came with the voice. Here was a man who, with his still-thick, sporadically greying blond hair and strong tan, had clearly been a good-looking youth, but was now the wrong side of fifty. The tiny crimson veins in his milky blue eyes betrayed his age, as did the heavy bags beneath them and the downward set of the lines around his mouth. Though from the ripple of muscle underneath his tightly buttoned shirt it was clear that he kept himself fit. His name was Nick Fourie, and he was a rock and roll manager.

'You've probably seen this,' he said, shoving across a *Mail on Sunday* with a front-page picture of Jonni K toppling off the stage in Hamburg. The lucky photographer must have been standing right below the star, as they had caught him in mid-air, legs akimbo, an expression of bewilderment on his famous features. Jonni had been pushed, the report explained, by a stranger who had been carrying a knife. The identity of this assailant was either unknown or unreported. Nor was it clear why he'd failed to use his weapon. Hefty security guards had scooped up the man immediately, as other pictures attested, and he had been subsequently arrested by German police.

Even though Jonni K was one of the most celebrated British pop stars of the moment, Francis knew little about him. He had stopped in a Costa en route to his meeting with Nick to educate himself over a flat white. A flickaround on his mobile had told him that Jonni was twenty-eight, over two decades younger than Francis. He had been one of the stars who had emerged from *The X Factor* after winning a place in the put-together band Facing Both Ways, which had come second in the competition. After two years, FBW had disbanded and Jonni had gone solo. He was a suitably contemporary icon: handsome, of course; lean and muscled, tick; tattooed, yes, though not heavily; and keen on cross-dressing, both on- and offstage. There were shots online of his all too masculine body in a turquoise camisole and tutu; others of him smiling broadly at an awards ceremony in a full-length crimson evening dress, complete with dangly pearl earrings and challenging stilettos. Not that he was transgender, or even transvestite; he was 'experimenting with established ideas of gender and fluidity', his website stated.

AZ Music occupied two floors of a warehouse in a mews just north of Oxford Street. Most of the company's young and mainly female personnel were working at a long, shared table at the centre of the large open-plan space. Others had desks against brick-faced walls. Nick, the ancient stag of the outfit, had a glass box to himself up steps at the back.

'We understand that you're the guy,' he continued now.

'The guy?' echoed Francis.

'Who can get to the bottom of these things.'

'I'm flattered. Where did you hear that?'

Even as Francis asked, he knew. The fame he had enjoyed after the Villa Giulia case (the 'mixed-race crime-writer sleuth', etc.), which he had then happily forgotten, had finally returned to haunt him. He had worried at the time that he risked becoming a cut-price Sherlock Holmes for the new age of fashionable diversity, but the weeks and months and then years had passed, and no one had bothered either him or his agent. He had lapsed back into the quiet obscurity of the minor author.

Nick gestured towards the buzzing beehive beyond the glass wall.

'My team know what they're doing,' he replied. He looked down at a single sheet of A4 in front of him, on which Francis could see his name. 'Crime writer and occasional detective,' Nick read out loud. 'Solved the sudden deaths of a critic and a journalist at the Mold-on-Wold literary festival, and murders at a creative writing course in Tuscany. He's rumoured to have helped the FBI with the puzzling deaths of American nationals on a cruise ship off West Africa.'

Francis laughed. 'Sounds like you already have a competent detective.'

Nick leant forward, his broad shoulders hunching over his empty desk. 'In confidence, Francis, the problem is that it's not just this incident.'

'I see,' said Francis. He didn't yet, obviously.

'I'm trusting that even if you turn me down, you won't go running to the papers with what I'm about to tell you.'

'I've always been discreet.'

Nick looked back at his briefing notes. 'So I'm informed. Unfortunately, the world I work in is full of crooks and shysters, so I've had to learn to be careful.'

'There are crooks and shysters in all worlds.'

'Probably more in mine than yours.'

'I wouldn't be so sure about that.' Francis chuckled, remembering a literary prize selection panel he had recently been on.

'OK,' Nick went on. 'I'm going to take a leap of faith and trust you. As I said, this is not the only incident. Strictly between ourselves, one of the crew was found dead on one of our sleeper buses when it arrived in Copenhagen four days ago. The second gig on our tour.'

'From natural causes?' Francis asked.

'He OD'd. They'd had a long journey down from Stockholm, and though we forbid class A drugs on the tour buses, we can't police everything. Rock and roll crews are not known for their abstemiousness.'

'No.'

'Although they're better than they used to be, believe you me.' Nick sat back in his chair, fingers threaded behind his neck. 'I don't know how much you've followed Jonni's career.'

'I'm ashamed to say, hardly at all. I was aware that he was a big star, but that's about it.'

Nick smiled. 'You're not a fifteen-year-old girl. But here's the thing. Jonni used to be something of a party animal. Alcohol, drugs, women, obviously – he liked a good time.'

'Rock and roll.'

'Exactly. Anyway, my partner, Adam, has been gently working on him for a while. Jonni's bad habits had been getting out of hand, to put it mildly. On his last tour of the US we had to cancel three stadium shows because he was too wasted to perform. It's not good for business.'

'No.'

'Eighty thousand refunds at an average of two hundred dollars apiece is a lot of money to burn.'

Francis did the sum in his head. 'Sixteen million.'

Nick nodded approvingly. 'That's hardly cash we can afford to lose, especially in these days of downloads, when almost all our profits are in touring and merchandising. Now Adam, fortunately, is a persuasive guy. He's also had his own drugs hell, but I shan't bore you with that. Suffice it to say, the man is made of stern stuff. He cleaned himself up and crawled back to the top. He hasn't touched so much as a dry sherry for almost thirty years.'

'Don't tell me. Now he's got Jonni clean as well.'

'Exactly. He's happier, we're happier, it's all good.'

'So how does this relate to your dead roadie?' Francis asked.

'We don't call them roadies these days, but good question. Ricky had also got clean at the same time as Jonni. This was important, as Ricky was a mate of Jonni's…'

'Even though he was a …what do I call him?'

'Crew member will do. It's quite an ecosystem, the rock and roll tour entourage,' Nick went on. 'Although by and large the crew and band don't mix much, you do get strange friendships springing up. Especially when illicit substances come into the picture.'

'You're saying…'

'He and Jonni were good mates who liked to party, put it that way. They hung out together quite a lot on tour. A bit too much for our liking, frankly. And on off-tour holidays too. But one thing you learn as a manager is that you can only tell your star what to do to a certain degree. Otherwise you risk everything. Especially with an erratic fellow like Jonni.'

'I see.'

'So we were very happy when Ricky agreed to join Jonni in getting clean. Adam took on the job of mentoring them. Got them both into rehab, saw them through a painful detox, and then did his best to keep them on the straight and narrow afterwards.'

'NA meetings and suchlike?'

'You know all about that? Good. For Adam, it's like a mission anyway. In his ideal world, everyone would be clean. I think he sometimes forgets the fun he had when he wasn't.'

'So how did Ricky manage to OD?' Francis asked.

'This is what we don't know. But smack – heroin, which

was one of his favoured substances, can be lethal when people have cold-turkeyed and then return to their usual dose.' The clipped, almost medical way Nick spoke suggested to Francis that he wasn't much of a drug taker himself. 'To be honest,' he went on, 'Ricky was always a bit of a liability, though he was a perfectly competent worker. We'd have got rid of him ages ago if it hadn't been for Jonni.'

'And how did Jonni take his death?'

'He was very shocked. Upset, too, obviously. We were all set to cancel the Copenhagen gig, which was scheduled for the night after Ricky's overdose, but then Jonni rallied and decided he wanted to perform. He wanted to do it *for* Ricky.'

'Which must have been a relief to you?'

'Quite apart from the financial aspect, cancelled gigs are never good news. There are always questions. Having a bad cold doesn't quite cut it with the disappointed fans, unless you're Morrissey, of course…'

Francis joined in politely with the manager's knowing chuckle, though he had no idea about the mononymous singer-songwriter's performance record. He hesitated for a moment before asking his next question. 'This Ricky thing, the over-dose. May I ask: did either of you feel that there was there anything suspicious about it?'

Nick met his gaze. 'As in?'

'Foul play.'

'We didn't. Not at the time. Why would there be? Ricky was a popular guy.'

'And no question of suicide?'

'That didn't seem likely. There was no note, no obvious reason. Sadly, it seemed more of a tragic accident.'

'And now?' Francis asked.

Nick shrugged and met his eye. 'That's the question.'

'There's been a post-mortem, presumably?'

'Yes, the Danish authorities require that, even though the

death might have taken place on Swedish soil. The results came back swiftly, and everything was as you would have suspected. It seems Ricky basically went on a bender, though what his lampy pals thought they were up to, I have no idea.'

'Lampy … pals?'

'Lighting crew. They all travel on the same bus. It's generally thought to be the wildest of the three buses. Ricky was actually a keyboard tech, but for some reason he always went with them. I'm afraid that night Ricky had alcohol, cocaine, Ecstasy and then, fatally, heroin.'

'So the authorities were satisfied?'

'There's an ongoing inquest, to which we're contributing.'

'But they let you go?'

'Luckily there was a scheduled day off in Copenhagen before the gig, so the police were able to interview all the relevant crew members then. We've committed to allowing them to call anyone back at any time if they want to. They were pretty understanding, from what Adam told me.'

Jonni's Hamburg incident had happened, Nick explained, on the night after the Copenhagen gig, the Saturday. Nick and Adam had then taken the decision to cancel the next concert, scheduled for that night, Monday, in Bielefeld. They'd had to, because the Hamburg police wouldn't let them go any earlier. So the band and crew were now going straight to Berlin, where another planned day off would hopefully give Jonni enough time to recover his mojo before his appearance at the Velodrom on Wednesday.

Which brought Nick to the point. Would Francis consider going out there and joining the entourage as an observer? If so, they would come up with a cover story, pretend that he was a journalist writing a feature for a magazine or something. As he'd done in the past, if Nick's research was correct. He would be given access to talk to anyone he wanted to.

'How serious are your suspicions?'

Nick shrugged. 'Our star act's best mate overdoses, and then he is pushed off the stage by a random stranger who is carrying a knife but refuses to tell the police why. As a tour, we are moving through jurisdictions on a daily basis. The German police are even more disconnected than we are, with largely autonomous regional forces. I'd just like to have someone of your calibre on site to try and find out if these incidents really are unconnected, or whether something more sinister is going on. Also, to be honest, to keep an eye out. We can't afford any more hiccoughs.'

'Hiccoughs,' Francis repeated with a smile.

'Perhaps that's not quite the word. Obviously we've tightened security considerably, but I'd be lying if I didn't say that everyone's extremely nervous. What our usual security guys thought they were doing in Hamburg, I have no idea, but letting a lunatic onstage with a knife is not part of their job description.'

There was a long pause. Nick looked down at his desk, then up again to meet Francis's eye. Francis got the sense that he was a seasoned, tough negotiator, used to getting his own way.

'So are you interested?' Nick asked.

Though Francis had come to the interview on a curiosity-only basis, he now found himself asking about money. Nick's answer changed his mind. Even in these depleted times, rock and roll clearly operated on a different scale from scribbling. It was now 12th February. The tour was scheduled to end on the 29th in Paris, having visited Germany, the Netherlands, Belgium and Austria en route. For seventeen days of what sounded like an intriguing assignment, Francis was being offered more money than he was for an entire George Braithwaite novel. There would be a bonus if he found out anything concrete. It was a no-brainer. Now here he was in Berlin, as the roadies – sorry, crew – finished setting up, then the band strode on and took their places for the sound check.

A short-arsed drummer with a mane of ginger curls was hammering away aggressively on the drums. A tall, lean guitarist joined in with some wild strumming. Another guitarist, female, skin just a little darker than Francis's, with a huge Afro and a dazzling smile, introduced a powerful bass line. A pair of backing singers, one white and blonde and one Black, with braided hair, added some tentative crooning. On the step above, the straw-haired technician was being embraced by a hunched, thoughtful-looking, bearded fellow in a retro blue denim suit, who then took his place at the keyboards. Around them, the white beams of spotlights roved in the hazy semi-darkness.

The excitement was mounting – even before the star had appeared. As Francis waited to see Jonni in the flesh for the first time, his mobile rang. It was Charmaine, PA to Nick's co-manager Adam, summoning him to the backstage canteen.

Chapter Two

'Please,' Adam said, 'do have whatever you want. I used to love a tipple in the old days. My only problem was, I couldn't stop.'

Jonni's other manager was something of a contrast to the tense, thin-lipped Nick: a big, roly-poly fellow, with chubby cheeks and large, sensitive brown eyes set off by a welcoming half-moon smile. His bushy pepper-and-salt eyebrows and the tiny V of beard at the bottom of his round chin contrasted with his gleamingly shaven head.

It was only after Francis had ordered an Asahi beer from the dark-haired waitress in the crimson crop top and it had arrived, glistening, on a tray with Adam's Perrier and Charmaine's freshly squeezed orange juice that he realised he had made his first mistake. Even though Adam had offered the alcohol, a flicker of disapproval – or even disappointment – crossed his face. In one foolish, greedy, unprofessional move Francis had ruled himself out of the teetotal gang, which was, round here, the inner circle.

Nonetheless, Adam clinked glasses with him. 'Welcome,' he said. 'We're glad to have you on board, Francis.'

'Thank you. I'm glad to be here.'

In the sudden, uncalled-for awkwardness, Francis was struggling to get beyond banalities. He cast his eye quickly around the rest of the catering area, which was, with its smart, stainless-steel-topped tables, chalkboard menu and waitress service, more like a pop-up restaurant than any works canteen Francis had ever been to. Two hours before the start of the gig – at 9 p.m. – it was busy with crew: presumably in a hungry lull between setting up and running the show. Adam, in his blue and yellow diamond-patterned Madiba shirt and baggy cream chinos, was just one of the guys: yet, quite obviously, from the invisible force field that hovered around his table, he was not. He wore two watches, Francis noticed with interest: a classic gold one on his left wrist, an up-to-the-minute white digi device on his right.

'Nick has filled you in on the situation, I believe.'

'Up to a point. I know about what happened on Saturday night in Hamburg … and also, er, Ricky.'

Adam winced.

Surely it hadn't been another misstep to mention the roadie? He was one of the reasons Francis was here.

But: 'Please be reassured,' the manager replied, 'we're here to help. Anything you need to know, just ask Charmaine or myself. You have the triple A lanyard – Access All Areas – which is given to very few. It even gets you into Jonni's dressing room – if Security will let you.' As he fingered his own lanyard, which had *AAA* prominently displayed beneath the words *Jonni K, The Ungendered Tour*, he chuckled and his sidekick tittered. 'And everybody,' he concluded, 'apart from myself, Jonni and Charmaine here, thinks you're writing a piece for *GQ*.'

'So I understand.'

Why they wanted to maintain this fiction was beyond Francis, but presumably they knew the people they were dealing with. Perhaps the very mention of the word 'detective' would have made everyone in the entourage clam up. Though in the real-life enquiries he had been involved with, Francis had never found that the role, even if unacknowledged, had stopped people talking, especially if there was a puzzling and upsetting incident to be solved, involving an individual that people cared about, as there was here. The irony was that in his previous cases he'd been unwanted and unacknowledged: now, for the first time in his life, he'd been called in as a professional.

He gave Charmaine a nervous smile. She, at least, was someone he liked and was ready to trust. She had been there to meet him when he'd arrived from the airport at the hotel where the band were staying, the luxurious Kaiser Grand in Charlottenstrasse, as cute a rep for this new world as you could have imagined in her high boots, skintight blue jeans and brown sheepskin jacket, complete with a pair of electric-blue Chanel specs that set off her dark skin perfectly, but which Francis suspected were unnecessary. She had been full of easy chat and laughter in the car that had whisked them to the Velodrom, and had left him to his own devices in the auditorium most gracefully, handing over her mobile number and promising a meeting with his new employer just as soon as he'd finished with Jonni.

'Jonni always needs a bit of cosseting before a gig,' she'd said, rolling her eyes like the teenager she probably only just wasn't. 'Especially at the moment.'

'We'll introduce you to Jonni after the gig, if that's OK with you,' Adam said now.

'Whatever works for you.'

'He'll be in a suitably relaxed mood then. After the Hamburg incident, as you can imagine…' He tailed off. The pretty waitress was upon them again. She had a left nostril piercing and another silver ring, complete with what looked like a tiny sapphire, in her exposed belly button.

'Now what can we get you to eat?' Adam asked. 'It's quite a

long time between now and our midnight feast back at the hotel. Flo already knows what I'm having, don't you, Flo?'

'The chicken Kiev, Adam?'

'The chicken Kiev. Or perhaps that should be Kyiv. And I might risk a sticky toffee pudding afterwards. Francis?'

Things loosened up a little over the meal. They didn't talk about Jonni, or Hamburg, or Ricky, or Copenhagen, or any fears about the future of the tour. Everything of importance seemed to be off the conversational menu. Instead, Adam asked Francis about his writing and his life in London, and confessed that he had once harboured a desire to be a writer himself.

'But I got to the age of twenty-five and I realised I had a couple of problems with that ambition. One, I couldn't write, and two, I had nothing to write about. Bit of a double whammy.'

Adam gurgled with self-deprecating laughter and Francis joined in, starting at last to relax. 'I'm sure that's not true,' he said, slipping easily into flattery.

'It was then. These days, maybe, I'd have more of a story to tell.'

'Of course you have, Adam,' Charmaine said.

Though Adam was a big bald bruiser of a man, there was something curiously child-like about him. You could imagine him in a romper suit, running amok in an oversized nursery. In that scenario, Charmaine might well have been his nanny.

On their way out, Adam introduced Francis to the tour manager, Bernie, who was sitting alone at a table, eating with one hand, holding his mobile in the other, his laptop open in front of him. He was lean as a whippet, with a full head of hair cropped short in a no. 4.

'Gotta go now,' he said, ending his call as Adam stood before him, swaying slightly on his pale blue Campers.

'Hope we're not interrupting, Bern. This is Francis, the journalist I told you about.'

'From *GQ*,' Bernie replied, giving Francis a stagey wink.

'That's the one.'

Bernie jumped to his feet and held out a hand, as well-mannered as an equerry.

'Bernie's the man,' Adam said. 'If you need anything, anything at all, just ask Bern, and he'll get it for you.'

'Wine, women, sheep, I'm not fussy.' His accent was raw South London.

Charmaine was rolling her eyes. 'Bern,' she cooed, registering appropriate Gen Z disapproval. 'He's a bit unreconstructed,' she muttered to Francis.

'Just make sure never to annoy him,' said Adam.

'No,' Bern agreed. 'Don't annoy me. That could be fatal.'

'Tell you what,' said Adam. 'I see the band are down. I might leave you in Bern's capable hands for a quick introduction, Francis. And after that, roam where you will. We'll see you after the gig. Backstage, in Jonni's room probably. Charmaine.'

And with that summons to his lovely daemon, he was gone.

'When Adam says probably, he means definitely,' Bernie explained. 'He also means keep well clear of backstage till after the show.'

'I gathered that,' said Francis.

'You'll soon pick it up. If you ask me nicely, I'll show you a little place you can watch the gig from that won't upset anyone. And with that lanyard round your neck, you can swing out into the arena anytime. You'll notice the Hell's Angels on the green baize door will give you suitable respect. I think there's only about five of us with the triple A pass. OK, so just let me gulp down this chilli and then I can familiarise you with our lovely artistes.'

Despite being quite a bit older than all of them, Francis felt as gauche as a teenager as he met the band, who were eating at a table over on the other side of the canteen. It felt like the first day at a new school, a closed and established community where it was essential to get on with everyone to survive. But perhaps because Bern was the introducer, they all seemed as easy as anything.

'Sit down, mate, make yourself at home,' said Vanko, the lead guitarist, whose face was as lean as his muscled torso.

Bern shimmied off, and Francis took in the rest of the group, even as they fired questions at him: Simon, hipster-bearded, tousle-haired keyboard player and composer, as Francis's research had told him, of many of Jonni's most famous hits; Topaz, she of the amazing smile, the bass guitarist, now dressed for the stage in a shiny black leather catsuit; Suzi and Thelma, blonde and Black backing singers; Scally, the short-arsed Mancunian ginge who was the drummer.

They all, clearly, had the upcoming gig on their minds. They ate quickly then peeled off one by one. Finally, Francis was left alone with Vanko.

'Another Nespresso, mate? I'm having one.'

'I'm fine, honestly. I had one when I had supper with Adam.'

'The big man. So, why *have* they hired you? Are you really a feature writer?'

'Of course.'

Vanko shrugged. 'It's just that they normally do their level best to keep journos away from us. The only exception to that rule is when Jonni suddenly adopts a tame one, which happens from time to time. They're usually the most terrible creeps, as far up the royal arse as it's possible to go. Which is quite a long way, believe me. They hang around for a couple of days until he gets bored with them, and then they get their marching orders.'

Francis laughed. 'Let's hope that doesn't happen to me.'

'It won't if you're Nick's idea. Or Adam's, maybe?'

'Your guess is as good as mine. I was recruited by Nick in London.'

Vanko nodded. His head was almost oblong, like an Easter Island statue or one of those wood or soapstone carvings you find in African markets. Come to think of it, though Vanko's skin was bone white, his features would have worked well with a darker epidermis; perhaps this was part of his appeal.

'It's been a bit of an odd tour, to be honest,' he went on. 'The security lapse two nights ago was weird. That so shouldn't have happened. I'm amazed Adam didn't sack Mitch and Omar on the spot.'

'Mitch and Omar being the security detail?'

'Yeah. Useless pair, if you ask me. I mean, where the fuck were they? That lunatic had a knife. He could have done for any of us.'

'Though it was Jonni he went for.'

'And why did he carry a blade if he wasn't intending to use it?'

'Nick seemed to think he was just some random nutter.'

'Plenty of those around a tour like this,' Vanko agreed. 'Females too. You should see some of the shit I have to put up with.'

'Such as?'

'Websites created by crazies. There's one who's got this whole wedding fantasy about me. I mean, seriously. She's mocked up photos, menus, the lot. I'll show you some time. It would be funny … if it wasn't.' He sat in silence for a few long seconds.

Watching him, Francis decided to go for broke. 'That's not been the only incident on this tour, has it?'

Vanko's eyes widened. 'By which you mean?'

'Copenhagen.' Francis was enjoying Vanko's expression.

'Gobsmacked' might have been the *mot juste*. 'Ricky on the lampies' bus…'

'So they told you about that, did they? Wow. They must like you. Is that going to be in your article?' Then: 'How much *do* you know?'

'That Ricky was a good friend of Jonni's. Even though he was just a crew member.'

'Not just any old crew member, mate. Keyboard tech. Important guy.'

'I also know that Jonni almost didn't go onstage in Copenhagen,' Francis continued. 'And then he did.'

'He did,' Vanko agreed. 'Almost as a two fingers up to fate – or whoever it was that did away with Ricky. Man, was he on fire that night! You should have seen it. Whatever people say about Jonni, that he's too corny or mainstream or whatever, when he pulls it out of the bag you just have to stand back and gasp.'

'I wish I'd been there,' said Francis.

'Funny, isn't it?' Vanko went on. 'If we were a small band in a van with a couple of roadies, we'd probably not have been allowed to perform in Copenhagen, let alone roll on to another country the next day, before the post-mortem was even concluded. But there you go. Arena tour. There's a lot at stake.' He rubbed his forefinger suggestively against his thumb.

'Money changing hands, you think?'

'I'm sure the Danish police are incorruptible.' Vanko's widened eyes didn't match his words.

'Who was interviewed?' Francis asked.

'Everyone, more or less. It was a blizzard of Nordic efficiency. Like a speed-dating session. With three of them on the go. In a string of offices backstage at the Forum.'

'So d'you really think someone might have done away with Ricky?' Francis asked. 'Or was it actually an overdose?'

'Who knows, mate? It just seemed a bit odd, to all of us,

that a guy like Ricky, who's been filling his face with every illicit substance known to man for years should suddenly get it so disastrously wrong.'

'Nick told me that happens sometimes. To people who've been clean and then go back to their usual dose. It's too much for them.'

'Dose, schmose. What would Nick know? He likes a nice glass of wine in a *ristoront* from time to time, but that's about it.' Vanko pronounced the word in harsh mockery of the manager's South African accent. 'I'd be more interested in what Adam thinks.'

'And what does Adam think?'

'Fuck knows. He's not exactly sharing. Certainly not with the likes of me.'

'Have you spoken to Jonni about it?'

'Hardly. Jonni's rather stepped back into the world of Jonni at the moment. As he does sometimes. There's not much I can do about that. Have to wait for my moment.' Vanko paused. Francis said nothing, as was his habit in situations like this. Usually, when people were in confessional mode, it was just a matter of time. Time, and perhaps the odd encouraging phrase. It was a constructive sympathy that Francis had learned years ago, doing interviews for magazines, and had developed since, so that sometimes even he was amazed by what he could pull out of people.

'It's funny with Jonni,' Vanko went on. 'You know, there are times when he can seem like your best mate, and then suddenly, if it suits him, he switches off. Looks through you, almost as if he doesn't know you.'

For a moment, Francis thought he was going to get more, then it was as if Vanko remembered himself, where he was, who he was with, despite his earlier openness. 'He's quite a guy,' he concluded with a tight smile. He shifted in his chair. 'I'd better go. Got a gig to get ready for.' He held up his hand in a high five. 'D'you know what, mate? Ricky liked his substances, and he had this wild child rep, but he was actually quite a careful guy. People who OD are a type. They're reckless. If Jonni had done it, in the days before he got clean, I would have believed it. He's got demons. Pretty big ones, although maybe a bit more tamed these days. But Ricky. He was like *No, Jonni, time to come down.* I've seen it. That's why it seemed odd to me. That he would have screwed up so mightily.'

Chapter Three

Out the front, excitement was mounting. In the time that Francis had been backstage having his supper and chatting to Adam and Vanko, the doors had been opened and the Velodrom had filled with fans. On the flat floor near the stage, they were standing pushed together in tight rows. Further back, things were looser, but it was still packed. In the huge circle of seats that surrounded the central arena, most were now taken. Francis stood at the top of an aisle, being bumped into by ebullient passers-by. He had never, he reckoned, seen so many teenage girls in one place: chattering, striking poses, laughing extravagantly, showing off, screaming.

The feverish atmosphere was encouraged by loud thumping music (not Jonni's, Francis didn't think) and dramatic announcements over the PA.

'Jonni K ... will be with you ... in ten minutes!'

'Jonni K ... and his band ... will be with you ... in eight minutes!'

'Jonni K ... is *almost ready* to join you. Tonight ... please let us inform you ... he is in a *very* upbeat mood.'

'Jonni K … cannot wait … to entertain you. He will now be with you in five. Minutes, that is.'

'Jonni K … is now … *very nearly* … ready to perform.'

Francis was trying to work out whose voice this was, and where it came from. Initially – idiotically, really – he thought it might be Bernie's, but then, looking at the bank of knobs and switches and slides and dials and monitors at the control station set one third back through the crowd, he realised that it must be coming from there. One of the two crew members standing, indeed gently boogieing, behind the desks, was either making the announcements or, more likely, given the smooth actorish-ness of the voice, pressing a button to activate them. Each was greeted with a screaming cheer from the floor, as the audience worked themselves up into a frenzy.

The lights started to dim. Spotlight beams roamed round the arena, criss-crossing the artificially smoky haze above the darkened heads of the crowd. Then, finally, the band were there, running onto the stage, up to their stations, grabbing their instruments. As they did so, the lights came up on the backdrop, a giant head portrait of the star, a typically quizzical expression on his handsome features, godlike yellow sunbeams radiating behind him.

Vanko's face was a mask of concentration as he strummed an opening guitar chord. Behind him, picking up the rhythm with a deeper sound, Topaz shimmied and smiled. Up at his keyboard, beardy Simon was nodding along mellowly, magiste-rially almost, as his notes tinkled into the mix. Suzi and Thelma boogied and cooed to one side. At the back, central, Scally's sticks flew as he thumped out the beat.

Bang! There was a brilliant yellow flash which turned into a glorious fifteen-second fountain of golden sparks. And there was Jonni, strolling smoothly through the smoke, radio mic in hand. How had he done it? Had he been hiding, bent double, behind a speaker case? Was there a trapdoor?

He was wearing a short black dress, suspenders, fishnet stockings, boots, a choker round his neck, long black gloves and a bowler hat with a fluorescent purple band. Of course! Homage to Berlin! He was Liza Minelli in *Cabaret*. He even had the heavy mascara. A laugh of surprise rippled through the arena, but it was in no way mocking. Jonni's stage presence wouldn't have allowed that. The raw energy of his personality was tangible.

The musicians paused. For a moment it looked as if Jonni was going to greet the crowd. But then his clear voice rang out:

I've been hiding ... in the wild...

As the words of the famous song began, the arena erupted.

Sometimes bitter, sometimes mild...
But I've missed you,
Hey, so much.
How's about it?
Let's go Dutch.

Gibberish, really, Francis thought, but with the music even the barely coherent lyrics succeeded in moving him, as well as all these thousands of people. Strange sensation, watching the crowd go crazy in delighted recognition of the tune that even Francis had heard – endlessly, in fact, last summer, pumping out from the open windows of white vans or on Bluetooth speakers in London parks.

Now he had tears in his eyes. Why? He hadn't even met Jonni yet. But still. There was something about the raw power of the man, as he strode along the front of the stage, conducting the crowd's response with his open hands.

'Hello, Berlin!' he shouted, and the returning cheers rang up to the roof. *'Guten Tag!'*

Another roar of appreciative laughter and then, with a signal to his band, he was straight into the second song, 'The Love That Tells Me', which even Francis knew was the greatest hit of the Tainted Idols, the quasi New Romantic Scottish band that had been so huge in the late 1980s. It had been a favourite of Kate, his long-dead wife, whom he hadn't touched outside of dreams in over twenty years. How she would have loved this! She would have been out there, hands waving, shouting, stirring it up, on his shoulders, her legs clenched tightly round his ears. After all this time, all those others, he still missed her. Idiot. He knew by now that his longing was pure sentimentality. If she had lived, God knows what might have happened. Perhaps, like so many of his friends, they wouldn't have stayed the course. Parted in acrimony over money or sex or family or housework or all the other things that drove once loved-up people apart.

Pull yourself together, he told himself. You've got a job to do. He clenched his jaw, wiped his glistening eyes with the pad of his little finger, then turned and walked slowly down the aisle towards the floor, his triple A pass gleaming.

Back in Catering during the fifth song of the set ('Sometimes the Moon'), Francis found Bern, still hunched over his laptop.

The tour manager looked up, saw him, and then, rather than returning to what he was doing, beckoned him over. 'All right, mate? Not lost, I hope?'

'I've just been out the front. With the fans. Watching the show.'

'You don't want to be down there with the riff-raff,

gorgeous though some of them are.' The tour manager winked. 'Come on, mate, I'll show you where you do want to be. Hang on a mo.' He called over to the waitress in the crimson crop top, who was working her way round the now empty tables with a J-cloth and a bottle of blue cleaning spray.

'Flo, darling, could you keep an eye on my laptop for five mins?'

After a few shiny-floored backstage corridors, Bern led Francis up steps, past a couple of hefty security guards, and round to a vantage point on the edge of the stage. From here you could see across to the band, with Jonni leading the action out front, the vast crowd beyond that, arms up, waving like so many pale grasses in a windy twilight.

'Magical, innit?' said Bern. 'The VIPs are the other side.' He gestured across the stage to where Adam was standing – or, rather, gently swaying – with little Charmaine right beside him. Next to them was a tallish blonde with dark lipstick wearing a patchwork jacket and a familiar, stocky-looking guy in a tattered denim frock coat.

'Taylor Swift,' Bern shouted into Francis's ear. 'And the legendary Zak, of course. There'll be a party after, so you might get to meet them. See ya.'

And with that, like the ageing sprite he was, he was gone, dancing away down the ledge to the steps beyond. Taylor Swift … and Zak, lead singer of the Tainted Idols, who amazingly – and amusingly – was slightly shorter than Swift in real life. Shorter, but just as blond, with that trademark mane of spikily youthful hair around those baggy, lined, unredeemably jowly features. Old he might well be, but you could still sense the raw power of the man, emanating from him like radioactivity. Even from here Francis could see those famous turquoise eyes, shining in the light reflected from the stage. (*Blue-green, blue-green, cruel as the bleak and empty sea*, Carmela had sung back in the day.) Why on earth was Zak, of all people, watching Jonni work? Did he hope to learn something? Or was it just a homage? To youth. To success. To Jonni's However Many Minutes He Had Left of Huge Fame. At least that explained why the star had sung 'The Love That Tells Me'. Perhaps the homage was flowing both ways.

When the gig ended, and Jonni had done two wild encores, and the band had finally scarpered in an excited gaggle down their own set of steps to backstage, Francis remained where he was. Now what? Should he follow Adam and the celebrities or head back to Catering in the hope of finding Bern?

'Francis!'

It was Charmaine, bless her.

'Enjoy that?'

'I did. Very much. He's quite a performer, isn't he?'

'That's what he does,' she replied. Her eyes were shining. 'Pretty awesome, isn't it? Especially when it goes as well as that. They just love Jonni in Germany. Totally mad for him. So anyway, now, since it's Berlin, there's a little party in the backstage bar here and then we'll be off to the hotel. You'll be travelling on the band bus, if that's OK?'

'I'll do whatever I'm told,' Francis said, with a smile.

'You'll get on fine if you stick to that. But hey, come and meet a few world-famous people first. Sir Simon Rattle was in tonight, of all people.'

'The conductor?'

'Him, yes, with his opera-singer wife. Zak, of course. You saw Taylor Swift.'

'Bern pointed them out. I didn't realise a man like Zak would do this kind of thing. Check out the younger competition.'

'He's an old mate of Adam's. You know that Adam managed the Tainted Idols at one point?'

'Is that so?'

Francis had been thrown, he realised, into the heart of the rockocracy.

Much later, after the party, and the champagne-fuelled trip back to the Kaiser Grand on the band bus, and the after-gig supper, in a panelled dining room where vases of white lilies and ranunculus topped black plinths on shiny orange marble floors, Vanko came up to Francis and tapped him on the shoulder. 'Good evening, man?'

'It's been fun.'

'Simon and I are heading out to a club. You want to join?'

After a day that had begun at 5 a.m., Francis was ready for bed. But he realised that this was an honour – and a seminal one, at that. If he turned Vanko down, he might never develop a key relationship with him in quite the same way as if he seized the bonding opportunity and went. There was also Simon to consider: he had been polite enough, but nothing like as forthcoming as Vanko, even during the hi-jinks on the band bus.

He had to go.

So all of a sudden he was on the plush maroon leather seat of a white limo heading across town. At one movie-like point, they were racing up towards the floodlit Brandenburg Gate before turning left, past a wooded park, then diving back into the busy city streets. Then they were out and being whisked past a long queue of hopefuls and some dour-looking bouncers, down more corridors, up more steps, and out into a VIP area above a throbbing dance floor.

Here there were little circular tables and a crimson rope that cordoned them off from the steps down to the noisy crush of dancers below. The waiters and waitresses were all wearing bright blue T-shirts that read *WELKOM JONNI K*.

'Where's Jonni?' asked a short, rather creepy-looking manager.

'He'll be along in a bit,' said Simon, winking discreetly at Francis.

'Our guys are all ready for him, as you see.'

'Brilliant!' said Vanko, high-fiving him. 'He's going to love it.'

Champagne was offered, and arrived in a jeroboam, a bottle large enough to keep the three of them going till breakfast time.

'But Jonni's not coming, is he?' Francis asked.

'No way!' said Vanko. 'He'll be drinking Evian with Adam in his hotel room. Still, we don't need to tell them that, do we?'

Were the uniformly beautiful young women at the other tables in this privileged section VIPs as well? Francis wondered as he gulped his champagne. Or were they just potential friends of VIPs? The ugly guy with the shoulder-length black hair, white sharkskin suit and elaborately patterned boots was presumably famous for something. Being a world-class shit, perhaps. Even though he had a pair of coiffured blondes hanging on his every grimace, he didn't look happy.

'How did you find Zak?' Simon asked Francis, after a bit.

So his encounter at the after-party had been watched, possibly by all of them. Adam had dragged Francis over and left him there to fend for himself with this squat superstar who was hardly noted for his good manners and easy charm. With someone that famous you are, of course, stripped of the usual conversational openers. 'What do you do?' wouldn't really cut it with the living legend that was Zak. Even a contemporary culture slouch like Francis knew that Zak had gone on from the Tainted Idols to be even bigger on his own, not just as a solo artist but also as an actor, with a run of successful films in the late 90s and early 2000s – *Possessing Anna*, *The Light That Shines* and *Bullyboy*, to name but three. Powerful, not to say sinister, roles which had always seemed oddly mismatched to his famously ethical off-screen persona: he insisted he paid a ten per cent tithe on his income, a glowing example of redistributive decency that he regularly, and at times aggressively, urged other well-heeled celebrities to follow. Where else to begin, with a man whose private life had for so long been so public? Had he really suffered from 'sex addiction' back in his heyday? And if so, how exactly had that been diagnosed? How much did he miss Goldie, his beautiful, if troubled, first wife who had battled depression, eating disorders and infertility before running off with Bones, the lead singer of Guitarmageddon, and dying in a tragic jet-ski accident in Antibes? What were his true feelings about Sunny, the Eritrean refugee child he and Goldie had adopted, who had confounded all expectations by becoming a pro-Brexit Tory candidate and now an MP? Did he have any regrets about his affair with the matchless Carmela, twelve years his junior, whose passion for him had engendered a string of acclaimed tunes, including the number-one worldwide hit 'Turquoise Eyes', whose lyrics had allegedly led to the end of their high-profile affair? Even, on a trivial level, how proud was he of the award-winning cheeses, organic craft beers and twelve-year-old malt whisky produced on his wind-, hydro- and solar-powered farm at Glenveray Castle, his Scottish estate?

No, rather than asking all the things a stranger would be desperate to ask Zak, given the chance, Francis had found himself humming and hawing like an inept student at the Goldfish Academy of Social Interaction. He had blathered, hopelessly, about why he was here: his journey out, his unfamiliarity with the rock and roll scene, his impressions of Jonni's 'amazing' performance, etc., while Zak had regarded him as he might a cockroach on the floor just in front of his boot. Then, without so much as a brusque Glaswegian 'excuse me', the great man had turned away to talk to Sir Simon Rattle.

'Not easy,' Francis replied now.

'You have to get to know him,' Simon said. 'Then he's OK. Up to a point. But it takes a while. Weirdly, considering how famous he is, he's basically a bit shy.'

That's one word for it, Francis thought. 'Does he come to a lot of your gigs?' he asked.

'He drops in from time to time. He and Adam are very old mates. You know Adam managed the Tainted Idols back in the day?'

'Charmaine told me.'

During this exchange Vanko had been staring, without subtlety, at a woman in a tight gold cocktail dress who looked, with her long shiny dark hair and big brown eyes, like a German version of Anne Hathaway. Now he got to his feet and necked his champagne. 'Excuse me, guys,' he said. 'Got to go and do my duty as a rock star.'

He headed over to Anne's table. After barely three minutes of chit-chat, they were off together, arm in arm, scuttling past the crimson rope to the dance floor.

Simon was laughing. 'You have to love the randy Bulgarian. He really can't help himself.'

'Bulgarian?'

'That's where he's from. Originally. Though he's lived in Deptford since he was about six. Vanko means "God's gift", apparently. Which is appropriate, I can tell you.'

'Was that girl at the gig?'

'Probably. They usually are. They're very persistent, the fans. They generally know before we do which club we're going on to afterwards.'

Francis felt suddenly awkward. Was there some obscure etiquette here? Was he holding Simon back? From getting out there to enjoy the rewards of his fame?

'If you…' he began. 'I mean, I'm fine here with the champagne and the view, if you…'

'Want to go and grab myself a shag? No, don't worry. I'm happily married these days, so I've rather given up on the feasting.'

'Feasting?'

'Sorry. Inappropriate tour slang for sexual activity with fans.'

'Groupies?'

'We don't call them that nowadays, but yes, I guess.' Simon nodded thoughtfully to himself and tugged nervously at his beard. For all his studied cool, there was something of the geek about him. 'Fun while it lasted,' he went on. 'But always skin-deep, if you know what I mean. You start to feel a bit empty after a while. Anyway, they're never after you. They're after this image of you. And that gets boring too. *Wow, amazing, you wrote 'Let's Go Dutch', that's so incredible, how does it feel to hear it sung everywhere all the time by everyone?* I mean, what do you say to that after the fiftieth time?'

'I guess it must be a bit tedious,' said Francis. 'Though plenty of people would fantasise about such a life…'

Simon wasn't listening. 'So you got to meet Jonni as well?' he asked.

'For about ten seconds.'

'That's something. Plenty of journos don't even get that. How did you find him?'

'We barely spoke. Just shook hands. Adam was hovering.'

'He does that. Don't worry. My advice with Jonni is, don't rush it. Let him come to you. He doesn't like wannabes and hangers-on.'

'As you'd imagine, in his shoes.'

One of the waiters was upon them, holding up the glistening jeroboam. 'A top-up, gentlemen?' he asked, in faultless Home Counties English.

'You're not really here to write for *GQ*, are you?' Simon asked when he'd gone.

Francis shrugged.

'I'm not expecting you to confirm or deny, particularly. Just to tip you off: Nick is famously paranoid. I mean, you presumably know all about Ricky.'

There was no point pretending. 'Yes, I was told about that.'

'By Nick?'

'Yes.'

'What did he say?'

'That he OD'd on the bus trip from Stockholm to Copenhagen. One of his mates found him dead in his bunk.'

'That is what happened, yes.' Simon was nodding thoughtfully, as if weighing up whether he should say more. 'The key word is OD'd. He had been clean, then he went on a bender and took a shitload of drugs and his body couldn't handle it. It's a classic. But it has no relationship, in my humble opinion, with some random nutter pushing Jonni off the stage in Hamburg.'

'No?'

'The two things are unconnected. But because Jonni loved Ricky and Ricky is dead, Jonni's basically got it into his head that someone's trying to kill him.'

'The Hamburg guy was carrying a knife, by all accounts.'

'But he didn't use it, did he? Clearly a nutter. I mean, why would you take a knife onto a stage and then not use it? If you just wanted to make a statement and push the star off the stage, you're setting yourself up, pointlessly, for a much longer jail sentence if you carry a weapon.'

'So the sense I got from Nick,' Francis said, 'was that Ricky used to perhaps supply Jonni with drugs – or help him out, anyway?'

'That's one way of putting it. The guy was basically Dr D, if you know who he was…'

Francis's face revealed his ignorance.

'Prince's supplier,' Simon went on. 'Worked backstage as

well. Whatever Jonni wanted, at any time, Ricky would get for him. Anywhere. I mean, he was quite amazing. We had an American tour where we were in the middle of nowhere, out in the Nevada desert, and Ricky managed to source the necessary. But he wasn't just Jonni's drug buddy; he was like Jonni's little mate. One he could rely on. You know, in the days when Jonni used to come out to clubs like this after a show, Ricky would be here too. Even though he was supposed to be backstage, doing the loadout with the others. Adam turned a blind eye, of course, as he always does, because keeping Jonni happy is what it's all about. Always has been. Forget about the rest of us. As long as Jonni's OK, then everything's OK. But then, when Jonni was talked into starting this new clean life, Ricky got rather left behind.'

'I thought Ricky cleaned up too. That's what Nick told me.'

'Did he? Up to a point, mate. I think he went to a few NA meetings with Jonni and Adam. But if you knew the guy, you would know that he was never going to leave the bad stuff behind. He was like the waster's waster. Seriously. A deeply fucked-up fellow.'

'So what are you saying? He hadn't really got clean? In which case, why did the drugs he took on the bus kill him?'

'D'you know what?' said Simon. 'I think he *had* sorted himself out. Somewhat. If only to be on the tour. I think Adam had read him the riot act and said he could only come along this time if he was going to take it all seriously and give Jonni a helping hand. So he'd probably got clean – for a while, at any rate. And then, inevitably, once he got back with the wild men on the lampies' bus, he couldn't help himself.'

'Nick told me in no uncertain terms that class A drugs were banned on the buses.'

Simon laughed. 'D'you think that stops the lampies? There's no one else on that bus except the driver, and he's not going to say anything, is he? More than his life's worth.'

'Why did Adam even let Ricky back on tour? If he was such an obvious liability?'

'You don't understand how this thing works, do you? Jonni cries, "If I don't have Ricky around, I'm not going to do the tour", and so Adam has to oblige. And now, Jonni's little friend is dead and Jonni is running around thinking someone's trying to kill him too. So he wants increased security. And not just that, it seems, but private eyes on the tour too.'

He raised an eyebrow. Francis met his gaze. Was there any point trying to deny what he was doing here? Did it even matter? It had been Nick's idea to have a cover story. In some ways, it might make things easier if people knew what his real role was.

'D'you really think that was Jonni's call?' he replied. 'I mean, I've been hanging around all day and he's shown no interest in meeting me.'

Simon smiled. 'Thanks for the confirmation, mate.' He tapped his nose. 'I'll keep it to myself, don't worry. But I'm afraid that's Jonni for you. Wants something. Screams for it. Then, when he gets it, he isn't bothered. He'll probably suddenly ask to see you tomorrow. You'll be on his bus on the way to Dusseldorf, I expect. Watch this space.'

Chapter Four

Next to his bed, Francis's phone was ringing. Ripples. The ringtone he'd installed a fortnight ago when the cold grey January in London had been getting him down, and he'd decided he needed something new in his life. Little had he realised how soon his wishes would be granted – and how. Now he reached over groggily to silence the weird quasi-Eastern sound.

'Francis.'

'Yeah.'

'You've only been with us a day and already you sound like a rock star.'

There was a tinkle of familiar laughter.

'Charmaine…'

'Sorry to disturb your beauty sleep. I thought I'd give you a heads-up that the buses leave in just over an hour, from the side of the hotel – that cobbledly bit. Eleven o'clock sharp. It's as well to be there a few minutes early, so as not to piss off Bernie. And the only food on them will be Pringles and biscuits and that kind of stuff. So if you want some proper brekky or anything…'

'Thanks. Nobody actually told me.'

The printed schedule, which had addresses of hotels, capacities of venues, travel times between hotels and venues, phone numbers of promoters, door times, concert times and so on, had omitted this crucial detail.

'People on tour kind of assume you know what you're doing, don't they?'

Energised by Charmaine's thoughtfulness, not to mention the prospect of a hotel breakfast, Francis sprang up, grabbed a rapid shower in his marble-tiled bathroom, then ran downstairs to the dining room. It was a shame he hadn't woken earlier, because it was just the kind of spread he liked. Cereals, mueslis, prunes, fruit salads, sausages, eggs, salami, cheese, croissants, more cheese, pastries, more cheese – well, it was Germany.

Over at a sunny table by the window sat the two fit-looking security guards he'd seen with Jonni at the Velodrom backstage party. One was Asian, Middle Eastern or possibly mixed-race, the other white with a jaunty little 'tache. They were laughing loudly together; then, it seemed, they had clocked Francis loading his plate and quietened down, almost as if what they had been joking about was off limits. For a moment, Francis had a bold idea that he should go over and say hello. But then, no. The appropriate moment would arrive, soon enough. No need to push it. So were these the actual guys, he wondered, who had been responsible for letting the Hamburg madman get so close to Jonni? Seeing them joshing with each other now, he'd never have guessed. They didn't exactly look contrite.

At a quarter to eleven, stomach full, bag packed, room double-checked for left-behind phone charger and toothpaste, Francis made his way down in the lift and out through the revolving doors to the side of the hotel, where two gleaming silver-grey coaches with black windows were parked, one behind the other.

Francis stood with his bag against the wall in the pale February sunshine, waiting.

'Come on, you arsehole, get on!' Bernie's chirpy face appeared at the door of the second bus. 'No need to stand on ceremony, mate.'

'I'm on this bus, am I?' Francis asked.

'You are. Yes.'

'The band bus?'

'This is the band bus, yes. Were you expecting another bus? A personal bus for "visiting journalists", perhaps?' There was mockery in the implied quotes.

'No, but one of the guys suggested that I might be on Jonni's bus.'

'Not today, mate. I wouldn't stress. He had a gig last night and he's got another tonight, so he'll be needing his down time. Anyway, you'll have more fun on here. It's sometimes a bit tense on Jonni's. Plus, you'd have to play Skyjo all day.'

'Skyjo?'

'It's a children's card game he likes. Is, you might say, mildly obsessed by. You have to let him win. That's true, isn't it, Steve? More fun on this bus.' Bern nodded towards the driver. He was a small man with an elf-like triangular face, perched in a huge black leatherette seat with the dials and switches and screens of an elaborate console in front of him, a brushed steel thermos in the cup holder to his side.

'Of course, mate.'

'This is Steve Parton, your friendly bus driver. Known as Dolly, for obvious reasons.'

Steve chuckled gamely: the dutiful response of the Englishman, obliged by his culture to put up with nicknames and wind-ups.

Down a corridor there was a lounging area with padded orange couches, a huge TV screen and a little kitchenette. Narrow stairs halfway along led up to a top floor with another, smaller lounge at the front and stacks of curtained bunks stretching away behind. 'If you fancy a kip,' Bernie said, 'just help yourself. We deliberately don't have dedicated bunks, otherwise things can a get a bit arsey, with people insisting they have top or bottom or middle or what have you.'

Topaz and the two backing singers were already upstairs in the front lounge. 'You can either hang with the ladies or come downstairs and watch telly with the lads. Oh, here he comes!' Bern was looking through the picture window towards the front of the hotel, where Vanko was embracing a leggy blonde in boots and a thigh-length suede coat. This was a turnabout. When Francis and Simon had left him in the club, probably as late as 3 a.m., Vanko had still been with the Anne Hathaway lookalike.

'Come o-o-on!' shouted Bernie through the window, as the three women gathered round him to watch. 'Do us a favour and skip the long goodbye. You're never going to see her again.' He turned to Francis. 'It's like a movie every time. Kissie kissie, strokey strokey. Brings tears to my eyes. I mean, how much sincerity can a man develop in a few hours?'

'He's got a big heart,' said Topaz.

'And a big dick,' said Bernie.

'Bernie!' said Suzi, in mock-disapproving tones.

'Just sayin',' said Bernie, skipping out the door. 'He's not called the Schlong for nothing.'

Francis hovered, not sure whether to follow him or stay.

'You're very welcome to hang with us for a bit,' Topaz said, favouring him with her wide smile. 'If you want.'

'Thank you.' He hardly knew where to put himself.

'I mean, we just look at our phones and chat and stuff, but it's quite chilled. Thelma does her knitting.' She nodded towards the backing singer, who was already clicking away with two long cream needles on a pale blue oblong.

'If that's OK,' said Francis, sliding into a seat. 'I've got a bit of reading to do.'

'Cool.'

Vanko was followed on board the band bus by Simon and Russell, the chubby-faced American tour accountant. Then Jonni appeared, with Adam, and made his way past a small crowd of cheering fans to the first bus. Scally the drummer was right behind him, revealing his gap teeth in a broad cartoon-character grin as he pulled a blue wheeled suitcase along behind him. Handing this to Jonni's driver, a thickset, good-looking Black guy who was standing by the door of his bus, he hopped up behind the star and the manager.

'So Scally goes with Jonni?' Francis asked.

'Most of the time,' said Topaz. 'He's like Jonni's little mate.'

Another 'little mate', thought Francis. How many did Jonni need? Or had Scally just jumped into Ricky's shoes?

The buses travelled in convoy out through the wide straight Berlin streets and onto the autobahn west towards Dusseldorf. Suzi offered coffee, then went downstairs and brought back three cups.

'Sometimes we play a little game,' Topaz said. 'Just to pass the time.'

'Is it always segregated like this?' Francis asked. 'You up here, the men downstairs?'

Topaz shrugged. 'It's not something I've really noticed. But I guess it is. They like to watch their violent movies and we prefer to listen to podcasts and gossip.'

Their game was called Room 101, and it was more of a conversation-inspirer, Francis thought, than a game. It was loosely based on the TV and radio show, and all you had to do was say what you would put in Room 101 and why. Topaz went first. Hers was a bit of a cliché, she said with a giggle. Rats. She couldn't abide them. Though where she lived in

Camberwell, you'd see them on the streets sometimes. In the dark. Rooting around bins. Ugh.

'They say,' said Thelma, smiling as she knitted away, 'that if you live in London you're never more than six feet away from a rat.'

'Six feet, is that really true?' Topaz asked.

'Sewers and stuff – they're everywhere.'

'Where do you live, Francis?' Suzi asked.

'In London too. Tufnell Park.'

'Oh, nice. I like it up there. Near Hampstead Heath?'

'Near enough, yes. That's where I go jogging.'

'Have you ever seen a rat?' asked Thelma.

'I had one in my flat.'

To squeals of delight, Francis told the story: how he had been working away in his living room one morning and had become aware of something dark moving quietly across the edge of his vision on the floor. Looking up, he realised it wasn't a shadow or even a small cat; it was a rat. Encouraged by his female audience, Francis went overboard describing how hopeless the local council had been; the useless jobsworth they'd sent out to deal with the problem; how he had eventually been forced to construct a makeshift rat-run with an ironing board; how of course that had only been the first of several sleek rodents that had escaped from the sewers through a broken toilet in his neighbour's basement and into Francis's flat that way.

'Euk!' cried Topaz. 'That is such a disgusting story. You've basically ruined my day, you realise that?'

They moved on to spiders, which was Thelma's phobia. Each of them had a scary spider story, though Francis's description of the huge, hairy huntsman spiders he'd seen in Australia was definitely up there.

Suzi wanted to put snobs into Room 101. 'Not that they're frightening. I just don't like them.'

Francis laughed. 'And how d'you define snobs?' he asked.

Suzi shrugged. 'I don't know. People who only value you for who you know, or maybe what you do, rather than what you are.'

'But isn't what you do part of what you are?'

'Of course. But you know the kind of people I'm talking about. They just literally rank you. Christ, we get plenty of them on tour. That after-party last night was full of them. Super-smooth PR people who only want to talk to Jonni. And if they can't do that, to Simon or possibly, at a pinch, Vanko. But if you're a mere backing singer, there's a total lack of interest.'

'*At a pinch, Vanko,*' Thelma repeated with a snigger. 'Is that man ever going to be as famous as he wants to be?'

'But isn't it true,' Topaz said, 'that who you know is, like, totally related to what you do? So it's kind of impossible to pull out that strand of who you are, underneath. I mean, take Jonni. He is what he is, at one level. Just Jonni, the guy we know backstage, the funny guy, the edgy guy, the insecure guy, the way-demanding guy, yeah? But he's also Jonni K, the super-famous celeb, like, all the time, not just when he's onstage. So you can't pull out Jonni and not have Jonni K, if you get me? He's also totally what he does, and to some extent the people he knows. I mean, weirdly, when people want to talk to Jonni, like at that party, the PR dudes and the famous people, like Taylor Swift or Zak or whoever, I think lots of them are trying to get beyond that, kind of, construct of fame. They would really like to get to know the real Jonni.'

'Is there one?' said Thelma, to laughter.

It was interesting how much they kept coming back to Jonni. It was almost as if they couldn't help themselves: he was the brooding presence on which their livelihoods depended. After a few minutes, Francis tried, perhaps without as much subtlety as he might have used, to turn the conversation to specifics. Not just Jonni in general, but Jonni now, on this tour. He wanted to know what these three thought of the Hamburg incident. Presumably they also knew about Ricky. But would they talk?

He was aware of them gently clamming up; realising what he was trying to do, sharing covert looks with each other, becoming circumspect.

'It must be very upsetting for you all when security breaks down,' he heard himself saying.

There was silence.

Suzi shrugged.

'Yeah,' said Thelma, and carried on knitting. Her pale blue oblong was getting visibly longer.

'I mean, that's what they pay those guys to do,' Topaz said eventually, 'so it's pretty crap if they can't keep that kind of crazy man offstage. We were all gobsmacked about Hamburg, to be honest. It's not just Mitch and Omar and Dead Ed. I mean, you've seen all those tattooed biker types they employ. German Hell's Angels or whatever. What were they all up to that night? Security, my arse.'

'Sorry,' said Francis. 'Who's Dead Ed?'

They all laughed. 'The third security guard,' Topaz explained. 'He travels with the crew and is supposed to look after them, though why that lot need a security guard, God alone knows.'

'And he's Dead Ed why?'

'Oh, he died or something,' said Suzi. 'In Iraq or somewhere.'

'What!?' Francis queried.

'He actually did die,' Topaz explained. 'In a drowning incident in Afghanistan. His tank rolled over into a canal. His heart stopped. Then they got him out and resuscitated him. You know what these army types are like with their nicknames.'

It was time to get direct. 'So, do you think Jonni is in danger?' Francis asked. 'When he's onstage?'

'Obviously he was that night,' said Topaz. 'In that the guy pushed him off the stage and was carrying a knife.'

'But in general, does he have enemies?'

The three of them were looking at each other again, eyes flicking round, as if assessing as a group whether they should speak.

'I don't think he does,' said Topaz after a few moments. 'Crazies, yes, that goes with the territory. Happens to all these people. Brad Pitt got attacked on the red carpet, Simon Cowell got eggs chucked at him, Kim Kardashian was flour-bombed, Robbie Williams was pushed off a stage too back in the day – you just have to hope that it's not like George Harrison or John Lennon, like a stabbing or a shooting. Look, there's a lot of adulation out there for a big star like Jonni. You've seen it already. Every city we get to, there's thousands of young girls going crazy. Every now and then, one of them's a bit *too* crazy. D'you see what I'm saying?'

'But this was a bloke,' said Thelma.

'Well, yeah. Maybe some girl's boyfriend.'

'Women don't do this attacking stuff much, do they?' said Suzi.

'Actually, it was a woman who attacked Kardashian,' said Thelma. 'I think it was to do with her wearing fur. She called her a "fur bitch" or something.'

'I don't think,' Topaz cut in, 'to answer Francis's question, that Jonni has many enemies. His rise to fame has been, like, effortless. Everyone accepts he's got the looks, the voice. More to the point, he's got the stage presence. He came up through that freakin' competition, didn't he? He hasn't exactly had to do anyone down to get here. I mean, to be honest, if somebody had it in for somebody on this tour, it would be more likely to be Adam–'

She stopped herself, as if suddenly realising who she was talking to. Suzi's eyes had widened, and Thelma was looking down at her knitting.

'Why?' Francis chanced. But before anyone could answer, the door burst open and the boys were upon them: Simon, Vanko and Russell the accountant.

'Movie's over,' cried Russell, his bulging eyes casting round the little cabin before settling, almost helplessly, on Topaz. 'We thought we'd come and annoy you.'

The conversation was finished. They ended up playing In the Manner of the Word. Who would have imagined, Francis thought, that seasoned rock 'n' rollers would sit around on tour buses playing old-fashioned party games? As if that wasn't enough, when that was done, there was a round of Happy Families. Topaz produced a pack of classic Jacques cards and insisted they all stick to an elaborate form of words when asking for family members: 'Do you *happen to have* Mr Bun the Baker?' Then, through the window, there was the amusing distraction of two carloads of fans who were chasing the buses. Teenage girls, having a great time by the looks of it, swerving from lane to lane, waving out of the side window as they over-took, shouting for Jonni. One of them had a blue and white megaphone. Had they come from Dusseldorf to meet the band? Or had they followed them down from Berlin? It wasn't clear, but Vanko's opinion of them was.

'Freaks,' he said, shaking his head with disdain.

Before Francis knew it, they were coming into Dusseldorf. Down off the autobahn and into the suburbs, along by the tram tracks and into the wide car park beside the sleek grey Mitsubishi Electric Halle, where banners proclaimed not just *JONNI K*, but *WEIRD CRIMES* and *DEUTSCHE CHEER-SPORT MEISTERSHAFTEN*.

The lounge door swung open and Bernie was there.

'Here we are, guys,' he announced. 'Dusseldorf. Straight

into the venue, please. You can leave your big bags on the bus, as it will be guarded by Dolly or locked, and we'll be heading out to the hotel from here straight after the gig. There are showers at the venue. And toilets. So you can finally release that toxic shit you've all been saving up since Berlin. Francis, could I have a word? Outside, if you don't mind.'

He led him along the corridor past the bunks to a space at the far end where there was a narrow desk and bench configuration, with a view out of the front of the bus. An open laptop sat on the desk.

'So,' he said, 'd'you want the good news or the bad news?'

'Both, I suppose.'

Bernie smiled. 'Very wise. Well, the good news is that the Steigenburger Park Hotel in Dusseldorf is a lovely spot. Nice rooms, delicious nosh after the gig, beautiful park right outside, great clubs just down the road. Even Russell stands a chance of getting laid. There's also a Maccy Ds for Scally round the back, so everyone will be happy.'

'And the bad news?'

'You're not joining us. Adam thinks you might like to watch the loadout, then travel to Rotterdam on one of the crew buses.'

'The loadout?'

'When the crew take the set down after the gig. While the band – and I, of course – swan off to the hotel for supper, the crew dismantle everything, bolt by bolt, nut by nut. Often it takes them till two, three in the morning. And then, if there's a gig the next night, they go straight on to the next venue and start putting it all back again four hours later. That, my friend, is the definition of fucking hard work. No one is suggesting you help them. But if you hang with them, Adam thought, it might be instructive.'

'I see,' said Francis, trying not to sound disappointed. Actually, this was exactly what he needed. Some time with the guys below stairs. A different perspective. Who knew how much they might tell him about the stuff he wanted to know?

'You will sleep – if you get any sleep, that is, which I doubt – on one of the three crew buses. Maybe even the lampies' bus, which is the bus Ricky used to travel on.' Bernie gave Francis a significant look. 'You may even, lucky man, have his bunk. I'm sure a keen journo like yourself would find that interesting. And as there's a day off tomorrow, and we don't set up in Rotterdam till Saturday, the crew may well be in party mood.'

'And you will let me know how and when to find this crew bus?'

'Not me, mate. I'll be too busy guzzling champagne from some German model's cleavage. But I'll introduce you to Pants, our friendly Production Manager.' Bernie yawned extravagantly. 'I look after the star and the band and the manager. Pants looks after the gang of assorted troglodytes known as the crew. Which would you rather do?'

Chapter Five

Jonni was wearing an electric-pink backless cocktail dress, its low neckline revealing his unreconstructedly hairy chest. It was a gender-challenging look, and tonight he was rocking it. Berlin had been good, but this Dusseldorf crowd was something else and the band were all on fire. Vanko and Topaz took turns to join in with the backing vocals, Vanko getting so close to the stand-mounted mic in front of him that he was, at moments, all but snogging it. He looked up, caught sight of Francis lurking behind the speakers at the edge of the stage, and gave him a smile and a thumbs-up. Then Bernie materialised beside Francis, shifting from foot to foot in time to the music. They gazed out together over the huge crowd, whose arms were swaying, phone torches and wristbands shining, a thousand stars dotting the darkness. Back in the day, when Francis had gone to gigs, it had been phone lighters; now, Simon had told him, the handed-out LED wristbands were centrally controlled, so every waving individual light could be turned up or down by Kylie at her monitor desk. She could even change the colour.

Dancing just below them, right up by the stage, were two very young girls holding up a placard that read:

JONNI
CAN WE FUCK YOU
FOR BLOW

What did they mean? Francis thought. Should it have been *OR BLOW*? Or were they offering to prostitute themselves for marijuana? Surely not, as they would know, as eager and informed fans, that Jonni no longer did drugs.

Bernie nodded at the sign, and laughed. 'No chance!' he cried. He made a devil's horn gesture with the upturned thumbs of his two hands, shook his head, as if in weary disapproval, then skittered off, teeth shining in the multicoloured stage lights.

Afterwards, Francis made his way back down into the arena. He watched as the audience covered up their party outfits with nondescript windbreaker jackets and hoodies and headed out into the winter night. The black-clad crew were already at work around him, dismantling the set. As the last punters drifted away through the back doors, the crew's shouts seemed to get louder in the empty space. Huge video screens were lowered, giant speakers were pushed to one side, lights carefully brought down from the complex network of roof girders above. Up on the stage, the backline team were packing away instruments, mic stands, amps and so on into the big black silver-rimmed boxes on wheels that Francis now learned were called flight cases.

'All right there, Francis?' It was Pants – real name Bruce Pantlin – the Production Manager, an Australian with cowboy good looks, who had given Francis all of a minute before the gig, just enough time to tell him which bus to sling his bag on.

Now, with the show out of the way and Bernie gone, he seemed altogether more relaxed.

'Just taking in your military operation,' Francis said. 'Very impressive. These guys up on the roof girders. Terrifying.'

'It is a bit military, isn't it?' Pants smiled, revealing a pristine set of white teeth, just one gold filling visible up left. 'For your information, we call them trusses, not roof girders. Not that it matters a flying monkey's.' He nodded towards a passing security guard, who looked like a seriously tough cookie: the thick neck, the jaw, the thin line of his mouth, the broken nose, the death-stare eyes. If Francis had been making a movie of this tour, he would never have signed off on such a clichéd bit of casting.

'Dead Ed?' Francis asked.

Pants chuckled. 'They told you that, did they? Yeah, that's him. But don't ever call him that to his face. It's Edmund to you – Edmund Cheeseacre. OK, so you wander round and do what you have to do, ask your questions or whatever. And when you're ready, or bored, feel free to go up and chill in the band hospitality room. Some of us'll be along there in a bit. Help yourself to a beer if you want.' He headed off, yelling up at a young rigger who was perched precariously on a truss above them.

The unravelling of the set went in clear stages. First to finish and go backstage were the backline crew: the guitar and drum and keyboard techs who looked after the band's instruments. Then the sound and monitor engineers and the catering team. Then, as Francis made his way up to band hospitality, the lampies, an altogether more raucous crowd. Finally, Pants reappeared with the riggers and carpenters and told the party – as it had now become – that the loadout was done and dusted. The five pantechnicons that carried the kit – everything from the stage sections to Jonni's gold radio mic – were packed up, and the three tour buses that carried the crew were ready on the tarmac outside. Francis followed the backline crew down to their bus, carrying two bottles of baksheesh band hospitality wine as instructed. They piled in, greeting their bus driver in exaggerated tones.

'Here we are, Bryn.'

'Evening, Bryn. Or rather, morning.'

'Let's hit Rotterdam!'

There were, as far as Francis could see, about eight or nine crew members who travelled and slept on the backline bus. Pants himself, who was clearly the boss. Ted, the straw-haired hobbit Francis had seen messing around onstage when he'd first arrived in Berlin, who was Scally's drum tech. His equally short, blonde colleague, Mel, who was guitar tech for Topaz and Vanko. Kylie, a skinny, dark-haired, rather tense-seeming Kiwi, who was the Creative Director and Lighting Designer; it had been her silhouette Francis had clocked, up by the mixing desks in the crowd, boogieing away solipsistically as she operated the controls. The catering department was represented by waitress Flo, she of the welcoming smile and sapphire-strung midriff, along with Darius, the shaven-headed St Lucian chef and his mumsy Cornish assistant Jemima. There were also a white-bearded, long-haired Irishman called Seamus, his muscled arms dense with elaborate tattoos, who was stage manager, and Laurent, costume designer and wardrobe mistress. She had bright blue eyes, a big nose, a lovely figure and nice suede ankle boots, and came complete with a comedy French accent. Snuggled up in their downstairs lounge, they were all being studiously polite to their overnight visitor, but their curiosity was tangible.

Seamus had rolled a fat joint before the bus had even got going. As they sped away through the back streets of Dusseldorf, whose lights and apartment blocks and rather flimsy trees were just visible through the darkened windows, he took a deep toke and passed the spliff to Ted on his left. There was a brief 'is this all right with the journalist watching?' flicker between Ted and Pants before he too indulged. Mel passed, without comment; she was drinking tea from a mug that read *HAPPY CAMPER*. But chef Darius inhaled, deeply and without a murmur, as did Jemima and Flo, who were also necking paper cups of red wine. When the half-smoked, damp-filtered spliff arrived in Francis's fingers, he felt it would be rude, not to say impolitic, not to join in, so he took a shallow puff, just enough to realise, with an embarrassingly uncool cough, that this was stronger stuff than the dope he remembered from his uni days at York.

This gesture of acceptance took the tension out of the little cabin like air out of a balloon. The journalist, if that's what he was, was now one of them.

'So, man,' Seamus asked him, as smoke poured from his huge, hairy nostrils in two beautifully distinct streams, 'how are yer finding it all?'

'It's interesting,' Francis replied.

'Interesting,' Seamus repeated slowly, in a Dublin accent that wasn't from the genteel south of that city. He pursed his lips and blew three perfect smoke rings, which sailed up, loosening as they went, to the roof of the hugger-mugger cabin. 'Is that all? Aren't we more than interesting?'

'Of course,' said Francis.

'What are you doing here anyway, man? What's this magazine piece you're supposed to be writing?'

'Well,' Francis began, 'it's a sort of in-depth look at a band on tour, with Jonni at the centre, of course–'

'Are you, by any chance,' Seamus interrupted, 'going to be looking at what happened to him four nights ago in Hamburg, or is that something you'll gloss over, in the best traditions of contemporary investigative journalism?'

He was trouble, this man, under his mellow-fellow grin. From the edge in his voice, even now that he was clearly quite stoned, Francis realised that Seamus probably had several axes to grind.

'No,' he replied. 'I'm very interested in what happened in Hamburg. That was the main reason I came out. People think that these assaults on celebrities happen all the time, but they don't really. You can count the number of attacks on rock stars over the last twenty years on the fingers of two hands.'

'Is that so?' said Seamus. The first joint had gone and he was busily constructing another, licking Rizla papers, tearing up a couple of roll-ups for the tobacco, then crumbling in some hash from a dark green block he took out of a small freezer bag in his pocket. Now he lit the twist of paper at one end and sucked until the spliff glowed a fiery orange before passing it to Ted again. 'It's all crap, really, isn't it?' he added.

'What is?' Kylie asked, after a moment.

'I mean, Jesus, the guy was pushed off the stage. Big deal. It wasn't like he was stabbed or shot. He got back up again too, fair play to him. But those managers'll overreact and make a huge deal about it. Cosset the poor lamb in frickin' cotton wool. Paranoia One and Paranoia Two, we call them.' He looked over at Francis, and there was heavy meaning in his bloodshot eyes.

'Seamus,' Pants interrupted, a warning note in his voice. 'This is all off the record, isn't it?' he added to Francis.

'Sure,' Francis replied.

'It's not going to be much of an evening if you're taking notes, is it?' Seamus said. 'Though I must admit I always fantasised about being the subject of one of those *Rolling Stone* or *NME* spreads. But – no offence, as my nine-year-old daughter Niamh would say – you're hardly Nick Kent, are you?'

'Seamus.' Flo giggled. 'You're stoned.'

'So are you, darling, with this very fine sinsemilla. The nice thing about this little trip, Francis, from Dusseldorf to Rotterdam – well, actually there are two nice things, but the first one is that once we're over the border into the Nederlands, this stuff is entirely legal and tomorrow we can get as wrecked as we like in the beautiful little coffee shops of Rotterdam.'

'And the second thing, Seamus?' asked Kylie, after a few moments of silence. There was another long pause before she followed up with, 'That's nice? About this trip?'

'I've forgotten,' Seamus replied. He raised his hand, like a kid in a classroom. 'Miss, miss, miss! Sorry, I've forgotten. Oh yes, I just remembered. The second nice thing is, it only takes a couple of hours. So we'll be there soon. It's not like that long haul from Stockholm to Copenhagen.'

With the mention of that trip, there was silence. It was on that overnighter that Ricky Fisher had OD'd, and they were all clearly thinking of that, even if they weren't saying anything.

Francis decided to try his luck. 'So what did happen to Ricky?' he asked. There was an intake of breath as the lumbering elephant in the room was finally acknowledged.

'Did he just OD?'

Seamus met his eye. 'Who knows?' he said, and there was a blank emptiness in his reply that was chilling, as if he couldn't have cared less. 'The sad truth of the matter is that he probably did. As I'm sure you know, he'd been clean for a while, keeping up with Jonni, as it happens. And when you've been clean, you've got to be careful. Because if you fall off the wagon, the thump can be harder than you expect. Especially if the wagon is moving. Poor old Ricky, for one reason or another, decided to join the lampies' party out of Stockholm. If you were ever on that bus, you'd know—'

'Seamus,' Pants interrupted, holding up a hand. 'Too much information.'

'Sorry, man.' He grimaced at Francis and ran his yellow-stained forefinger over his lips in a zipped gesture.

'The case is still in the hands of the Danish police,' said Pants.

'Sarah Lund,' said Seamus. 'One of the junior coppers that asked us questions was a dead ringer for Sarah Lund. Remember her? From *The Killing*. Chief Inspector Sarah sexy Lund. She didn't have the Faroe Isle jumper, though. Sadly. The real Sarah. Or rather, the real not-Sarah.'

'What did the police want to know?' Francis asked. 'Out of interest.'

'Out of interest,' Seamus repeated slowly. 'Or in interest? I'd say in interest.' He nodded significantly. 'What d'you expect, my friend? They wanted to know if there were drugs on the buses. Obviously, since they're frowned upon in–'

'Illegal,' Pants cut in. 'In Sweden.'

'Exactly. Illegal. There were no drugs on the buses. Certainly not on this one, eh, Pants?' Seamus took a lingering toke of the joint which, with perfect timing, had just been put into his hand by Flo. 'I couldn't speak for those naughty lamp-ies. Wild men, those electrical people. It's actually a moot point who's wilder – the lampies, or the carpenters and riggers? That's the third sleeper bus.'

'The lampies,' Ted piped up. It was a surprising comment, because his eyes had been closed for several minutes.

'Anyway,' said Seamus. 'We told the Danish fuzz there were no drugs on the buses. Beer, we said. Just nice Swedish beer. Mariestads. Norrlands Guld. They hate the Swedes, the Danes. They even hate their beer. It's something to do with the war, I can never remember what.'

'Jesus,' said Ted. 'My neck is melting.'

Francis took another small puff, just to keep up. But it was clear that while Pants was in the room, the subject of Ricky was closed. Francis was ready for his bunk now, but he hung on in there, hoping that the Production Manager might peel off and leave him with Seamus. Unguarded, might the old roadie tell him more about the keyboard tech's death? Not to mention Ricky's special friendship with Jonni. What were they all trying to say? That he and Jonni were just drugs buddies? Or was there more?

'I mean,' Seamus was saying now, 'sometimes, man, you have to ask yourself. Why does one star succeed and another doesn't? Why is Jonni up there, and countless others like him, pretty boys with passable vocals and an equal amount of attitude, aren't? Is it because he dresses as a woman, is all woke and supposedly gender-*fle-e-e-e-ewid*?'

'Because, to be fair on 'eem,' Laurent cut in, in that caricature French accent, 'Jonni 'as that performance thing. You know. 'E works the crowd, 'e loves the crowd. You may not like 'eem, Seamus, but 'e is totally electric. And they love 'eem back, *bien sûr.*'

'Who's saying I don't like him?' Seamus gave Francis a stagey conspiratorial wink. 'I love him, man. How would I fund my feckin' life partners and kids without him? But you have to say he's a puppet. It's Paranoia and Paranoia who pull the strings.'

'Seamus, man,' said Pants. 'Enough of this already. Jesus.'

'I mean, there's another one.'

'What are you on about now?' asked Kylie.

'Jesus is what I'm on about. The Good Lord. The Lord Good. Jesus.'

'*Jesus?*'

'Yeah, Jesus. It's the same feckin' thing.'

'What eez?' asked Laurent.

'I mean, consider this,' said Seamus. 'First-century Palestine was full of nutters wandering around saying they were the Son of God. You've seen *The Life of Brian.* So why was it Jesus who managed to pull it off, and be believed, while all the others crashed and burned? Then you get the early Christians, dodging the lions. Then you get the Roman emperors, signing up to the whole deal. Next thing, the Normans are building massive stone cathedrals, then a load of Italians are painting amazing pictures, and before you know it you've got a world-famous freaking religion on your hands. Fait a-feckin'-compli. But it was touch and go at the beginning, is all I'm saying.'

'Seamus, you're not making a great deal of sense.'

'Pants, man, I'm just *starting* to make sense. Take the rock legends, the Beatles, the Stones, the Who, you know – set in stone these days, aren't they? Pub music, lift music, tinkle tinkle, they're part of the feckin' fabric, like it could never have been otherwise. But it wasn't always like that. The ones who got famous are just like the ones who got lucky. There were plenty of others, equally as good, if not better, man, who didn't make the cut. Maybe because they were in the wrong place at the wrong time, or maybe just because they were *too* feckin' talented to get their shit together.'

Now Kylie was laughing, a high-pitched Kiwi titter.

'I'm not joking,' Seamus went on, a frown creasing his forehead. 'You don't believe me, Kylie, but I knew guys like that when I was getting going. Like, the real talents. They just never got through the sieve of feckin' fame. Look, if the Beatles hadn't met Epstein, or the Stones met what was his name, Loog Oldham – I mean, forget it. They'd have been playing clubs in Richmond for a few years and then got proper jobs. Look what happened when Keith got fed up with Mick and tried to go it alone. D'you even remember what his band was called?'

Seamus was staring directly at Francis, his spooky, deep-set eyes holding him with the deep sincerity of the extremely stoned.

'I don't, no.' Francis didn't even know that Keith Richards had formed his own band.

'There you go,' said Seamus. 'There you feckin' go.'

'So what was his band called, Seamus?' Flo asked.

'I can't remember.' Seamus laughed, a hollow, self-absorbed, long-drawn-out cackle. 'See what I mean? I can't even feckin' remember.'

'The X-Pensive Winos,' said Ted, without opening his eyes.

'Nice one, Ted. The X-Pensive Winos, that was it. What kind of a shit name was that? Seriously. That's what I'm talking about. Noel Gallagher, there's another one. Couldn't stand his brother so he sets up the what d'you call it–'

'High Flying Birds,' said Ted.

'The High Flying Birds, brilliant. High Shitting Birds, more like. And what about that insane egotist Lennon?'

'The Plastic Ono Band,' Ted cut in.

'Awesome, my man. Are you with me, Francis? It's all touch and feckin' go. I mean, if things had gone differently for me, I might have been one of those people.'

'Dream on, Seamus,' said Kylie.

'I'm not dreaming. I was in a band once.'

'What was it called, Seamus?' Flo asked: not for the first time, Francis thought.

'The Flaming Buzzards.'

''E can remember that one,' said Laurent.

'Not the Flaming Buzzcocks,' teased Kylie.

'That joke has been made before, my darling. In all fairness, we were pretty good. Folksy, but good. That's my point. It's just a question of which way reality goes. Sliding doors, man. The dice might have tumbled in a different direction. It might have been me that got the three lemons.'

Shortly after that, Francis made his excuses and retired to one of the empty bunks, up on the top deck of the bus. However relaxed his cheesy smile made him appear, Pants was clearly not going to leave him alone with Seamus tonight. Now, like a child listening to their parents talk as they fall asleep, Francis could hear the conversation and laughter filtering up from below. Was it his paranoia, or did they now sound more relaxed? No, of course it was. He was an outsider, put there to snoop on them – they all knew that.

Some time later, he was aware of the bus stopping. And not just for a minute at a traffic light. They had arrived in Rotterdam. He sank back into sleep and woke with the light. He lay there for a few minutes, listening to heavy snoring from a bunk just below him. Then he crawled out, found his bag and dressed quietly.

Downstairs, he said good morning to bus driver Bryn, who was revealed in the cold morning light as a stocky Welshman whose rugger-playing days were over. He was sitting up in his big black leatherette driving seat doing crosswords and eating a bacon sandwich. 'With avocado,' he enthused. 'As you'd expect in the Netherlands.' They were parked up, he explained, in the car park of the Rotterdam Travelhotel, where the crew were berthed for their day off before they started on the next bout of set construction at the venue first thing tomorrow. 'Just walk into reception and you'll find your name on the rooming list. So you're a writer, are you? What's a famous Irish novel based on a Greek myth? Seven letters. U dash Y dash dash dash S.'

'*Ulysses*,' said Francis.

'Sure about that?'

'Has to be.'

Francis spelled it out and Bryn filled in the squares. 'Thanks, bud.'

'Sweet little pencil,' Francis remarked before he headed off.

Bryn smiled. 'It's from IKEA. They're free, so I collect them.' He pointed to the little plastic well next to him, which was supposed to hold a drinking cup. 'I've got a load here, if you want one.'

He had, too. About thirty short pale brown pencils, tumbled on top of each other.

Francis's room was high up on the twentieth floor, with picture windows revealing a dreary view out over warehouse roofs and apartment blocks and trees and high rises, with the cranes of the port some way off. At least up here there was sunlight.

He took the lift back down to the ground floor and found the restaurant, imagining that it might be full of crew stocking up on a free breakfast. Not a bit of it. He was alone with the tea and coffee and ham and salami and cheese and salads and pastries. Where were they all? Smoking weed in one of their rooms? Asleep? Out and about, already, at quarter past nine?

Upstairs, Francis fell back on his bed and snoozed for a while. What now? he wondered when he woke. What did the crew get up to on a day off like this? Did they do cultural stuff, if indeed there was cultural stuff to do in Rotterdam, or did they just hit the first coffee shop they came to and get high? A quick look on his phone told him that the port city had a zoo, a maritime museum, a boat tour, and some odd 'cube houses', painted bright yellow and grey, that looked like giant children's toys. This being the Netherlands, you could see the whole lot on a two-and-a-half-hour bike tour, but Francis didn't imagine the crew would be signing up for that. What an image! The guys in black, all in wraparound rock 'n' roll shades, veering round the docks and back streets in a stoned posse.

He had enjoyed the smoking session with Seamus and the gang, but he felt now that he had failed to find out what any of them thought about anything, let alone a detailed take on the demise of poor Ricky. Maybe if he just went out for a wander, he would run into one or more of them. In a coffee shop, even. Maybe alone, or in a pair, without Pants hovering like a schoolmaster, they would talk more freely.

His phone was ringing. *BERNIE*, read the screen.

He clicked on it to hear a familiar chuckle.

'So how was your night?'

'Comfortable enough.' He refused to let Bernie gloat.

'Pants's bus?'

'It was.'

'Mm-hm. You learn anything?'

'Maybe.'

'Very discreet, you are. So d'you want the good news or the bad news?'

Francis was getting wise to the tour manager's teasing style. 'Give me the bad news,' he said.

'Nice one. OK, Adam wants to see you. Here, now. He's just off to an NA meeting with Jonni, but you're next on his agenda. So, soon as you can make it, please, which should be in just over an hour if there's no traffic. By the time you get downstairs, you'll find your car is waiting. A white Toyota Prius.' He spelled out the registration number. 'Got that? Mohammed is your driver.'

You had to hand it to Bernie. He was quite an operator. 'So what's the good news?'

'The good news is that you can stay. In Amsterdam. At the lovely five-star Hotel Du Monde. We've managed to find a room for you. And I expect you won't mind joining us all for dinner later. With Jonni. In the Michelin three star round the corner.'

Chapter Six

Adam was all alone. No Jonni in sight. The manager was lounging on one of the cream-gold sofas in his suite, legs wide apart, reading *The Economist*. The rooms were stylishly done out: antiques, deep pile carpets, views through big windows of the sunny canal below. The Hotel Du Monde was like the bow of a big cruise liner, surrounded by water on three sides.

'Sit,' he said, as Francis shuffled in. 'What can we get you? Tea? Coffee? Something stronger?'

Francis didn't fall for the teetotaller's trap this time. He asked for coffee.

'I might have some too,' Adam said. He reached over to the hotel phone and placed the order. 'They always bring these nice little home-made biccies. A bit of a contrast to the crew bus, I imagine. Which one did Pants put you on?'

He probably already knew, Francis thought, but he would play along. 'Backline,' he replied.

'Backline, eh? That's Pants and his gang, isn't it?'

'The instrument technicians, the catering guys, Kylie, the Creative Director, the wardrobe mistress–'

'The lovely Laurent. Such a clever young woman she is. Jonni would be lost without her. She always somehow manages to channel his wilder ideas into something that works. Onstage. We're obviously keen that he's as gender-bending as he wants to be, but there are limits. She stops him looking ridiculous. Not that I would ever dare make such an old-school remark in front of either of them.' Adam chortled. 'They think they've reinvented the wheel, this lot, but we went through all this kind of thing in the 70s, when I was a mere teenager. Bowie, Bolan, the New York Dolls – *The Rocky Horror Show*, for goodness' sakes! Anyway, you had fun?'

'It was different.'

'I imagine. You know, Francis, I wouldn't mind being you in this role. A fly on the wall. I've managed bands for forty years, but I've never spent the night on a crew bus. So, did they enlighten you in any way? About either of our little incidents?'

So Adam was prepared to talk about this stuff. After Francis had met him the first time, in Catering, he hadn't been so sure. That initial evasiveness had made him wary. So how much was he going to share with him now? Not that Seamus called his bosses Paranoia and Paranoia, he didn't think.

'A little,' he replied. 'They were quite cagey.'

'Glad to hear it. As we say in this business, "What goes on on tour stays on tour." Did any of them even mention Ricky?'

'Yes.' It wouldn't be fair to name names. 'They seemed to think that he had OD'd. But that that had nothing to do with the Hamburg incident. The feeling I got was they didn't think that was such a big deal.'

'Didn't they? But it was a big deal, Francis. Jonni being chucked off the stage. By an intruder with a knife on his person. Shouldn't have happened.'

'Do *you* think there's a link?'

Adam's features cracked into his half-moon smile. 'That's why we've got you here, Francis. To check this stuff out. I sincerely hope there isn't a link, because if there is, what are we looking at? Something quite sinister. Jonni is naturally worried. I've told him not to be. But when one of your best friends dies, and then some apparently random nutter has a pop at you out of the blue, it would be hard not to take it personally. Don't you think?'

Pretty much the whole band party met for dinner in the Rive Gauche, with its swanky white tablecloths, funky contemporary furniture and three gleaming Michelin stars. Only Jonni's place remained empty. But then, miracle of miracles, as the huge octagonal monogrammed plates were being cleared away after the main course, the front door swung open and there he was, sweet chaperone Charmaine beside him.

'Jonni!' called Topaz, enthusiastically. The star looked around, almost shyly, then slid down past Francis to take his place next to Adam at the end.

Despite himself, Francis found his eyes drifting towards him. There was something mesmeric about his presence, which cast a self-conscious pall on all other conversation and interaction. At one moment, Francis caught his eye. Not wanting to gawp like a punter, he looked hurriedly down and away. But it was too late. There hadn't been so much as a flicker of acknowledgement on Jonni's face, but he had noticed him all right. Presumably this is what celebrities had to do to survive. Be aware of the ever-watching eyes, but not necessarily formally accept them.

After scoffing down a hamburger and a Diet Coke, he was off again, taking Adam with him.

'See you later, Jonni-boy,' the band members crooned. All very normal and friendly, but once he'd gone, you could sense the company relaxing, like a tautened wire slackening off.

'So,' said Bernie from across the table. 'How was your night with the crew, Francis?'

'Interesting.'

'Interesting?' Bernie scoffed. 'Is that all you're going to give us?'

'OK, there was one important thing I learned.'

'Don't tell us,' said Vanko. '"No shitting on the bus."'

Francis laughed. 'That was it! Actually, Seamus was telling us that in the old days…'

'The very old days if Seamus was involved…'

'Before they had toilets on the buses, they used to shit in a bag and throw it out of the window.'

'Yuck,' said Topaz. 'Too much information.'

'In the old days,' said Bernie, 'they used to shit in a bag and throw themselves out of the window.'

After they had finished eating they moved into a side area of sofas and armchairs. Francis found he was next to Topaz. She had remarkable features. Big enough to register as beautiful on the stage's wide screen, yet lovely in an intimate setting too. Her dark brown eyes pulsated with feeling: confident and humorous, but curiously vulnerable.

'Were they indulging?' she asked.

'Indulging? In what?' he replied mock-innocently.

'In more than just alcohol?'

'What do you think?'

'Obviously, yes. But just a spliff, was it?'

He nodded. 'I'm sure my presence ensured they were on their best behaviour. No danger of overdoses last night, I don't think.' There was chatter in the background, laughter and music, the clink of glasses. 'May I ask you a question?' he said.

'If you want.'

'What did you mean, yesterday on the bus, when you said that if some crazy fan had it in for somebody on this tour, it would most likely be Adam?'

Topaz shrugged, as if her remark had been no big deal. 'I didn't say "some crazy fan", Francis. I don't think the fans give a toss about Adam. Most of them don't even know who he is. What I meant was' – she leant forward towards him and dropped her voice – 'if someone seriously wished the tour harm, it would more likely be Adam they were trying to get at than Jonni. That's all.'

'Why?'

'You'll have to ask me another time. When we're alone.' She let her hand rest briefly on his wrist; despite himself, her touch sent an electric charge of desire right through him. 'Put it this way,' she went on, 'he's a legendary rock and roll manager, Francis. The bands and artists he's looked after: Zak and the Tainted Idols, Guitarmageddon, Tender Plastique. I mean, the list is fairly awesome. But you don't do that for forty years without upsetting people.'

'What do you mean, people?'

She didn't reply.

'The artists? The other managers? Who?'

She leant right in. 'There is – at least, there was – a lot of money swimming around these legends. Maybe somewhere along the line, somebody didn't get their fair share.' Her eyes widened. 'Who knows?'

Much later, Francis was back in Vanko's room, having a late drink. The guitarist had apologised for not going clubbing; he was more in the mood for a quiet night in. 'We've got a gig tomorrow night. I never like to do too much before. All that sexual stuff, it's more like an after-show thing. You know, you come off that stage like a conqueror. But also, in a weird way, a bit insecure. You kind of need the validation. And one has to say, a good fuck is validation. But I've had it now. That Berlin girl was fairly crazy, but nothing compared to last night. Dusseldorf. You didn't see her, did you?'

'Sadly not. Your Berlin girl looked nice enough.'

'She was, wasn't she? Gertrude. A sweetie. We're actually in touch on WhatsApp. But Dusseldorf. Jesus, who would have thought it? She was the whole nine yards, a fantasy woman.'

'In what respect?'

'In every fucking respect. Looks, intelligence, laughter, appetite. Jesus, she wrung me out like a cloth. I haven't got a single sperm left in me. Truly. Every last one has left the building. It's like a crisis down there. They've got to start manufacturing again from scratch.'

'She was German?'

'Yeah. Some kind of demonic student. There's an art school in Dusseldorf apparently. Not being vulgar, but boy, was she an artist. What she did with her tongue and lips was pure poetry. The Schlong certainly got attended to, put it that way.'

'I'm glad to hear it,' Francis said, cutting him off before he became any grosser.

'Even Russell got lucky last night. Not a great looker, but he was happy. Shame you weren't with us.'

'Don't worry – that sort of thing isn't for me anyway.'

'Are you actually gay, Francis? I hope you don't mind me asking.'

'I'm not, no. I just don't think it would be very professional of me … to get involved. In that kind of way. My objectivity would be compromised. Anyway, you lot would never leave me alone.'

'This is true,' Vanko agreed.

'Plus, I'm a bit older. #MeToo, you know. All that.'

'Fuck that shit! You're in good shape, mate. How old are you, anyway?'

'Late forties.'

Vanko laughed. 'I'll take that as early fifties. I get your

point about being objective, though. Have you been round the red light district here in Amsterdam?'

'No.'

'You should. It's bizarre. It's legal, so it's all above board. No pimps, allegedly, though I find that hard to believe. Anyway, you see all these women posing in their underwear behind picture windows. Standing, sitting, lying back, bathed in red light. So you can basically see exactly what you're getting. I probably shouldn't say this, but I quite like that sort of sluttishness. Especially if the women really are in control. I find that a turn-on. But I went for a stroll through those streets tonight and I felt nothing. My poor old pecker's had it. Even if one of those lovely ladies had opened her booth and offered me a freebie, I would have had to turn her down.'

Francis wasn't quite sure where this odd confessional was leading, but his instinct was – somewhere.

'Another nice thing about them,' Vanko went on. 'Those whores. They're not fans. At least, as far as I know. You go with a fan, you're never quite sure what you're going to get. Most of them are fine. They've seen you onstage. They like your playing, they're into you as this, like, wild performer. Fair enough. But there's always the risk that you're going to get one of the psycho ones. And they really aren't funny. You should see some of the shit they come up with.'

For whatever reason, Vanko was determined to show Francis some examples. He switched on his laptop and found one of what he called 'the most offensive websites'. This was the fan he had mentioned before, who was publicly living out a fantasy of marrying him.

'A *fan*-tasy.' Vanko chuckled darkly. 'The *tassie*' – he slipped into a caricature Scottish accent – 'of one of my more extreme *fans*.' In the central image, this young woman had photoshopped Vanko into a picture of her in a wedding dress. It was all spookily realistic, complete with shots of her family drinking champagne, menus and a guest book with comments.

'It almost looks as if you did marry her, Vanko.'

'Seriously disturbing, right? She's not the only one of these freaks. I mean, people outside this mad world talk about groupies sometimes. But I don't think they have any idea what these girls are like. You saw those ones chasing the bus yesterday. That's really nothing. I mean, Jonni point-blank refuses to tour in Italy and Spain any more, because they're even crazier down there.'

'And Topaz doesn't have the male equivalent?'

'It's something in the adolescent female psyche, man. In my humble opinion. My theory is that they're at a stage where they're still looking for the ideal man, the dream man, before they settle down with the compromise. I mean some of these fruit loops actually kid themselves that they're going to be with Jonni, you know, in the future. Like, for good. I'm not joking.'

He'd opened up another website, this one devoted to photos of Jonni, around the caption *My husband, though he doesn't know it yet.*

'Have you shown him this?' Francis asked.

'He wouldn't be arsed.' Vanko paused, clearly thinking through his answer. 'His attitude is that it's none of his business what people think of him.'

'Really?'

'We've talked about it. I happen to disagree. However weird they are, these people are for real. You have to take them seriously.'

'So what about the bloke in Hamburg?' Francis asked. 'Where does he fit in? I know he was supposed to be insane. But what was his motivation? Deep down. Is he jealous of all the attention Jonni gets? Did he do it for someone else? Or what?'

Vanko didn't reply. 'D'you want to know what he said?' he said eventually.

'What who said?'

'The Danish nutter. As he pushed Jonni off the stage. This is totally off the record, man, you didn't hear it from me.'

'He was Danish?'

'Yeah. Nils something or other. You knew that, surely?'

'I do now. So what did he say?'

'*This is for Sandra.*'

'Who told you that?'

'Jonni.'

'Who else knows?'

Vanko shrugged. 'I was sworn to secrecy. So, Adam maybe. Charmaine. I doubt he's told Simon.'

'So why are you telling me?'

'You're "the journalist". Who's "writing the story". Perhaps you ought to know.'

Francis ignored this teasing suggestiveness. Had Simon shared his thoughts about what Francis really was with Vanko during a boozy night in Dusseldorf. Or on the bus to Amsterdam?

'So who is Sandra?' he asked.

'He didn't say.'

'A fan Jonni slept with?'

'Maybe.'

'And abandoned. Or did something bad to. Is that possible?'

Vanko met Francis's gaze. 'I really don't know, Francis,' he said flatly.

'A jealous boyfriend takes revenge?'

'The thing is, we never know about that sort of stuff. You have to accept the fans are all adults. If they shag us and have some difficult explanations to go through later with a boyfriend, that's their problem.'

'*Are* they all adults, though? Some of them look pretty young to me.'

'What are you saying? That they're not old enough to make their own decisions?'

'I don't know. I was just quite shocked, I suppose, by how young some of those ones up at the front are. With their signs.'

'*Fuck me, Jonni*, you mean. That kind of thing.'

'That kind of thing, yes. I was surprised. In this day and age.'

Vanko shrugged. 'It's mostly a tease. You know, that age group. Out to shock and be daring. Without understanding what they're even doing half the time. He doesn't, though. Fuck them. Nor do I. Hand on heart, those really young ones are not a turn-on for me.'

'But how do you know? How old they are?'

'You can tell. There's a certain – how can I put this? – savoir-faire that comes in as they get more mature. Anyway, the ones you end up with aren't usually the ones in the front rows. That's all just a game, those signs, saucy T-shirts, all that stuff. You usually hook up with older girls in the clubs afterwards. I mean, they might have been to the gig, but they're not the babies. Those ones go home in a giggling gaggle to Mummy and Daddy.' He held up both palms defensively. 'Honestly, man, I'm not a paedo.'

'I'm sure you're not.'

It had been an odd conversation to end with, Francis thought, as he peeled off to his room a short time later. And where had it come from? Out of nowhere. Or rather, out of some speculation about *This is for Sandra*. And why had he had to wait to hear about that key detail from Vanko? How many of the rest of them knew? There was this strange combination among these tour folk: (a) they mostly all knew anything that one of them knew and (b) they didn't want to tell anyone else, certainly not an outsider like Francis, even if he'd been employed by their boss to get to the bottom of things – especially if he'd been employed by their boss to get to the bottom of things. There was an *omertà*. What went on on tour did indeed stay on tour, however controversial.

With the exception of Vanko, who seemed to be on a mission to share stuff. Why? Did he actually know that Francis was in detective mode? Or was he trying to tease a confession out of him? Perhaps that was it. I'm honest with you, you be honest with me.

But *This is for Sandra* changed everything, didn't it? It gave the Hamburg assailant a motive. Perhaps what Francis needed to do was give up on the tour and head straight to Hamburg to try and interview the assailant. Would the German police let him do that, if he had Adam and Nick's backing? But even if they would, who was to say that he would have any luck in finding out who Sandra was, and why she needed avenging?

As he lay there in bed, he was seriously considering this course of action. But then again, wouldn't it be better to stay with the tour? *Omertà* notwithstanding, Vanko and Simon had been open enough with him, and other tantalising titbits had already dropped out. Not just this Sandra thing, but Topaz's remarks about Adam. *Maybe somewhere along the line somebody didn't get their fair share.* There had been a definite suggestion that she might say more about that. If the time and place were right. What was she driving at? And why? Did she actually know of someone whom Adam had done down at some point? It certainly felt like it.

Tomorrow night, they were to play Rotterdam. That was almost halfway through the tour. After that there were just eight more gigs and fifteen more days before the entire entourage returned to London. Every day that passed, he was getting to know them all better. Maybe there was a whole lot more stuff he hadn't been let in on.

This is for Sandra. Maybe Jonni was usually more of a

womaniser than had been apparent so far on this tour? Maybe being clean had changed his behaviour. Was it even conceivable that this had something to do with Ricky too, and there was a link between the two 'incidents' after all?

As Francis drifted off to sleep, all kinds of thoughts scurried around his brain. One thing he was sure about: they all knew more than they were letting on; and his challenge was to somehow get under their skin and find out what it was.

Chapter Seven

I n London Francis rose at seven most mornings, woken by the *Today* programme on his radio alarm. He set it for 6.58, so he got the cheerier weather before the depressing news. A quick cup of tea with the headlines, then he'd be into his running things before he had time to think. Off out onto the street, avoiding the freshly laid dog shit as he ran down the little hill and turned right up York Rise, then left down one of the pretty streets that led across to Highgate Road and the open Heath beyond. Back home, after his hour-long circuit, he'd shower before heading out to the Roasted Bean for a flat white and breakfast while he read the paper. Living alone, he needed to start his day with company, even if it was only Tom and Julie, the bickering couple who ran the café, and assorted faces he knew on his walk there and back: the saturnine Indian newsagent by the Tube, the big smiley Middle Eastern guy in the halal butcher and greengrocer.

Now, as he rolled over in the huge hotel bed, he felt like an adolescent again. Rootless between the sheets, curtains blocking out the morning sunshine. So this was what it was like for rock 'n' roll bands. Very late nights; long, bleary, introspective mornings. No wonder half of them went mad.

His phone was ringing. He reached over to locate it, on the antique mahogany cabinet beside the bed. *NICK FOURIE*, read the screen.

'Aren't you up yet?'

'Nearly.'

There was a disembodied South African chuckle. 'I see you're settling into the rock and roll routine.'

'They like late nights, don't they?'

'And you've been keeping up with them? I hope all your ligging along's been fruitful.' Nick sounded almost jealous. What did he expect from his hired tec? Someone who *didn't* get stuck in?

'I've been getting to know them a bit better, that's for sure.'

'Though Adam tells me you think they've been a bit reticent with you.'

'Yes, well, what goes on on tour stays on tour. There's been some of that.'

'Bound to be. To begin with. Though if they start to think you're part of the gang, they may loosen up.'

Exactly, Francis thought. That's why I've been hanging out with them in the way that I have, you idiot. But he wasn't going to grass up Vanko, even to make a point.

'So what have you found out?' Nick asked.

Francis trod carefully, giving the London-based manager a carefully edited account of what he now knew – and suspected. That almost everyone in the band and crew whom he'd spoken to seemed to think Ricky really had OD'd, and that his death had nothing to do with the Hamburg incident. As Francis filled Nick in, he decided he would give him one trial titbit: not Seamus's nickname for the managers, but that – in confidence, and obviously not to be shared with Jonni, please – some of the crew thought Jonni had overreacted to being shoved off the stage.

'Overreacted!' replied Paranoia One. 'To being thrown off a stage by a man carrying a knife. Who exactly is saying that?'

'I think I need to protect my sources.'

'Why? We're employing you.'

'Sure. But at this early stage, I wouldn't want…'

'Don't you trust me?'

'Of course I do.'

That had decided it. He certainly wasn't going to share *This is for Sandra* with Nick just yet. Adam might have done, but then again he might not even know, let alone have decided to share. How close were the managers, anyway? So, Francis would take his chances and keep schtum. As for Topaz's suggestion that unknown malevolent forces might have it in for Adam and thus the tour too – no, that neither. 'I mean, Nick,' he said, hoping to divert him by changing the subject, 'it's been quite hard convincing them that I'm writing a piece for *GQ*, or even that I'm a journalist.'

'I hope you're sticking to your story, whatever they think.'

'Of course,' Francis lied.

'It's down to you, Francis. You've got to convince them.'

'OK.'

'It would be awkward if any of them thought we didn't trust them, that we'd actively put a spy in the mix.'

'Of course.'

'I'll have to hope that you're going to get a bit more feed-back very soon. Otherwise I'm going to be questioning the wisdom of sending you out at all.'

Excuse *me*, Francis thought, as he clicked off. You pretty much begged me to do this. I almost didn't accept. I'm doing my best, and I'm getting somewhere, even if I haven't shared everything yet with you, you controlling arsehole.

To add insult to injury, Francis realised he'd now missed the hotel breakfast, which stopped at half past ten. By the time he'd had a shower and got dressed, he was condemned to a coffee and a Danish (did they call it that, here in the Netherlands?) in a canal-side coffee shop. Ah well, there were worse fates. It was a sunny February day, one of those early, glowing ones that you get in London too, when spring suddenly seems just around the corner.

He strolled out of the hotel and along by the canal, which was, if not exactly glassy, at least still enough to reflect the bare-branched trees to either side, the colourful little houseboats moored up by the black railings, the clear blue sky above.

On a bridge a hundred yards or so up he spotted a familiar figure, albeit in an unfamiliarly glam black coat. The band's bass guitarist was standing between two chained-up bicycles, leaning over, contemplating the watery mirror. She was carrying two boxy shopping bags, one of which was a bright orange. As Francis was debating whether he should say hello or just slope quietly by on the other side of the bridge, she turned. She had already clocked him and was waiting for her moment.

'Hiya,' she called. She looked almost shy.

'Hi, Topaz. Been out shopping already?'

'Some great little places here. Although some of them don't open till eleven, which is a bit weird. Hey, d'you fancy a coffee? I was just going for one. Though coffee shops here...'

'Are a bit different.'

She raised her eyebrows. 'Some of them, yes. I'm not personally planning to indulge on a show day.'

'Me neither.'

'Then we need a *koffiehuis*, not a "coffee shop". Anyway, they often have rubbish coffee, the dope cafés.'

They found a little place on the other side of the canal. There were clean wooden tables, brown vinyl stools, framed prints on the wall, a red-lipsticked waitress with a crimson and white spotted bow in her hair – and no marijuana menu. The concentration on varieties of product had to do entirely with beans, not leaves.

They ordered flat whites and brownies and sat down at a table in the window.

'I just hope Vanko doesn't do something stupid and get off his tits somewhere,' Topaz said.

'He's probably not even up yet.'

'That's true. The bus leaves for the venue at half three. Maybe we'll be spared.'

'So does he … ever?'

Topaz made a face. 'Normally he's sensible. Just every now and then, like, once a tour, he seems to feel the need to be Keef or Ozzy or Kurt and arrives in no fit state to play. It's a bit boring of him, to put it mildly.'

'I'm sure he'll be fine,' Francis said. 'He seemed quite low-key last night.'

'You didn't go out clubbing again then?'

'He was worn out.' Francis grinned. 'We had a quiet drink in his room.'

'Poor lamb. After all his random ladies…'

'He does rather go for it, doesn't he?'

'He's keeping the flag flying,' Topaz replied with a laugh. 'For rock and roll chauvinist pigs everywhere. You know, I think that's why they have him. In the band. They've got sensitive, gender-fluid Jonni, who's very respectful of his female fans, but it's like they need Vanko too. For the old-school macho element.'

'"They" being the managers?'

'Of course. We're a constructed artefact. Not a band that got together organically. That's why we all get on so well.'

They sat in silence for a minute, sipping their coffee. Francis forked up a portion of brownie. It was delicious: crisp on the outside, gooey within.

'Let's hope this isn't a space cake,' he said.

'Too yummy for that.' Topaz looked down thoughtfully, then up again, quite suddenly. 'You're not really writing a piece for *GQ*, are you? That's your cover story. You're trying to find out what happened to Ricky, aren't you? And why Jonni was pushed off the stage? Jonni's deeply paranoid, as we know. He thinks something weird's going on. So he asked Adam to employ a detective figure. You. I know you're a writer – George Braithwaite and all that. But you're actually better known for the murder cases you've solved, aren't you? I checked you out.'

Francis said nothing. He hoped his face had remained relatively poker-like during this barrage. This was always what he'd feared: in this age of maximum information, there was no escaping the reputation he had never wanted. Not as the crime writer, you could bring that on any time, but as the successful amateur sleuth.

'It's all there, isn't it?' he admitted. 'Or most of it, anyway. So, if I tell you, in confidence, what's going on my end, will you tell me what you were going to say about Adam last night? Why you think somebody might have it in for him?'

'Maybe,' she replied – and was he imagining a flirtatious edge to that smile of hers?

So he confirmed that her guess was true: that he had nothing to do with *GQ* or any other magazine and that Nick and Adam were employing him in an investigative role. 'Your turn,' he concluded.

She sighed deeply, but it was clear that at one level she did want to unburden. 'OK,' she said eventually, 'so what do you know about Zak?'

'As in super-famous Zak who turned up in Berlin? What I know is what everyone knows: that he was the lead singer of the Tainted Idols, and then later went solo and became a famous actor, gives ten per cent of his income to good causes, makes award-winning cheese and whisky on his net zero Scottish estate, has a troubled/tragic personal life, never had kids of his own but adopted a couple, one of whom freaked him out by becoming a Tory MP.'

Topaz smiled. 'Not bad.'

'So what's that got to do with my question about Adam?'

'As you know, Adam managed the Idols. Back in the day. Before he crashed and burned. Before he got together with Nick. Anyway, strictly between ourselves, and not to be repeated for fear of scary consequences that even I can't guess at, Zak is not the hero he's so often depicted as being. Yes, he's very ethical and publicly pays that tithe, but the bottom line is, he's a massive hypocrite. Back in the day, he basically took all the money from the Idols for himself.'

Francis laughed. 'You're joking?'

She shook her head.

'How d'you mean, all the money? In what way?'

'In every way. You know, the dear old Idols, they were all great musicians – unlike Zak himself, it has to be said – but none of them were very savvy businessmen. Do you under-stand the difference between recording royalties and publishing royalties?'

'Not really, no.' The truth was, he hadn't heard of either; he didn't even know there was a difference.

'In a nutshell, bands make their money from live shows, particularly these days, and from royalties. Recording royalties get paid to bands when they record a song, and are generally split equally among the band members, but they often get swal-lowed up in the costs of touring and so on, especially if the band doesn't survive very long. It's the publishing royalties that are where the money is, even though, at first sight, they may look smaller. They get split between the publisher and then the writer of the lyrics and the composer of the tune, usually fifty–fifty, but in any percentage they all agree on. Zak cottoned on to this from the start, and took not just the publishing royalties for the Idols' lyrics, which was fair enough, since he wrote most of them, but for a load of the tunes as well. Which was wrong of him, as the band composed the music together, even if Zak was in the room at the time.'

'So he ripped off his own band?'

'Exactly.'

'And manager Adam was aware of this?'

Topaz shrugged. 'He knew that Zak was cornering the lion's share of the publishing royalties, but he didn't stop him and he didn't tell the others in the band. Who knows exactly what he got in return, but put it this way, he gets his percentage whatever the split, so he did OK. It was the band who were left with nothing.'

'Really *nothing*?'

'That's why they split up. Because they eventually cottoned on to what was going on. Even as the band was running out of money, unable to afford the sets for the tours and that kind of thing, Zak was buying Glenveray, his castle in the Scottish Highlands. There's a funny story about the Idols touring Europe on their last ever tour, and they were so broke by this stage that they were having to paint their own sets and stuff, could barely afford to buy takeaway pizzas, meanwhile the back of the tour bus was filling up with priceless antiques for freakin' Glenveray. At that point the brilliant Scotsmen suddenly realised that something was a bit wrong. How wrong, they had yet to discover.'

'How do you even know this?' Francis asked, once he'd stopped laughing.

'Bobby told me. He was on the bus.'

'Bobby?'

'Fairhurst. Lead guitarist? Of the Idols?'

'Oh right, sorry.' Francis's ignorance of pop history was shocking. 'Bobby … Fairhurst. I see. So how exactly d'you know him?'

'He's my godfather.' Topaz grinned proprietorially.

'The lead guitarist of the Tainted Idols is your godfather. In a proper religious sense?'

'Maybe not that religious, but yeah, he is my proper godfather. He's like one of my dad's best mates. They used to be in a band together before Bobby joined the Idols. Up in Glasgow.'

'Your dad is a musician?'

'Yeah. Where else d'you think I learned to play?'

'But you don't come from Scotland, do you?' Francis laughed. 'Where's your accent?'

'Dad moved down south before I was born. But he and Bobby stayed mates. So we used to see him quite a lot when I was growing up. Bobby's a larger-than-life type, you know, and very droll. You should see him do his Zak impression. That mad dancing, the intense, groaning delivery. Hilarious, he gets it right off.'

'So where are they all now? The other Tainted Idols?'

'Nowhere. In terms of fame or whatever. They went their separate ways in the mid-90s. Bobby has this little tourist farm near Wigtown. You know, goats that the children can stroke, rare sheep breeds, llamas, that sort of thing.'

'He's given up on music?'

'He plays down the pub with the local folk band. Swapped his guitar for a *clàrsach*, which is like a Celtic harp, massive great instrument. He's grown a beard, looks like some angelic old hippy.'

'And the others?'

'Dan the drummer went back to Shetland, I think. Frankie Freak, the keyboard player, remember him?'

'Vaguely,' Francis replied, not wanting to lose face.

'Super-skinny, used to wear this Pierrot outfit. No? He ended up in Italy. With an Italian wife and a bunch of kids. Pigged out on pasta and now looks like a fat Mafia boss, according to Bobby.'

'And Adam knows all this? Your connection to Bobby?'

'I'm not sure he does. We've never spoken about it. Anyway, why would he?'

'Because you used to hang around with your godfather back in the day. When you were a child and the Tainted Idols were up there.'

'The Idols predate me, I'm afraid. Do I look that old?'

'Sorry, my grasp of rock and roll history isn't what it should be.'

'The Tainted Idols were late eighties, nudging into the nineties. They split up finally in '95, I think. The year before I was born.'

'OK.'

'The point is, I don't think Zachary – Zak – and Adam realised quite how pissed off they all were. About the "appropriated" publishing income. Bobby and Frankie in particular. There were various tunes they felt they'd all contributed to … you know "The Love That Tells Me"?'

'Of course. Jonni's been singing it at the gigs.'

Topaz nodded. 'The keyboard carries the tune,' she went on, 'and there's a reason for that, because it was Frankie's melody. One hundred per cent. And he didn't get a penny for it. Zachary claimed the whole thing, told poor Frankie he would get a "suitable reward" further down the line.' She made the quotes with scornful fingers. 'Frankie, being a trusting guy, thought this amounted to a "verbal agreement", but that turned out not to be worth the paper it wasn't printed on.' She laughed bitterly. 'Uncle Bobby even tells this story about Frankie's mum telling him she couldn't understand why Frankie had never got anything for the song, because she remembered him playing it as a teenager, at the upright piano in their house in Paisley.'

'You call him Uncle Bobby?'

'Yeah.'

'And Zachary is Zak's full name.'

Topaz was rolling her eyes, as if everyone in the world should know such a thing. 'Er, yes. Zachary McWhirter.'

'So how could he do that? Zachary, Zak. Get away with it? Claim a tune that was known, by everyone, to be someone else's?'

'Hard to understand, isn't it? They signed stuff, that's the problem. Like I said, they were musicians, not lawyers. They trusted Zak and Adam to do things right. And then by the time they realised what had happened, it was too late. They let it all go for years, but then, you know, "The Love That Tells Me" is such a huge and perennial hit, covered by all sorts, that in the end, encouraged by Bobby and others, Frankie tried to take Zak to court.'

'And how did that go?'

'Not well, for Frankie. Adam rang him up a few days before the hearing and told him that if he lost he'd have to pay all Zak's costs, some supposedly massive figure, like half a million quid or something, which would have bankrupted him.'

'Adam rang him up?'

'Yeah. They work together, those two. The evil twins. So Frankie dropped the whole thing.'

'Really?'

'Yeah. Settled for some nominal sum and having his costs paid. Didn't even ask for recognition, like, you know, Matthew Fisher.'

'I'm sorry. I'm not with you.'

'Matthew Fisher. Keyboard player for Procul Harum. Sued Gary Brooker over the tune of "A Whiter Shade of Pale". He got credited, but no royalties, because he'd waited thirty-eight years to pursue his claim.' Topaz laughed. 'That melody was nicked from Bach, anyway, so maybe that had something to do with it.'

'I remember people saying that,' Francis said.

'Anyway, Dad thought Frankie was an idiot, because his

case was so cut and dried, and the backdated royalties were worth a lot–'

'How much?'

'I don't know. Millions, probably. It was a huge hit.'

Francis nodded, remembering the times he had danced to 'The Love That Tells Me' over the years. With Kate, too, back in the day. It was a song to end an evening with. *It's the love that tells me / All I need to know.* Who hadn't boogied to that? A beloved partner in their arms. How many nights of passion had that set up, in discos up and down the land? Around the world, even?

'That's why the costs gambit was so evil,' Topaz went on, 'because it totally wasn't fair. But bottom line, Frankie was scared off, and his Italian wife was terrified they'd lose their house.'

'When was this?'

'A year or two ago.'

'That recently?'

Topaz nodded.

'So what are you saying, Topaz?' Francis asked. 'That having failed to get legal redress, Frankie or one of the others is having a retrospective go at Zak … and Adam … by trying to mess up the tour or something?'

Topaz shrugged. 'I don't know, Francis. Just, like I said before, that if anyone had enemies, it would be Adam, not Jonni. You know, Jonni is a bit up himself sometimes, and he annoyed a few people with his crazy behaviour when he was caning the substances back in the day. And then, obviously, there are things about his–' She stopped abruptly.

'There are things about his what?' Francis asked after a few moments.

'Nothing.' Topaz was shaking her head, almost to herself, as if to say 'I shouldn't have said that'. 'But he doesn't have enemies,' she went on. 'As such. Not like Adam and Zak.'

Francis decided not to push her on whatever it was she wanted to keep quiet about. She might come back to it, in her own time. But not, he didn't think, under pressure. 'So Zak is still involved with Adam in some way?' he asked.

'He part-owns the company, for fuck's sake. AZ Music. Adam–Zak, get it? Nick came in later. He's Adam's partner, does most of the work, but he doesn't have as much of a share as Zak. Zak basically rescued Adam when he crashed and burned in the late nineties.'

'Yes, Nick mentioned that. What happened?'

'He didn't tell you?'

'No. Nor did Adam. Hardly surprising, given that I've only had two short chats with him since I got here.'

Topaz shrugged. 'It was pretty heavy, I think. He was basically this big, showy rock 'n' roll manager with a country mansion, collection of classic cars, huge Harley-Davidson, all the trimmings, and he lost the lot. His marriage went tits up. Then Zak came along and bailed him out.'

'I thought that was Nick.'

'Nick was part of it. I think Nick might have got him into rehab and stuff like that. But he never had Zak's financial clout. It was Zak who put him back on his feet again. One of the few genuinely nice things he's done in his life. Although canny too, because Adam is an awesome manager. Talent-spotter, talent-nurturer, big daddy, big bruiser if need be. So yeah, you hurt the tour, you hurt Adam. But even more than that, you hurt Zak. There's a reason why he was hanging around backstage in Berlin. He was finding out what's been going on. These tours make a lot of money. In these days of digital downloads, tours make most of the money, in fact. They can't risk losing that.'

And why on earth, Francis thought, did neither Nick nor Adam tell me this? It made his embarrassing encounter with Zak in Berlin feel even worse. He was surprised he hadn't been sent straight home. *You've got me a backstage detective? He didn't even realise I was financially involved. What kind of a useless prick did you manage to find?*

'If there's one thing Bobby's told me about Zachary,' Topaz continued, 'it's that he cares about the bottom line. Over and above all that public stuff about his famous ten per cent tithe, which I don't think he actually pays anyway, his profits matter to him.'

'So how would they have done it? These enemies of Zak and Adam? Got onto the tour bus – or inside security? I mean, did they pay that guy to push Jonni off the stage?'

'I don't know. Maybe what you should be looking for is someone on the inside.'

'And what about Ricky? Does he have something to do with all this? Do *you* know something, Topaz? Is that what you're trying to tell me?'

She laughed, that ebullient, infectious explosion that made you want to say something to amuse her. 'Don't be silly, Francis. I'm just saying that if there *was* something weird going on, around messing up the tour, there's enough people on the inside, among the crew perhaps, who don't like Zak, or Adam, to make things happen.'

'You're not talking about anyone in particular?' he asked.

'The band and the crew don't mix that much,' she replied, rather airily. 'We live in our own bubbles. Here we are in Amsterdam. What's going on down in Rotterdam isn't for us to know, really, is it?'

Chapter Eight

Francis sat in Catering for the first few songs of the Rotterdam gig, sipping black coffee and eating a passion fruit cheesecake in tiny nibbles while chatting to Flo as she cleared up after the early evening meal, spraying and wiping down the tables. It was actually one of Francis's private bugbears, waiting staff who cleaned tables right next to you in restaurants with stinky blue fluid while you were still eating, but in this case he wasn't complaining, rewarded as he was with Flo's chirpy banter, naked midriff and tight red satin shorts. Jesus Christ! What kind of a tragic perv was he becoming? But it seemed as if sex was everywhere in this rock 'n' roll environment. There was barely a woman backstage he didn't at some level fancy, quite apart from the anonymous hordes of dolled-up fans. Not that he was going to give in to temptation, even if temptation came seriously calling. As he had explained to Vanko, any actual involvement would be highly unprofessional, as well as leaving him exposed to mockery from the entire entourage.

Pre-gig, Francis had tried to speak to Jonni, but yet again Charmaine had put him off. Maybe later, she said, after the show. Yeah, right, Francis thought. You would think that at some point they would want me to actually talk properly to the living victim in the case, who also happened to be the dead victim's 'very close friend'. If they don't, what can I say? Or do? He had decided that he would give it one more night, then phone Nick and give some of his attitude back, ask for some action. Whatever Adam was up to, with his ever-genial corralling of his little star, it wasn't exactly helpful.

The only other people in the works canteen at this dead time were a couple of the bus drivers: Bryn the stocky Welshman was drinking tea with a twinkly-eyed, pink-cheeked fellow, who looked, with his round gold specs and sailor's navy flat cap, like a muscly reincarnation of Benny Hill. All he needed was a cravat and a posse of saucy ladies in skimpy underwear and he'd be a dead ringer.

'All right, Bryn?' Francis ventured as he walked past to refresh his coffee. Benny graced him with a sideways smile, but the Welshman wasn't doing introductions right now. The pair of them were bent over a mobile screen, indulging in a bit of online gambling by the look of it. Three of the other guys, including diminutive Dolly, and Jonni's handsome Black driver, had been at their table earlier, but had headed off into the arena when the show started, in harnesses and yellow vests. They earned a bit of extra cash by being follow-spot operators during the gigs, Bernie had explained, climbing high into the rigging on rope ladders.

Song five on the set list tonight was – yes, indeed – 'The Love That Tells Me'. Francis left his now empty plate as soon as he heard the famous piano intro. He headed up to his regular viewing spot, just behind the bank of huge speakers stacked to the right of the stage (right for the audience, that was, though in fact stage left). This useful location seemed to stay the same regardless of the venue, as did the matching one on the far side, where Adam and Charmaine made their base during the gigs, the PA bopping up and down enthusiastically while the boss man swayed gently from side to side. They looked like Piglet and Pooh at a pop-up disco in the Hundred Acre Wood. Both were always ready with a grin or a thumbs-up when Jonni looked over towards them for mid-concert reassurance.

Jonni did hardly any covers, yet he did 'The Love That Tells Me' at every gig. It was almost as if Adam had licensed him to take over the great Idols hit as his own. Or did Zak insist that Jonni sing it, so that the publishing royalties kept flowing into his bank account year after year? Francis had listened to that haunting piano, tears pricking his eyes, even before he knew that the tune had originated with Frankie Freak, who still hadn't got proper justice, by all accounts.

'That's the lovely thing about the Netherlands,' came a voice in his ear. 'They're mostly completely stoned, so it's a very laid-back crowd.'

It was Bernie, with his trademark cackle. He stood beside Francis watching as the tiny phone and wristband lights danced back and forth, dotting the arena like a thousand mobile stars.

There was a sudden loud crack, like a gunshot. A yellow flash lit the stage.

Vanko, who had been playing his guitar and singing at the same time, pretty much snogging his mic as usual, fell backwards, like a puppet whose strings had been cut. His guitar dropped with a crash as he crumpled to the floor and lay still.

'Jesus Christ!' cried Bernie. 'Vanko!'

Topaz was the first to react, laying her guitar down carefully and running to him. Now Jonni had turned, seen his bandmate on the floor and stopped singing. As the drums stopped too, the noise in the auditorium rose. Francis heard shrieks of '*Oh mijh God!*' and '*Wat is er gebeurd?*' and then a shout that sounded like '*Geël-ektrocute-erd!*'

The band were all around Vanko now, shielding him from

view. Adam was onstage too, leaning over him protectively. Bernie had run from this side, shouting back at Francis as he went. 'Electrocuted!'

Francis followed, but hung back from the immediate group around the prone guitarist. Now there was a paramedic onstage, in a green and white jacket with *MEDIC* written on his back in green fluorescent letters. He was at the centre of the action, bending over. Crew members Ted and Mel and Seamus were scurrying around with torches, rescuing the fallen instrument, testing plugs and cables. Finally, it seemed, Vanko was moving. Then, miraculously, he was up on his knees, then on his feet, waving away offers of help from all around him. He walked over to Jonni and put his arms round him. Jonni reciprocated with a stagey hug. They were talking urgently. Another hug. Then Jonni moved back across to his microphone, looking over to check with Ted, then touching it quickly with the back of his hand to nervous, admiring laughter from the crowd before picking it up from its stand.

'He's all right,' he announced, to a huge cheer. Then: 'Ladies and gentlemen, boys and girls, we've had a small incident, involving a bad electrical connection or something. God knows how that happened. But the good news is, our unstoppable guitarist Vanko Angelov is back on his feet.'

More cheering, rippling around the stands.

As Jonni spoke, Vanko's guitar tech Mel was holding out his instrument. Vanko leant forward and spoke to her. Mel was gesturing down towards his foot pedal, then waving negatively towards the mic. Apparently reassured, Vanko took the guitar and slung the strap over his shoulder.

'He's going to play,' Jonni said.

Everyone's attention was on Vanko as he began strumming, quite slowly, then faster, then suddenly he had riffed his way into a Hendrix-style solo. Jonni stood watching, nodding, grinning, as the guitarist got wilder. After two minutes the grin was starting to crack. With a crazy flourish, Vanko finished.

'Vanko Angelov!' shouted Jonni, gesturing at him in apparently respectful homage. 'The Jimi Hendrix of our time. A mere matter of electrocution is not going to stop our Vanko. OK, let's pick up where we left off, shall we? Take it away, man.'

The guitarist's fingers were playing the famous tune again. Simon was joining in with the keyboard, Topaz with the bass, then the drums crashed in. Finally Jonni, with a reprise of Zak's famous lyric:

It's the love that tells me
All I need to know
Wherever you may be
Wherever I may go...

The audience were going berserk. A near-death, and now their favourite song repeated. Phones and wristbands waving, they yelled back the chorus line.

Backstage, afterwards, the shock kicked in.

'What happened, man?' Jonni was asking.

'I've no idea,' Vanko replied. 'One moment I was just there, strumming away, the next I was, like, thrown back.'

'Did it hurt?' asked Charmaine.

'It was kind of weird,' said Vanko. 'Like a really hard punch in the stomach. The medic told me I was lucky I was wearing rubber-soled shoes. But Jesus, it makes you wonder, doesn't it? I've been playing an electric guitar for seventeen years.'

'What's going on?' said Jonni, turning to Adam, who was

trying to look calm and collected, and visibly failing. He looked like a nervous blancmange, pale and trembling.

'Come on, Jonni,' he replied, taking his arm. 'Everything's being thoroughly checked out. It was an unfortunate accident, that's all.'

Jonni was looking directly at Francis, eyes wide. 'Someone's out to get me,' he mouthed. 'Us.'

At least he knows who I am, Francis thought.

Vanko was taken off to hospital for a check-up and the band went back to the hotel – no champagne on their bus tonight. Simon went with Jonni. Drummer Scally came with the band.

'Don't you have to write something on this story?' he asked, as they sat in a tight huddle in the downstairs lounge, speeding back up the motorway to Amsterdam.

'I'm not that kind of journalist.'

'No? What kind of a journalist are you?'

'With a magazine piece, you keep your powder dry till the end.'

'What the fuck does that mean?'

'It means that I've been lucky enough, I suppose, to see some eyewitness stuff that a newspaper journalist would kill for, but I'm not going to use it just yet. I'm going to keep it back for my piece. So it creates a bigger impact when the time is right.'

As Scally nodded, Topaz was smiling quietly to herself. Francis longed to get her alone, to ask her what she thought about the electrocution, given everything she had said earlier. But the dynamic wasn't allowing that and Topaz was making no effort to help, sticking with the two backing singers as they got off the bus and made their way back into the hotel and along the plush corridors to the dining room that overlooked, through heavy peach silk curtains, the glinting canal at the back.

The remaining band members sat around with the accountant and tour manager, discussing famous rock and roll electrocutions as they ate. Keith Richards had come close to death, according to Bernie, at Sacramento in 1965, or was it 1963? Anyway, he too had been saved by rubber-soled shoes – blue suede ones, appropriately.

'Were you there, Bern?' teased Scally.

'Don't be silly. I'm not that old.'

'Maybe Seamus was.'

'Ha ha. I wouldn't make that joke with him if I were you.'

'Wasn't Moby electrocuted one time?' asked Thelma.

'Rings a bell,' said Bernie. 'Kesha was, for sure. In her, ahem, vagina, as far as I remember. George Harrison, of course.'

'I thought he was stabbed.'

'Electrocuted before that. From his mic, while filming *Let It Be*. You can see it in Peter Jackson's documentary *Get Back*. And Les Harvey was killed. Touched his mic with wet hands and that was that. Didn't live to tell the tale.'

Francis had no idea who Les Harvey was, but he wasn't going to let anyone know that, or ask what group he'd been in. Nor was he going to be a pedant and point out that to be electrocuted you had to die. Otherwise it was just shock.

'It must have been something to do with Vanko's mic,' said Suzi. 'I was watching him. He was singing, then he kissed it, then, like, just crumpled.'

'It was his guitar,' said Thelma. 'You know how he insists on a cable and an amp.'

'But they let him back on the guitar,' said Topaz. 'So it wouldn't have been that.'

'Mel was waving him away from his mic,' Suzi added.

'It's still a fucking mystery,' said Bernie. 'He kisses that mic every single night.'

'Several times,' said Thelma.

'Snogs it,' said Scally. 'The lunatic.'

'Has to be something to do with the guitar,' Bernie added. 'To make the circuit. But how you feed mains into that without the backline guys noticing, I've no idea.'

A little later, as they were toying with puddings, Vanko reappeared, to table-wide applause.

'Jesus Christ!' said Scally.

'...is risen again,' added Bernie. There was laughter.

'I could seriously use a drink,' said Vanko. 'D'you know what? I hate hospitals, even nice Dutch ones.'

'Shag any nurses?' asked Scally.

'Give us a break.'

'I thought you might have gone for the sympathy vote, mate.'

'Scally!' cried Topaz. 'Vanko nearly died this evening.'

Adam was in the room, hovering a little way off, watching his band relaxing again. When Francis caught his eye, he was rewarded with a beckoning hand gesture. He got up and went over.

'How's it going?' he asked. 'Learning anything from this lot?'

'I don't think they know what happened, to be honest.'

'I'm surprised you stayed with the band,' Adam replied. 'I would have thought the crew might have had more insights. Into how a guitar could become live in the middle of a concert.'

'I got swept up backstage,' said Francis, honestly enough.

He could see what was coming. A midnight flip from his comfortable bed, just three floors up in the Hotel Du Monde's luxuriously carpeted lift (which came complete with a padded and monogrammed seat) and back out down the motorway to the wide empty spaces of the Ahoy. Then another small-hours bus ride.

He was right. Adam had a car ready for him. It was just a matter of collecting his bag. As Francis came back downstairs, he could see, through the side door to the dining room, that Jonni had now joined the party, was standing supportively next to Vanko, his hand on his shoulder. Simon was with him.

'Good luck!' said the manager, who was waiting for him in the foyer, smiling his broadest, cheesiest smile. 'Nick and I are very keen to know what happened.'

The usual geniality had returned to the surface, but under that there was a new and tangible tension. Whatever was going on, Adam wasn't happy about it.

So did Adam really want him to quiz the crew, or did he just want to keep him away from the band? What was he up to? Francis wondered as he sped reluctantly back through the night to Rotterdam, chit-chatting intermittently with his bulky Surinamese driver Cherwin, who seemed keener to talk about Rotterdam than his home country. It was a far better city, he said, than Amsterdam, even if Amsterdam was more popular with the tourists. The football team Feyenoord was better than Amsterdam's Ajax, that was for sure.

Francis arrived at the venue just as the crew were taking down the last items of the set. The waiting trucks were almost fully loaded and the backline crew were already backstage, enjoying what was left of the hospitality wine and beer.

'Ooh, la la!' cried wardrobe mistress Laurent. 'A very late arrival. What are you doing 'ere, Mr Journalist/Detective? Did the band get fed up wizz you? Or are you trying to find out 'ow Vanko could nearly get fried onstage, given all the checks the crew 'ave to do zese days?'

'Yes,' Francis replied wearily. There didn't seem much point denying what he was in front of the others. Most of them weren't paying attention to Laurent anyway, used as they were to her extravagant personality.

'I'm keen to get all sides of the story,' he added.

'The trouble eez, nobody really knows what 'appened. Your best bet is to ask one of zose backline people when they come in. Or maybe you could travel with them tonight, if they 'ave a spare bunk.'

But after a word with Pants, it emerged that the order from above was that Francis was travelling on the fabled lampies' bus. Not that there were going to be any wild parties tonight. Nor were any of them even up for a pre-kip chat, as it was 2 a.m. before they left Rotterdam, and the Brussels load-in began at 7 a.m.

'Sorry, mate,' said Garry, the Lighting Crew Chief (also known, apparently, as the Gaffer). 'I'd love to speculate with you all night long, but I've got to get me beauty sleep, otherwise nothing's going to happen tomorrow. Come and find me in the morning, though, and I'll tell you what I know. I always like a bacon sarnie about nine.'

Here was a challenge. Francis followed the five zombies upstairs and inserted himself carefully into 'the empty bunk', which was on the bottom rung of three. Nobody had said it was Ricky's, but there seemed little doubt that it was. Did Adam's insistence that he sleep on this bus have something to do with this? Francis just hoped the sheets and blankets had been changed since Ricky's death. He lay there, trying not to inhale what might or might not have been the stench of death, trying not to think about his lovely king-size bed in the Hotel Du Monde, with the fresh, starch-scented sheets and the view out through the heavy satin curtains to the civilised glimmers of the dark canal below. Above and around him came a *Symphonie Fantastique* of snores and farts from five lampies, dead to the world after their long day of loading, lighting and unloading. But they weren't as dead to the world as their colleague Ricky, who had once stared upwards at this sagging fabric above him too. Had this dark, criss-crossing, shiny plastic thread been the last thing he'd seen, as the drugs had overwhelmed him and destroyed the miraculously complex functions of his exhausted body?

Chapter Nine

Francis had been half-aware of the bus stopping. Slowing and stopping and starting up again. Then slowing and stopping and drawing into a parking space. Shortly after that, of the cacophony of mobile phone alarms. Of not-so-quiet grunts and bodies shifting and feet thumping onto the floor. Of dressing and clattering down the narrow stairs and some shushing and laughter – for his benefit, presumably. Then a loud, ironic cry of 'Don't shit on the bus!' Then more laughter. Then an operatic rendition of the same command. Then doors opening and silence.

Francis had drifted back into a heavy sleep, only to be startled by his own mobile alarm. It was 8 a.m. Time to get up and go looking for Garry's bacon sandwich. Was this going to be the way to get the answers he needed, if he was going to get anywhere with this bloody case and prove himself effective to the managers who had employed him? Jesus, he thought again. One moment I'm the amateur solver of mysteries, dragged in by curiosity and circumstance, with no need to prove anything to anyone. The next, I'm the incompetent employee, running around getting nowhere fast. Oh to be Sherlock, with his brilliant intellect and all-seeing eye. Now, it seems, I've even lost the one thing I ever-so-discreetly prided myself on: the ability to get people to open up to me.

Downstairs, he splashed cold water on his face in the toilet sink and said hello to the driver, who was lounging in his huge black leatherette seat with an iPad on his knee. It was the Benny Hill lookalike, no less.

'Francis,' Francis said, holding out a hand.

'Ray,' the driver replied, taking it and giving it a surprisingly firm squeeze. He wasn't wearing the navy cap this morning, though he'd made up for it with a stripy matelot top and a gold stud, in the shape of an anchor, in his right ear. 'You're the last up there, I hope,' he cooed.

'I am.'

'So I can get off – finally.' Ray/Benny rolled his eyes in a mock-grumbly fashion. Francis was all set for jaunty music to start and five scantily clad ladies to come leaping out of the downstairs lounge.

'Apologies,' Francis replied. 'I didn't realise I was keeping you.'

'Someone's got to lock the fucking door, haven't they? You never know what kind of people lurk around pop venues, do you?'

'I guess you don't.'

'Still, I'm not complaining. Just had a little windfall. On the gee-gees.'

'Are they running already?'

'They are in Melbourne.' Ray giggled.

'Glad to hear it,' Francis replied, internal eyebrows raised. 'I don't suppose you'd know where I'd get a bacon sandwich round here?'

'Bacon sand-*witch*. There's a couple of caffs up that main

road there, but this is Belgium, matey. You'd be more likely to get a croque monsieur. A crooked mister, as I call it.'

Ray was right. Up among the apartment blocks and leafless trees of the Avenue Victor Rousseau, Francis found a little café, but it didn't sell bacon sandwiches, and the idea of a croque monsieur as a takeaway was clearly not in their remit. In the end, having gulped down a hot, milky *café crème* and a rich, flaky almond croissant, he decided to take a repeat order of the same into the venue for Garry.

It was all go in the empty, echoing Forest National, where the eight thousand bright orange seats were arranged in a giant circle, a steep stalls area rising from ground level and then a higher dress circle above, stretching back. The heavy black flight cases were being wheeled across the gleaming grey central floor. Chunky sections of stage were being slotted together. There were shouts from high up on the girders – sorry, trusses. The sound and light desks were already in place, side by side, a third of the way back down the hall, huge banks of monitors and slides and knobs in many colours. Here Francis found Creative Director Kylie tapping away at the keyboard of a laptop.

'How was your night on the lampies' bus?' she asked. 'Wild?'

'Sadly not. They were all asleep five minutes after we got on.'

'Farting and snoring.'

'That was about it.'

'You can see why I prefer the backline bus.'

He chuckled. 'Well…'

'Not a word of disloyalty to your new friends.' Kylie smiled and looked up. 'So that was something exciting for your piece, wasn't it? Vanko's little incident.'

She tossed over a copy of the morning's newspaper. *Het NiewsBlad* it was called, with a very large white N in a blue box in one corner. *JONNI'S PARTNER STAAT OP UIT DE DOOD* read the headline. And there was Vanko, curled up on the floor, with Jonni leaning over him, and then, in a second picture, back up again, playing like a demon.

'Wow, front page,' Francis said.

'They love Jonni even more than we do. All good for Vanko, though. I think that means he rose from the dead.'

'Do any of you know what went wrong?'

'It so shouldn't have happened. I mean, Seamus may be a bit of a stoner, but the safety checks that go on before the band even get to sound-check are prodigious. Foolproof, or should be.'

'So what are you saying? That it was sabotage?'

She shrugged. 'And some. God knows. Another extremely strange incident on this extremely strange tour.'

'And who would want to electrocute Vanko?'

'Excellent question. Me, obviously. No, I'm only kidding. My dislike for him doesn't run that far.'

'You're not joking?'

'He's not that popular with the crew, Francis. Hate to disillusion you.'

'Why's that?'

'He can be a bit of an...' She paused and lowered her voice. '...*arsehole*. But a selective one, like all arseholes. He's always terribly nice to Mel, who looks after his guitars for him. And Laurent, who he fancies, I suppose. Ditto lovely Flo. Anyway, I shouldn't keep you. I'm sure you've got people far more important than me to talk to.'

'I was actually looking for Garry,' Francis said.

'The Gaffer? Why?'

Francis held up his paper bag. 'Got him an almond croissant.'

'That was nice of you.' Kylie reached in, grabbed the pastry and took a bite. 'Yum,' she said with a smile. 'Creative

Director's privilege.' She turned and pointed across towards the back of the arena. 'He's over there somewhere.'

'He actually wanted a bacon sandwich,' Francis said. 'I hunted around the local cafés, but I couldn't find one.'

'They do them here, you idiot. In Catering. At nine o'clock. Didn't he tell you?'

By the time Francis found the Lighting Chief, the takeaway *café crème* was cold. Not that it mattered. Garry laughed at Francis's misunderstanding and was happy to finish off the almond croissant before heading up to Catering. 'Come and have a quick coffee. I could do with a break.'

Catering was only half constructed. But Flo was in a white apron, dispensing bacon sarnies. The Nespresso machine was in action, as was the kettle: boiling water not just for PG Tips, but camomile, green, ginger and lemon tea too. They certainly looked after their staff on this tour.

Up here they were reading, not just *Het NiewsBlad* but also the *Mail Online*, on their phones. *JONNI'S JINXED TOUR* ran the headline, with a mugshot of Jonni looking concerned (possibly library), then a sequence of pics of Vanko getting back up and playing, ending with the guitarist triumphant, head thrown back, singing, while Jonni watched from the mid-stage background. Was that envy in his eyes? Surely not.

Garry made himself a double espresso and sat down with a sigh. 'Sorry about last night. We all tend to be a bit knackered after the loadout. So what did you want to know, mate? How it came about that the great Schlong got electrocuted?'

Francis smiled at his directness. 'That's about it.'

'None of us know. I've got nothing to do with backline, but the checks would all have been done. Mel is well upset, obviously. It seems it was a damaged foot pedal somehow putting mains power up into his guitar. And Vanko has a wired mic, like all the instrumentalists, so when he did his usual trick of snogging it – bang, he created a circuit and was down on the floor.'

'Mains into a guitar? That sounds pretty serious. How did that happen? By mistake? Or did someone tamper with the foot pedal?'

'Looks like it, doesn't it? I'm surprised the safety circuit-breaker didn't trip, to be honest. Cut the power to backline. You should talk to Mel, really. It's her job as guitar tech to keep an eye on all those bits and pieces.'

'Could *she* have done it?'

Garry's face was a picture of astonishment. 'What? Why? She loves Vanko. With a burning flame. No, I really don't think it would have been Mel setting up any rogue mains feeds.'

'But how would any outsider get onstage to set this all up while you were loading in?' Francis asked. 'I mean, even if he got through Security, surely he'd stick out like a sore thumb.'

'Or she,' Garry replied. 'Sometimes it's easier for a she to get through the ring of leather than a he, if you follow me.' He put a clenched fist to his mouth and mimed fellatio, his tongue pushing against the inside of his cheek. 'But it's odd. Because Dead Ed is pretty incorruptible. And he's always prowling around.'

'So if it was sabotage, it was an inside job?'

Garry shrugged, but didn't reply. Did he know something? Francis often got the feeling with this lot that he was being quietly excluded. Even if bad things were going down, none of them were snitches, were they? It was like a school, in which he was the inquisitive new junior master.

'May I ask you another question?'

'Feel free.'

'You all move around, don't you?'

'How d'you mean?'

'You crew for Jonni, for example, then you move on to some other band and work with them?'

'Of course.'

'And how d'you get employed?'

'Word of mouth, I guess. Production managers talking to each other. Recommendations. Kylie's a brilliant lighting designer, that sort of thing. In this job, as you can see, you can't afford timewasters. There's no slack. Speaking of which.' He looked down at his watch. 'I'd better get back.'

'I don't suppose,' Francis said, realising he was grasping at straws, and too late in the dialogue too, 'you'd happen to know if any of these guys ever worked for the Tainted Idols? Back in the day.'

Garry was on his feet. He gave Francis a look that was part admiring, part warning him off. 'With the legendary Zak,' he said with a chuckle. 'Maybe you should ask him who he remembers from the old days. Nice to chat, mate.'

And he was off. Just like that. There was no way that Francis was going to be able to ask Zak which, if any, of the current crew he had ever worked with. He would have to follow his instincts. And keep asking questions. Maybe spend another night on a crew bus. After tonight, Brussels, there was a day off in Frankfurt for the crew (while the band had a day off here in Brussels). Which presumably meant another party on the bus tonight. And who knew what a stoned Seamus might divulge this time?

On the other hand, Francis also wanted to talk to Vanko. How was he feeling after the shock – literally – had worn off? Was he scared? Did he feel targeted? If so, by whom? And what was Topaz thinking? She had been weirdly quiet last night. And the rest of the band: Scally, Suzi, Thelma, not to mention Jonni himself. Anyway, Adam, for whatever reason, had closed down that particular avenue. Had he really wanted Francis to interrogate the crew? Or was that just another cover story, in this increasingly weird set-up, where he'd been employed to look into this case by Paranoia

One, only to find himself actively frustrated by Paranoia Two?

He knew where he'd like to be tonight, given the option. In Brussels, with Topaz, continuing the one-to-one they'd had in Copenhagen. Get over yourself, you silly man. Where do you need to be? Obviously, on the backline bus. There would be time enough to talk to individual members of the band at the venue before the gig.

Chapter Ten

Francis spent the long morning watching the crew set up. It was hard work, but not for him. He felt like a total spare part, wandering around trying not to get in the way. Up on the newly constructed stage he found the backline crew, Mel and Ted, working on the instruments. Mel was tuning guitars; Ted was on his knees among the drums, checking each component. Stage manager Seamus was, meanwhile, going over Simon's keyboards; once, presumably, this had been Ricky's work. Then, without a word, he walked down to the drums, took Scally's seat and gave each skin a battering with the sticks. As he finished an undeniably skilful solo, he nodded at Francis. As if to say, 'Not bad for a roadie, eh? Those dice might after all have tumbled in a different direction.'

Francis took advantage of the opening. Taking out his notebook, he asked Seamus if he could name the drums for him.

'For your magazine piece, is this?' Scorn and disbelief mixed in the old Irishman's voice.

'If you don't mind.'

Seamus pointed at them, one by one, unceremoniously.

'Kick drum, snare, floor tom, small tom, large tom, crash cymbal, ride cymbal, hi-hats.' Then he walked off. There was clearly going to be no chance for questions about whether he'd once crewed for the Tainted Idols, let alone how Vanko's electrocution could have come about.

Ted followed with a shrug and a grimace, and Francis found himself alone with Mel. He was tempted to make some snarky remark along the lines of 'friendly pair', but decided against it. He didn't want to risk pissing her off as well. Group loyalty was important to this lot.

'Quite a business, isn't it?' he ventured, having watched her silently for a couple of minutes.

'Lots of double-checking today. Can't have a repeat of last night, can we?'

'That was a bit unexpected, wasn't it?'

'We're not actually that keen on electrocuting our stars, no. Kind of takes away the point of putting up the set for them in the first place.'

'So what happened?'

Mel met his eye. 'Looks like something went wrong with one of his foot pedals. Though how and why, none of us know.'

'But it was touching the mic that did for him, is that right?'

'Yeah. Well, you need a circuit, don't you? So if there's a dodgy wire in the foot pedal, and the mains got up into the guitar, and then he touches his mic, which is also wired, bang, route to earth, you're away.'

'So what are you saying? There was a loose connection or something in the foot pedal? How did that happen?'

'It's a total puzzle. Especially as I checked that unit only a couple of days ago.'

'Aren't all the units they use checked every night?'

'No. Why would they be? They're all secure. I mean, it's not like you open your kettle up every day to see if it's properly wired, do you? That's what you'd need to do to cause an incident like last night. Open the unit up and rewire it.'

'Lucky he was wearing rubber-soled shoes, I guess.'

'What's that got to do with it? He could have been in bare feet. The stage is made of wood. Non-conducting. The mains would have been in the guitar. Up from the foot pedal.'

Francis's mobile was ringing. *NICK*, read the screen.

'Sorry, Mel, I'd better get this.'

The manager was at the AZ Head Office in London. Adam had told him that Francis was out with the crew in Brussels. How was it going? Had he got any insights into what had happened with Vanko last night?

'The latest I've got,' Francis replied, in a low voice, keeping an eye on Mel, who had wandered off across the stage, 'is that it was something to do with a foot pedal not being wired properly. And then Vanko kissed his mic, as he does, and ker-bam, off we go.'

'But how does a foot pedal not get wired properly, in this day and age? Am I going to have to sack someone?'

'No, they're all completely baffled. The tech I've just been speaking to says she checked the unit only a couple of days ago.'

'You'd think they'd check all the units every day.'

'It's not something that normally goes wrong, apparently.'

'Is what they've told you?'

'Yes.'

'So it sounds as if someone did tamper with it.'

'Yes.'

'Keep asking the questions, Francis. I hardly imagine the guilty party is going to own up for the hell of it.'

'Nobody knows who the guilty party is.'

'Nobody knows,' Nick repeated scornfully. 'Or they're not telling?'

'Maybe they're not as one hundred per cent open and

candid as I'd like, in an ideal world, but I don't think they're deliberately hiding stuff from me.'

'And in general, d'you feel you're any the wiser? About what's going on, or perhaps I should say going *wrong*, with this tour? This is the third incident, the second public incident. The papers have started to write about "Jonni's jinxed tour".'

'I saw.'

'Can't say I'm happy. That kind of press makes everyone nervous.'

'Of course.'

'God knows what they'd write if they knew about Ricky. Luckily the lid's still on that one for the time being. Though it only takes a greedy Danish policeman. Or one of the crew, acting anonymously…'

'They strike me as pretty loyal–' Francis began.

'I'll see you tomorrow, Francis,' Nick cut in. 'In Frankfurt. If you had some answers for me by then, that would be terrific.'

'I'll do my best,' Francis replied, trying to ignore the sneery spin that Nick had put on 'terrific'. But he was, he realised, talking into thin air.

He looked up to see that Mel had made herself scarce. Damn. So that pointless and aggressive call had actively slowed him down. He should have squared up to Nick: 'One of the things that's holding me back is your partner. Whom frankly I don't trust. Why is he shielding me from Jonni? And why did he insist I left the band party last night? He must have known that the crew on a night between a loadout and a load-in are not talkative. I continually get the feeling that he doesn't want me around. What has he been telling you? And by the way, where exactly do you stand in the loop with Adam and Zak of AZ Management?'

Tomorrow, when Nick arrived in Frankfurt, Francis needed to put his cards on the table.

Around 6 p.m., he made his way past the latest heavy-duty phalanx of German Hell's Angels and up into Catering. What a wonderful pop-up affair it was, this friendly little café reconstructed in every venue they got to, with its cheery gingham tablecloths, its chalked menu board, smiling Flo, and the two chefs, Darius and Jemima, working away in their white hats in the background.

There was no band in evidence. But Russell, the American accountant, was making his way through a plateful of one of the specials: boeuf bourguignon, it looked like. Seeing Francis, he gestured to a chair. 'How's it going, dude? Getting anywhere with your enquiries? I'm sorry not to be able to keep up the crap about the piece you're supposed to be writing. But we all know you're a snoop. An in-house one, is the general feeling. Who's employing you? Nick? Or Adam? It's not the same thing, as I'm sure you've already found out.'

Francis looked across at those smug and gleaming pink cheeks and realised there wasn't any point, or even mileage, in continuing to pretend. At least with the band party.

'Did Topaz say something to you?' he asked, after Flo had come over and Francis had ordered a cheeseburger.

'Sadly not. I worked it all out for myself. Sorry, dude.'

By the same token, Francis thought, it wouldn't be wise for me to share my concerns about Adam, would it? Russell hardly seemed like a model of discretion.

Vanko joined them. 'Hi, man,' he said, reaching out a hand to shake Francis's. 'You, like, vanished, last night.'

'Yes,' Francis replied. *I was vanished. Forcibly. By Paranoia Two.* But: 'I thought I'd better see if the crew had any idea what had happened.'

'And did they?'

'The ones I spoke to thought it had something to do with your foot pedal. And the fact that you kissed the mic.'

'I always kiss the mic. They know that.'

'And so does everyone else. That may be the problem.'

'Which foot pedal anyway? I've got six.'

'One that was wired for mains, apparently.'

'They're all connected to the mains, one way or another. Francis, I've never had anything like this before, in all my years of playing. And that includes some well dodgy outfits, let me tell you.'

'Surely you must be scared? That someone's after you? Don't you have any idea who?' These were the questions Francis wanted to put. But he didn't feel he could. Not while Russell was there.

'How's Jonni?' he asked instead.

'He's cool. I guess. He made a brief appearance at supper. Just after you left. But I've not seen him since. None of us went out last night.'

'I should think not,' said Francis.

His cheeseburger had arrived, and Vanko wanted the same, so there was banter with Flo and then, after she'd gone, some decidedly unreconstructed chat between the accountant and guitarist about whether they would 'do' Flo if she was (a) a fan and (b) single. They decided they would.

'Hardly the biggest revelation, Russ.' Vanko laughed. 'You'd do anyone on this tour, given the chance.'

'Not the guys, FYI.'

'Really?'

'And I'd draw the line at some of the crew.'

'Some of the crew might draw the line at you, mate.'

'I very much doubt it.'

'Is Flo not single?' Francis asked.

'Oh no!' said Russell. 'Our undercover tec has got the hots for the Silverbird.'

'Really, I haven't. I'm just asking.'

'For a friend. Don't be shy, dude, she's pretty cute.'

'I appreciate that,' said Francis. This made Russell howl with laughter.

'I appreciate that,' he repeated, in a poor imitation of Francis's accent. 'Really, you are too hilariously English for your own good. You "appreciate" what? That our lovely wait-ress is as tasty as the food she serves? D'you think she would "appreciate" you? That's if you were in the market to be "appreciated". Which we understand you're not. For reasons of professionality, allegedly.'

Francis decided to leave them to it. Vanko wasn't going to open up to him with Russell around. He would go up and see what the women were thinking, and then hopefully catch Vanko alone later, when Russell had retreated to the mobile office where he kept track of the tour finances. Maybe he could finally get to speak to Jonni, if Adam would let him – and if he wouldn't, that would give him the ammunition he needed for when he saw Nick tomorrow.

He found the band hospitality room empty. But he heard female laughter from down the corridor, in a room with a piece of A4 tacked on the door. On it was written *FEMALE – PRIVATE.*

He knocked. 'Who is it?' came Charmaine's voice.

'Francis. May I come in?'

The door opened a crack to reveal Topaz, in loose black trousers and a lacy bra. As Francis tried not to stare, she grinned. 'No men allowed.' She waved a mock-admonitory finger at him.

'I just wanted to talk to Charmaine about Jonni.'

'Charmaine!' Topaz called, turning, then she turned back and met his eye before she sashayed away.

The PA appeared at the door.

'Sorry,' Francis said. 'I was just wondering if there was any chance of getting to speak to Jonni before the gig.'

'I'll check with Adam,' Charmaine replied. 'Jonni's in a strange mood at the moment. Post the Vanko thing.' She gestured towards the door of the hospitality room. 'Wait there, Francis, and I'll see what I can do.'

Chapter Eleven

There was wine and beer on the makeshift bar in the hospitality room, but Francis wasn't going to touch that before a possible interview with teetotal Jonni. He sat down on one of the battered leather sofas and picked up a copy of *WOW!* from the pile of celebrity gossip mags littering the long low central coffee table. At Candide's baby shower, Poppy Pink had shown off a seven-stone weight loss in a leopard-print dress. Jamsie Flint had hit rock bottom after finding out that her boyfriend Thebes had been texting other women. Timmy Trent's wife Sharene was breaking her silence after being seen out and about without her wedding ring. And yes, even if you couldn't meet the man himself, you could read about him. *FROCK OFF!* In a four-page spread Jonni K was showcasing some of the 'mandrogynous' outfits he was wearing on his tour of Europe. Appalled though Francis's inner pedant was at this toe-curlingly tautological coinage, he was learning more about what the star thought, reading this piece, than being with him on tour.

After a couple of minutes Adam appeared, his grin a couple of paces ahead of the man himself.

'Hi, Francis.' He seemed very genial today, as if Francis had just returned from a successful hike to the South Pole. 'How were the crew?'

'Good.'

'Glad to hear it. Did you get any insights into what the hell happened with Vanko?'

Francis filled him in with a summary of what he'd learned. *If I'm straightforward with you*, he thought, *maybe you'll reciprocate.*

'Keep asking the questions,' Adam said when he'd finished. 'I'm not happy about this, not happy at all. It's a total mystery, to be frank, and not a good one. Now, Charmaine tells me you wanted to talk to Jonni.'

'Yes.'

'About all this?'

Francis smiled, as patiently as he could manage. *Among other things, mate, yes.* 'If he's amenable,' he replied. 'If you're amenable,' he added cheekily.

'Jonni's in an odd place at the moment,' Adam replied. 'As you'd imagine. He's got it into his head that all these … er … incidents are linked. Not that the press are helping.' Adam produced a print copy of that day's *Sun on Sunday*, which he tossed down on top of the *WOW!* Francis had been reading.

ELECTROCUTIE! read the headline.

Now Jonni's gorgeous guitarist Vanko hits the deck

Further down, in a banner: *JONNI'S JINXED TOUR: p. 4, 5. Editorial, p. 13.*

'Luckily they haven't found out about Ricky,' Adam said. 'Though I fear it's only a matter of time.'

'D'you think they are?' Francis asked. 'Linked?'

Adam put both his hands down on his left knee and leant forward, his manner like that of the family doctor making a home visit. 'I actually don't,' he said. 'I think we've just had a lot of bad luck. I remember, back in the early nineties, when I was touring America with Guitarmageddon, one thing after another went wrong. It wasn't just a roadie who OD'd on that occasion, it was the lead guitarist. And then the tour bus over-turned in the middle of the night on the interstate and the drummer broke his arm. And then a stalker went mad with a gun. Everyone thought we were jinxed. Just like this time. We had headlines. TV reports. Journos chasing us on motorbikes. But we still carried on.'

'With a new guitarist and a new drummer?'

'Of course. Guitarmageddon was all about the lead singer, Skin. You remember him?'

No. 'Vaguely,' Francis fibbed.

'Hugely energetic presence. Built like a brick shithouse. Beard like a rug, and not one you'd want to sit on. As long as Skin was OK, the fans were happy. It was a bit like Jonni here. Different look, but the same phenomenon.'

Now's the time, Francis thought. I may not have Jonni, but I have Adam. Softly, softly, and I can sound out some of Topaz's wilder accusations. 'So was Guitarmageddon your most successful band?' he asked.

Adam paused, cocking his head as if he sensed a trick question. 'Difficult to say,' he replied. 'Perhaps in terms of impact it was. And posterity.'

'But not financially?'

Adam gave him a sharp look. Then, 'No,' he replied.

'That would have been the Tainted Idols, presumably?'

'Probably so, probably so. Look, we're rather wandering

off the subject, aren't we? Perhaps it's time I fronted up to you about this. Nick was keen to get you out here because he – and this is no secret – was never sure poor Ricky had OD'd. Naturally, if you follow me.'

Not exactly what he told me, Francis thought. 'What did he think had happened?' he asked.

Adam shrugged. 'Heaven only knows. But to me, I'm afraid, it's open and shut. The guy was a big user. He stopped for a while, which was great, we were all pleased, but then he fell off the wagon. And that, I'm afraid, is always the time for disaster. You go back to the dose you're used to, it can prove a bit too much. That's my take on it. But if my partner has other ideas, I have to respect that. Respect is very important between us.'

'I'm sure it is,' Francis replied tactfully. 'Isn't that always the case, in the best partnerships, business or otherwise?'

There was no answer to Francis's leading question and the silence grew to a point where he wondered whether he'd gone too far and the interview was over. But then: 'You know,' Adam went on, 'strictly *entre nous*, Francis, Nick saved me. Twenty years ago I was literally at rock bottom. I'd flushed all my cash down the toilet. The big houses. My classic car collection. I had a hundred, man. In this great big eff-off barn in the grounds of my place in Monmouthshire. Just up the road from the Rockfield studios, if that means anything to you. Beautiful gaff. Views to die for. Across to the Black Mountains and the Skirrid. That's another mountain. Looks like a big tit. One of the reasons I liked it. And that was in addition to the penthouse flat in Covent Garden and the villa in Calabria.

'But my mind was on this stuff.' Adam put his index finger to his nostril and snorted suggestively. Then he mimed knocking back a glass of wine. 'And that stuff. Any freakin' stuff, to be honest. So I kissed it all goodbye. Bedtime stories with my lovely girls, riding pushbikes with my little boy, good times with my beautiful wife Olivia.' He shook his head, slowly, as if mentioning her name had conjured her up, like a genie he suddenly missed. 'I pissed the whole lot against the wall.

'You know, Francis, when you're riding high you have endless mates. That's such a cliché, but it's true. When I had Guitarmageddon, and the Tainted Idols, and Tender Plastique, and a couple of others, in the eighties and nineties, everyone was my friend. Elton had me to his birthday party. I danced with Princess Di. Charley boy wanted my advice on the Prince's Trust. Everybody was up my arse. Seriously. It was like a party going on up there. "Excuse me, how do I get a VIP ticket to Adam Ainslie's back passage?"' He chortled. 'That was genuinely what it was like. And then I went too far. Way too far. I mean, that was OK if you were an artiste. Ozzy Osbourne once pissed in his record company executive's wine glass. Standing on a restaurant table in Germany. But that kind of behaviour's no good if you're the manager. It's an unforgiving world, the rock business. In the end, I had one friend left. You know who that was?'

Francis wasn't going to spoil this sudden, remarkable flow by even risking getting it wrong. Though as he sat there with his best 'tell me all' face on, he guessed who Adam was going to nominate.

'Nick,' Adam said, settling his big, brown, troubled eyes on Francis as if the very name was a confession. 'He was the only one that came to see me in that terrible rehab place. Outside Harrogate. Where I went through twelve weeks of shuddering hell. Jesus. And when I came out, stone-cold sober, with literally nothing, he was the one who looked out for me.'

There was silence as the manager stared blankly down at the floor. For a moment, Francis thought he was going to cry. There was some distant laughter from the women, but that was it. What about Adam's 'old mate' Zak? Francis thought. Where had he been in all this?

'I don't know why I told you all that,' Adam went on, recovering himself. 'Except that I wanted you to understand why I have to go along with him if he thinks there's something iffy going on and insists on calling in his latest idea of help – a private detective with a five-star reputation. You. My main problem in the here and now is that Jonni, my little star, agrees with Nick. He's young enough, and inexperienced enough, and frankly paranoid enough, to think that something is going on. That there's a pattern. And that what happened to Vanko is part of it.'

'And do you?' Francis chanced.

'I have no idea what happened to Vanko. Wish I did. Maybe it was just an accident. Let's hope so. So yes, I would like you to talk to Jonni. Tonight, if you can make the time. But not now. I don't want him upset before I've got him onstage. And off again. There's eight thousand lovely young Belgians out there who've forked out between one and three hundred euros for the privilege. We don't want to disappoint them, do we?' Adam's eyes glinted like diamonds, as well they might. 'But later,' the manager went on, 'in the hotel, come up to his room and play games with us. Our latest favourite is Skyjo. D'you know it?'

'I don't.'

'Great fun. You can learn in a minute. It's meant for nine-year-olds.' He rolled his eyes, the first time Francis had seen him be even vaguely disloyal to his star. 'So maybe we'll leave you two alone together at that point. And if I explain to Jonni what you're really doing here, perhaps you can tell him that, in your professional opinion, there's nothing going on. His mate OD'd, some jealous weirdo had a go at him onstage, Vanko's wiring was cocked up: a sequence of unfortunate accidents…'

Can I? thought Francis. He was suddenly on the spot and he didn't know what to say. He was longing to have a one-to-one with Jonni. But could he really tell him things he didn't believe?

'I should just say,' he replied, 'that I already asked Pants whether I could go on one of the crew buses tonight. There's some stuff I'm keen to follow up on.'

Adam sat forward. 'From what you just told me?'

'Maybe. I'm kind of stumbling around a bit at the moment. But I'd like to ask the questions.'

'Such as what?'

'I'd rather not say.'

'To the people who've hired you?'

A bullying tone had crept into his voice. But it was interesting, even odd, that after what he'd just said, Adam didn't dismiss Francis's suspicions out of hand.

Francis thought fast. 'I appreciate you've hired me, even if you don't personally think there's anything to see.' *Touché, mate, get out of that one if you can.* 'But I've told you everything I've found out. There's nothing else to report. As soon as there is, you and Nick will be the first to know.'

Adam was eyeballing him again. 'You don't even want to give me a rough clue what you're looking at?'

You, mate. And your old pal Zak. And possibly some vengeful member of the Tainted Idols, Frankie Freak or Bobby Fairchild maybe, whom you both allegedly screwed over big time. Back in the fabled day.

'Not at the moment, no,' Francis replied. He let out a little laugh, in an attempt to keep things light.

'You don't trust me?'

'No, that's not it, I do,' Francis lied. 'And that's saying something, in this environment.'

'By which you mean what?'

'*What goes on on tour, stays on tour.*'

Adam nodded thoughtfully at this restatement of the old mantra.

'But at the same time,' Francis went on, 'everything seems to get around the entourage.'

It was Adam's turn to laugh. 'That's a fair summary,' he said. 'Now I'm not pulling rank on you, Francis, but I want you with us tonight, OK? I think it would be useful for you to talk to Jonni. Calm him down a bit, whatever you think. Did Pants actually give you a confirmation about your place on the crew bus?'

'Not yet, no.'

'Little heads-up for you. We have fairly strict rules about what the crew are allowed to do on the buses. But then again, if they've been working for two or three nights on the trot and there's a day off tomorrow, we don't exactly monitor everything that goes on, if you follow me. So I don't imagine, on the lampies' bus particularly, that they would welcome an agent of management, which is how they'll see you, joining their little overnight party.'

With that, Adam pulled his mobile from his quaint little leather waist pouch and pressed a single number. 'Pants,' he said, smiling as he looked over at Francis. 'Did you manage to find space for Francis on the lampies' bus tonight?'

Francis couldn't hear the garbled answer, but it wasn't a straightforward yes, and Adam was chuckling.

'Much as I thought. No worries, mate. Francis will stay with us tonight.'

There was more gabbling from the other end. Even though Francis couldn't make out the exact words, he could still – bizarrely – hear the Australian accent.

'OK, mate, have a good one. And we'll see you in Frankfurt on Tuesday evening.' He clicked off and turned back to Francis. 'Where's your bag?'

'Where I left it. On the lampies' bus.'

'You'd better go and retrieve it then.' Adam smiled and

pressed another single digit. 'Bern, sorry, mate, busy time I'm sure…'

His curt nod indicated that he meant right now. Francis got to his feet and left the manager to it.

He made his way along the gleaming corridors, out round the edge of the stage and down to front of house. It was eight o'clock now, an hour before the official start of the gig, and the floor of the Forest National was filling up fast. Young women, very young women – could you call them girls? You certainly could – were already ten deep up by the long series of metal barricades that ran below the front of the stage, making an alleyway for the row of Security beyond. There they stood, the 'ring of leather', arms crossed in their battered and studded jackets. Long-haired or shaven-headed, tattooed, nose-pierced hard men, staring out over this chirpy sea of pubescent girls with the sour expressions of those who had been there, done that and set fire to some long-forgotten T-shirt many moons ago.

Jackets and coats bundled up inside dainty little backpacks, the girls, by contrast, were every teenage boy's fantasy, with every cliché of a sexy look on bold display: crop tops, shorts, miniskirts, tights, stilettos, funky boots. Watching them, Francis felt almost fatherly. So fresh-faced and wide-eyed, did they really have any idea of the power and precious loveliness of their youth? And who were they all so alluringly attired for? Themselves and each other, yes; TikTok selfies, for sure; even maybe some poor sap of a boyfriend; but Jonni most of all. *My husband, though he doesn't know it yet.*

Francis hardly saw himself as sexist. He had always liked the idea that he had held, quite determinedly, over his teenage and uni years, that even if their instincts were different, their hormones, their experiences, the minds of women and men were the same. But looking at this lot, he had to wonder if Vanko was right. Were the gigs of similar female artistes packed with spotty teenage boys, wired on testosterone, a crazy few of whom thought they might be in with a chance of a long-term relationship with the star?

The set was pretty much up. A couple of skinny riggers were high above, spidery silhouettes, adjusting lights on the criss-cross trusses. Halfway back down the hall, Creative Director Kylie was behind her huge console, headphones on, boogieing gently as she pushed and turned the numerous slides and knobs in front of her. Spotlight beams ranged through the artificially smoky gloom. White, yellow, pink, green, blue, geeing up the expectant crowd along with the thumping pre-show music menu.

Francis decided to leave them all to it. His walk out to the crew buses was, for him, a walk of shame. The lampies didn't want the spy at the feast: fair enough. Adam wanted him with Jonni, or he said he did. He was a powerless employee who just had to get on with it. He would have to ask Seamus and Garry his follow-up questions another time. If the managers didn't want to let him be where he needed to be, what could they expect? There was no huge urgency. The tabloids were slavering over the Jonni and Vanko incidents, but nothing had come out about Ricky. Nor, more to the point, had they realised that *he* was here. It wasn't, as yet, 'Francis Meadowes' next case'. Would it ever be? Perhaps the sensation-seeking vampires had forgotten all about him after a year and a half.

He snuck out of a side door past a dutiful German security man and made his way towards the three crew coaches, which hadn't moved all day, though the rest of the car park was now full. It was raining lightly, and the wet tarmac gleamed with bright reflected light. Which coach was it? He peered through one front door at an empty driver's seat. But there was someone in the next coach. Headphones on, snacking on some kind of takeaway while reading a book. It was the good-looking Black guy whom Francis had seen at the door of

Jonni's bus and in Catering, with Bryn and Ray, strapped into a lighting harness. He should surely recognise him, let him in?

Francis waved, then tapped on the door. The driver looked up, saw him, and leant forward to press a button. The big shiny door slid open.

'Can I help you?' he asked.

'Just got to pick up my bag. I was on here last night. With Garry and … the lampies.'

'Aha. You're that journalist guy, aren't you?'

'Francis.' He stepped up and held out a hand.

The driver shook it, warmly and firmly. 'Gideon,' he said. 'Not joining us tonight then?'

'I'm staying in the band hotel.'

'Moving on up, eh?'

'I do what I'm told.'

'Don't we all?' Gideon laughed, a rich, gurgling belly laugh.

'I thought Ray drove this bus.'

'Oh we swap around, us two. Between this and Jonni's bus. Jolly gets the day off in Brussels this time. Not that I'm complaining.'

'Jolly?' Francis queried.

'Ray. Rogerson. That's his nickname. Jolly Roger, it's a pirate thing. Also, that's what ex-Marines get called, isn't it? That or Bootneck.'

'So what do they call you?'

Gideon grinned, sheepishly, almost as if his nickname was his responsibility. 'OJ. I was a bit of a footballer in my younger days.'

'Playing for?'

'Boston United. We never got out of the third division, I'm afraid.'

'But you didn't murder your wife?'

'Not yet, I haven't.' The belly laugh was reprised, which

was lucky, as Francis's joke could easily have been taken amiss. 'To be fair, she's more likely to murder me. Anyway,' he went on, 'Frankfurt's an interesting enough place. A bit short on waffles, but there's a beautiful old town. One of my favourite churches is there. Old St Nicholas Church. Lovely vaulted ceiling and windows. You should have a look at it if you get a chance.'

'Maybe I will,' Francis said, noticing that the heavy black book Gideon was reading was none other than the Bible. He was working his way through Psalms. 'May I?' he asked, nodding at the stairs.

'Be my guest. I'll put the lights on for you. There's a couple of crew in the downstairs lounge, but you've no need to disturb them.'

As Francis made his way along past the kitchen area, he could smell weed drifting down the corridor. Squashing his curiosity, he tiptoed past and up to the first floor and retrieved his bag from the twisted bedding on Ricky's bunk. He was all set to scarper. But as he came back down he heard laughter that was unmistakably Topaz's, in counterpoint to a voice that was rumbling and male.

He couldn't help himself. He stood outside the door. There was silence now, and then, God help him, the unmistakable sounds of sex. Christ! What was going on? Topaz and … who? One of the crew. Which? How? Why? But then, as he stood listening, he heard the same sequence of erotic gasping repeated. Exactly. A man grunting, high-pitched female squeals. It was porn. Had to be. Topaz was watching porn with a male member of the crew. Francis couldn't help himself. He knocked.

'Yeah?' came a male voice.

He pushed his way in.

The beautiful guitarist was on the couch. Lying back next to her, a fat, glowing joint between his fingers, was Seamus.

They were watching something on a laptop that lay between them.

'Francis!' Topaz cried. 'What are you doing here?'

Her left hand reached out to close the laptop. Francis glimpsed naked flesh, but that was that. He could hardly draw attention to it. Topaz was, in any case, trying to make her measured swipe at the laptop look like a casual gesture. She didn't succeed.

'I was just getting … I'm sorry…' Francis stuttered.

'I'm hanging with my old mate, Seamus,' Topaz replied.

'Fair enough,' Francis managed, clocking the unwelcoming look on the stage manager's face. 'Sorry. I heard … your voice. I was getting my bag. I've been transferred to the band hotel.'

'Lucky you,' said Seamus. 'You'd best be hurrying along then. Leave us plebs to our buses.'

Francis had Seamus right here. But it absolutely wasn't the moment to quiz him about any possible links he might have to the Tainted Idols or even – who knew – Guitarmageddon, let alone talk to him about what he made of the Vanko electrocution incident. The answers Francis was after wouldn't come now, would they? You could have cut the tension with the proverbial knife.

He paused for a second. Stubborn and contrary as ever, he suddenly wondered if he could, after all, push the boundaries.

'Toodle-oo,' sang Seamus, in a mock-posh accent. Was there a smidge of good old-fashioned racism lurking in there too? Towards him, if not, obviously, for his mate Topaz?

'Laters,' said Topaz. Her cool, slightly scared look wasn't inviting him to stay. 'By the way,' she added, 'I wasn't here.'

'No worries,' Francis replied. 'I'm not sure I was either.'

'You weren't, mate,' said Seamus. 'Nor was I. Got that?'

Chapter Twelve

F rancis didn't surface the following day until almost lunchtime. Finally he got fed up with staring blankly at the sunlight on the heavy curtains, like some superannuated teenager. He rolled over and pressed the room service button on the phone by the bed. He ordered a coffee and a bacon sandwich from the rather sexy French-accented receptionist, wondering to himself what she looked like, then chuckled about something Vanko had said about being on tour. That when he went home, for a couple of days at least, when he woke up in the morning he'd reach out automatically for the phone, to hit the room service button, only to realise there was no phone, no room service, and he would have to get his own effing coffee.

It was very rock 'n' roll of him, but why was he still in bed? Last night had hardly been debauched. Adam had, amazingly, stayed true to his promise. After the gig and supper in the back dining room of the Excelsior, Francis had been invited up to Jonni's suite for a game of Skyjo. Was *this*, he'd wondered, going to be the moment he was finally left alone with the star? But no, it wasn't happening. Adam was there, Simon was there, along with Scally the drummer, Mitch and Omar the security guys, and two twitchy record execs from the US, who looked as if they'd be far happier out clubbing with Vanko than stuck with Jonni drinking Evian and playing a game meant for nine-year-olds.

Jonni took charge, briefing the guys on the rules of Skyjo, then excitedly leading each round. In between, he chatted about aspects of his life on tour, almost as if he had been briefed to by Adam. Some of the highlights of the tour wardrobe. The traditional dirndl Bavarian dress he was saving for Munich, the awesome magenta ballet tutu he was looking forward to wearing in Paris. Pretty much every time Jonni opened his mouth, Adam shot Francis his 'significant' look, as if Jonni was revealing crucial information, which he wasn't. Eventually, realising he was never going to get solo time with the star, he made his excuses.

'Goodnight, man,' Jonni said, high-fiving him.

Adam had joined in. 'Sleep well. I bet you're glad you're not on the lampies' bus.'

'Was he going to be on the lampies' bus?' Jonni asked, almost as if Francis wasn't there.

'At one point, yes,' Adam replied.

'Nice one. Sorry you got stuck here with me, mate.'

'No worries,' Francis heard himself saying; he almost felt grateful to be addressed directly.

Now he had a long afternoon and evening in Brussels. Doing what, exactly? After last night, he didn't really feel he could call Adam and demand a proper interview with Jonni. He badly wanted to talk to Topaz too. But he didn't have her number. Even if he had had it, what was the etiquette? Was he allowed to hassle one of the stars on their day off? Probably not. Maybe, he thought, one or more of them might be down-stairs in the public areas of the hotel. Or they might pass through.

Showered and dressed, Francis drank a slow coffee in the central lobby of the Excelsior, gazing idly up at its unusual domed high ceiling. After an hour of looking at social media and news apps on his phone and waiting for a random encounter, he decided he might as well do some sightseeing. What was there to do in Brussels? There was a hop-on, hop-off tour on a red bus that looked remarkably like a London bus. Riding round on this, you could visit the 'world-famous Atomium', with its giant silver balls representing the provinces of Belgium; or the Royal Museum of Fine Arts; or the European Parliament (though you couldn't, sadly, enter without prior booking). Another attraction of the tour was the '360-degree view from the top deck of the bus'.

In the end he went for a stroll around the flat-cobbled, pedestrianised centre of the city, treating himself to a strawberry and whipped cream waffle and marvelling at the sheer number of shops selling near-identical chocolates. There was a huge central square, the Grand Place, surrounded by splendid, long-windowed buildings in who knew what architectural style. In the hushed interior of St Michael and St Gudda Cathedral, there were fine stained-glass windows and a gleaming gold madonna. Up in the gardens of the Mont des Arts there were neatly clipped low hedges and a statue of a man on a horse: King Albert I, no less, once burnished copper, now weathered to a pale green, the grey stone base spoilt by unintelligible graffiti. Further on there were cafés with crimson and green parasols outside, and on a corner behind some railings an odd little statue of a peeing boy – the Manneken Pis – which even in February had attracted a crowd of tourists taking selfies.

At 6 p.m., there was still nobody Francis recognised back at the Excelsior. He returned to the lobby and ordered a beer. Nothing. There was a limit to the amount of time you could watch elegantly attired people greeting each other and heading off to more interesting places. Maybe, he thought, I'll just go up to my room, order a club sandwich and watch a film.

He was back on his huge empty bed and about to hit the room service button again when his mobile rang.

'Hi, man.' It was Vanko. 'There's bugger all to do in this city. D'you fancy getting a bite to eat somewhere?'

They met in the lobby and strolled out together to find a restaurant. How much nicer the alien streets were in company; and Vanko, tonight, was in a lively mood. There had been a vague plan for him to hook up with Jonni, he said, but then the star had dropped him in favour of an NA meeting. 'Boring git. Adam makes him do it.' Then he'd been asked to go out with all the others to some swanky Italian place, but he didn't fancy it. 'You get to this stage on a tour,' he said, 'where you get a bit sick of everyone. Little niggles. You know, man.'

'I imagine,' Francis replied. He was flattered that Vanko had seen fit to call him, though a tiny bit miffed that none of the others had wanted to include him in their group meal. He hoped he hadn't offended Bernie in some way.

'Especially with all this bullshit in the papers about the jinxed tour and everything…'

'Yes.'

Now was the perfect moment to ask about Vanko's take on the electrocution. But no, he would wait till they were sitting down and had drunk at least one glass of wine.

They walked on. Vanko had read about this French place that was supposed to be awesome. Le Plat Sacré, which served 'classic French cuisine', apparently. They found it eventually, at the end of one of the many paved, pedestrianised streets. Vanko looked delighted with his choice: wood panelling, glass-topped tables, white linen napkins, a chalkboard menu, a wall of wine bottles and a suitably haughty sommelier, complete with a theatrical Poirot-style moustache. Would Vanko suddenly pick up the table and hurl it, Axl Rose style, over the bar? No, he studied the menu quietly and ordered a pricey bottle of wine. 'Might as well have something decent,' he said with a grin as the man bustled off, newly deferential. 'Plus, I like to surprise these arseholes sometimes. They don't expect someone dressed like me to spend a hundred quid on a bottle. The booze is on me, by the way.'

Was Francis going to be obliged to get a second bottle at a similar price? Maybe the revelations in store would be worth it. He got the feeling that Vanko was warming up to something special. It was funny how you could always sense it in interviewees: the need to unburden.

Poirot returned, and they observed the opening and tasting ritual. Vanko took his time swirling the costly purple liquid round his glass. Poirot stood obedient, like a dog waiting for a treat. Vanko nodded. All was fine. A waiter appeared. Vanko ordered the *nougat de foie gras* followed by the *entrecote*; Francis the *raviole de homard* and the *onglet de boeuf*.

'Classic French,' Vanko repeated. 'No choice. At home you get these places with fifteen things on the menu, all done badly.'

This was indeed a very different Vanko from the wild man of the stage, head thrown back, guitar up towards the sky.

'So how did you get on with the crew?' he asked. 'When you spent the night with them? After the Rotterdam fuck-up?'

They had got to it, and it hadn't been Francis asking the question, which was a relief.

'They were all tired that night,' he replied. 'Just went straight to bed without saying anything much.'

'Really? Even though it was their responsibility to make sure the electrics are safe?'

'Not sure they'd have said anything to me anyway. You know. The outsider.'

'The detective,' Vanko corrected. 'Sorry, mate. None of us buy that *GQ* bullshit any more. You realise that?'

'Russell made it pretty clear to me the other night.'

Vanko laughed. 'Not exactly known for his subtlety, our American friend. So did you get anything out of the crew at all?'

'A bit the next day.' Francis thought of Kylie and her answer to his question about whether it had been sabotage or not: *And some. God knows.* 'Don't you have mates among the crew, Vanko?' he asked, deflecting the question.

'Scally's drum tech, Ted, is a good guy. And Mel, obviously, who looks after my guitars. Seamus, the stage manager, is a bit of a legend. He was great mates with Ricky, of course...' There was a short pause, then Vanko went on. 'I know Pants a bit. But the truth is they're mostly people I nod to, rather than talk to properly. A bit of banter here and there, and that's it. That's how it tends to be between band and crew.'

'And yet Ricky and Jonni were great friends?'

'That was a bit different. They were drug buddies, as I'm sure you know.'

'Ricky would get stuff for Jonni?'

'And the rest! Back in the day, Jonni was a serious user. He didn't have time on tour to procure his own substances. Adam's happy to get him most things he wants, but not drugs. Not with his history. So there was a kind of tacit arrangement with Ricky, if you like. A great big blind eye.'

'And Ricky was happy to do it because Jonni paid, presumably? For the gear?'

'And he loved Jonni.'

'What are you saying?' Francis asked. 'Presumably just as a friend?'

'It's not for me to talk about Jonni, is it? He's a big hit with the ladies, as you know. Which is kind of important in this business. Commercially and historically.'

'Historically?'

'It's that female psyche again, innit?' Vanko's 'innit'

mocked his adopted roots, as a newly assimilated immigrant could: it was a delivery that was somehow helped by the swanky surroundings. 'The guys have always had to be available.' The guitarist smiled and took a slow sip of his wine. 'When Keith Moon got married,' he said, 'in the sixties, to his pregnant teenage girlfriend Kim, it was all hushed up. Only one of the band turned up to the wedding. In the meantime, the management was coming up with stories about what a naughty boy around town Keith was. When he went out, poor Kim was left at home. Even after she'd had his kid and was living with him in Primrose Hill she had to leave their flat by the back door, so as not to disillusion the fans out the front. One of them found out the truth, and waited for Kim down the road with an axe. You could repeat a version of that story a hundred times. I mean, that's one of the reasons I don't have a girlfriend. A partner.' He invested the word with quiet scorn. 'Call them what you will. You know, I have fun on tour, but there's no one waiting for me at home, wondering what's going on. I wouldn't want to be put in that position, so I don't do it to anyone else. Also, you know, man, I have to say I don't get it. If someone doesn't do it for you, like one hundred per cent, why would you want to be with them anyway?'

This was a fair articulation of Francis's own philosophy about relationships. He found himself warming to the promiscuous guitarist.

'So what are you saying, Vanko? That Jonni's gay?'

Vanko's eyes widened. He put his forefinger to his lips and looked around the crowded restaurant. The well-upholstered, grey-suited types who were troughing away at the tables around them looked more like European Commission apparatchiks than earwigging tabloid journalists.

'I'm not saying anything, mate. Certainly not that. In any case, there are more options than boring old gay and lesbian these days, aren't there? B … T … Q … plus plus whatevs. Did you know that the K in that list stands for kink?'

'I didn't.'

'The Kinks were ahead of their time.' Vanko chuckled dryly. 'But I'll ask you just one question. Does Jonni take advantage of all the undeniably gorgeous creatures who line up for him night after night?'

There was, it had to be said, a stark contrast between the star, up in his room playing cards with Adam and the security guards, and Vanko, out on the town.

'Not that I've seen, no.'

'There you go. Something to think about, maybe.' Vanko raised his eyebrows and the expression on his face was close to a smirk. 'Anyway,' he went on abruptly, 'you were supposed to be telling me what more the crew have told you. About my electrocution "incident".'

Francis decided that he wouldn't push him on Jonni; you had to let people reveal what they wanted to reveal, and there would be time for that later. 'I only spoke to a couple of them,' he replied. 'If you really want to know, in the spirit of swapping confidences freely, they didn't seem to think it was an accident. There are too many checks.'

'So, what *are* they saying? Sabotage?'

Francis gave him a shrug-nod.

'Of what? One of the foot pedals, you said…'

'That was Mel's theory.'

'Well, she should know. So someone *is* out to get me.'

Either he was a fine actor, or Vanko was genuinely worried.

'You?' Francis said. 'Or someone else?'

'Who else are they going to hurt by electrocuting me? I was lucky, the doctors at the hospital said. If I hadn't been wearing rubber-soled boots, I could have been a goner. I've been sitting up in my room reading up on electrocution deaths. Watching videos. Rock 'n' roll is full of them.'

'Yes, Bernie was going through them the other night.'

'Was he?'

'While you were in hospital.'

'Nice timing. But you didn't answer my question. Who else are they possibly going to hurt by electrocuting me?'

'Adam, Nick … Zak even.'

'How does that work?'

'It's an attack on the tour,' Francis said. 'Each of these events puts the tour into greater jeopardy. If it has to be cancelled, for insurance reasons or whatever, the managers stand to lose a lot of money.'

'*Events*!' Vanko scoffed. 'Glad to be of service. So they try and kill me to get at Adam and Nick. Or Zak – why? D'you really think that's likely?'

'I don't know what's likely. I'm just doing what I always try to do in these situations. Keep an open mind.'

'Who would want to attack Adam anyway?' asked Vanko.

'You tell me. By all accounts, he's made a few enemies over the years.'

Vanko nodded thoughtfully. He knew, he said, that Adam had had a chequered past: that he'd managed some very famous bands and made a great deal of money before going down the tubes of addiction and losing it all. 'But the only person he hurt was himself. Unless you think his ex-wife and kids would be on some revenge kick.'

Vanko clearly hadn't had a conversation with Topaz on this subject.

'From what I understand,' Francis said, 'Adam was fairly unscrupulous in the old days. As a manager.'

None of this made sense to Vanko. Adam was tough as a manager, yes. You had to be in this business. Rock and roll was not a place for lightweights. 'But he's fair. We all know where we stand. Yes, in this set-up Jonni gets the lion's share, but then Jonni's the lion. We're just hired hands, really.

That's the way it is these days with pop bands, more often than not.'

'What d'you get paid? A session fee?'

'Sort of thing. A monthly retainer. It's pretty generous, especially as we get it at home too. And then *per diems* on top of that. When we're out on the road.'

Francis knew about *per diems*: the daily allowance for expenses that came on top of all the free booze, food and hotel rooms. You didn't need to spend it. If you were careful, or tight, like Thelma or Scally, and lived on McDonald's rather than fine French food and hundred-euro bottles of wine, it was another way of saving.

'And who gets the publishing rights?'

'Jonni, obviously. Since he writes the songs. Si usually gets a share for the music.'

'And you're OK with that?'

Vanko shrugged. 'How long have you got?'

'As long as you like.'

'Look, Simon writes the tunes. Mostly. Maybe some of us feel that a bit of financial recognition for our input would be nice. But there are recording royalties, which we all get a share of, which we really don't have to, so that's generous. Anyway, it is what it is. Si runs the band. I mean, to be perfectly honest, I'd rather take the retainer and get on with my own stuff, that nobody can touch – when the time comes – than get steamed up about whether this or that riff or whatever might be mine. You can chew yourself up that way if you're not careful.'

But no, Vanko didn't get that either of the managers would be a target. He was more worried about his own fans, the ones he'd told Francis about, that night in Amsterdam.

Did he really think, Francis asked, that some rogue fan would have the resources to get through security and meddle with the electrics onstage?

'I obviously didn't show you enough the other evening.

Some of these freaks are terrifyingly focused. If anyone's likely to get through security from outside, it's going to be a woman. They're mostly blokes, the crew, and security too.'

'I get that,' Francis said, before Vanko resorted to obscene gestures. 'But with all due respect, Vanko, this sounds like a pretty crazy scenario.'

'They are crazy, man! That's the point. There's already a website up there celebrating the attack on me. Vanko Fries, it's called. I won't show it to you now. Put me off my entrecote.'

'And your fries.'

'Ha effing ha. Lucky I like you, man, or I might take offence at that. Anyway, they're *frites* here.'

'Vanko *Frites*.'

The guitarist was shaking his head dolefully. 'You've got to see it, man. See what I'm up against.'

'But if it was just you these people were after, why would they want to chuck Jonni off the stage?'

'Separate incidents, mate. Or, more likely, someone pushes Jonni off, for reasons undisclosed, in my view just a random nutter, then my personal gang of international fruit loops are encouraged by it. Hey, let's go for Vanko. What can we do that's a bit different? Electrocution, brilliant. Maybe it will kill him, maybe it won't. Hours of fun.'

Vanko's phone was ringing. It was Russell. The other band dinner was over, could he join them?

'The horndog,' said Vanko, clicking off. 'He's unstoppable. He probably wants to go to a strip club. Why he needs me to hold his hand while he tries to get his horrible Californian rocks off, God only knows.'

His guess was right. 'Oh come *arn*,' the accountant enthused, settling in next to them, cradling a big glass of five-star cognac. 'It's a night off.'

'In Brussels!' Vanko scoffed. 'Hardly famous for its scintillating nightlife. Anyway, Francis and I are having a civilised evening. For a change.'

Nonetheless, when the *moelleux au chocolat* and the *nougat glace aux amandes* were finished and more brandy had been drunk and the bill settled, Russell's goatish energy had the three of them tramping wearily down the gleaming pavements of the European capital, looking for something that ticked the American's 'nightlife' box.

Two streets away stood a bearded man in a big windbreaker jacket waving flyers. He smelt faintly of pee and was super-persistent about the bar he was standing outside. 'Very nice *gu-u-u-u-urls*,' he repeated, like an automaton.

Russell shrugged and they went in. The place was empty, apart from a couple of bored-looking young women in pale blue nighties sitting up at the bar. There was no stage.

'Uh-oh,' said Vanko. 'This doesn't look good.'

'Let's have a beer,' said Russell. 'Just the one. *Petit*,' he directed the bartender, the one word enough to reveal his execrable accent.

More *gu-u-u-u-urls* were now arriving, all in the same sad outfit. As the beers were put up on the bar, two pushed themselves up next to the three men, demanding champagne.

'A *piccolo*,' the one next to Russell insisted, with a simper. 'Just for me.' She had an accent to match her flashy Italian good looks, though there was something haunted about her dark eyes. Her long-fingered hands, nails bright with purple varnish, were now on Russell's chubby denimed thigh, massaging it as if it was a lump of dough.

'You know what,' said Vanko. 'This isn't a strip club.'

Russell laughed. 'You're right.'

'Neck those and let's piss off,' said Vanko.

'No champagne from us tonight, girls,' Russell added. 'We're tired. Beddy-byes, you understand.' He made a head-on-hands pillow gesture. 'Sorry, dude,' he added to the bartender, 'we want to go somewhere we can look at girls, not fuck them.'

'Jesus,' said Vanko as they got back outside. 'That was a whorehouse. How much were the beers?'

'Thirty-five euros each.'

'For Christ's sake!'

'No worries, I'm paying.' He laughed. 'Or rather, Jonni is.' He waved a shiny black credit card on which could be seen the silver name R.J. KNIGHTSON. Jonni K! Francis wondered what the R stood for. Something unsexy and unstarry, surely? Roger? Richard? Rudolph?

'Let's get back to the hotel,' Vanko said.

It was altogether cosier on the leatherette couches of the back bar of the Excelsior. Russell had moved on to vintage malt whisky, but Vanko wasn't staying. 'Gig in Frankfurt tomorrow. Need to conserve my energy.'

'First time I've ever heard him say that,' said Russell, when he'd gone.

'He's still shocked,' said Francis.

'Shocked is the word.' Russell laughed. 'A highly scary thing to happen to anyone. Is that what you guys were talking about tonight?'

Francis took the opportunity to steer his reply towards what he wanted, which was the accountant's take on the jinxed tour. Was it possible that these incidents were an attack on one or both of the managers, by some ex-employee or musician who held a long-standing grudge?

'Sorry, dude, I see what you're trying to do, but it's not for me to spill the beans on my employers, is it? They're rock and roll managers. That means they're tough. You don't get on in this business as a pussycat. But they're not rip-off merchants. And frankly,' he took a deep swig of his whisky, 'whatever Adam did in his youth, he left behind with the drink and the drugs.'

'So Adam *was* unscrupulous in his youth?'

'Dude, the guy pays my wages. Ask some other people. I'm sure they'd be happy to fill you in.'

'Doesn't it concern you? That someone might be trying to create havoc with this tour; that there've been three life-threatening incidents and there might be more?'

'*Life-threatening?* Tell that to poor Ricky Fisher. The bottom line for me is that the Yank accountant is not a target. I'm a bean counter. I'm lucky enough to get to go on tour with a major pop star and have some fun, but realistically, what am I? The guy who pays the wages, keeps the local promoters happy, checks that we don't go over budget. It's freaking boring work, which is why I need some perks. Like those two over there.' Russell raised his eyebrows like Groucho Marx, indicating the two young women sitting to one side of the bar, dressed up for a non-existent party, having a visibly self-conscious conversation. 'Bless them, waiting in a hotel bar on a Monday night, on the off chance that Jonni might pop down for a ginger beer.'

He rubbed his hands, got up, and went over. Francis watched with silent amazement as the accountant struggled to impress, at one point taking out, it seemed, Jonni's credit card to show them. What was he up to? Reassuring them that he was the real deal? Offering to pay them? At this rate he was going to get arrested for harassment.

He returned, alone.

'Nothing doing. I thought she might be tempted by the possibility of a meeting with Monsieur K, but no. She couldn't give a toss about him. She's doing a philosophy major at the Vrije University. Now that turns me on, dude. A philosophy major who looks like that.'

'And isn't interested in you.'

'That too, tragically. Hey, hey, what's this?'

Three more women had arrived, dressed up, older, and

altogether noisier. They were up at the bar, ordering drinks, looking around.

'Much more promising.'

'Hate to be a party pooper,' said Francis. 'But I'm off to bed.'

'No way, dude! You can't leave me on my own.' But Russell didn't really seem to mind.

Chapter Thirteen

Francis was back on the band bus, speeding down the busy E40 towards Frankfurt. 'I thought I might be on Jonni's bus today,' he'd said to Bernie outside the hotel, as they all trooped over the cobbles, carrying their bags.

'You thought wrong, mate,' the tour manager replied. 'Sorry. I'm only following orders. Like the Nazis.' He winked.

Then they were waiting for Russell. 'Where – is – he?' shouted Bernie, his speech peppered with his usual expletives. 'Don't tell me someone's tried to do in the accountant. That's all we need.'

But Russell was fine – in fact, better than fine. He emerged a minute later, in the company of one of the women from the bar.

'Jesus!' cried Bernie. 'Come and look at this. Russell's scored.'

'D'you have to be *quite* so gross, Bernie?' said Suzi.

'No, but seriously, look at this.'

They all gathered round, giggling, as the accountant went through a Vanko-style hugging and kissing farewell. Arriving in the downstairs lounge, he punched the air and high-fived Vanko.

'OK,' he said, 'so I got the pig. But at least I *got* the pig.'

'Russell,' said Suzi, 'is that a nice way to talk about a woman? Specifically a woman you've just spent the night with?'

'Loosen up. She knows she's a pig. And she knows I'm one too. Oink, oink, we had fun. Actually quite a lot of fun.'

'I really don't want to know.'

'She was pretty cool, as it happens.'

'He's in love,' joked Topaz.

'Pur-lease. This is the twenty-first century, dude. There is such a thing as an enjoyable, mutually agreed, one-night fuckathon.'

'Did you take her phone number?' Suzi asked, grinning as she held up her hand in a phone gesture.

'Maybe.'

'Ah, sweet. Invite me to the wedding, won't you.'

'There isn't going to be a–' Russell's phone was ringing. 'Oh, hi, sweetie.'

As the accountant retreated towards the back lounge, they all laughed. There was a visible blush on his shiny cheeks.

The women stayed upstairs, as usual. Francis joined them, but there were no games today. Despite the earlier jollity, his attempts to start a conversation about Vanko's incident were rebuffed. Topaz wasn't up for a one-to-one either.

'I don't think there's much to chat about, is there, Francis?'

He slunk back downstairs and joined the boys watching a movie, though Russell soon fell asleep, snoring with his mouth open. As the bus approached Frankfurt, Bernie appeared at the bottom of the stairs and beckoned Francis with a silent finger.

'A word to the wise,' he said, when Francis had followed him to his cubbyhole at the front of the top deck, with its fine view of the autobahn rolling out before them. 'When we get to the venue, don't go hassling the ladies in their dressing room. If it says *FEMALE – PRIVATE*, that's what it means. Especially these days, mate.'

That was grossly unfair. When he'd knocked on their door before the Brussels gig, Topaz had been nothing but friendly. And amused. Charmaine ditto.

'I didn't–' he began, but Bernie cut him off.

'If the talent say you did, you did. Understood?' He held up a stern finger.

There was no point, Francis realised, in protesting further. Was this Topaz's reaction to his unscheduled visit to the bus, catching her with Seamus and the porn, or whatever they had been watching?

'I'm very sorry, Bern. I had no idea they–'

'I don't personally give a chipmunk's dick, mate, but there you go. You don't want to get a reputation for being some kind of #MeToo perv, do you?'

Francis sat quietly in the armchair in his room at the Frankfurt Schlupfwinkel Hotel checking out the YouTube videos that Vanko said he'd been watching, post his 'incident'. There were more victims of faulty electrics than Bernie had identified, and they weren't all in ancient rock history either. French singer Barbara Weldens had died onstage when her bare foot touched a piece of electrical equipment during a festival in 2017; Grimes had survived shocks from her earpieces in Dublin in 2016; Argentinian Krebs singer Agustín Briolini had died after touching a live mic in 2014; Frankie Palmeri of Emmure had fallen onstage during a gig in Moscow in 2013; the bass player of Rubber Fingers had had a shock during a performance in 2011; same with the guitarist of Hot Heat in 2009 and Kelly Jones of the Stereophonics in 2005. It was a roll call of technical cock-ups stretching all the way to George Harrison leaping back from a microphone on the documentary *Let it Be* in 1970. What they all had in common was the sudden surprise of the shock and, in the serious ones, exactly what he'd witnessed with Vanko. That helpless crumple. The body folding up.

Well, if the band weren't talking to him, perhaps he should display some initiative and head down to the venue, try and get what he wanted from the crew. Might Seamus or Ted change their tune and give him time while they were setting up? Wasn't it worth a try? 'Yes, mate, I fixed the electrocution. It was easy enough, I'm always on and off the stage. I was doing it for my old mate Frankie Freak, who was massively short-changed years ago by Adam and Zak. For a long time he suffered in silence, but recently, after the failure of his court case, he's wanted his pound of flesh. It was, frankly, a privilege to help him.'

Dream on.

Nonetheless, he called Bernie and asked how he could get out to the venue.

'Did you hear of a contraption called a taxi?' the tour manager replied. 'They invented it a couple of hundred years ago, I believe. For gentlemen – and ladies – who need to get to places.'

'There's no earlier bus?'

'You're right. There's no fucking earlier bus. Or a later one, for that matter. If you want to go to the venue by the designated bus, it's three thirty sharp or nothing. Now if you'll excuse me, I have some German Hell's Angels to shout at.'

Francis sat back, trying not to feel demoralised. It was paradoxical that this time, on his first professional outing as a commissioned detective, there was so little to go on. He hadn't even seen the only body in the case – if it was indeed in the case. Maybe, as Adam had suggested, this was just a 'bad luck tour' and Nick was being paranoid about nothing, because there was no crime. A tragic overdose, a crazy fan, and an accident with the electrics that no one wanted to own up to.

Or maybe there were different perpetrators for each incident. First off, it was perfectly possible that someone could have bumped off Ricky, making it look like an overdose. The man had clearly been close to Jonni, though exactly what Vanko had been driving at last night in the restaurant wasn't clear. BTQ plus plus. What was that all about? They were all so … if not evasive, then elusive – not just about Jonni, but about everything. Francis supposed it was only natural. Unlike the ordinary folk he had dealt with in the past, who had opened up with their concerns and points of view quite easily, this lot were constantly under siege: from the press, from fans. They knew what the consequences were of letting your guard down, allowing the temptation to be indiscreet to get to them.

Say Ricky and Jonni had been super-close – lovers, even: did that explain why Adam was keeping Jonni away from him? Was it even possible that Adam, or one of Jonni's security detail, trained killers both, had had a hand in Ricky's demise? He had to consider everything, even the darkest scenarios.

Say Adam was behind the overdose: could he also have had something to do with his own star being pushed off the stage by a man with a knife? And if so, why had this alleged lunatic said *This is for Sandra*? Was it even possible that the manager had come up with such a line to cover his tracks? Released to a couple of the band, making them swear to tell nobody, a foolproof way of making sure they would (a) tell everybody and (b) give it significance. It was a hell of a question. Especially as Adam so clearly doted on his little prince. Who had, by his own admission, the talent he didn't have. In some ways, Adam was the biggest groupie of them all. He so clearly loved the vibe, the whole razzle-dazzle of gigs and tours and musicians and music and fans and phones being held up and waved in the air to a tune created by someone he had discovered, made into a star – and yes, saved from themselves.

No, get real, that was a ridiculous scenario. So was it even possible that the incidents were unrelated?

1) Ricky, either overdosed or yes, murdered.

2) Jonni, pushed off the stage by a man with a grudge: he might have been crazy, one of the fantasists that this kind of operation attracted (e.g. Vanko's weirder fans); or else someone who had a credible reason, who knew or was even involved with someone called Sandra, who was/had been a fan, a groupie, a disappointed shag – or worse, a girl he'd got pregnant, who'd killed herself, even. It was perfectly possible.

3) Vanko, the victim of an accident? Or an act of sabotage by (a) one of his crazed fans, getting in under the radar; (b) a suborned member of the crew acting for same; (c) ditto acting for a ripped-off ex-client/band member of Adam's? (Which could circle straight back to the all-three-are-related scenario.)

Francis buried his head in his hands. It was all as clear as mud. What was he going to say to Nick when he saw him, presumably tonight, if he was flying in for the gig? The manager's impatience was going to be off the scale.

The band seemed cheerful enough on the three thirty bus going out to the Festhalle, but it was all on the surface. Not one of them met Francis's eye.

'Er, Topaz,' he said, catching up with the guitarist as she strode off towards backstage. 'Could I have a word?'

She turned to him with a flat, dead smile. 'Stuff to do, mate, sorry. Got a gig tonight.'

He decided to leave them all to it. He cut down past Security and into the auditorium. The crew were all working, doing their thing, shouting, making final adjustments to their great daily construction. Seeing Seamus alone onstage, on his knees, fiddling with wires and plugs, Francis reckoned he had nothing to lose. If he waited for the 'right' time to talk to the old stoner, he might be waiting forever, especially if Adam had anything to do with it.

'Hiya,' he said, hovering nearby.

Seamus didn't even look up.

'Did I miss a good party on the crew bus?' Francis persisted.

Seamus shrugged and got to his feet. 'How do the words "none of your fucking business" sound?'

'I was hoping we might have a little chat sometime.'

'Were you now? About the musical instruments? Or how we set up the stage? Or was it Vanko's electrocution you wanted an insight into?' Seamus laughed, hollowly.

'No. More about you. Stuff you've done in the past, bands you've worked with, stories, a bit of colour for my piece.'

'Your *piece*, of course.' The Irishman paused, though. 'What's the magazine again?'

'*GQ.*' Francis could hardly bear to repeat the lie.

'Uh-huh. I don't read that sort of posh stuff myself, but the Paranoia Brothers must love it to give you so much access. We've had journalists with us before, but they're usually packed off after a day or so. And here you still are, hanging around like a bad smell.'

He turned back to his work; Francis stayed where he was.

'Tell you what, mate,' Seamus said, looking up after a bit, 'I'm quite within my rights to tell you to fuck right off to Fuck-land, but I almost feel sorry for you, floundering around. So how about this? I'm usually on the backline bus for half an hour or so after seven thirty. After I've had my tea. All right? That work for you?'

'I could always meet you in Catering.'

'Let's stick to the bus. Quieter there.'

It almost seemed, Francis thought, when the old roadie

had gone, muttering something about grip screws, that there *was* something he wanted to tell him. Why else had he relented – unless of course he'd suddenly thought his animosity might be seen as racist? What the hell, swings and roundabouts. Francis was excited as he went for an early supper, then back out into the auditorium. It was tempting to go backstage, but he didn't want to jinx things or risk any more complaints to Bernie about him going places he shouldn't go.

At seven twenty-five, he made his way out of the stadium into the car park. There were the three buses, parked up in a row in the coach section. Which was backline tonight? He nosed round the front and saw Bryn, in his big driving seat, bathed in the flickering light of his laptop. He tapped on the window. The Welshman looked up, saw him, pressed a button and the door slid back.

'Backline?' Francis asked.

'I'm always on backline,' said Bryn, eyes barely flicking up from his screen. His crossword book was open on his knee, and he had one of his little IKEA pencils in his hand.

'Seamus here?'

'Haven't seen him. Mel's in the lounge though, if you want to go in.'

Damn. This was all he needed. Bloody Mel getting in the way.

'OK, you literary fellow,' Bryn asked. 'What's a Shake-spearian duke magician? Seven letters. P dash dash S–'

'Prospero,' said Francis.

'I was going to say dash dash dash O, but you got there before me. Lovely jubbly.' He wrote the answer in. 'Not my area of expertise, unfortunately. I'm better on the rugby.'

'Which I wouldn't be able to help you with at all.'

Vanko's beloved guitar tech was curled up in a corner of the downstairs lounge, a cup of tea in her *HAPPY CAMPER* mug beside her. She was reading a thick turquoise paperback by Marian Keyes.

'Oh hiya,' she said, looking up. 'Lost in my family saga. How can I help you?'

'It's Seamus I'm after. We had a rendezvous here for half seven, if that's OK.'

'Did you now?' She chuckled knowingly. 'When and if he turns up, I'll make myself scarce. You after his story too? He's got plenty to say, if you get him going. Been in the biz almost as long as Adam. Worked with all sorts.'

'So I hear. The Tainted Idols, I think…'

'Yes, all Adam's bands – the Idols, Tender Plastique, Guitarmageddon, too, back in the day. Get him on the stories about the American tours if you can. That was proper rock 'n' roll, not the sedate world we live in now.'

'Yes,' said Francis, thrilled that his little gambit had paid off and the info he'd been after had slipped out so easily. Seamus *had* worked with the Idols. So he would have known Bobby and Frankie. And who knew how well?

Mel gave an odd little laugh. 'Presumably you've talked to Adam too?'

'A bit.'

'He's worth pursuing. If I was doing what you're doing, I'd certainly try and get his story. You know, it was something I always wanted to be: a journalist, or a writer.'

'But you didn't pursue it?'

'It didn't pursue me. Sadly. So here I am, running around after bands, checking guitars and organising fireworks and such like.'

'I thought the light show was Kylie's area.'

'Is that what she told you? No, I do the pyrotechnics. We always discuss it together, but it's my baby. I enjoy it. Jonni appearing from a cloud of smoke and so on.' She looked up and met his eye, suddenly looking rather nervous, he thought.

'No, Adam's lovely, if you don't cross him. Of course, he learned a hard lesson, back in the day.'

'Too many illegal substances, by the sound of it.'

She shrugged. 'I'm sure he'd be happy to tell you about it, if you catch him at the right moment. He's a sweetie, really.'

'Really?'

'No, he is. As well, obviously, as being a tough cookie. Which you have to be, in that job. I couldn't do it. All those big egos…'

'People squabbling over who wrote what and how much they should get paid for it.'

'Of course. Not that that happens with this lot. This is a manufactured band. Apart from the star and the composer, they're all session musicians, basically. They're on a retainer, so you don't get those problems.'

It was good to have this confirmed, and from a crew source this time.

'The problem arises, presumably, when they're all supposed to have an equal share. Like Zak and the Idols.'

'You know about all that?'

'I'd heard something.'

Mel was looking down again; it was clear she wasn't going to be drawn.

'No, Adam's brilliant,' she said. 'And persistent. That's why he came back from … the dark place he came back from. He's brilliant at seeing what works. Zak and the Idols, Guitarmageddon, now Jonni, all huge. And bringing Simon in, of course. Who would have thought of putting a pretty boy like Jonni with a washed-up genius like Simon? Don't get me wrong. Jonni's a good singer – he didn't win *The Voice* for nothing.'

'*X Factor*,' Francis corrected her. How impressive was his knowledge of celebrity trivia these days! 'And the band he was in came second.'

'So many of the guys from those talent shows just vanish,

don't they?' Mel continued. 'But you put Jonni's ability for getting teenage girls excited together with Simon's tunes and Vanko's amazing guitar, and you've got gold dust. That's how I see it, anyway.'

'You rate Vanko?'

'He's the best. I would say that, though, wouldn't I? As his tech. Lovely voice too – not that you often get to hear it properly.' She dropped her voice to a whisper. 'Better than Jonni's. Which one day the world will hear, I hope.'

'Vanko the star.'

'He deserves it. Really. And he's got the looks.'

'You sound very objective, Mel.'

The poor woman was blushing. 'Just saying.'

'Of course you are. So what went wrong with the Tainted Idols?'

Now she was laughing. 'I can see why you're a journalist,' she said. 'And why I could probably never have been one. You're like a terrier with a rat. Look, it's hardly a state secret. You look through the history of rock bands, you'll see that the ones who stayed together were the ones who divvied things out fairly. Or even unfairly. But equally, anyway. Like U2. You know, did Bono contribute more, creatively, than the Edge?'

'The Edge?' queried Francis.

'U2 lead guitar. Did he contribute more to the music than one of those guys whose names you can't remember – perhaps in your case never knew? Maybe. But they split the proceeds, the royalties, both recording and publishing, equally, right from the start. So they stayed together. Ditto, up to a point, Coldplay, REM, Radiohead and the Doors. Otherwise, inevitably, it can so easily end with bad blood. Ask Seamus about it. Just how cross Bobby and Frankie used to get…'

'About Zak?'

'There you go again. Ask Seamus. He was witness to it all.'

'Speaking of which,' said Francis, looking at his watch.

'Where is Seamus? He said he'd be here at seven thirty. I have got the right bus?'

'Oh yes. This is his bus all right. That's his mug over there.' She waved at a white one on the shelf that said *PISS AND LUST* in big red letters. 'That's his take on peace and love. Charming, eh?'

'He was on the lampies' bus yesterday,' Francis said.

'He moves around. But he almost always sleeps on here. He prefers the fragrant young ladies to the snorers and farters. Don't worry, he'll be here, but he's not the world's greatest timekeeper. Irish, you know what they're like. They say they'll meet you for "just the one" at eight o'clock and then they don't turn up till nine thirty. Then they keep you out till three. He's probably got chatting to someone in Catering.' Mel laughed. 'On the other hand, he may be avoiding you.'

'So what's his relationship with Topaz?' Francis asked, looking round towards the door despite himself. 'Just friends? That's who he was with yesterday.'

'You weren't imagining anything else, were you? I think he's known her since she was a little girl. He's great mates with Bobby Fairhurst. Who's her godfather, did you know that?'

Francis's phone was buzzing in the front pocket of his jeans. He pulled it out. *NICK FOURIE*, read the screen. He ignored it. This time, the manager could wait.

'Yes,' he said. Then: 'It's funny that Adam wanted her in the band, really. Given the bad blood between them.'

'Adam and Bobby?'

'Yeah. Well, more like Zak and Bobby.'

'Topaz would have been Simon's choice,' Mel said. 'She's beautiful, she's another guitar wizard, plus she has that incredible voice. So you can see why he wanted her. And Adam would have been OK with that, unless of course he's clumsily trying to make it up to Bobby after the event. You know, "I'm sorry about what happened with Zak, but I'd like to help your friend's daughter." There might be a bit of that going on.'

Ping. Now there was a message on his phone.

Where are you? I'm in Catering with Adam.
Let's talk. Now, please. Nick.

There were footsteps on the stairs. Seamus at last? But no, it was only Ted, Scally's drum tech, with the lopsided grin and wild straw hair. 'Oh hi, Mel,' he said, looking away from Francis. 'I'm not disturbing anything, am I?'

'No,' Francis replied. 'It's fine. I was just off anyway.'

Chapter Fourteen

Francis strode back across the Festhalle. The doors were open and fans were pouring in, running across the wide expanse of floor to get up the front by the stage. Others, older, were taking their places in the surrounding banks of seating: a stalls area at one end of the 'standing room only' central oblong, then a dress circle and an upper circle going right round. Beams of light were already raking the dark stage.

Francis waved his AAA pass at one of the Hell's Angels and went on up to Catering. There was no sign of Nick. Or Seamus, for that matter. He headed off into the corridors and ran slap bang into Topaz, hurrying the other way.

'Can't talk now, sorry,' she said before he'd even spoken. And then, weirdly, she paused mid-step, looked around, and went right up to him. So close he could smell the muskily alluring scent she wore. Diorella? Something like that. She ran a forefinger across her neck in a throat-cutting gesture. 'Walls have ears,' she whispered. She squeezed his shoulder, gave him a rather arch look and left him standing there.

Unsettled, Francis made his way towards where the band hospitality and dressing rooms must surely be. Yes, there was

FEMALE DRESSING ROOM – PRIVATE. He wasn't going to mess with that again. Or, tonight, even *MALE DRESSING ROOM*, which for some reason didn't have the *PRIVATE* qualification. Perhaps it should read *MALE – PUBLIC, ALL COMERS* he thought with a silent chuckle.

Jonni's dressing room had no sign at all on it. It didn't need one, with beefy Omar posted outside.

Francis could hear Adam's rolling laughter coming from within.

'Is Nick in there?'

'He is.'

'He sent me a message to come over.'

Omar nodded, unsmiling. 'Wait a moment,' he replied, looking up and down the corridor before sliding in the door, sideways, almost as if he was expecting Jonni to be waiting for him with a primed grenade. The laughter stopped and Omar returned.

'In you go,' he said.

'Thanks.'

'Francis!' said Adam, genial as ever. 'Where've you been hiding, mate?'

Jonni was lounging on a big armchair. 'All right, man?' He nodded, then looked away.

Nick was standing to one side. 'Here you are. So you've finished with the crew?'

'Sorry, Nick, I was just chatting to a couple of guys on the backline bus.'

'Francis is thick as thieves with the crew these days,' joshed Adam. 'I can't keep him away from them.'

'Probably more fun than the band,' said Jonni. 'Eh, Francis?'

'I wouldn't say that. The band are good fun too.'

'Just a shame I'm not,' said Jonni.

'Don't be silly, Jonni. You're glorious fun.' The jovial

response hovered on Francis's lips, but he didn't say it; he just wasn't on those kind of matey terms with him – yet. Would he ever be?

'Shall we pop down to Catering, Francis?' Nick cut in. 'Have a coffee and a chat?'

'Sure.'

Adam stayed behind with the star, rather to Francis's surprise. He followed Nick back down the corridor.

Catering was pretty much empty now. A couple of the crew were hunched over puddings. Three bus drivers sat chatting in their lighting harnesses and yellow vests. Francis nodded perfunctorily at Steve 'Dolly' Parton, who obliged him with a nod back, albeit one that acknowledged he was with their joint employer, so should be left alone. He didn't get the feeling that Nick had a clue who any of the bus drivers were, or even about the scary stuff they did up on the trusses for extra money.

'Coffee?' asked Nick, standing by the Nespresso machine. 'You probably know how to work this thing better than me by now.'

'It's easy enough,' said Francis. He made them both coffees and they sat, opposite each other, at a table to one side.

'Hi, Francis,' said Flo, sashaying past with a smile.

'So,' said Nick, 'you seem to be getting on with everyone pretty well.'

'They're mostly easy enough,' Francis replied. Once again, he sensed a weird competitiveness in Nick; almost envy. As if, having employed him to find out all these things from the band and crew, he slightly resented Francis for being successful in that task.

'That's all good,' Nick went on. 'But can we cut to the chase? Are we getting anywhere?'

Francis hesitated. He had to be careful with Nick. If he brought up suspicions about Seamus, for example, he didn't trust the hands-on manager not to dive in feet first and mess everything up. As for his misgivings about Adam, he hardly thought that now was the time.

'I'll level with you,' he replied. 'They've all been friendly, as you see, but…'

'Not telling you everything you want to know?'

'Certainly they're cagier than on some of the other cases I've been involved with. I'm not sure many of them still believe I'm writing a piece for *GQ*.'

'I hope you're sticking to your story?'

'I've done my best.'

'But you've had *some* feedback about the Vanko incident?'

'Of course. Opinion is divided – between those who think it was just an accident and those who think something sinister is going on.'

'What does Vanko think?'

'That it's something to do with his fans. He's a bit obsessed with them. Having said that, he's got some pretty weird ones.'

'He really thinks a fan might have got through Security and tried to electrocute him?'

'Or got in with a member of the crew. Somehow.'

'*Somehow*,' Nick repeated, lingering dubiously on the word. 'What do you think, Francis? You've been hanging around with them all.'

'I really don't know, Nick. To be honest, I'm still waiting for a breakthrough.'

'And what do they all think about Ricky?'

'They mostly think he just OD'd.'

'But not all?'

'No.'

'Are you going to tell me who doesn't think … that?' And with that single word, Nick's face expressed all the suspicions he had about this incident. Watching him, Francis decided he might as well be direct in his answer, give the impression of some progress on his side.

'Vanko,' he replied.

'OK.' The manager smiled and nodded. 'And Topaz?'

'I've no idea.'

'You haven't spoken to her?'

'I have. But not about that. Actually, she's been weirdly distant with me recently.'

'Has she now? So what did you talk about when you did talk?'

'This and that.' Francis wasn't about to level with Nick on that. 'Where she grew up, that sort of thing. I hadn't realised her dad was a musician too.'

'Yes. With the Flaming Buzzards. Funny little folk band, weird mixture of Irish and Scots, based up in Glasgow. Good enough, but they got nowhere, though they did produce Bobby Fairhurst.'

And didn't produce Topaz's dad, Francis thought, or unlucky Seamus. Bingo! So the old roadie would have known Bobby even before he worked for the Idols. Did Nick know about that too?

'And what about Jonni?' Nick was asking.

'Haven't you spoken to him?' Francis replied. 'Don't you know what he thinks?'

There was a pause.

'I'm interested in what he's told you,' Nick said.

'I'll have to level with you, Nick, and say that I've hardly spoken to Jonni about anything. I don't know why, but Adam hasn't exactly encouraged me to be alone with him. Yes, I've joined in with a couple of the games evenings, but it's always in company.'

Oddly, Nick didn't look surprised. 'Well,' he said, 'he's a sensitive chap, as I'm sure you've realised. And the bottom line is that he has to be kept on tip-top form. Certainly on tour.'

'I do understand that.'

'I'll have a word with Adam.'

Up onstage, they could hear the gig beginning. The intro music and announcements had reached a crescendo, and now there was screaming from the waiting hordes. Clearly the band had either just arrived or were about to.

'Let's carry on with this later,' Nick said. 'I ought to get down and catch the gig, having come all this way to see it.'

'Of course.'

Francis let him go. He didn't immediately follow. He knew the set backwards by now. 'Let's Go Dutch', 'The Love That Tells Me', 'In the Park', 'Identity', 'Sometimes the Moon', 'Cambodian Girl', 'Little Me'. The running order switched around, but they did the same songs every night.

Catering was empty now. Flo was going round cleaning tables with her spray fluid.

'Finished, sir?' she said, reaching for the two coffee cups. The 'sir' was a joke, he hoped.

'Certainly have.'

'You OK?'

'I'm fine.'

'You look a bit troubled, that's all.'

'Just stuff to work out.'

'You coming back on our bus again sometime?'

'I hope so.'

'Me too.'

Two tall riggers had appeared. One cantered in front of the Nespresso machine like a horse. 'Flo Flo Flo Florence!' he sang. Trying not to look put out by this easy familiarity with his favourite waitress, Francis left them to it and headed up to the side of the stage.

Jonni was coming to the end of 'Cambodian Girl', giving it his all. What a beautiful song it was! Touching, melodic, he had the audience in the palm of his hand. Now he sprang round and somersaulted across the floor, chased by Vanko with his guitar. Topaz seemed on a high too, immensely cool in her tight top and leather skirt, pacing around with her guitar like an oversexed panther. Then Jonni was back on his feet and down the front again, whipping the audience up to a frenzy with his outstretched hands. How he must love this, Francis thought, watching his fingers doing a tickling motion like a fisherman trying to catch trout. Then he was leaning down to hold the outstretched hand of some girl in the front row. Then moving along to another. And another.

The band were all as high as kites after the show. It had been a blast, nothing untoward had happened, group confidence was returning. Nobody was going out clubbing tonight, but there was a general invitation up to Jonni's suite after the post-gig supper at the Schlupfwinkel. Jonni himself seemed on very easy form, apparently quite relaxed about half the band drinking beer and champagne around him. A noisy game of Skyjo was in progress at the central table. Even burly security man Mitch was taking part.

Adam came over to where Francis was sitting, in an armchair to one side. He was part watching the game; part listening to Topaz, who was playing gentle, rather jazzy melodies on an acoustic guitar; part gazing out of the floor-to-ceiling picture windows at the lights of Frankfurt laid out below them: a clutch of City-like skyscrapers to the right; on the left the river Main, glinting under dark bridges. Was the manager about to tell him that he had to get off, right now, and join the crew? But no, they were already in Nuremberg, so God willing he was safe.

'Nick tells me you'd like a bit more time alone with Jonni,' he said.

'That would be great,' Francis replied. *As if you didn't know.*

'We'll do what we can to get you on his bus tomorrow morning. It's a three-hour drive down to Nuremberg, so there should be a bit of time for you to have a chat. He's in a very good mood tonight, so let's hope that lasts.'

Then Nick was in the room too. He seemed a little flustered, as if he had stuff to do, but wanted to be equally as fun and laid-back as his charismatic co-manager after the gig. 'I've got to get back to London first thing,' he said to Francis. 'But we can speak on the phone. I spoke to Adam about Jonni—'

'I know, thank you, he just came over.'

'Let me know how that goes. And if you need anything else.' He made the 'call me' gesture with his thumb and little finger. 'I'll see you in a week anyway. In Vienna. Let's hope we've got some answers by then.'

'I'll do my level best.'

'I'm sure you will, Francis. I didn't want to seem impatient earlier, but—'

'You are impatient,' Francis replied. 'That's fair enough. So am I.'

When he'd gone, Francis sat watching Topaz fingering the strings of her guitar. What a gift she had! Such speed and agility. One moment her right hand was holding chord shapes while the left was strumming; the next the fingers of both hands were running wild, plucking, tweaking, twanging – he didn't have the right musical words to describe her playing, but with a tall flute of champagne in front of him he was mesmerised.

Her strange hostility of earlier seemed to have worn off too. Topaz was smiling back at him as she played. Now it was an acoustic version of 'The Love That Tells Me'.

'Frankie Freak … wrote this,' she mouthed, looking directly into Francis's eyes. Was she even a little tipsy?

Eventually she put the guitar down and leant forward. 'You want a nightcap?'

He held up his champagne. 'I've got this.'

'I mean, out of here. In the bar or somewhere.'

Was this the moment she was going to tell him all about Uncle Bobby and Seamus – that she did, after all, know something about why the tour had been attacked?

'OK,' he said.

'Quick exit now,' she said quietly, 'before they finish their game.' She gestured with a sideways flick of her eyes towards the central table, where the Skyjo players were lost in their battle, shrieking with frustration as they failed to keep up with the triumphant Jonni.

Francis got to his feet and followed her out through the door and into the corridor, where Omar stood guard like an impassive sentry.

'Where are we going?' he asked. 'Down to the bar?'

'D'you fancy a spliff?' She grinned wickedly. 'I picked some stuff up in Amsterdam. I've been dying to try it. My room's just along here.'

So he was going to Topaz's. For a spliff. Serendipity seemed to have kicked in big time.

'In the old days we used to do it in front of Jonni,' she said, when she'd clicked her door open and retrieved her little stash from the bottom of the big red shell suitcase that sat on the luggage rack to the side of the room. 'But sadly no longer. Or actually, not sadly, as Jonni would have had most of it. He was such a drug monster, back in the day.'

She laughed, as her deft fingers fashioned a little filter from a strip of rolled-up card, lowered it onto a flat Rizla paper, pulled tobacco from a broken cigarette, crumbled in some grass, then rolled it all up into a fat joint.

She picked up a lighter and put a clear flame to the twisted paper mini-fan at one end. Then she put her lips to the filter, sucked hard and inhaled.

'Wowsers!' she cried, laughing as smoke poured from between her teeth. 'That's quite something. I asked for medium. God knows what strong would be like.'

She passed the spliff to Francis. He wasn't usually a great one for marijuana, but this wasn't a party he didn't want to be at. He took his own, less substantial puff, and drew it slowly into his lungs.

'Pathetic,' she said. 'You can do better than that.'

'Do I have to?'

'Of course. Go on.'

He took another, deeper toke, then realised, as he handed it back to her, that he was suddenly quite wrecked. This dope was as strong as Seamus had had on the bus. Perhaps, given her intimacy with the stage manager, it was the same stuff?

They were relaxing, having fun, chilling out. As if the joint wasn't enough, Topaz had opened the free bottle of champagne from the fridge. Part of him wanted to use this time as an opportunity to quiz her further: about her dad and 'Uncle Bobby' and Frankie Freak and Seamus; about what she thought of the Vanko incident; about why she'd been avoiding him; about that bizarre throat-cutting gesture from earlier.

But they were side by side on one of the plush hotel sofas and he didn't want to break the spell.

You should walk away now, he told himself. There may be info coming from her, but it's so unprofessional to be here. With her powerful musky scent pulling you in. Her laughter. She's such a honey and if she... This is classic, a man like you, bit older, gets confused, signals wrong, bad enough anyway, but with the guitarist of the group you're supposed to be looking into, disaster, surely? You've got to stay on the tour to get the money.

But she had put her hand on his: her lovely long guitar-strumming hand, with its bright scarlet fingernails, trimmed surprisingly short.

'Are you OK?' she asked, and in her open smile there was something almost needy.

'Yuh,' he managed.

'I was worried about you. You seemed sad.'

'No, not sad.'

'Not sad? That's funny.'

They were both laughing.

'Shall I roll one more?'

He shook his head. 'It's a bad idea. We've got to get up tomorrow. Go to…'

He had temporarily forgotten where they were going.

'Where to, Francis?'

'I can't remember.'

'Nuremberg, you idiot.'

'Nuremberg, yes, Jesus, that's it.'

'You're definitely one of us now. You get to that point on tour where you can't remember where you're going any more. Or where you even are sometimes. Where are we now, for example?'

Francis thought hard: skyscrapers and the river Main. 'Frankfurt,' he said.

'Brilliant. The danger is you say the wrong thing to the audience, like Guns N' Roses did in Melbourne. They shouted out *Good to see you, Sydney*. Disaster. Especially with those two cities.'

Francis chuckled. 'What's Nuremberg like?'

'Spooky.'

'I imagine.'

'Right next to the new stadium, where we perform, there's this old stadium where Hitler used to have these, like, huge Nazi rallies. It's falling down, but it's still there. I'll take you and show you, if you like.'

'Will you?'

'Yeah. Let's have another.' She sat forward and reached for her Rizlas. 'Actually, can you keep a secret, Detective?'

'Is that really how you see me?'

'That's not how I see you. It's what we all call you. It's what you are.'

'So what's the secret?' he asked.

'Coke,' she replied. 'I've got a small stash. That Seamus got me. Is that, like, something you can keep quiet about? From your bosses. 'Cos we're not supposed to have it. The management turn a blind eye to spliffs, but *co*-caine' – she lingered over the first syllable – 'is a sackable offence.'

Francis nodded his agreement.

'So why did you go all quiet on me?' he asked. 'What was all that *walls have ears* stuff?'

She rolled her eyes. 'You're unstoppable, you are. They do, Francis. Even in places like this. Even in places where we're only staying a night or two, or a stadium with walls we're only going to see for a few hours before and after the gig. They still have fuckin' ears.'

'By which you mean, that you don't want Adam or Zak finding out that you told me some of the things you told me before?'

'Maybe.'

'What were you watching with Seamus anyway? On that laptop?'

'Francis,' she said with sudden emphasis. 'It's really not important, OK? Some silly YouTube thing Seamus wanted to show me. No biggie.'

'It sounded like porn.'

'Yeah, well, Seamus has strange tastes.'

Topaz got to her feet, went over to her bag, brought out a small wrap of coke and chopped it out into two fine lines on the glass table in front of them.

Now she presented Francis with a rolled twenty-euro note: blue, with two gothic church windows below a big bland *20*.

'You first,' she said. 'Then I won't feel so bad.'

In for a penny, in for a pound, he thought, leaning forward.

He snorted up the white powder. Felt that forgotten tingle at the top of his nostrils, then the bitter taste of it trickling back down his sinuses into his mouth. Then the rush hit him. Watching Topaz leaning over in a long sensual curve to snort her line, all he could feel was raw desire.

'Christ!' she said, wiping her nostrils with finger and thumb. 'Seamus always gets the best.' She stretched back on the sofa beside him, like a big cat.

'So … Topaz…' he said.

She met his eye. Was it his imagination, or did she feel the same? *No, don't be idiotic, you're two decades older than her. Wrecked as you are, this is a total #MeToo moment. Stay professional.*

'So, Topaz … what?' she replied, with a giggle.

'Are you going to tell me what I want to know? The stuff you held back when we were in Amsterdam. About Adam and Zak and Seamus and your father and Bobby…'

'How d'you know I held stuff back?'

'*Walls have ears.*'

'Touché. Maybe in a bit. But d'you know what I fancy right now?'

'What?'

'A shower. I'm still a bit sweaty after the gig. I don't really want to fuck you if I'm all sweaty.'

'Whoever said…'

'Oh, come *on*,' she replied. She put her long forefinger out and ran it slowly under his chin.

'I thought you had a boyfriend in London.' He could barely speak, he was breathing so fast.

She shrugged. 'I'm seeing someone. Some of the time. But I'm not really into that whole possession narrative. I mean, like, nobody owns my body, do they? Except me. And maybe you, for one glorious night only.'

It was time to leave. Really. Every fibre of his sober, sensible self told him to get up and go.

Chapter Fifteen

'I thought I was on Jonni's bus today,' Francis said to Bernie as the tour manager waved him, once again, towards the steps of the band bus. 'Adam promised,' he added.

'If he did, I'm afraid I haven't been informed. Sorry, mate, default position. You're on with your pals in the band.'

'May I just speak to Adam?' Francis moved towards the star's bus.

'He's not on yet, mate. Still closeted with Jonni. Who's in a weird mood this morning, let me tell you. So if I were you, I'd take it easy for the time being. I'm sure there'll be plenty of time to chat to the star backstage in Nuremberg.'

Yeah, right, Francis thought. If he hadn't been in such a sublimely blissed-out state, he might have just walked off the case there and then. Let them keep their money. Instead, he nodded, in as friendly a way as possible, at Steve 'Dolly' Parton, waiting in his driving seat, and headed on up, past the upstairs lounge, to Bernie's private area at the far end, where he phoned Nick.

There was no answer. Paranoia Two was probably still in the air. Francis left a terse message expressing his disappointment about the promised bus journey. It wasn't even as if he thought a chat with Jonni would be that revealing. If the star didn't want to talk to him, he wouldn't talk to him, even if Francis was shoved in his face. But still. He wanted the opportunity to try.

Eleven thirty-three. Three minutes after the scheduled departure time. Simon and Vanko and Russell and Suzi and Thelma were now all on board. Downstairs, Bernie was on and off the front step of the bus like the proverbial blue-arsed fly.

'Where – are – they?' he yelled at Francis, though those three simple words were of course extended to a sweary seven.

It wasn't just Jonni and his manager who were late coming down; it was Topaz as well. Unable to do much about the star, Bernie called upstairs for Russell and dispatched him to the guitarist's room to see what the heck was going on.

'You got any idea, Francis?'

'No.'

'Thought you might have. Somehow.' Bernie gave him a slow and unwelcome wink. Had his exit with Topaz been that obvious? None of the others had said anything. He didn't want them all knowing or, even worse, teasing. He wanted very much for it all to remain private, just between her and him – though how it would be when he saw her again, in daylight, dressed, normal, no longer his, God alone knew. There would be no post-coital embarrassment; they were too grown-up for that. Maybe it really had been what she'd said it would be, a one-night stand, and that was going to be that; if anyone was going to have to deal with disappointment, rejection, a burning desire for more – oh yes please – it was going to have to be him. The single one.

In the night, in that first delicious half hour of rest and recovery, he and Topaz had chatted, desultorily, as new lovers do.

'You do have something to tell me, don't you?' Francis had said.

'Maybe I do, sweetheart. Then again, maybe it would be wisest of me to keep my trap shut. Like I've been told to.'

'By whom?'

'By whom,' she repeated, lingering on the 'm'. 'You're so intellectual, I love it.' She giggled.

'Whom is correct,' he heard himself reply.

'Of course it is, darling. Anyway both Who and his heavy mate Whom have told me to mind my gob. So I'll be doing that. For the time being. There's no huge hurry, is there?'

'The only hurry is that I'm being employed by the managers to find out what the fuck is going on.'

'Shh,' she replied, putting a finger to his lips again. 'No need to get worked up. All in good time. Maybe later, if you're nice to me.'

He had crept away in the dawn without learning more. He hadn't left because he thought anyone would find them together, or his bed empty, but you never knew. In any case, while she lay there beside him, gorgeous and golden, he wasn't going to get any sleep, was he? He wanted to get back, shower in his own room, and then be down in time for breakfast with the security guards, and maybe Adam too, to make everything look professional and normal. He could always get some more kip on the bus.

Finally, Jonni was there, in a rather magnificent fluffy grey coat: the kind of coat, Francis thought mischievously, that his own adoptive granny Irene might have worn, back in the day. The grandmotherly impression was only added to by the double string of pearls the star wore around his neck. Not that Francis was in any way critical of Jonni's garb. Of course a star of his magnitude had to stay on trend; that was pretty much the job description. Anyway, forget gender-fluid: why shouldn't men dress more exotically? They had done throughout history. It was one of the things he wanted to ask Jonni about, when he finally got him alone: whether he found his gender-challenging dressing addictive, or did he just enjoy the buzz of being able to create fads? How did it feel, for example, to have made the bowler hat fashionable again, so that people of all genders were now seen wearing it, although not yet with the Liza Minelli-style frock and suspender combo Jonni had famously worn in Berlin?

Adam stuck close to him, as always. He gave Bernie a thumbs-up, but he didn't smile at Francis. Nor did he say 'Come on, mate, I thought you were on our bus today.' Instead: 'Good to go,' he said curtly, turning to greet his bus driver – Ray this morning, in his usual sailor's cap and top, albeit without the anchor stud in his right ear. Surely he didn't need to conceal his sexuality from Jonni, of all people? Ray grinned back, Benny Hill-style, and once again Francis imagined the famous jaunty music, the saucy seventies ladies dancing around him.

'But we are not good to go,' said Bernie. 'Where the fuck is Topaz?'

Now Russell had reappeared. He looked worried.

'The door's locked. She's not answering. Has she gone AWOL?'

'Right,' said Bernie. 'You guys stay here. I'll go and check this out.' He headed back towards the revolving front doors of the hotel, with Russell padding along next to him.

Francis went with them. He didn't think he'd be particularly welcome, but who cared? Topaz was normally completely reliable. Had their night of passion discombobulated her that much?

Bernie was at the front desk, asking for assistance. Francis kept his distance. A neat, grey-suited, blonde female manager appeared with a key card. The trio headed for the lifts. Francis followed, diving in next to them just as the doors were closing.

To his credit, Bernie didn't object. 'He's with us,' he said to the manager. 'You don't have any idea where she is, do you, Francis?'

'No.'

'I thought you might.' There was no wink this time, nor even the slightest smile, though Bernie undoubtedly knew exactly what had gone on. But the expression on his face now was more serious than Francis had ever seen it. Russell's chubby features, too, looked spooked.

'It's not like her,' Bernie said. 'She's normally first on. The bus,' he added unnecessarily.

They got out at the fifth floor. They followed the manager along the corridor, the opposite way from Francis's happy tiptoeing journey back to his room just six hours before. The pictures on the walls, big anodyne commercial abstracts, looked very different now.

Room 539. The card slid down. The tiny green oblong flickered. They were in.

'Topaz,' called Bernie softly.

There was a horrible silence. Surely she'd just got up and gone out? Maybe she was in a coffee bar in town, or shopping, and had simply forgotten the time. Francis felt fear catch at his throat.

'To-paz,' echoed Russell.

She wasn't in the bedroom, but all her stuff was. Her big crimson suitcase was on the carpet by the bed, half full; she had started packing. The maroon satin robe she'd worn last night lay on the crumpled sheet. There was still the heavy scent of the massage oil she'd produced for their second, gentler, more teasing session: orange and geranium.

'Don't touch anything,' Francis heard himself say.

Bernie marched into the bathroom, the hotel manager and Russell right behind him. Francis heard two sounds in canon, like sound following light. Bernie's quiet, matter-of-fact, 'Fucking shit', followed by an air-rending scream.

As Francis ran in, the hotel manager was throwing up in the sink.

Topaz was in the bath, face down, her beautiful hair streaming around her like Ophelia. A single bottle of hotel shampoo, half full, floated bizarrely next to her.

'None of us must touch a thing,' Francis repeated.

'Copy that,' said Bernie.

The hotel manager was wiping her lips with toilet paper. 'I will call the police,' she said. 'You are right. We must leave everything as it is.'

'Thank you,' said Bernie.

'And an ambulance,' said Francis.

'Of course,' she agreed.

'I'd better phone Adam,' said Bernie.

'I'll go and tell the band,' said Russell. He hadn't been sick, but he looked desperately pale.

'Shit,' said Bernie, as the door clicked shut behind the accountant. 'She didn't deserve that.' He was shaking his head, looking at Francis with an almost brotherly sympathy. 'You OK, mate?'

Francis nodded. And then, suddenly, he could feel his guts heave. He ran back into the bathroom and just made it to the toilet. For a moment, the thought occurred that he shouldn't be contaminating the crime scene any further, that he should just chuck up on top of the manageress's uncleared sink puke. But then he was on his knees by the porcelain bowl. And there was his breakfast, stained with black coffee, a half-digested lump of croissant perched oddly on top.

As he knelt there, on the verge of tears, he felt Bernie's hand on his shoulders, massaging them lightly. 'All right, mate?'

'Thank you.'

The tour manager was holding out a glass of water.

Francis smiled. 'Thanks,' he said, taking it and gulping it down.

As he got to his feet he could see Bernie back in the other room, on the phone to his boss. Adam was on his way up.

Francis decided to stick around. If this horrible death was another accident, it was a most unlikely one. Yes, rock stars had drowned before, even in baths, but surely they had been drunk as skunks, or catatonic on drugs. Francis knew exactly how Topaz had been when he'd left her. Like him. Sobered, frankly, by all the sex they'd been having.

He felt angry now. Angry at whoever had done this to Topaz: beautiful, talented, rare, special, gorgeous, passionate, crazy Topaz. On the previous cases he had been involved in, he realised, his emotions had not been engaged. Yes, he had been sad for the elegant, courageous old lady Eve, prematurely dead in her cabin on the West African cruise, and gutted when the body of his favourite creative writing student had been found, surrounded by a halo of wild mushrooms, at the Villa Giulia in Umbria, but it hadn't been a visceral fury like that he felt now. He would have to be careful, he realised. Bernie knew he had been in here last night, or if he didn't know, he'd guessed. Francis would be obliged to tell whoever was doing the formal investigating what he knew. God help him, he might even be a suspect.

Now Adam was here. Let into the room, he marched straight to the bathroom.

'Jesus Christ!' he said, emerging a minute later. He turned to Francis. 'I am prepared to believe that this is no longer a chapter of accidents.'

'No, boss,' Bernie agreed. 'It certainly fucking isn't.'

Downstairs, they could hear sirens. The police were already here.

'What are we doing about Nuremberg, boss?' Bernie asked.

Adam was trying hard to look composed. Only his eyes

showed how freaked out he was. 'It'll be half set-up by now,' he replied. 'Let's see what the police have to say. I don't imagine they're going to want to let any of us go just yet. It'll be like Copenhagen and then some, I fear. So who was the last to see her?'

Adam had no idea, Francis realised, about his night with Topaz. Bernie met his eye, raised his eyebrows a discreet fraction, then looked down.

'I was,' said Francis. 'We spent the night together.'

Adam looked stunned. He turned to Bernie. 'Is this true?' he asked slowly.

Francis nodded. 'I left her at about five. She was in bed. She was fine, absolutely fine.'

'Was this a regular thing?' Adam asked.

'No. Just … a one-off.' And it really was a one-off now, Francis thought, tears rising up behind his eyes. He gritted his teeth and got control.

'You're going to have to tell the police this.'

'Of course. I appreciate I shall probably be a suspect. Being the last one on the scene. But I could hardly compromise any of you. I think Bernie guessed, anyway.'

'You knew I had, mate.'

'I did.'

'Leaving together like that. And then the look on your face this morning.'

There was a light tapping on the door. It was the hotel manager with two police officers: a tall, lean, dark-haired young man and an older woman, shortish, thickset, blonde, with rather flushed red cheeks. Both were as neatly turned out as you would imagine German police to be, in dark-blue uniforms with a white *POLIZEI* insignia on their shoulders. They were both carrying chunky-looking dark-blue flat caps, with a big star badge on the front, just above the peak.

'*Guten Tag*,' they said as they came in and stood just inside the door.

'*Guten Tag,*' the hotel manager replied. She was echoed by Adam, Bernie and Francis, who were standing in a line by the window.

The hotel manager spoke rapidly in German, explaining, it seemed, her name, rank and situation. Frau Schröder. The policewoman introduced herself and her assistant. She was the boss, it was clear.

'*Die Leiche ist im Badezimmer,*' said Frau Schröder, pointing through to the bathroom. '*Wir haben alles so belassen, wie wir es vorgefunden haben.*'

'*Gute Arbeit,*' the policewoman replied.

There was a further exchange in German, at which the policewoman made a face. '*Vollkommen verständlich,*' she concluded. '*In einer solchen Situation.*'

There was a mention of *Forensikern mitteilen*, then an understanding nod. The policewoman went through, followed by her sidekick. Bernie followed, then re-emerged. There was the sound of one of them being sick: presumably, Francis thought, the male greenhorn.

'Frau Schröder?' Bernie said to the waiting manageress.

'*Ja,*' she replied.

'We're going to need to speak to the police urgently about what they need from us, since we've already checked out and are supposed to be driving immediately to Nuremberg for a gig – a concert – that's scheduled for tonight.'

'Of course,' she replied. 'But these two are just from the Polizei, the uniformed police. I am thinking they will probably want to call in the Kripo – the Kriminalpolizei, the investigative police, if they haven't already.'

Kripo. Hadn't that been the name for the Nazi police? Francis pushed down the thought; it was certainly not one he would dream of articulating, even in jest, and his mood was a long way from jest at the moment.

'Presumably,' Adam was saying, 'the Kripo will need to decide ... if this ... is a criminal matter.'

Frau Schröder shrugged. 'Of course they will have to consider this angle. I suppose we must hope that it will, very sadly, just be *Unfall*. I don't know the English for this. An accident. Not intended.'

'Misadventure,' Francis said.

'Miss Adventure,' Frau Schröder repeated slowly.

Bernie was shaking his head. Francis detected a very subtle, if still respectful, slide of his eyes in Adam's direction.

'I don't see how we're going to play Nuremberg tonight, boss.'

'Let's see what the police think,' Adam replied. From the bathroom came the sound of the female officer speaking in rapid German on her radio. Francis was fairly sure he heard the word 'Kripo' in there.

'Are they aware,' Adam asked Frau Schröder, 'of the situation? Of who we are?'

'I explained that you were the band of Jonni K. And entourage.'

The police had emerged.

'We have called in the Kriminalpolizei,' the female officer announced, po-faced, but with barely concealed excitement. 'They will need to take the case over from here.'

'Of course,' Adam replied. 'I think Frau Schröder has explained who we are and what we're doing here. Our immediate problem is what we do now. In the normal scheme of things, we would already be heading for Nuremberg, where Jonni K is supposed to be playing this evening, to a crowd of nine thousand. Some of whom will already be queuing outside the venue as we speak.'

The policewoman nodded, clearly unfazed by this passive-aggressive and frankly heartless appeal. 'And where is Jonni K now?' she asked.

'In his tour bus, outside,' Adam replied. 'The band are in a second bus.'

'With the, how do you say it, *roaties*?'

'We say "crew" these days, but no. They are already at the arena in Nuremberg, setting up for tonight.' Adam looked meaningfully at his gold watch. 'They started at 6 a.m. this morning.'

This was a slight exaggeration: 7 a.m., more like.

'OK,' said the policewoman. 'So you have a problem.'

Adam looked almost relieved. 'We do.'

'Nuremberg is nearly three hours away.'

'Exactly.'

'What time is this … concert?'

'Nine o'clock tonight.'

'So you would need to leave here by 4 p.m. at the latest? To arrive there in good time.'

'Yes.'

Francis saw the hope in Adam's eyes, flickering nervously. Was German efficiency going to triumph? Would the Polizei be able to interview the people they needed to super-quick and then let them all go? Was he really asking for this?

'Ideally earlier,' he went on, 'as the band – and Jonni – need to prepare before going onstage. Have a meal and so on.'

For a rock and roll manager of long experience, Adam was away with the fairies, Francis thought. How on earth did he imagine that he was going to get the famously twitchy Jonni and the other musicians up onstage when one of their fellow band members, probably the universal favourite, lay dead in the bath? Had he over-estimated his persuasive powers? Did he really think they were so professional they would be able to put their emotions to one side for the sake of "the show must go on"?

'It will be a decision for the Kripo,' the policewoman replied. 'The Kriminalpolizei. Normally they would want to interview all the witnesses immediately. Where do you go after Nuremberg?'

'Bernie?' Adam asked.

'Stuttgart,' said the tour manager. 'Then Munich, Vienna, Zurich. But we have a day off in Stuttgart, which could provide a window if necessary.'

Adam shot him a critical look.

'But you are, how do you say, on the *roat*?' the policewoman asked. 'Not coming back here to Frankfurt?'

They were interrupted by a loud, urgent knocking on the door.

'Are the Kripo here already?' said Adam.

'I think this will be the *Rettungsdienst*, the ambulance service,' said Frau Schröder. After her understandable first reaction, she was the very model of the calm professional, Francis thought, taking it all in her competent stride. He wondered how routine a matter death was at the Schlupfwinkel.

She was right. The door opened to reveal another female/male duo, this one reversed in age, in red and yellow fluorescent uniforms with red crosses on a white circle on their shoulders.

'*Guten Tag.*'

'*Guten Tag,*' Frau Schröder replied. '*Sie ist dort drinnen.*'

She nodded at the open bathroom door. The paramedics went through without another word.

'With your permission,' said Frau Schröder, 'I should excuse myself now. I have things to do downstairs. If you need me, I will be contactable through reception. I can come straight up. Shall I hold all your rooms for the time being?'

Adam looked over at the policewoman, who nodded.

'We need to work out what's happening,' he said.

'OK,' she replied. 'I'll hold them. Luckily it's not a particularly busy time.'

Adam beckoned to Bernie as he followed the manager out into the corridor. Through the open door, Francis could see them having an urgent discussion. Their voices were low but it was clear that it was about the Nuremberg gig. Francis was amazed they were still debating it.

'Are you staying for the time being?' he asked the police-woman, who was standing silently with her colleague, two half-silhouettes against the bright sunny morning outside.

'We must wait for the officers of the Kriminalpolizei,' she said. She too looked at her watch. 'They should be here in any minute.'

You had to hand it to the Germans. Even if they sometimes got it slightly wrong, their attempts to speak English properly, colloquially, were impressive. Once again, as so often in Europe, he was ashamed at his lack of language knowledge. He had a smattering of French, and that was it.

The *Rettungsdienst* duo had come out of the bathroom, and were now conferring urgently with the police.

'Francis!'

It was Bernie, at the door, beckoning. Francis went out to join the huddle in the corridor.

'As you can imagine,' said Adam. 'We are trying to work out how to play this.'

'Yes.'

'Do we cancel tonight, and maybe Stuttgart as well?'

'Well…' Francis began, but he was cut off before he could state what seemed to him the bleeding obvious: that however difficult it was, and however expensive, they would have to cancel tonight.

'Obviously,' Adam went on, 'what we decide will depend in part on what the police want, need, from us. The Kripo, the detectives. I assume you yourself are going to tell them everything.'

'Yes.'

The *Rettungsdienst* duo had emerged from the bedroom. Without a word, they headed off down the corridor towards the lift.

'I imagine your witness statement will be more important than anything the rest of us have to say,' Adam said.

'I'm sure it will be,' Francis replied. He suddenly felt a little pissed off. Was Adam about to try and make a sacrificial lamb of him? So that he could then try and talk his star and band into keeping the show on the road?

'On the other hand,' he went on, 'if the police do end up thinking this is suspicious, it's not going to be just me they're wondering about.' He gave Adam a level look. 'I know what I did last night, and it has nothing to do with this terrible situation.'

'Of course not, Francis. But the police might not see it that way.'

'Maybe not. But they're still going to want to talk to the rest of the band party who were in the hotel last night. Just for starters.'

Francis remembered his first-ever real-life case, at the Mold-on-Wold literary festival, when the police had closed down the hotel where the body had been found and insisted on taking statements from all the guests. Would that happen here? In more efficient Germany? Surely it would.

Bernie was looking thoughtful. 'I think we might have to postpone Nuremberg, boss.'

'Let's just see what the Kripo have to say.'

As if on cue, another suited German appeared in the corridor, looking purposeful. But this wasn't a lone representative of the Kripo, the waiting policewoman explained, as he too went through the bedroom and into the bathroom. It was a doctor.

'The *Notarzt* … the doctor of emergency,' she explained. Before she could say more, another pair appeared: a youngish woman with severely cut black hair over a square face, and an older, balding guy with gold John Lennon specs perched on a beaky nose. They were casually dressed, in clean-cut jeans and lightweight jackets. The Kripo.

The two detectives nodded at Adam, Bernie and Francis and spoke in rapid German with their uniformed colleagues. Then they too went into the bathroom, and Francis could hear an urgent exchange with the *Notarzt.*

After a minute they returned.

'Good morning,' said the older detective.

'Good morning,' Adam and Bernie replied in unison.

'This young woman is from the band of Jonni K?'

'She is. The bass guitarist. Topaz Brown.'

The dark-haired female detective was now taking notes in a small black Moleskine notebook.

'We will need to take her for post-mortem,' the older guy continued, 'to establish if she perhaps drank too much alcohol. Or maybe there were other substances involved. I have asked the *Gerichtsmediziner–*'

'Forensic specialists,' chipped in the uniformed policewoman.

'To attend this scene. They are coming now. Their analysis will help us. But what are you thinking? That this is a very unhappy accident? Or something worse?'

God help me, Francis thought. Perhaps I should have kept my trap shut after all. He could see, down in the ashtray on the table, the spliff stub. Would he get a chance to discretely pocket that when Polizei backs were turned – or would that be a mistake? Perhaps he should hide the ashtray too. Or perhaps it would be better to leave it, deny that he had been involved. Topaz might well have had a quiet joint by herself in the morning, after he'd gone. And what about the coke? There were no obvious traces of that. But forensics didn't need obvious traces.

Adam, meanwhile, seemed lost in thought. For a man who

wanted the band to be in Nuremberg tonight, things weren't going well. 'I'd assumed it was an accident,' he said.

This hardly tied in with his earlier reaction, Francis thought. What was he playing at?

'There has been quite a bit in the newspapers about this tour,' said the female Kripo. 'Jonni K being thrown off the stage in Hamburg. Then the guitarist being electrocuted in Rotterdam. They have been calling it, in Germany, the *verhext* tour.'

'*Verhext?*' Adam queried.

'I don't know the translation for this.'

'It is, like, bewitched,' said the uniformed policewoman.

'Aha, bewitched,' said Adam. 'We would say "jinxed". We've had the same nonsense in the UK press. I've been a manager in this business for many years, and this is what happens if anything goes wrong with a big tour like this. The press just love making a drama out of it. But, believe me, I've had much worse – in the US, with Guitarmageddon, another of my bands.' For a moment, Francis thought he was going to reprise the whole story: the overdosed lead guitarist, the overturned tour bus, the stalker with the gun. But: 'Thankfully the state police dealt with all that very swiftly and efficiently…' He held out his hands, then seemed uncertain what to say next. He looked involuntarily towards the bathroom door, then back again, directly at Francis. 'Sometimes bad things happen.'

'You managed Guitarmageddon?' the older detective asked.

'I did, yes. Among others.' Adam grinned self-deprecatingly.

'I love Guitarmageddon. Skin and Bones, what a pair!'

'Thank you.'

'Apart from Blind Guardian and Led Zeppelin, maybe Ozzy Osbourne, these are my favourite band.'

'Well, there you are.' Adam shrugged in a 'you're welcome' fashion.

Ice broken, they got down to business. As the two plain-clothes officers had said, the *Gerichtsmediziner* would soon be here. This room would remain sealed off until they had finished their investigations. At some point, the body would need to be removed for post-mortem. Regardless of the press dramatising the *verhext* tour, the Kripo pair would need to inter-view everyone from the entourage who had been staying in the hotel last night, Jonni K included. Of course they realised that this was a tour, and that Jonni was supposed to be in Nurem-berg tonight, but they didn't see how they could release everyone by four o'clock this afternoon. Perhaps by tomorrow morning, if all went well. They would be as helpful as possible. But they must take statements, and every member of the entourage must be available for recall at any time.

After five minutes of this, it was clear that Adam had capit-ulated. He was now looking at damage limitation. Perhaps, he suggested, the Nuremberg gig could be postponed till tomor-row. How, Francis thought, had he ever thought otherwise? Bernie was dispatched to the corridor to make phone calls.

Frau Schröder was summoned back. She was informed that this room, 539, was now secured as a crime scene. A meeting room downstairs would be turned over for police interviews, which would begin immediately.

Bernie returned with good news. There was no other event booked at the Nuremberg Arena for tomorrow. The scheduled day off in Stuttgart, the next venue, could be cancelled. The gig could be postponed for twenty-four hours.

Under the serious mask of an experienced manager dealing firmly with a horrid unexpected crisis, Adam looked delighted.

'So perhaps,' he said to the Kripo pair, 'we could do our level best to aim for that. We will make everyone available right now, and hopefully we can get away this evening, at the latest tomorrow morning.'

Whatever the detectives needed in terms of assurances, he went on, legal, financial, would of course be made available. Adam clearly wasn't going to try and bribe German police – that might be counterproductive – but he did, Francis noticed, rather linger on the word 'financial'. Meanwhile, Frau Schröder was going to keep all their rooms free for tonight. For the time being, Adam suggested, the band could hang out in a meeting room next to the one designated for police interviews. Jonni would return to the suite he'd vacated.

'I must go and speak with him now,' Adam said. Forget the others, Francis thought. Presumably they were contracted to perform, whatever their feelings. As long as the golden goose was on side, everything was OK.

Adam hurried off with Bernie and Frau Schröder. Francis was left with the two uniformed police, who now had the task of securing the room. He'd had an idea that he wanted to go in and say goodbye in private to Topaz, but he couldn't, when it came to it, bear it.

And then, all of a sudden, he could. Promising not to touch anything, he asked the blonde policewoman if he could make one final visit. She nodded. She had a kind face, he decided. And why shouldn't a German policewoman have a kind face? Ridiculous stereotyping and prejudice.

He tiptoed in. It was incongruous. This bathroom had a high window, through which the morning sun shone, casting a bright parallelogram of light on the marble-effect mosaic tiles.

Topaz lay in the gloom of the bath below. Someone had turned her over. *Rettungsdienst*, checking she was dead? The *Notarzt*, doing whatever it was that *Notärzte* do? The Kripo? Were they even allowed to manipulate a body at a crime scene? But there she was, floating, he supposed, face just above the surface of the water. There was no mottling, no bloating, nothing in the condition of her smooth and lovely skin to indicate that she wasn't alive, wasn't about to sit up, smile, and summon him back to bed. Only her big empty brown eyes, wide open, unseeing, gave her away. Hardly believing he was managing to do this, he peered down to look at her neck. If someone had strangled her, they hadn't left a mark.

In the depths of the night, they had joked about their colour. Francis was indeed, on comparison of wrists, a little paler than Topaz. Mixed race or dual heritage? Topaz preferred the former: 'It's straighter. That's what I am. "Dual heritage" makes me sound like some kind of antique.' To be honest, she hated the fact that there had to be terms at all. 'Why can't we just be ourselves? Why all this endless categorising and labelling? Did you have to put up with a lot of shit when you were younger?'

'What do you think?' he replied. 'Growing up in the 1970s and 80s, it was non-stop.' He shrugged. 'Routine.' But he'd boxed it up and left it behind, long ago. From the moment he'd got to uni there had been respect, at least from his contemporaries, for his colour. He never let the other, incidental, public abuse get to him, or allowed himself to succumb to fearful anticipation. And now, he thought, his skin tone sometimes even worked in his favour. 'In the literary and media world, anyway. Not that I'm complaining. It's payback time. I can't tell you how many worthy committees there are who want me on board as a writer of colour.'

'Wowsers, committees – lucky you!' Topaz laughed.

Funnily enough, of the casual insults he'd endured over the years, he'd been called 'Paki' far more often than the N-word, or that other almost-forgotten insult, 'coon'.

'You are rather a pale coon,' she'd said, stroking him gently. Then, in the early morning silence, she had sung him India Arie's 'Brown Skin'. It felt magical, that powerful voice low, tamed, right next to his ear.

They had talked about Botswana, where Francis's father originated and had returned to before Francis knew him, and how, even though he'd been within five hundred miles of that country, working at a school in Swaziland during a post-uni year off, Francis hadn't, in the end, gone there to try and find his father. He hadn't even wanted to visit the place. 'Was that odd?' he asked her. 'I often think there must be something wrong with me, not seizing the opportunity while I was out there. I suppose I was just happy with my existing family. John and Sheila. I didn't want to compromise all that.'

'You do what you want to do,' Topaz replied. 'No shame in that.'

Now, from nowhere, tears came. Francis was sobbing, then holding on to the shower rail for support. How could this have happened? Who had done it? Not Topaz. He knew it wasn't Topaz. So full of life, of passion, of music, she wouldn't have allowed herself to die like this. To be drunk. To overdose. To drown in a bathtub. Jesus, none of this lot knew this, and he certainly wasn't going to tell them now, but his wife Kate had also drowned, twenty years before, in a terrible storm on the Upper Nile. Completely different circumstances, but her body, when they pulled it from the river, had been the same. Even though Kate had been bruised from her awful fight to escape the felucca's cabin, her eyes had been wide open and empty too.

That had been an accident and, like all accidents, sudden, unexpected, unreal. But this wasn't a freaking accident. No way. Someone had killed Topaz. Deliberately. Between 5 a.m., when Francis had slipped back into his clothes and leant down to plant a last kiss on her smiling lips, and 11.30 a.m, when she had failed to make it to the bus. A six-and-a-half-hour window.

Those Kripo guys better know what they're doing, he thought. Or they will have me to answer to.

Chapter Sixteen

An hour later the band were gathered in a meeting room downstairs in the hotel. It was incongruously civilised, with sun streaming through tall windows, and coffee and biscuits on a long side table, almost as if they had gathered to discuss corporate strategy or attend a brainstorming session on effective ways to brush up their brand.

They were all in deep shock, even if they didn't realise it. Vanko was ostensibly the cheeriest. 'So we're going to give our statements and then get on the road to Nuremberg this evening, with the idea of doing the gig tomorrow night? Is that seriously Adam's plan?'

'He doesn't want to let the fans down,' said Simon, who as unofficial leader of the rest of the band had been privileged to a one-to-one with their manager in Jonni's suite upstairs.

'And Jonni's cool with that?'

'I have no idea. Adam's up there with him now.'

'It's ridiculous,' said Vanko. 'They should cancel Nuremberg at the very least.'

'I agree,' said Thelma. 'Topaz hasn't had a post-mortem –

we don't even know whether it's an accident or … something worse … and we're supposed to be able to perform?'

'Unless you guys could somehow see it as doing it for her. Like, in her memory,' said Russell.

'Nice try, Russ. Thinking about the money, as always.'

'I hate to disillusion you, dude, but the money is an issue. Your very healthy retainer doesn't come from nowhere, you know.'

There was silence. From outside, faintly, through the double glazing, came the hooting of horns and engine revs of mid-morning Frankfurt.

'So you actually saw her?' Vanko asked Francis.

'Yes.'

'Was it very…' he paused, 'shocking?'

'She didn't actually look dead. She looked like she might have been washing her hair. Apart from her eyes.'

Thelma was sobbing quietly. 'I'm sorry,' she murmured.

'That's more than OK,' said Suzi. 'D'you know what? Can we not talk about her? In this way?'

'As dead, you mean?' said Vanko. 'Well, she is dead, and we might as well face it. Just as we should face the fact that someone tried to kill me four nights ago. In Rotterdam. I mean, what the fuck is going on?'

'Nobody knows, dude,' said Russell. His patina of bonhomie had gone; he looked gutted. Well, he had been very fond of Topaz, hadn't he?

The door pushed open and Bernie had joined them. 'OK,' he said. 'So how's it going in here?'

'I guess we're all just trying to make sense of it all,' said Russell.

'Yup,' Bernie replied. 'Doesn't make a lot of sense, does it?'

'It does to someone,' said Vanko. 'To whoever's orches-trating this shitshow, it makes very good sense. I just wish I knew who it was and what exactly they're trying to achieve.'

'Vanko,' said Bernie. 'The police haven't even ruled out accidental death yet.'

'Well, I have. Ricky, Jonni, me, Topaz. There's no accident about it. The only question you lot should be worrying about is: who's next? I'm personally hoping it's not a second crack at me. What other classic rock and roll deaths haven't they tried yet? If I were you, Simon, I'd be careful about that flight from Vienna to Paris you're taking in a few days' time. It might end up not being such a perk, after all.'

'Oh fuck off, Vanko.'

'Just saying.'

'OK, kids,' said Bernie. 'The reason I popped into the kindergarten was to advise you that the police are ready to see the next member of the entourage for interview and statement. And that lucky person is … Vanko.'

'Great.'

'You've got plenty to say, Vanko,' said Simon.

'I certainly have. Am I supposed to tell the whole truth? And nussing but the ze truth?' he added in caricature German.

'I would if I were you,' said Bernie.

'Some of you better watch out, then.'

'Meaning what?' asked Simon.

'Zat vill be between me and my therapist. Correction, my detective inspector of ze Kripo.'

Suzi was quietly rolling her eyes.

'Follow me, then,' said Bernie.

'He's in a right state,' said Suzi, when he'd gone.

Ten minutes later, the guitarist was back, and it was Simon's turn.

'So how was it, dude?' Russell asked Vanko after the bearded band leader had left the room.

'Just basic questions, as Bern said. When did I last see her? Her state of mind from my point of view, that sort of thing. Whether she had any rivals or enemies in the entourage. Did she have a favourite? Did she have a boyfriend?' Vanko looked pointedly at Francis. Francis had confessed to Adam and Bernie, and he would be straight with the police when it came to his turn, but he wasn't going to get into all that with the band right now. God alone knows, Suzi and Thelma were emotional enough without him telling them about last night. Twelve hours ago. It seemed so distant now. And why, why had he left her? For the sake of some ridiculous scruple – of being found out; when half of them knew anyway? He could have saved her. He could have fucking saved her.

'Isn't it possible?' said Suzi after a few moments, 'that she just fell asleep in the bath? That in fact all these things are a sequence of terrible accidents. Like that Cranberries singer. Didn't she drown in the bath of some posh London hotel?'

'Dolores O'Riordan,' said Vanko. 'The Hilton. She was extremely drunk. By all accounts.'

The door swung open.

'Russell,' said Bernie. 'Your turn.'

'Where's Simon?' asked Vanko. 'Have they arrested him?'

'Gone upstairs to the suite in the sky.'

'Have they done Jonni yet?'

'No.'

Vanko raised his eyebrows, but said nothing.

When Russell returned, he looked happier; whatever he had said to the Kripo appeared to have calmed him a little. But now Bernie was back and it was time for Francis to face the music. He had done nothing wrong. He would tell them everything he knew.

It was the two Kripo officers from earlier, with the flushed blonde in uniform sitting to one side with a notebook.

The younger female detective with the severely cut black hair did the talking. This was just a witness statement, she said, which they were taking from everyone who had been staying in the hotel the night before. First, though, they asked him to stand still while they examined him. Was this a normal German procedure? If he really were just a witness, it was certainly odd. There was no touching, and after ten seconds of studying, it seemed, his face and neck (for what – scratches?), the pair looked at each other and shrugged, as if to say 'He's OK.' Then they asked him to sit and go through things one by one: name, occupation, his role – and then his honest account of what he'd done yesterday and last night.

There was no avoiding the truth – or most of it, anyway. They had already spoken to Bernie and Russell and Adam. Bernie knew what had gone on. He had told Adam. Vanko clearly had his suspicions. The all too easy segue from flirtation in Jonni's room to getting high in Topaz's, and then, and then … what had happened, so perfectly natural at the time … was now a sequence of suspicious events for inquisitive outsiders to pick over forensically.

'There was the gig at the Festhalle,' Francis began. 'Which went very well. Not that I saw the first few songs, because I was talking to one of our managers, Nick, who has now returned to London. But when I did go up to the platform on the side of the stage, my eyes were, frankly, all on Topaz. She's a corpse now, just a heap of flesh and bone and hair in a bath, but she was sex on legs when she was up there. What a performer! Who knows how many years of practice in her teenage bedroom she did to get to that standard, but believe me, when you saw those fingers racing so wildly and skilfully over the strings, you'd have wanted her too…'

So his thoughts ran, as his mouth gave the three police officers the mundane account of watching the gig and heading home on the band bus. He didn't bother with the scene of flirty Topaz joking that Francis could take the role of 'band butler' and open the freaking champagne. Nor did he go into detail about the cold-meat supper in the oak-panelled back dining room of the Schlupfwinkel. Nor how he, Francis, had come to love the post-gig camaraderie, when the band were in a great mood, their anxieties about their performance over for another night, their egos recharged by the wild applause of nine thousand pairs of hands. He described the move up to Jonni's room, but not that it was a first for the band on the tour so far. He mentioned the Skyjo, but not the weirdness of all the adults being forced to play a kids' game because that was what the star demanded.

'And then,' asked the older, balding, male detective, 'at the end of the evening, you left Jonni's suite in the company of Topaz Brown?'

'I did, yes. We'd been chatting together and she suggested a nightcap, so I thought–'

'A nightcap? This is a phrase for…'

Despite the tense atmosphere, Francis struggled not to laugh at the expression on the policeman's face. No, it wasn't a euphemism for sex, he explained. Just a drink. 'I thought we might go to the bar, for a bit of peace and quiet, away from the others, but then she invited me to her room. To be honest, I went with her because I was hoping she might open up, tell me some things I was keen to know.'

Had Adam – Mr Ainslie – explained to them his role on the tour? he asked. Yes? That he had been employed by the managers as an investigator, to try and find out who had pushed Jonni off the stage in Hamburg and then attempted to electrocute the guitarist, Vanko Angelov, in Rotterdam.

'And also, I think,' said the female Kripo, 'the death of the crew member who overdosed in Copenhagen?'

'So you know about that?'

'Herr Ainslie has briefed us comprehensively.'

Her look was significant. 'It's really not worth trying to hide anything from us,' her penetrating dark eyes seemed to say. 'So what was it that you thought Topaz might have been about to tell you?' she asked.

'Obviously, the main thing I've been looking for is motive,' Francis replied, hoping to strike a chummy, professional, detective-to-detective tone. 'Who would want to do these things? Were they all done by the same person, or group of people, and if so, why?'

'So what are you saying? You suspect an individual within the … *Gefolge*?' She looked across at her colleague.

'Entourage,' he translated.

'I've been keeping an open mind,' Francis went on. 'The guy who pushed Jonni off the stage in Hamburg was nothing to do with the band or crew. Having said that, who knows what individual members of the band or crew might know? Like people who might have it in for the managers, for example, for one reason or another.'

'So you think this series of incidents is motivated by an attack on the managers?'

'I've no idea. I'm still trying to find answers.'

'And Topaz Brown had some of these answers?'

'Maybe.' Was now the moment to explain about Uncle Bobby and Frankie Freak and the appropriated publishing royalties? Or would that just confuse things? These two had an immediate job to do. Decide whether there had been foul play in relation to Topaz's death – and then, if so, to work out suspects. 'Would you like me to explain the various leads I've been following?'

'Thank you,' said the senior detective. 'That might be useful. For the moment, though, perhaps you could tell us exactly what happened with Topaz after you left Jonni's suite.'

Francis obliged, though he glossed over any incriminating details.

'And this sort of thing hadn't happened between the two of you before?' the female detective asked.

'No.'

'To an outsider, this seems unlucky. After your very first time.'

Francis checked out the older cop for sympathy. In his gentle eyes under the glinting round glasses, he thought he found it. Certainly the other woman in the room, the blonde uniform, looked as if she weren't a hundred per cent supportive of her plain-clothes colleague's interviewing technique.

'But that's what happened,' he replied. 'I'm as shocked as anyone. To be honest, I didn't have to tell any of them that I'd spent the night with Topaz. It might have been easier to keep that to myself. But … up there … in the room … I just thought … I should.'

'It's always sensible to tell the truth. When people try to hide things, they can get themselves all twisted up with lies. As you must know from your own detective work.'

'I do.'

'So I have one more question for you, which it would be sensible to give an honest answer to. You say you had this drink, this "nightcap", with Topaz Brown. Did you also take drugs, the two of you?'

Francis had to answer immediately. Any pause might look suspicious. So what had they found? Joints in the ashtrays, definitely. Meanwhile forensics had been there for, what – he glanced at his watch, realising even as he looked at it that he was hesitating – an hour already, so who knew what else they had found? The coke had seemed so innocent last night, a little secret treat, laid out on the glass table top of a private room. Hardly a criminal activity, he thought, though of course it was, class A, and presumably in Germany too, and now he was severely compromised.

'Yes,' he said. 'We did. Topaz had some marijuana. I'm not sure what type. I think she'd got it legally in Amsterdam when we were there a few days ago. It wasn't a lot. Just a spliff. Which we had with a drink.'

The older detective nodded; he seemed happy with this confession.

'And that was it?' asked the younger. 'Nothing else? Nothing stronger?'

Francis met her uncompromising eye and very nearly lied. What was the attitude of the German police – correction, the Hesse police – to drugs? Did they take a gentler attitude to spliffs, as at home? Did they make a distinction between possession and use on the one hand, and supplying and dealing on the other? He had no idea, but he guessed from her tone that she already knew about the coke.

'After we'd finished the spliff,' he replied, 'Topaz produced a small wrap of cocaine. I've no idea where she got it from. So we had a line each.'

'Just one line?'

'You asked me to tell you the truth. I am telling you the truth. Maybe Topaz took more drugs after I left in the morning. But while I was there, that was it: one joint, a line of cocaine each, and then we went back to the hotel champagne. Another drug, but a legal one.'

The female Kripo looked over at her colleague. 'To recap,' she said, 'you were employed by the management as a detective?'

'Yes.'

'You went to Topaz Brown's room hoping, perhaps, to get some information from her?'

'Yes.'

'And you took drink and also the illegal drug, cocaine, in her company before having sex with her?'

'Yes.'

'Were you at any point concerned that you were being unprofessional?'

She was annoying, this woman. She had a point, of course she did. Hadn't he told himself, right at the start, that he would not get involved with anyone on the tour? He had broken his own resolution, albeit in very special circumstances. But actually, how dare she question how he did things? He was a free agent, not a member of a police force or investigative team. He could make up his own rules.

'I never intended to spend the night with Topaz,' he replied, truthfully. 'It was a mistake. I got carried away.'

She nodded, coolly. Give her an inch, he thought, she'll take a mile.

'Do you know what would happen to me if I was caught taking drugs on the job?' she said, and her tone was so smug she looked for a moment as if she might self-combust. 'Let alone having sex with suspects?'

'I'm afraid I don't.'

'I would be put under investigation. Probably have my career terminated. Maybe be sent to jail. Depending on the amount involved. This is what happens to corrupt police. Correctly, from the way I am thinking.'

'As I said before,' said Francis, 'I am not a policeman. I was employed in a private capacity.'

That seemed to silence her. At any rate, her older colleague took over at this moment, telling her, Francis thought, that enough was enough and she should pipe down. '*Genug jetzt. Ich denke wir sollten es dabei belassen.*'

Then, with a smile, and without taking Francis up on his kind offer of a recap of his own leads, the older detective produced his card and handed it to Francis with the standard request that he should get in touch if anything further should occur to him.

ERSTER POLIZEIHAUPTKOMMISSAR FISCHER, the card read. Francis had no idea what rank that was, but it sounded long enough to be fairly grand. Fischer shook his hand, and the look he gave Francis as he did this was quite something: frank, open, enquiring, as if he was expecting a call sometime. By contrast, his black-haired female colleague only nodded. Whether this was because she disapproved of Francis, or was merely the junior and so didn't do the honours, wasn't clear.

At this moment Francis realised that, despite so many surface similarities with home, he was adrift in a completely different culture.

Chapter Seventeen

Interview over, Francis returned to the other room, with instructions to send Thelma in. The Kripo pair were getting down to the last few people in the witness/possible suspect roster. For who else was there? The crew were two hundred and twenty miles away.

Adam had just been talking to the band, Bernie explained. A decision had been taken to postpone the Nuremberg gig till tomorrow. The band party would stay one more night in Frankfurt and then leave in the morning at the usual time. The rooms they had had last night had been serviced and were now available again. Suzi, the last interviewee, could wait here or outside the police interview room along the corridor.

As the others got up to leave, Adam beckoned to Francis and summoned him to the far end of the room, where sunlight was streaming through a window onto a long, pale brown suede couch. Bernie followed, trotting along like a loyal hound.

'Everything OK?' Adam asked.

'Fine, thanks, yes.'

'How did you get on with the Kripo?'

'OK. Have to say I preferred the man to the woman.'

'I think we all did.' Adam looked sideways at Bernie.

'She was a bit hardcore,' he agreed. 'Even for a seasoned old see-you-next-Tuesday like me.'

'You presumably told them everything?' Adam asked Francis.

'I did, of course. Let's hope they have some insights or skills that I don't.'

'Do you have *any* idea what's going on?'

'All I'm sure of is that it wasn't an accident,' Francis replied. 'I left Topaz at around 5 a.m. and she was fine. She wasn't drunk, she wasn't taking drugs, there was no reason for her to pass out in the bath.'

Adam was nodding, thoughtfully. 'Nick is flying out as we speak,' he said. 'He'll want a meeting later, I expect. I'll call you on the mobile, shall I?'

'Please do. So presumably the Kripo wouldn't let you go?'

'Actually, they've been very accommodating. Our main problem was Jonni. There was no way he was in a state to go on tonight.'

'Fingers firmly crossed for tomorrow,' said Bernie.

'We'll do it as a kind of memorial gig,' Adam said. 'Once he's got over the shock, Jonni will be up for that. Like he was with Ricky.'

In memoriam Topaz, thought Francis. Let us remember this wonderful guitarist who meant so much to us that we decided to let the show go on, and give all you lovely Nuremberg ticket-holders what you've paid for. A mere twenty-four hours later than planned.

'So what do you want to do?' Adam asked now. 'The police are fine with you having access to whatever's going on in Topaz's room, if you want to.'

Francis shuddered. Maybe this was yet another instance of him being unprofessional, but he didn't need this. Presumably whatever the *Gerichtsmediziner* found out would soon enough be shared with the managers – and him. He didn't need to hang around as poor Topaz's body was poked and prodded and eventually taken off in a bag.

'To be honest,' he replied, 'I'd like to go back to my room and then maybe go for a walk to clear my head.'

'Fully understood,' said Adam. 'This was one of the reasons we decided to stick around here. To give people time and space to get their shit together before we move on.'

He was such a fraud, Francis thought. Such a reasonable, nice, caring, thoughtful, teetotal, greedy old fraud.

In the centre of Frankfurt's Old Town, where the steep gabled roofs and colourful timbered frontages looked like something from a Grimm Brothers fairy tale, Francis considered visiting the beautiful old church recommended by Gideon the bus driver. Perhaps he could find the peace and quiet to think in there. But he was so exhausted and strung out, he needed a strong coffee and something sugary to eat, so he dived instead into an incongruous modern café, with funky lights hanging in a group from the ceiling, pale green walls, deep maroon curtains and dark wood tables with stylish black leather chairs. *BITTE BESTELLEN SIE AM TISCH* said a sign on the long glass case of cakes and pastries. *Please order at the table.* He chose a luscious-looking chocolate cheesecake topped with berries in a sweet purple jelly. Topaz would have liked this place, he thought, remembering their coffee together in Amsterdam less than a week ago – though it felt like a month. Then she had told him he wasn't a journalist, he was a detective, and she had obliged him with Zak's backstory. She had been very keen he know that. And now she was dead.

Tears filled his eyes as he gulped down his first strong *Kaffee*. To distract himself from his despair, he ordered another, then took out his notebook and started jotting down thoughts about the key characters in the case. It was a process he had gone through each time he'd done this, and it helped clarify his ideas, though he had to admit that on the last two occasions – at the Villa Giulia in Italy and on the Golden Adventurer cruise in Africa – his speculations on paper had been way wide of the actual result.

This case was a little different. Because it wasn't one hundred per cent clear that one of the victims was a victim anyway, and there were two other attacks on the band, neither of which had ended in anything more serious than a bruised elbow and considerable shock (in all senses of the word). For clarity, though, he would include everything.

VICTIMS

RICKY – Keyboard tech but, more important, Jonni's great mate/one-time drug buddy. Found dead on the lampies' bus on arrival in Copenhagen. Had supposedly OD'd on a cocktail of drugs after an all-night party. Perfectly possible, in that he had recently got clean, but had fallen off the wagon a couple of times too. But a strong suspicion from some that it wasn't an accident. And what exactly was Ricky's relationship with his 'close friend' Jonni?

JONNI – star of the show, centre of the travelling players, golden goose, pushed off the stage halfway through the Hamburg gig. By Danish Nils, a supposed 'nutter' who said he was doing it for Sandra. *Who knows this, apart from Jonni and Vanko? Adam? Has anyone even told the police? So who is Sandra? A fan/groupie who had been taken advantage of by Jonni? Or just a crazed obsessive who thought she had? As the unautho-rised Vanko websites show, there are plenty out there. And what of Jonni's link with Ricky (see above)? Is he, as Vanko seemed to be suggesting when we had dinner in Brussels, actually gay?*

VANKO – lead guitarist, subject to severe electric shock from guitar in

Rotterdam. Another accident? How likely is that, especially after Topaz? Vanko suspected one of his crazier fans, but how does that tie in with the rest of the incidents? Wasn't the guitarist just one in a series?

TOPAZ – oh beautiful Topaz, drowned in your bath at the Schlupfwinkel. How likely is that to be self-inflicted? Surely not very likely at all, given how she was when I crawled away from her in the pre-dawn darkness. Half-asleep, sober enough. Would she then spring up and start drinking and taking drugs, before climbing into the bath and passing out? No. It has to be foul play.
After she told me the story of Zak, Adam and the Tainted Idols' publishing royalties, she clammed up. Wouldn't talk about it – or anything else. Even last night, though we talked freely about so many other things, she steered clear. And what had that throat-cutting gesture backstage at the Festhalle been all about? Walls have ears, *she'd said. Why, why didn't I push her on this? How could I be so stupid to assume I had time? Today, later. There never was a later.*

SUSPECTS

NILS, THE DANISH GUY
A lunatic, or a man on a mission? The Hamburg police haven't, suppos-edly, been able to find out more. Nils has now been charged with assault and bailed. But he's not explained anything beyond 'Sandra'. So was the Jonni attack a one-off, nothing to do with the other incidents? If not, I can't exactly see how or why Nils would be working with anyone from band, crew, wider pissed-off ex-band community, etc.

SEAMUS
The roadie who once worked for the Tainted Idols, and knew them all well: had at one point been in a band (the Flaming Buzzards) with Topaz's dad and Bobby Fairhurst, famous lead guitarist of the Idols and godfather to Topaz, who was allegedly screwed over, along with keyboardist Frankie Freak and the other musicians, by Zak and almost certainly Adam

too. A recent attempt at a settlement, instigated by Frankie after many years, was foiled by Adam's bullying tactics, according to Topaz. Is it possible that one (or both) of them decided to punish these two another way, by spoiling their tour? Could Seamus be a part of this? He's on site, as stage manager and fill-in keyboard tech, so could easily have done something to Vanko's foot pedal after Mel had finished checking it. But why take it out on Vanko? Or did he set it up so that Vanko only got a small shock, enough to frighten him – and the management – but not kill him? And what about Topaz? She was Seamus's good friend, but was that all? What had they been watching on that laptop? Whatever it was, she really hadn't wanted Francis to see, had she? Or know, as she avoided the subject later. However, thankfully Seamus was miles away in Nuremberg when she died, so couldn't have been involved.

BOBBY/FRANKIE FREAK, *etc.*
See above. Good revenge motive for the ex-Idols, but none of them are anywhere near the tour. Unless working with/through Seamus and/or very undercover. And they would hardly kill their beloved Topaz.

ADAM
Something suspicious about him, as if he knows something he's not telling. He may well be guilty of ripping off all kinds of people – ex-band members, etc., but what motive would he have for sabotaging his own tour? And why has he been keeping me away from Jonni? Because he has, hasn't he?

ZAK
Even though, yes, he is a key part of AZ Music, why does he feel the need to lurk constantly around the tour? Thick as thieves with Adam, to the apparent detriment of Nick. What are they up to, the pair of them? He wasn't there last night, though. So couldn't have been directly involved with Topaz's death.

NICK
Is it slightly strange that the one night he's over, and travelling with the tour, there's a death? The opportunity was there, especially with a neat alibi of catching an early flight. But he couldn't have done it himself (could he?), and again, why would he sabotage his own tour? Unless Topaz knew something she didn't tell me? And that throat-slitting gesture referred to him. At our chat in Catering, he was very interested in what Topaz had said to me.

VANKO
Simon made a joke that Vanko would like Jonni out of the way so he could be lead singer, and yes, he does have a lovely – frankly, better – voice. But he's a jobbing musician on a retainer, so he wouldn't be promoted anyway. If Jonni went, the band would be dismantled. Also, very realistic about his own chances, how he needs to concentrate on his own music and career. In any case, you can hardly electrocute yourself. Can you? And he loved Topaz. Didn't he?

A PISSED-OFF FAN OR FANS
Working with the Danish guy, Nils, or just a lone maniac? Perfectly possible, in terms of motivation, as the Vanko fan websites reveal. But access? Hard to see how he or she would get that? The security guys were in the hotel all last night, one in with Jonni, the other at the end of the corridor outside.

WHO ELSE?
Any single member of the crew could have been in the frame for any of the first three incidents. But Topaz's death changed all that – they were all in Nuremberg. Unless there's more than one saboteur/murderer and they're working together. But why? Seems unlikely. So who are you left with, if the same person was responsible for all incidents? Management, band members, and – wild card – security guys. No one else there.

Francis looked up from the scrawl in his notebook to see the two backing singers, Suzi and Thelma. They had just come into the café and were looking at the display of cakes, then at the *BITTE BESTELLEN* sign. Now they were coming towards him, looking for an empty table. They had seen him. There were two empty chairs at his table. The place was busy, with just one other small table free over by the door to the toilet. He waved at them and they came over.

'Sorry,' said Thelma. 'Not meaning to disturb you…'

Of all the cafés, in all of Frankfurt, you walk into mine, Francis thought. But he wasn't in the mood for a Bogart impersonation. 'Please,' he said, gesturing to the empty chairs opposite him. 'Join me. I could do with the company.'

They looked at each other, then back at him, then they sat down together.

'They come to the table,' Francis explained.

'I saw,' said Thelma.

'We were doing some shopping,' Suzi said. 'Window-shopping, really, just needed to get away from the hotel.'

'Me too,' said Francis.

'I'll bet,' said Thelma.

A waitress appeared, and they ordered coffee. Then they decided they'd share a 'comfort cake' and there was some dithering over choices.

'How did you get on with the police?' Suzi asked, after they had finally decided and the waitress had gone.

'OK, I think. I preferred the man to the woman, have to say.'

'Christ, yes,' said Suzi. 'The black-haired automaton. She was a right bitch, wasn't she?'

'What did they ask you?' Francis asked.

'Oh, they were nice enough. Just a few basics. When I'd last seen Topaz. What she was like. What my relationship with her was. That sort of thing.'

'And you?' Francis asked Thelma.

'Yeah, similar. The woman detective wanted details about her character. How up and down she was, if there might have been any chance of suicide.'

Francis was shaking his head. 'So not. I know she was quite an emotional person–'

'She was,' Suzi cut in. 'But…'

'When I left her,' Francis continued, 'she was hardly in a depressed state.'

'I should hope not,' said Suzi.

'Seriously, what are they thinking? That she got out of bed at five in the morning and decided to top herself? Or that as soon as I'd gone she started drinking and/or taking drugs before getting into a bath and drowning herself?'

'I don't think it was an accident either,' said Thelma.

There was silence. The waitress appeared with coffee and cake.

'By the way,' said Thelma, tucking in, 'we don't think you had anything to do with it. If that's any consolation.'

'It is,' Francis said gratefully. Coming from Topaz's special friends, that meant a lot. At least, he felt, he could trust these two. 'You could mention that to the police, if you liked.'

'I already did.'

'So they asked about me?'

'Of course.'

'What in particular?'

'What we all thought of you and so on.'

'The journalist,' said Suzi with a sudden giggle.

'Is that what they called me?'

'Yes.'

'Interesting.'

'They were keeping to the cover story,' said Suzi. 'Even though everyone knows what you're here for really.'

'Did you tell them? That you thought I wasn't a journalist?'

'Knew you weren't, more like. No.'

There was another pause. The women, in tandem, took forkfuls of their shared cake and gulps of their coffee.

'So if you don't think it was an accident,' Francis asked, 'what do you think?'

'I'm scared,' said Thelma. 'To be honest. Jonni, Vanko, now Topaz. Who does that leave? Simon, Scally and us.'

'You really think some weirdo is working their way round the band?'

'What else are we supposed to think?' said Suzi. 'I never thought the Vanko thing was an accident. Not after what happened to Jonni. Adam assures us that they're stepping up security. But I can't say the existing guys have done that brilliantly so far. What do you think, Francis? Weren't you supposed to be working out what's going on?'

Francis had nothing to lose, he thought, by explaining about the leads he'd been following up. Maybe he would even prompt the backing singers to add stuff they had been keeping back from him. So he told them about Topaz's theories about her Uncle Bobby and Frankie Freak. As he'd imagined, her two close friends knew exactly what she'd thought. But they didn't buy the idea that Bobby Fairhurst, based up in Scotland on a rare breeds farm, or Frankie, now resident in Italy with a large family, would be bothered or even able to manage a vindictive campaign of mayhem with a rock and roll tour miles away in Germany. They didn't think that anyone else was trying to have a go at Adam. If he had behaved badly towards his employees in the past, that was in the past. He was a great manager now. He treated the band and crew fairly, if not generously, and they were mostly happy with him. As for Zak, OK, so he had an interest in AZ Music, but that was only one of many irons he had in various fires. He had Zak Films and

Zak Media, quite apart from the Glenveray cheeses and craft beers and whiskies and all that. Attacking Jonni K and his tour was hardly the best way to get to him.

'So you're as baffled as I am,' Francis concluded.

Chapter Eighteen

Nick looked drained. He had flown back to London, but hadn't even gone home. When he'd switched on his phone at Heathrow and heard the news, he'd turned round in Arrivals and got the first flight back.

'I don't think any of us can pretend any more that nothing's going on,' he told Francis, as they sat opposite each other in his room in the Schlupfwinkel. 'Adam was a little blasé about it for a while, but I think I've been proved right now.'

Blasé, thought Francis. That's only the half of it.

Nick was going to facilitate a meeting with Jonni today, he said. Immediately, in fact. 'When we've finished here, we'll go straight to his room. The gig's been cancelled tonight. He doesn't have to perform. You can't be pussyfooting around any more. You know, sometimes, between ourselves, I think Adam can be a wee bit too understanding of Jonni and his moods. Which is not to say that he isn't brilliant with him. He is. But the danger with these performers is that they start to believe their own publicity. The limelight is so strong, they forget it won't be on them forever. They revert to being toddlers. You remember Van Halen and the no brown M&Ms?'

'Er, no,' Francis replied. Van Halen was presumably a band.

'It was a clause in their contract. The promoters had to provide the sweets backstage, but sift out all the brown ones. Turned out it was just a clever way of checking they had read the rider properly, but it was not unduly outlandish, believe me. The Beach Boys demanded Bic lighters backstage, but not green ones. Prince required that everything in his dressing room was covered in plastic wrap. Paul McCartney wouldn't have leather furniture. Mariah Carey has to have two vases of white roses. Kanye insists on a barber's chair…' The manager paced up and down the beige carpet, chuckling, but in an almost unhinged fashion.

Francis hadn't seen him like this before. Nick had always been calm and collected, if a bit menacing underneath. Now he seemed seriously on edge: as if he really needed to get this problem sorted, and soon.

'So have you told me everything, Francis? I got the sense when we spoke last night that you were holding something back. You need to tell me all you know at this stage.'

'OK,' said Francis slowly. As a way of dodging the bullet, he told him that he'd spent the night with Topaz.

'I knew that. But thanks for being honest with me.'

'I also told the police.'

'I knew that too.'

'I was completely straight with them. She had a spliff up there, and also a wrap of cocaine.'

'That you partook of?'

'I'm afraid I did.'

Nick was shaking his head: in disappointment or under-standing, it was hard to tell.

'They were hers,' Francis went on, 'as I explained to the Kripo guys. I shouldn't have gone to her room. It was unprofessional of me. And for that, I apologise. I've always managed to walk away from situations like this before, where I might be compromised. But I don't know, I was just ambushed, I guess, because Topaz…'

'Was so fucking gorgeous,' said Nick.

Francis nodded, and suddenly tears flooded his eyes.

'It's OK,' Nick said, taking his hand. 'You just spent the night with her. And now…' He couldn't finish the sentence. 'I'd be concerned if you weren't crying,' he managed, finally. He was holding out a white handkerchief, surprisingly clean. Francis took it.

'It was totally unexpected,' he went on, as he wiped his eyes. 'She was one of my key leads. I went to her room because I was hoping that she would tell me stuff.'

'And did she?'

'No, not really. We never got round to it.' Despite this new intimacy between them, Francis decided not to tell his boss about his conviction that Topaz had been warned off.

'So what did you want to know?' Nick asked. 'From Topaz?'

So Francis told him about Uncle Bobby and Frankie Freak and Adam and Zak. 'Which you're already aware of, presumably?'

Nick nodded – impressed, it seemed, that Francis had found out so much. 'But that's all history now. It never had that much to do with Adam, anyway. It was more Zak's issue.'

'But Adam let him do it, by all accounts?'

Nick shrugged. 'The Adam–Zak relationship is complex,' he said. 'They go back a long way. In any case, never forget that Zak made the Idols. Believe me, that ramshackle bunch of Scotsmen would never have got out of Paisley without him. They were fine musicians, but they needed his energy and drive. And vision, frankly. So to some extent you could say he took what he deserved. The other point was that they all signed their contracts, the numpties. So they only ever had themselves to blame.'

'Contracts that they presumably took in good faith from Adam?'

Nick shrugged. 'Maybe. But they were all grown-ups. It was amazing to me that Frankie got his claim as far as he did.'

'But he wrote all the music for "The Love That Tells Me",' Topaz said. His mother remembered him playing the melody on the family piano as a teenager.'

Nick yawned. 'So she said. It was her word against anyone else's. Mothers. You know. It could have been something similar. Tinkle tinkle. Anyway, Frankie got what he wanted in the end.'

'Topaz didn't seem to think so.'

'Frankie was offered his day in court and he turned it down. Or rather, he took what he was given and ran. I really think that was the end of it. In the annals of rock and roll, this hardly ranks as a big scandal, Francis. Read about Procul Harum or the Smiths or Spandau Ballet.' He chuckled darkly. 'Let alone some of the stuff Allen Klein and Don Arden and their ilk got up to, back in the day. Where there's a hit, there's a writ, as they used to say in Tin Pan Alley.'

Francis decided to continue with his almost-full disclosure. Telling Nick that he'd been concerned that Adam had been moving him around a lot, quite deliberately. First, shifting him to the crew bus in Dusseldorf, when he was trying to talk to Jonni; then later, when he was trying to follow something up with the crew – he didn't say 'interrogate Seamus' – moving him back to be with the band.

'When was that?' Nick asked.

'After the Brussels gig, when the crew were going on ahead to Frankfurt. I was told that after two gigs on the trot they'd be having a party and wouldn't want me around.'

Nick nodded understandingly. 'Obviously on paper we

have to have strict rules about what they get up to, but we try not to keep too close an eye on them when they've worked hard and have a day off. The danger is that if you remove the fun element, you lose your best people to another band. Aerosmith had that problem, when they cleaned up their act and banned alcohol on tour for everyone. Half their crew scarpered. Shall we go up and see Adam and Jonni now?'

They found the star and the manager upstairs in Jonni's suite. It was hard to believe that this was the same view that Francis had sat gazing at as Topaz had played guitar – had it really been just last night? Now the bridges over the Main were clearly visible, and the clutch of central skyscrapers gleamed like toys in the bright February sunshine.

Jonni was in white shorts and a T-shirt that read *King of the Road* in red cursive script, above a blue line drawing of an American-style convertible. It showed off his tanned, gym-toned physique perfectly. He stumbled up to Francis and high-fived him. 'Hi, man!' he said. The sympathetic, curious, knowing, almost respectful look on his face suggested he was aware of Francis's intimacy with poor Topaz.

Nick took Adam aside and walked him off down towards the bedroom area. Their voices weren't raised, but you could tell there was some kind of an argument going on.

Jonni smiled beatifically, like a child who is trying to pretend his parents aren't rowing. 'Adam says you'd like to talk to me,' he said.

'I wouldn't mind.'

'Come and sit soft.' Jonni led him over to a long suede couch and gestured. Francis was now so close to the star that he could smell his aftershave: surprisingly masculine and tangy for someone supposedly gender-fluid, was Francis's unsayable thought.

'Topaz,' Jonni said, shaking his head sadly. 'What a thing … I totally can't get my head round it…'

'Me neither,' Francis replied.

'She was an immensely cool woman.'

'She was.'

'Crazy, sometimes. But cool. I'm so sorry, man.'

There was a silence. It was up to Francis to break it. He was the older man, by some years. It was ridiculous that he felt tongue-tied in Jonni's presence. Especially now, after everything that had happened. Jonni was just a guy in his late twenties, albeit extremely famous, albeit with an undeniable presence, which was hardly surprising given that he was able, on a routine basis, to get ten, twenty, eighty thousand people up on their feet, hands waving madly in the air.

'D'you have any ideas?' Francis began. 'Any thoughts at all about what's been going on?'

'What might be behind all this? No, man, I'm as puzzled as you are. That's if you are puzzled. I'm kind of assuming you are.'

'I am a bit.'

'But you've been talking to everybody. Apparently. You must have some theories?'

'Not really,' Francis said, looking round to see if the managers were about to return. 'I guess I do have a question for you. Which you don't have to answer, but–'

'Cut to the chase,' said Jonni.

'It's about Ricky. What did he mean to you? Do you think he OD'd … on that bus?'

Jonni was nodding. 'Yeah, well, as they've probably all told you, Ricky was a mate. A very good mate, actually, back in the day. You know, sometimes on tour it can get a bit lonely. Especially if you're the man in the middle of the circus. You're like the boss, only you're not.' Jonni's smile cracked open. Close up like this, it was very winning: he looked exactly like his own poster. 'But you can't really go off and hang with one member of the band and not take the others. They all notice.'

'I imagine.'

'But if you've got a little mate in the crew, that's different. It's like Ricky was just a keyboard tech, so fine. He's not competition. I'm not bigging myself up here, but you get the picture.'

Francis nodded. He was praying that the managers would continue their urgent discussion at the far end.

'Also, he was, like, someone you could talk to about things. As you probably know, I got clean at the end of the last tour, and Ricky was, like, a big part of that. We were both up against it, so we decided we'd do it together. We'd kind of both been to the end of the road ... with the, like, bad stuff, the illicit stuff.' Jonni looked down, then slowly up again, to meet Francis's eye. 'I was pretty high, most of the time. And if I wasn't high, I was low. But it was all artificial, if you get me. And when I stopped to think, which wasn't often, I was going, why? Why don't I like reality? I've got a pretty good life. I'm successful at what I want to do. People sing my songs, up and down the nation. As Adam kept telling me, people love me. Or at least the idea of me. Which is good enough, isn't it? I mean, who in life is ever really loved for themselves, truly themselves, and not some idea of them? No one. We all have fantasies about those close to us, all the time. I just had it on a bigger scale.'

He pulled out a little black notebook. It was a Smythson, Francis noticed. Well, of course.

'Quite like that, actually,' Jonni was saying, as he scrawled down a note. 'Could be a song. So where was I? Yeah, I was asking myself, what's so wrong with my reality that I need to be out of it all the time? Why is it that so many of the great rock stars were so out of it for most of their lives? Keith, Syd, Brian, Ozzy, Bobby, Iggy, Kurt, Whitney, Snoop, Amy ... the list goes on and on, doesn't it? And they had it so good, in so many ways. Talent recognised, every chance to perform. What the fuck were they escaping from?'

'Good question,' Francis said.

'But do you have an answer?'

Francis shrugged. 'Who knows? Maybe the pressure. Of all the adulation. Being the big "I am" all the time.'

'Yeah, that's good.' Jonni looked as if he was really considering this thought. 'The big "I am". I am … big? Am I?' He chuckled, pulled out his notebook and scrawled again. 'Thanks, man. In any case, with a little bit of encouragement from Adam, actually a lot of encouragement from Adam, I decided to ditch all that stuff. Drink, drugs, altered states. Face the music. Literally. I mean, he was right, it was dragging me down, I was missing out on real sensations, you know. Life. Although we did have quite a bit of fun, back in the day, in our crazy world, Ricky and I.'

The managers were upon them.

'Don't let us interrupt,' Nick said.

Jonni smiled up at Adam, like a son might to a father. 'I was just telling Francis here about getting clean.'

'Please, carry on,' Adam said. 'I'd like to hear this.'

This was hopeless. There was no way Jonni was going to talk honestly with Adam around. But what could Francis say?

'Come on, mate,' Nick said to Adam. 'Let's pop downstairs for a coffee.' The look that passed between the two managers was worth a million dollars. Literally, Francis thought. Adam got up and followed his partner out of the room, looking back twice, like a reluctant dog.

'Silence is golden,' said Jonni, tapping his fingers on the arm rest. 'Where were we?'

'Drugs dragging you down. You and Ricky deciding to get clean. But how you'd had fun, back in the day.'

'Nice one,' said Jonni. 'And you don't even take notes…'

'Mental ones, maybe.'

'That's a skill. It also tells me you're not a journalist. With their little notebooks and tape recorders. "D'you mind if I put this on?" All that shit. I fuckin' hate it – and them. They tape every word you say, and then they go home and make it all up. What's that about? So many lies – and people believe them, that's the strangest thing. Just because it's in print in front of them. Cunts. Sorry, it's a bit of an obsession of mine.' He breathed in deeply. 'So yeah, we'd come to the end of that road, Ricky and I. The drugs road. The road of white and brown powder.' He jotted in his notebook again. 'You're inspiring me, man. So yeah, I was messing up too often. Being too wrecked to perform, even missing gigs. You've read about it, I'm sure. That was my rep. Messed-up but lovable Jonni. I mean, all good rock star stuff for a while, but in the end it gets in the way. You don't want to end up like Elvis, do you? Or all the others. That's what Adam said, and he should know, since he nearly died himself at one point. He was right. It's sad, for a young man, loved by millions, to be on the run from himself. So yeah, now I'm good. Clean as a washed-up spoon.'

'And you've stayed clean, while Ricky slipped off the wagon?'

'Ricky slipped off, he did.' There was a long pause, as Jonni struggled visibly to contain himself. He put out a finger to wipe his eye. 'Sorry, man.'

'That's OK. He was your friend.'

'He was. Poor silly fucker. Thought he could handle it. Fucking hell, has this been a tour.'

Francis nodded.

'I'm sorry I've not given you much time, man, but you know, it's been hard, just keeping my head together, and performing, with all this bad stuff going on. First Ricky, then that nutter in Hamburg trying to kill me, then Vanko, now this. I mean, what the freaking fuck is going on?'

'I wish I knew.'

'That's your job, isn't it? Aren't you some kind of ace detective, under that journalist pose?'

'I have solved a couple of cases,' Francis replied, feeling like a pompous prat even as he spoke. 'Which were in the news. But it doesn't mean I have all the answers.'

'Who does, man, who does? Adam goes on about some Guitarmageddon tour he did in the US, back in the day, which was much worse than this. But I don't know. It all seems pretty weird to me.'

There was another silence. Francis did something he often did when people started to get into confessional mode: say nothing. Just wait. Jonni had started to trust him now. And he wanted to talk, that much was clear.

'No,' Jonni went on, after a full thirty seconds. 'I don't know how I got onstage. In Copenhagen. Once I'd heard the news about poor Rick. But then I thought, I've got to do it. *For* Ricky, in a way. What's the point of stopping all that shit in order to be able to do the performance thing properly, and then not performing? Pointless. D'you ever watch that show?'

'I'm sorry.'

'Daytime TV. *Pointless.* I guess you're too busy doing real stuff. It amuses me. When I've got nothing better to do.'

Keep him focused, Francis thought. His mind was like a jumping flea. 'And then,' he prompted, 'immediately after Copenhagen, Hamburg?'

'Yeah, Hamburg.' There was another long pause for thought. 'I lost it at that point. Had to get Adam to cancel the next one, wherever it was. Some nondescript German shithole. I just couldn't have done it, sorry. I was actually bruised. Physically. And mentally, too. My sadness about Ricky suddenly hit me. Slap.' He slapped himself on the cheek, surprisingly hard, then looked over at Francis for a reaction.

'But he did OD, though,' Francis said. 'In your opinion?'

'If he didn't, man, someone killed him. And that would

imply a whole lot of other crazy stuff. Has someone got it in for me? And if so, why? I'm a crowd-pleaser. I may have my faults – yeah, I may, but I'm getting on top of them now, that's the thing ... all of them. It's good, I'm feeling good, you know ... about myself, going forward, leaving the bad stuff behind, really I am.' He looked at Francis with a look of piercing sincerity. But Adam had returned, bustling towards them without his partner. Jonni was now yawning, ostentatiously, like a bored child.

'All right, guys,' Adam said. 'Had a good chat?'

'Yeah, good,' Jonni said, giving Francis an inclusive smile.

'I think we'll leave it there for today,' Adam said. 'Did you get what you want, Francis?'

No, definitely not. But he could see from the expression on the manager's face that pushing for more right now wasn't going to work. He would just have to be happy with what he'd got and take that short interview as a tantalising teaser, not to mention a trust-building exercise. To be returned to, sooner rather than later.

'I guess so, yes. It was good of you to talk, Jonni,' he said.

'Any time, man. Let's do it again soon.'

The golden goose turned towards his minder, and that was it. Shut down immediately. What was it with Adam? Why couldn't he let his little prince open up? Was he worried that Jonni, left alone, would say too much?

Chapter Nineteen

F rancis returned to his room. Despite Frau Schröder's promise that it had been serviced, it was the same as when he'd left it this morning; though both his suitcases had been returned from the coach. He slumped down in an armchair by the window. So he had finally got to talk to Jonni – and a great deal of help that had been. What had he found out? That behind the mystique the guy was quite sweet, he had a whimsical philosophical side, and he used his undoubted charm to avoid answering difficult questions. If Francis was going to get to the truth about Jonni and Ricky, for example, he was going to have to talk to somebody else. He had been hoping that his Jonni interview would be the key that would unlock the mystery. But it hadn't been. Why had he thought otherwise?

So where am I, Francis asked himself, on my first proper paid case? *My name is Sherlock Holmes. It is my business to know what other people do not know.* Fat chance. The leads he had followed up and at one point been quite excited about had just slipped away. What if he continued to get nowhere? What if the Frankfurt Kripo cracked it ahead of him? Would it matter?

Not really. Except that he wanted justice for Topaz. That was his driving force now.

His phone rang. It was Nick, summoning him to the lounge downstairs.

'So how was it?' he asked when they were sitting opposite each other, their matching *Kaffes* in front of them. 'Did you get what you wanted?'

'He told me a bit,' Francis went on, 'but not a lot. It's clear he's been pretty shaken up.'

'Of course. So I hope you're not still thinking that Adam, having hired you, has been trying to obstruct you?'

'It wasn't easy to share that with you, Nick. But you don't get anywhere with these cases unless you think of every possibility. The fact is, you hired me. You were in London. Adam kept telling me there was nothing untoward going on. I was just wondering why that was.'

Nick was nodding. 'I understand. And thanks for letting me know. We were both impressed. That you were prepared to think the worst of our partnership.'

'You never know, though, do you?'

'What do you mean?'

'About those close to you.'

'We're pretty solid, mate. We go back.'

'I know you do. But if I was thinking this wasn't just a chapter of accidents, I needed to find a culprit, and there weren't any very obvious ones in view.'

'So you thought of Adam. The big bad wolf manager who would disrupt his own tour for who knows what reason.'

'Put like that, it sounds silly. But I was trying to make sense – of why he seemed to be frustrating me. But I get it now that I've finally spoken to Jonni. He was protecting him. I suppose I didn't realise how much Jonni calls the shots.'

This appeared to rile Nick, as Francis had thought it might.

'He doesn't call the shots,' he said. 'But we have to treat him with respect. He is the star.'

'The golden goose.'

'You could say.'

'I didn't get the feeling,' Francis went on after a moment, 'that Jonni was going to open up any more about his relationship with Ricky.'

'He's a very private person, Jonni. Which is fine, in my view.'

'But they were close?'

'I'd say they were.'

'How close?'

'Friends, Francis, friends. Has anyone been telling you any different?'

Francis shrugged. He wasn't going to reveal his sources. 'You're not just keeping a myth alive?' he asked. 'Of a beautiful, talented, heterosexual guy? To keep the fans happy.'

Nick chuckled loudly; it didn't sound like genuine mirth. 'You're barking up the wrong tree on that one,' he said. 'Now what I wanted to tell you is that I've just been in with the Kripo. They're going to send poor Topaz away for a postmortem, but having interviewed everyone, they think it perfectly possible, given the traces of drugs they found in her room – confirmed by you, I understand – and the amount of drink she'd taken, that she drowned in an intoxicated state.'

'No!' said Francis, and it came out almost like a yelp. 'I've already told them I don't believe that.'

'I know you have. Obviously, since you were with her, you don't want to believe that. But Dolores O'Riordan of the Cranberries drowned in a bath–'

'In the London Hilton. Yes, yes,' Francis said wearily. 'The comparison has been made.'

'The diagnosis of O'Riordan's death was accidental death by drowning following alcohol intoxication. In the room were five miniatures from the minibar and one bottle of champagne. It's a fair amount, but not that much. Especially for a heavy drinker, as she was apparently. And there were no drugs. Topaz, on the other hand–'

'Nick,' Francis interrupted, 'what you – and they – need to understand is this. Yes, we had a spliff, and a line of coke, and a glass or two of champagne. But that was all at the beginning. When I left her, at five in the morning, she wasn't drunk. Not to put too fine a point on it, there had been a certain amount of physical activity during the night and she'd sobered up. Unless she'd hit the minibar, all by herself, after I'd gone, she wouldn't have been even vaguely tipsy.'

'Maybe you tired her out so much that when she got into the bath she fell asleep.' There was the slightest smirk on the manager's lips, but Francis wasn't going to rise to it.

'I think unless you're very pissed,' he replied, 'you'd wake up, wouldn't you? If you were actually drowning.'

'I wouldn't push this too hard, Francis. If the Kripo do have a suspect, it's you.'

'Don't be ridiculous.'

'I'm not. I've been working quite hard on your behalf. Pointing out your impeccable credentials and that, as our hired detective, you hardly have a motive. But (a) they're not that impressed that an investigator would sleep with a witness, not to say a suspect, and (b) you were the last one with her.'

'Why would you spend the night with someone and then drown them?' Francis replied. 'It makes no sense. Surely they can see that.'

'Whatever,' Nick said briskly. 'They have done all their interviews. We have talked to them. Sureties have been left, financial and otherwise. For the time being they're satisfied, and we – and you – are good to go. I'd be happy with that if I were you.'

'The whole band. To Nuremberg?'

'Yes. Though any one of us could be summoned back at any moment.'

'I thought the plan was to leave tomorrow morning.'

'Better safe than sorry. If the coaches go at five, the band can be at the hotel by eleven. Then they can take it slowly tomorrow.'

'You're not staying with us?'

'I need to get back to London. But I'll see you in Munich at the weekend.'

'And Jonni is cool with all this?'

'Jonni is a pro. He wants to finish the tour. His album isn't going to promote itself.'

They left it there. In his deep frustration, there was one other thing niggling Francis: the neat-looking woman across the lounge reading a newspaper and having coffee on her own. Perhaps she was just a random punter, enjoying some quiet time in the lobby of a busy city centre hotel. But there was something about the way she had glanced over at him and Nick just once too often, that worried him. But then again, if she was a police spy or whatever, would she have made herself quite so obvious?

Chapter Twenty

They were driving through the dusk towards Nuremberg. For a change, they were all together in the upstairs lounge of the band bus: the men, Simon, Vanko and Russell, and the two remaining women, Thelma and Suzi. Topaz had left a huge hole.

Scally was on Jonni's bus. Funny, Francis thought, how the star had said he couldn't have favourites among the band, otherwise they'd all notice. And then there was the drummer. Always on his bus. Not that any of the others minded. In fact, talking to Simon, you got the feeling they were quite relieved not to have to deal with Jonni's edgy presence. Had Scally in fact replaced Ricky as a special mate?

Bernie was in his cubbyhole at the front, as usual, hunched over his laptop, phone hooked to his ear, working hard.

There was an extra diversion today. Two more carloads of fans following them. Through the big tinted picture window of the lounge, you could just about make out their faces, in the dusk, as they swerved joyously from lane to lane, screaming, waving, singing.

'Weirdos,' said Vanko. 'They spent all day by the hotel in Frankfurt just waiting for Jonni to go.'

'You would have thought,' said Thelma sadly, 'they'd have more respect. For Topaz.'

'Listen,' said Simon.

They all listened.

'Vanko! Vanko! Vanko!' came the cry.

'They're shouting for you.'

'My,' said Suzi.

Vanko laughed. 'Christ, I hope Jonni can't hear them.'

'I'm sure he can,' said Simon.

At Suzi's suggestion they put down their phones and played Happy Families, in memory of Topaz. They had to stick to her rules as well. 'Do you *happen* to have…'

Thelma was crying. 'I'm sorry,' she said. 'I just can't believe … she's not here.'

Suzi stroked her hand.

'It's OK,' said Russell, as gentle as Francis had ever seen him.

'It's not OK,' said Suzi. 'And I'm scared. Who's next on the list? Us? You, Simon? I don't imagine an accountant counts.'

'Thanks,' said Russell.

'I don't have any enemies,' said Simon. 'That I know of.'

'Those are the ones you have to watch out for, dude,' said Russell. 'The ones you don't know about.'

'What are you saying, Simon?' Suzi asked. 'That Topaz had enemies?'

'I don't know,' said Simon.

'What d'you mean, you don't know? Who could possibly hate Topaz?'

Simon was looking over at Francis. 'I don't think anyone hated her. But they might have been frightened of her.'

'Who could be frightened of Topaz?' said Suzi.

'The murderer,' he replied. 'Or attempted murderer. Because she knew something.'

There was silence.

'So what do you think, Francis?' Suzi asked. 'You're supposed to be the one that solves these mysteries.'

'I've solved three murder cases in my life. Because the last one was reasonably high profile, I got this little reputation in the media. I thought it had died away, but then Nick suddenly comes out of the woodwork and wants me to have a look at what's going on here. But there's no magic trick. I'm as likely as any of you lot to work out the truth.'

'But you think it was murder, right?' Suzi went on. 'Topaz? You've given up on thinking this is just a strange string of accidents.'

'Someone was trying to kill me in Rotterdam, for sure,' said Vanko. 'I've said that from the get-go. No way was that an accident.'

'Yes,' said Francis, answering Suzi. 'I was trying to keep an open mind. But I'm not a huge believer in coincidence.'

'Don't you have any leads?' Suzi asked. 'Or even ideas?'

Francis shrugged.

'Not ones he's gonna share with us, eh, dude?' said Russell.

'I thought you thought it was one of the crew,' said Thelma.

'Who said that?'

'Topaz. She thought you thought it was Big Seamus or someone.'

'Did she?' So he hadn't been that subtle, after all.

'But it couldn't have been any of the crew,' said Vanko. 'For Topaz. Because they were all in Nuremberg last night. We have to face it: it's one of us. On this bus. Or the managers.'

'Or Mitch and Omar,' said Suzi.

'What possible motive would they have?' said Simon scornfully. 'They're paid security.'

'Exactly,' said Vanko. 'Paid security. They protect us – not very well, I'd say – for money. Maybe someone else is paying them more *not* to protect us.'

'They've certainly got the skills,' said Thelma. 'Ex-soldiers.'

'Being a soldier doesn't make you a murderer, dude,' said Russell. 'That's actually quite offensive.'

'Omar was a mercenary,' said Vanko.

'Was he?' said Suzi.

'He was a soldier in Iraq,' said Russell. 'Come on.'

'And a mercenary. After he left the army. In Somalia or somewhere. One of those African places.'

'You sure about that?'

'Yes.'

'If you've killed once,' said Suzi, 'it's surely not so hard to do it again. Whether it's for money or not.'

'So what was this theory of yours, Francis, that Topaz knew about?' Simon cut in. 'Apropos the crew.'

So Francis told them Topaz's story about publishing royalties, and Zak, and the Tainted Idols, and her Uncle Bobby and Frankie Freak. And how Seamus had once been in a band with Bobby and had worked for the Tainted Idols, and knew them all.

'That's all very well,' said Russell when he'd finished. 'But there was a court case. That royalty issue was sorted out.'

'But it never got to court,' said Francis. 'Frankie settled. But he still felt betrayed. That's what Topaz told me.'

'It was a lot of money,' said Vanko. 'That he never got.'

'But why now?' asked Simon. 'And if someone was going after Zak, or even Adam, why would they attack Jonni? And Vanko? And…'

'Topaz,' Thelma concluded. That silenced them all again.

'And what about Ricky?' said Russell.

'Back to square one,' said Suzi.

'This is basically where most of the aggro in the music

business comes from,' said Vanko. 'Dividing things up fairly. If it's fair, it's OK, everyone's happy. Look at U2. Or the Red Hot Chili Peppers. They've always split the money equally, no matter what the individual musical contribution. So they stay together.' He was echoing what Mel had told Francis on the bus. 'But,' he went on, 'as soon as one person says, "That's all mine, even the bits I didn't write", then things go tits up. Forget the Tainted Idols. Look at us.'

'I thought you guys all got paid a retainer,' Francis said. 'And Jonni was the star who got the royalties.'

'That's roughly right,' said Simon.

'Roughly right,' said Vanko. 'That's one way of putting it. Simon has a special arrangement. In that he gets half the publishing.'

'For the songs *I* write, yes,' said Simon.

'But *do* you write them?' said Vanko. 'I mean, who came up with the legendary guitar riff on "Sometimes the Moon"?'

Simon's face was a picture of restrained fury. But before he could answer, the door swung open and Bernie came in.

Just in time, Francis thought.

'All right, kids,' he cried. 'We are now one hour out of that famous historical centre of Nazi rallies, Nuremberg. We are going straight to the hotel, the charming Meridien Grand. A light supper will be provided after check-in for anyone who is hungry. You should also be aware that Topaz's story has got out and there are now a large number of gentlemen – and ladies – of the press waiting for us outside the hotel. We will do our best to park right outside the front door so you can just march straight through into reception, scowling or smiling blandly, as pop stars do. Do not engage with any chat with these inquisitive folk, please.'

'And what about Jonni ?'

'His bus will go round the back. So you guys are acting to some extent as a decoy, for which we thank you. Tomorrow you have the morning off, and there will be a bus out to the venue at 3.30 p.m. as usual. You are welcome to look around the delights of Nuremberg, which are limited, but should any member of the press try and surreptitiously engage you, particularly gorgeous ones with big tits, Russell, please politely ask them to naff off. Or refer them to me.'

'And you will tell them less politely,' said Thelma.

'Naturally. I thank you and goodbye.' The tour manager did a little bow to accompany his music-hall delivery, then backed out through the door to laughter, even from the women.

'You know he was once a rock star himself,' said Suzi.

'A performer,' said Simon coolly. 'Hardly a star.'

'He had his own band.'

'Sadly, they didn't divide the royalties equally and split up,' said Vanko with a dry laugh.

'What were they called?' asked Francis.

'The B-roots,' said Vanko.

'Was that it?' asked Russell.

Vanko nodded. 'The B-roots. Quite big in the Bromley area back around the millennium.'

Chapter Twenty-One

Francis stood behind the shoulder-high chain-link fence, contemplating the flight of grey stone steps that led up between two of the long rows of squat towers that overlooked the famous oblong amphitheatre, the Zeppelinfeld, where Hitler had once rallied his followers. The steps were stained and crumbling, overgrown with a filigree of blanched dead weeds, the slope to either side a mass of tangled brown undergrowth. They led nowhere now, but the huge structure of which they were a part was still standing, right next to the gleaming new arena. The band party had driven past it coming in on the transfer bus, and needless to say the opportunity for Hitler imitations had been too much for Bernie, Vanko and Russell to pass up, despite the mock-shocked cries of the ladies.

'You can't do that!' Suzi cried. 'You'll be cancelled.'

'I was cancelled years ago,' Bernie replied with a laugh. 'Before being cancelled was even a thing.'

Jonni was hardly a fascist leader bent on world domination, but it was the same thing, wasn't it? Francis thought. The slavish adoration of a single iconic champion. Males in rows of helmets for Hitler, females in party gear for Jonni, they were all yearning for a hero, and if Adam and Nick could monetise that yearning, they would, even if their beautiful guitarist had been killed less than forty-eight hours earlier. Another nine thousand people were turning up tonight, a day later than planned, paying between fifty and three hundred euros, a rough average of, say, €150, bringing in close to a million and a half quid in a single night. You weren't going to stop that juggernaut full of dosh if you could help it, were you?

This was, Francis thought, as he strode on by the rusty fence, the worst puzzle he had yet encountered; novel, too, because for the first time he was on his own. Yes, Nick and Adam had employed him, and in theory he could share all his suspicions with them. But something instinctive held him back; deep down he didn't quite trust either of them. For a moment back there, he had felt he could start to share his thoughts with Topaz – but who could he confide in now? The Frankfurt Kripo seemed to be working on the ridiculous theory that her death was an accident; in any case, they were four hours away. They were also looking at the incident as just that: a single incident. They weren't linking it up to what had happened in Rotterdam (a different country), Hamburg (a separate police force) or Copenhagen (a different country). Whereas Francis, now that he was sure that Topaz had been murdered, knew, in his gut, that Ricky had been killed as well, and that the attacks on Jonni and Vanko had had an equally sinister intent.

So was someone else in danger now, as Thelma feared? Him, even? If the murderer really was one of the band party, they would know his role, and they would want to stop him. Perhaps they would even think his protestations of bafflement were a way of protecting himself.

In theory, the tour stretched ahead for another week, ending on the 29th February in Paris. Already there had been jokes about leap years and women proposing to men at the last gig. On the night, if Jonni had recovered from all this and was back on form, he would have fun with all that, doubtless. But would they even get there?

Back up the road and through the gleaming glass doors of the modern arena, Francis climbed through the steep rows of blue flip-up plastic seats that formed a kind of dress circle above the more basic concrete tiers of the encircling lower area (weirdly reminiscent of the Zeppelinfeld). From here he could see all the crew at work, from the riggers high up in the trusses down to the backline crew on the stage.

There were Mel and Ted working their way round the instruments, tuning, checking, twanging, testing.

'Tee yah yee hey hey hey hey hey one one one hey yeah,' called Ted, and Francis was transported back to the first afternoon he'd seen them all, at the Berlin Velodrom. That too had been his first sight of Topaz: slinky in leather, her wide smile, her wild hair.

Mel joined in. 'Jonni's vocal, one two.'

'Vanko's vocal,' came Ted.

'He certainly is…' came the Kiwi voice over the sound system. Kylie, of course.

'Ricky's joke,' said Ted quietly.

And yes, of course, Ricky would have been up there too, once upon a time. Watching them from afar, Francis had a sudden flash of inspiration. Was it possible that Ricky had been removed so that the murderer – or murderer's representative – had free access to the stage? To do their worst: first with Jonni, then with Vanko? Had the intention in both cases been worse than what had actually happened? And could that implicate Mel and/or Ted even?

No, don't be silly. But then again: if Ricky hadn't been a party to the plan, whatever it was, it would have been hard to get round him, wouldn't it?

As he crossed the gleaming grey floor, Francis could see Pants briefing the local security guys. Next to him was the hunky, straight-backed figure of 'Dead Ed' Cheeseacre: the man who had, like Topaz, drowned, but who, unlike her, had come back to life. The local security guys looked equally terri-fying. German's Hell's Angels, Bernie had said. Looking at them now, mustering like buffaloes just below the front of the stage, another niggling question returned. How on earth had the nutter of Hamburg got past them, the famous 'ring of leather', to get onto the stage? Especially as Mitch and Omar had been up there too. There had been the element of surprise for that attack, but what about Vanko's? More and more, that at least felt like an inside job.

Everyone was on edge tonight. Did anyone other than the Frankfurt police think that Topaz had drowned accidentally? She had been killed because she knew something. About the murderer or murderers; and why he, she or they had had to get rid of Ricky. The safest thing to do was keep your head down and do your job. Wasn't it? Unless you were Francis and your job meant that you couldn't keep your head down.

Up onstage, Mel was bent over Simon's keyboard, a brace of screwdrivers at her belt.

'Not tuning any guitars today, then?' Francis asked.

'Half my work's gone.' She made a sad face. 'So I'm giving Si's keyboard the once-over. I quite enjoy it – takes my mind off everything.'

'Yes,' Francis replied in his usual fashion: saying nothing to allow his subjects the space to unburden.

Sure enough, 'What do you think, Francis?' Mel asked after a few moments. She was looking at him in a way that suggested she knew a lot more than she was saying.

'About Topaz?'

'Yes. Did she really just … drown?'

'I don't know, Mel,' he replied. 'I wish I did.'

She reached down to pick up a tool from her toolbox.

Written on it in small neat white letters was the single word *SANDRA*.

'Why Sandra?' he asked, his heart beating fast. 'Is that some nickname for you I don't know about?'

She laughed. 'This was Ricky's box. You know he was Simon's keyboard tech? Seamus and I had to take over from him when … after … you know … Copenhagen.'

'Ricky was called Sandra?'

'By the crew, yes.'

Did Mel not know what Jonni had been told onstage in Hamburg? Surely she must.

'Why?' he asked, treading carefully.

'I don't know. That was just his name. Gay man, you know, usually has a girl's nickname backstage. Among the other gay men,' she added, almost apologetically. 'And then we all kind of take it on.'

'I didn't even realise Ricky was gay.'

'Well…'

'And best friends with Jonni.'

She shrugged and looked down.

'May I be blunt?' he said.

'Fire away.'

'Is this something that everybody backstage knows about except me? That Jonni is in fact gay?'

Mel smiled. It was a solid but uncooperative smile. If she knew something about this, it said, she wasn't going to share. 'That's a question above my pay grade,' she said, fiddling aggressively with a screw. 'Bloody little thing. And yet essential. Actually,' she went on, 'I'm not one to talk out of turn, but Jonni is many things. As Keith Richard said of Mick Jagger, *He's an interesting bunch of guys*. Ooh, look, here come the lovely fans. Bless their darling cotton socks.'

She turned away towards the empty arena. Across the floor,

shrieking and laughing, came the first wave of the audience, the very young ones who wanted to be right up by the stage. They were dressed in jackets or coats and clutching their little bags and backpacks. Soon they were forming rows, chattering like starlings. Then they were stripping down to party gear and their mobiles were out. They were taking selfies, phoning, texting, Instagramming, WhatsApping, TikToking. Their enthusiasm was infectious.

'Thanks, Mel,' said Francis.

'My pleasure,' she replied. Then, after a pause, 'Are you OK, Francis?'

'Yup,' he replied. 'I'm fine.'

'Good.'

She stepped towards him and gave him a hug. It was surprisingly firm.

'Thanks, Mel,' he repeated.

He turned and walked up and away towards backstage. She knew about him and Topaz. They all did. But more to the point, did she know what the Danish nutter had said to Jonni? Even if she did, she wasn't going to tell *him*, was she?

Chapter Twenty-Two

Z ak was back. Down on the platform by the side of the stage. Why on earth was he here? Wanting to show respect for Topaz? Offering Adam solidarity at a difficult time? Or for a more sinister reason?

Every last body in the Nuremberg audience surely knew about the guitarist by now. The newspapers had been full of the *Verhext Tour*, *Topaz Ertrank*, etc., etc. Out of respect, or perhaps because he just wasn't in the mood for fun, Jonni was dressed simply in black tonight: leather trousers and a loose silk shirt, with a single string of pearls around his neck to hint at another gender. After the first song, 'Let's Go Dutch', he came down to the front of the stage and looked slowly, hauntingly, around the suddenly silent crowd. They had been waiting for something like this, and their eyes were all on him.

'As many of you here may know, we had a very sad loss two nights ago. A dearly beloved member of our band, Topaz Brown … erm…'

Francis could see him looking across the stage to where Adam stood, pate gleaming in the spotlight. The manager nodded back and Jonni continued. 'Erm … drowned … in fact

… in her bath.' As Jonni paused again, the fans hushed into a respectful silence. 'She was a wonderful guitarist and a wonderful singer and a wonderful human being. To be honest, we very nearly packed up and went home. But we didn't…'

Because Adam our manager stood to lose several million quid. So here we all are, still raking it in, as we will continue to do as we progress shamelessly on around Europe, Francis thought irreverently.

Jonni continued with his sincere and moving valediction: 'But we didn't – because we thought about you, our lovely fans, and we didn't want to disappoint you. And we knew as well that Topaz, God rest her soul, wouldn't have wanted to disappoint you either. So partly in her memory and partly because she believed that the show must always go on, here we are, and we are not stopping now. We love you, Nuremberg, and we are going on. To Stuttgart. And Munich. And Vienna. And Paris.'

With each destination there was another cheer.

'Just as we always meant to. And the spirit of Topaz is coming with us.'

Jonni stood stock-still for a moment. Very slowly he held up a fist, then lowered it and wiped away a tear with his little finger. You could hear the matching sobs of emotion throughout the arena. A few fists were raised, but for a few moments no one knew what to do, how to behave. Adam was looking down at his shoes. Zak was gazing round, nodding, taking it all in: he looked more quietly excited than properly sad, Francis thought. He gulped back a sob, closed his eyes, and squeezed his nose between forefinger and thumb to keep himself under control.

Now, Jonni announced, he and the band were going to sing a tribute to Topaz. And that tribute was of course the song she had loved the most: 'The Love That Tells Me'. With music, Francis thought, by Frankie Freak.

Excited by his outpouring of emotion, Jonni switched up a gear. Ten gears. The pierhead pro had taken a back seat, and that raw, wild Jonni had danced back onto the stage. Oh, who could not love him when he was like this? His every pore exuded empathy and true feeling.

The crowd were with him, singing along to the famous words, waving their lit-up phones in unison. Many of them were weeping openly for this woman they had never known. They had loved her nonetheless, just as she and Jonni had loved them. As Jonni himself had said, *who in life is ever really loved for themselves?* Francis had hardly known her either; the passion they had shared so briefly had all been about discovery.

Bernie was in his usual position, just along from Francis on this side of the stage. But he wasn't dancing like a pixie tonight. He was sobbing too. Francis looked away, not wanting to embarrass him.

After the show they went back to the hotel for the post-gig supper. There was another neat-looking, suited guy sitting looking at his phone in reception. Obviously, he was just a neat-looking, suited guy looking at his phone in reception at 11.30 p.m. – as you do in Germany. But there was something about him, and the way he looked away when Francis glanced at him, that made Francis wonder.

The band were quiet tonight. Hardly surprisingly. After the wild onstage release of earlier, they were back to the shocking reality: could it really be one of them? There was no request from a libidinous Vanko to go clubbing out in Nuremberg. 'I'm going to get my head down,' he said, sloping off first.

Francis followed soon after, leaving Simon behind with Thelma and Suzi. Francis wasn't sure how to play it. He had his (strong) suspicions now, but no proof of anything. And it wasn't as if he was working closely with the police, as he'd done last year in Italy and before that during the literary festival murders at Mold-on-Wold. Even if he hadn't shared everything with them, he had at least known what track they were on; he'd had their input, even if it hadn't been that helpful, and their support. Here, he didn't even have an idea what the Kripo were doing in Frankfurt, which was in Hesse, a separate state. Nuremberg was in Bavaria, which had a different force.

So should he even bother to phone the Frankfurt Kripo, tell them what he suspected – no, more than that: what he knew? Then again, weren't they working on the idea that Topaz's death was an accident? Perhaps he should put in a call to the Nuremberg Kripo. But what did they know? Would the Frankfurt lot have even communicated with them? Or perhaps they had, and the man downstairs was working for both of them, or for some other interstate detective agency that Francis knew nothing about? Francis felt out of his depth, alone and scared.

This is for Sandra, Nils the Dane had told Jonni. Ricky was Sandra. In Nils's eyes at least, Jonni was implicated, at some level, in Ricky's death.

Say Jonni had been having a relationship with Ricky, something that Vanko had hinted at during their dinner in Brussels, but which now seemed possible, if not likely. Say Nils also had been Ricky's lover, or at least had known him well enough to care about his sudden death. If Jonni had been in any way responsible, everything about the Hamburg attack suddenly made sense. This didn't mean that Jonni had killed Ricky, or even sanctioned that. He could have treated him badly, dumped him unceremoniously, driven him to take his own life.

If that had been the case, the management would hardly be keen for it to come out, would they? Jonni gay, and in a love triangle that had gone fatally wrong.

If so, that would help explain the first two incidents. What it didn't account for was the attempted electrocution of Vanko. Unless of course Vanko knew too much and was being warned to keep his trap shut. Rotterdam had, after all, been only one night after he and Vanko had had dinner in Amsterdam, when the guitarist had told Francis about *This is for Sandra*.

If Topaz had also known too much about Ricky and his demise, that explained everything: the throat-cutting gesture, the refusal to talk. Christ, even during their night together, she'd been avoiding the issue. She was scared – quite rightly, as it had turned out.

So who exactly might be involved with all this 'incident management'? Adam, surely, whom Francis had never quite trusted, ever since their first chat, in Catering in Berlin. Let's face it, he had never wanted Francis out here. How much did the old rocker communicate with Nick, holding the fort in London? Did he report everything back? Francis's hunch was that he didn't; that he knew a great deal more about the entourage than he let on.

So what was Francis to do? Could he, should he, confront Adam, his notional boss, with his suspicions, suspicions that might well turn out to involve him? If he had tried to electrocute Vanko and then succeeded in drowning poor Topaz, he was hardly going to stop at silencing a man who had rumbled him, even if he had paid him to do so.

The alternative was obviously to phone Nick. But what if he had misjudged the Nick/Adam relationship and Nick was in on whatever was going on? Francis would be in just as much danger. But then again, if Nick was in on it, why had he employed Francis in the first place? It made no sense.

Francis paced up and down the hotel room. He was on the verge of phoning Nick when his mobile rang. It was Adam.

'Hi, Francis. Are you still up?'

'Yes.'

'Dressed?'

'I am.'

'I don't suppose you'd like to pop up here for a nightcap, would you?'

It wasn't an invitation; it was an order. Another 'nightcap'. Would this one be fired from a gun? Francis studied himself in the long mirror behind the door. Don't be silly, he told himself. Even if your latest idea was true, they're not going to try to do you in, here and now, in the Nuremberg Meridien Grand, not when the Kripo have been called in, even if they are in another German state.

For a moment he thought about phoning the number on the card he had in his wallet and letting Erster Polizeihauptkommissar Fischer know the state of play, what he was about to do. Then he decided against it.

He ran his hands through his hair, then he headed out into the corridor.

Chapter Twenty-Three

Zak and Adam were waiting for him, slumped on opposite sofas in Adam's top-floor suite.

Even in this soft, late-night light, Zak looked tired and, frankly, old, the smooth semicircle of his chin set forward against the surrounding jowls and turkey neck. He'd clearly had work done on the bags under his eyes, but you could never eradicate the radiating deeper wrinkles. His spiky blond hair had, worn long, been a feature of his rebellious youth, but now it made him look like an old bag lady – albeit a bag lady of preposterous and revealing vanity. By contrast, Adam gleamed like an egg, and a relatively youthful egg at that. As Francis approached across the deep pile carpet, their eyes followed him hungrily: Adam's as brown as chestnuts, Zak's the famous blue-green.

'Can I get you anything?' Adam asked. They were beyond trick questions now, Francis reckoned. If he wanted a proper drink, they weren't going to hold it against him. Adam had a little pot of tea in front of him, but the tumbler in front of Zak looked as if it contained whisky.

'I'm fine,' Francis replied; it was classier to remain sober, professional. *I never drink on duty, guvnor.* Especially after everything that had happened.

'Sit down,' said Adam. His grin was not its usual steady self; it was flickering like a faulty lightbulb. 'So what we wanted to know was, how are you getting on?' He looked sideways at Zak, who sat immobile. 'Obviously we've got our own ideas, but we'd like to know yours. Strict confidence on both sides, of course.'

Francis nodded and took a deep breath. Should he wing it and try and make up something plausible that didn't involve them, or should he dive in and share what he really thought? He decided to play it straight, even if selectively, telling them about *This is for Sandra* and his suspicion that Jonni might have been involved in Ricky's death, and that – how could he put this tactfully? – there was, it seemed, more to their relationship than just friendship. He decided not to bring up Frankie Freak and the royalty dispute issue; not yet, at any rate.

Adam denied nothing. They were clearly talking turkey now. 'I didn't even realise Ricky had that nickname on his toolbox,' he said.

'But you knew his nickname was Sandra?'

'Jonni told us, yes. But as far as I know, Nils's words haven't got out beyond our immediate circle. I don't imagine Jonni will be thrilled with Vanko for passing them on to you.'

So you didn't know Vanko had told me, Francis thought, or is that just another bluff? 'I don't want to get Vanko into trouble,' he said. 'Compromising my sources isn't going to help me going forward. It's been a long, slow process building up the trust for people to share things with me.'

This was a fib, but a necessary one. It wasn't for him to tell them how weirdly indiscreet Vanko had been, from the very first time he'd met him in Catering.

'I get that,' Adam replied, looking sideways to check in with Zak again. 'Of course. Schtum's the word. On both sides.'

Francis didn't trust these two further than the end of the plush gold sofa they were sitting on, though he doubted whether he could throw either of them as far as that.

The manager leant forward, matily. 'Here's the thing, Francis. Ricky had put us in an impossible situation. He didn't want to break up with Jonni, even though Jonni had moved on. Getting clean was obviously a game-changer for him, and part of the game that was changing was Ricky. So "the Ricky thing", as we called it, had to stop. But Ricky was not going to accept that. His first position was that he was going to get clean too, and for a while we thought that might work. Admirably, he did rehab, and made an initial success of it. He came with Jonni to a few NA meetings – as you know, we go most days. But it wasn't working. They had been drug buddies, and once Jonni sobered up he could see that. So we chatted about it and we all agreed that the easiest thing would be to let Ricky go. We gave him his notice, and I may say a pretty generous payoff, and a reference that was considerably kinder than it could have been.'

'The story I heard,' Francis said, 'was that he was good at his job.'

Adam shrugged. 'He had been. But he was off his face half the time. That doesn't mix well with the technicalities of keeping keyboards in good shape. Simon was pretty fed up with him too.'

'OK,' said Francis, thinking that once Ricky had got clean, he was presumably back to being competent.

'But this was when the shit hit the fan,' Adam continued, 'because Ricky wasn't going to go gracefully. He'd decided he was in love with Jonni, though I have to say that for a man in love he was perfectly capable of putting it around all over the place. There were times, before all this, when I've seen poor Jonni down in the dumps over Ricky's behaviour. Then he started getting seriously arsey. He was putting all kinds of pressure on Jonni and telling us that if we let him go, he'd go to the press. Effectively, Francis, he was blackmailing us to keep him on, and we couldn't have that. So to defuse that little time-bomb, we told him he could stay on if he agreed to an NDA, for which we'd pay him.'

'NDA?'

'Non-disclosure agreement.'

Of course. Francis knew that. What an idiot for asking. 'Preventing him from talking about…?' he went on, as seamlessly as possible.

'Everything,' Zak cut in.

'Obviously we didn't want him running to the press with salacious tittle-tattle,' Adam continued. 'He signed, so we kept him on. Rather reluctantly, I have to say, for this tour. He came with us to Stockholm, and then, as you know, he lapsed again.'

Adam got to his feet and paced away across the carpet towards the dark window.

'It might seem convenient for us that he overdosed, but I don't want you to get the wrong end of the stick. We're not murderers, Francis, even though we have at times been tempted, haven't we, Zachary?'

He laughed hollowly. Zak didn't join in.

'How do I know that you didn't give in to temptation?' Francis said.

'If we'd gone down that route,' Adam replied, 'I hardly think we'd have bothered with the NDA. No, I'm afraid poor Ricky obliged us by doing it for us. He took more than his usual dose of heroin, which is particularly risky, as I'm sure you know, when you've been clean for a while.'

'And there wasn't anything that prompted that?' asked Francis. 'I mean, in Jonni's behaviour?'

'How d'you mean?' the manager asked.

'It wasn't a gesture of protest,' Francis said. 'A cry for help that went wrong?'

Again Adam was looking over at Zak. Francis had, he reckoned, hit the nail on the head.

The genial smile made a return. 'They were splitting up. Jonni had refused to see him. Ricky was upset, yes. There were some texts. But none of us foresaw that he'd actually … go through with it.'

'But he threatened to? In these texts?'

'No,' Adam said firmly. 'It was all pretty vague. Some of them talked about going over to the dark side. You know, suggestive stuff like that. But he and Jonni had a private language, a whole world of their own. It didn't really mean anything.'

'But Jonni would have known what the threats meant? That they were real.'

Now, finally, it was Zak who spoke. In his deep, resonant Glasgow accent, the name of the star cut through the silence like a threat. 'Jonni,' he said, 'as well as being an enormous talent, is a very decent fellow. He didn't want to upset Ricky any more than he had to. But he'd got clean at considerable cost to himself, hadn't he, Adam? He couldn't allow himself to slip back, just for the sake of a – to put it mildly – histrionic ex-lover.'

So he'd said it – or rather, spat it out. And looking straight back at him, Francis realised he'd meant to say it. In this case, the truth was a warning. You are in on this now, so don't screw with us, or you're next. No, Francis had to believe that these two meant what they said. They were tough, yes; unscrupulous, of course; but not actual killers.

Or were they?

'No,' Adam agreed. 'It was a shame, a terrible shame that he felt he had to do that. But…' He too shrugged, as if to say 'that's enough now'.

'Was there a note or anything?' Francis asked.

'No. Just the texts. A few missed calls.'

'You were there?'

'Jonni was with me, yes.'

What? Francis thought. When Ricky was threatening to OD? 'So were you aware,' he asked gently, 'what was going on?'

'I wasn't leaning over Jonni's screen, Francis, no. But we were in the same suite. Ricky was on a crew bus, surrounded by friends. However bad he sounded, we didn't think for one moment... You know, Francis, this journey to getting clean isn't an easy one, and I've had to be there for Jonni, one hundred per cent. I'm his sponsor, and his professional mentor as well. So...'

He looked over at Zak, whose expression was quite clearly telling him to can it.

'I understand,' Francis replied. He also understood that if Zak hadn't been present, Adam would have said more – would have admitted, perhaps, that he had sat alongside Jonni throughout and actively encouraged Ricky's suicide attempt (which Ricky may not even have wanted, at one level, to be successful). Seriously shocking, but Francis wasn't going to compromise any more revelations by pointing out the legal implications of what Adam had just told him, even though he wasn't going to let either of these two get away with anything, if he could possibly help it.

'Moving on,' he continued. 'What did Nils have to do with all this? What was he? Another lover of Ricky's, or what?'

Before Adam could speak, Zak answered. 'I can see now why Nick wanted to employ you, Francis. You're asking exactly the right questions. As Adam has said, even when they were "together"' – Zak made the quotes with his gnarled fingers – 'Ricky didn't comport himself well. There were always others. And you're right. Nils was one of those. I don't think Ricky had a boyfriend in every port, but he'd been touring for years with different bands, so he had many mates and connections around Europe and America, as you do.'

'Did Jonni join in on these friendships?' Francis asked finally, when neither Zak nor Adam volunteered any more.

'You know how it is,' Adam said. 'Or perhaps you don't. The world of drugs. This was one of the reasons Jonni was so hooked on Ricky. Because he could always access the stuff, Ricky could. And not just the stuff – the fun. Ricky was the original lord of misrule. Off-tour, they even went on holiday together. Jonni had never ventured out of Europe really, or at least America, Australia, comfortable post-tour First World stuff. But Ricky took him backpacking, to places where he could rough it and be more or less anonymous: Thailand, Vietnam, Cambodia, Morocco–'

'"Cambodian Girl",' said Francis.

'Quite,' said Adam, looking away, then nervously down at the floor.

'Anonymous being the big thing,' Zak cut in. 'Being recognised all the time can get very wearing.'

'I imagine,' said Francis. Zak, of all people, would know about that. 'So the chances are,' he went on, 'Jonni might have met Nils before. On a previous tour?'

'It's possible. Though his last tour of Europe was two years ago.'

There was silence. It was as if, Francis thought, the pair were taking stock of where they'd got to. Francis had given them something: had they now given him too much in return? He decided to press on before they clammed up, as they surely would. His long experience of interviewing, from the celebs and others he'd once tackled professionally for magazines like *Loaded* and *GQ* and *Man Alive!* to the suspects and witnesses he'd encountered on his unofficial career as an amateur sleuth, had taught him that.

'So how much of this do the police know?'

'As I'm sure you know,' Adam replied, 'the forces in Germany are all separate. Obviously, the police in Copenhagen, where Ricky finished up, are another outfit again.'

'Don't they talk to each other? Surely there's some sort of German central control? What about Interpol?' Francis fired questions into the silence.

'When we were in Hamburg,' Adam replied, 'the police were well aware of the background. That was one of the reasons they let us go so quickly.'

'You told them that Ricky and Jonni were … special friends?'

'Of course. They had to know that to understand Nils's motivation.'

'And what's happened to Nils now?'

'They let him off with a warning. We didn't press charges.'

'With nothing in return? At all?'

'There was the small matter of an NDA agreement,' Adam said. His face was deadpan.

Another one! 'This is all fairly key information,' Francis said. 'May I ask why you didn't share it with me before?'

Adam looked over at Zak. They really were thick as thieves, the pair of them, speaking a language that didn't require words.

'To be honest, Francis, this isn't even something I've shared with Nick.'

'What!' Francis replied. 'That Jonni's gay, that he was with Ricky–'

'Not that, obviously…'

'So, what? That Nils had been Ricky's friend, lover, whatever?'

'Yes.'

'And that he had said that stuff about Sandra?'

'Nick knew about the words, but not what they meant…'

Francis was incredulous. The key information, that made

sense of at least half of the puzzle, kept away from his so-called partner. Really? Francis was angry too. If this was true, it made a total patsy of him. No wonder Adam had kept him away from Jonni. No wonder he'd kept moving him around.

'I see,' he replied, looking from one to the other of them in as measured a way as he felt able.

'Sometimes discretion is the better part of valour,' Zak said slowly. He was quite something, Francis thought, managing, with his Glaswegian accent and the measured sincerity of his tone, to make this ancient cliché sound both original and significant.

'It makes me wonder why you bothered to go along with Nick's idea of hiring me in the first place,' Francis said. 'If I wasn't going to be briefed properly. Or, really, at all.'

'To be perfectly honest,' Adam replied, 'when Nick said he'd decided to bring you in, I didn't think you'd get anywhere. I suppose, in an odd kind of way, I was intrigued to see what you would dig up. Not that it mattered, as we knew the score, and I didn't think anything else would happen.'

'But if Nick knew about Jonni and Ricky, why couldn't you share the Nils stuff with him? I don't get it.'

'You don't need to,' said Zak.

'OK,' said Francis. He was tempted to get up and walk off the job. But (a) there was the amazing money, with bonuses dependent on results, and (b) he was in deep now, and it wasn't just professional curiosity that was motivating him.

He looked back at Adam. 'So am I going to be allowed to chat about all this stuff to Jonni?' he asked.

'Of course,' Adam said.

'Maybe tomorrow morning,' he suggested, taking his chance. 'If I came on his bus on the way to Stuttgart?'

'Perfect,' said Adam. 'I'll be there, but I'm happy to keep out of your way.'

Zak said nothing. Francis pressed on. 'So then Vanko went

257

and got himself electrocuted,' he said. 'How does that fit your picture?'

'It doesn't,' said Adam.

'But do you have any inkling how it happened? Or why?'

'No,' Zak replied.

Did Francis really believe that? 'Was it, perhaps, a warning?' he asked. 'To an indiscreet member of the group who was talking too much to the visiting detective?'

'There's a thought,' Zak said. 'But no.'

'Electrocution is a serious business, Francis,' Adam added. 'If you sabotage the stage electrics, you don't have any control over what's going to happen. That incident could easily have been fatal. If Vanko's hands had been sweatier or whatever. There's a good few musicians who've died—'

'Yes,' Francis cut in. 'We talked about that in the hotel afterwards. Bernie knew them all, as well as the ones who survived…'

'The great rock 'n' roll archivist,' said Zak.

'The point is,' said Adam. 'You would hardly fiddle with the onstage electrics just as a warning.'

'So it was an accident?'

Adam shrugged, then met Francis's eye. 'No. We don't think it was.'

'We being you two?'

'Yes.'

'And Nick?'

'To be honest, Nick tends to go along with our thinking. Given that we're on the spot.'

Francis nodded. On the spot and not telling him everything. Of course he does. 'So who was responsible then?'

'That's the mystery. We were tempted to call you in, especially since you were on site, but that would have meant filling you in on all the earlier stuff. Then we were starting to think, maybe it was just an accident, one of those things, and eventually the jinxed tour would stop being jinxed. But then … poor Topaz.'

'Not another accident? As the Frankfurt Kripo seem to think.'

'We don't think so,' said Adam. He looked both serious and, for a change, sincere. 'But who knows? It's a possibility.'

'And have you shared what you've told me with them? The Frankfurt Kripo?'

'Not yet, no.'

'Presumably withholding information from the police is as much of a crime here as it is at home.'

Adam said nothing.

'I reached a stark, and perhaps rather obvious, conclusion this afternoon,' Francis went on, 'while the crew were setting up. Topaz's killer has to be one of the band party, because when Topaz died, the crew were already in Nuremberg. So that narrows the field considerably, doesn't it? The band, the managers, the security guys. Nobody else was there.'

'The security guys!' said Adam, laughing he did a double take. 'What possible motive would they have to murder Topaz in her bath?'

'I have no idea,' Francis replied. 'But they had the opportunity.'

'We employ Mitch and Omar to look after us. Why on earth would they want to do away with one of the people they're supposed to be protecting? They are, for your information, mortified about everything that's happened.'

'If it wasn't an accident, and it wasn't them, then it's either one of the band, or Bernie … or you,' Francis replied. He was too tired to go on placating these two. He had no idea how much they knew about everything that had happened, but it was more than they were letting on, of that he was certain.

Chapter Twenty-Four

The buses left the Nuremberg Meridian Grand at noon. It was a short hop down the A6 to Stuttgart, barely two and a half hours, though they did cross into a new state, Baden-Württemberg, which meant, Francis realised, yet another police force.

But it was still a good long time to talk to Jonni, and that was definitely going to help him put the pieces together, he thought. He had stayed in his room for breakfast this morning and worked out not only his questions, but his strategy too. He was going to go very gently, do whatever it took to soften the star up for the really difficult questions: about Nils, about enemies, about Ricky, their break-up, what exactly he might have texted his friend from his hotel room that night. And if the road journey proved good for talk, as road journeys often do, perhaps he might even try the gentlest probe into Jonni's sexuality.

But he was in for a disappointment. 'The powers-that-be need Jonni to be on form tonight,' Bernie said, as Francis arrived outside the buses. 'So you're with us again, I'm afraid, mate.'

'Adam specifically said last night,' Francis protested, looking over angrily at Ray, who was guarding the steps of the star's bus, neatly attired in his usual outfit: blue sailor's smock, dinky captain's cap and, Francis noticed, a gleaming new gold hoop in his right ear (he, at least, was nothing if not open about what he was!).

'Sorry, mate,' Bernie insisted. 'I've had my instructions.'

Ray shrugged and made a 'que sera, sera' face.

'Can I speak to them?' Francis asked.

'No,' Bernie replied. 'When they come down, they come down, and straight onto the bus, OK. No chit-chat from visiting journos.'

'Sounds like a fait accompli, matey,' Ray cooed. 'A very accomplished fate.' He giggled, annoyingly.

Francis didn't even grace the driver with a smile. He turned away crossly and climbed the steps onto the familiar band bus, doing his best to nod politely at Dolly as he went. What were Zak and Adam up to? Did they actually want to prevent him discovering that the story they had told him last night was rubbish? Maybe the twist was that Jonni was in fact a rampant heterosexual, as billed to his public. In his interview with the evil twins (as he now saw them), Francis had failed to double down on what exactly they had wanted Ricky – and Nils – not to disclose. That Jonni was gay? That he'd had a long-term relationship with a roadie? Could it really be true that a successful pop star *still* had to conceal stuff like this? OK, back in the day, when Francis had been young, Elton John, George Michael and Freddie Mercury had pretended for a long while to like the ladies – Christ, Elton had even got married – while others like Boy George, Marc Almond and Jimmy Somerville had made their own waves by being openly out. But thirty years on, well into the twenty-first century, such a PR strategy would be ridiculous. Wouldn't it?

Francis climbed the familiar stairs and found that everyone

was, once again, huddled in the upstairs lounge: Simon, Suzi, Thelma, Vanko and the ever-upbeat Russell. Today, they were all looking at their phones or laptops in silence, though there was sporadic banter as they drew away from the green awnings and stern grey façade of the Grand Hotel Meridien and headed down a broad, dreary highway of apartments and office blocks then up onto the busy A6 west towards Stuttgart.

'So how are your investigations going?' Suzi asked after a bit. 'Are you getting anywhere?'

'Some things are becoming a little clearer,' Francis replied truthfully. And then he thought, to hell with it, why shouldn't I just throw it open and see what they know? So, having got their attention by explaining that he was going to speak in total confidence, he told them about his meeting with Adam and Zak the night before, and what they'd discussed. Had they all known about Jonni being gay? he asked. And Ricky? And about the break-up? And Nils?

They looked from one to the other in a silence so heavy it could have fallen to the floor with a clatter. It was Russell who eventually spoke. 'I think, dude, it's fair enough to say that we don't talk about Jonni's private life. He likes to keep it that way – and we obviously respect that.'

'But why is it a secret at all?' Francis asked. 'I mean – gay? For fuck's sake, why on earth should that be an issue for a pop star these days?'

More silence.

'Dude,' Russell said eventually. 'The awful truth is, it *is* still an issue, for some. It's like footballers: their fan base still don't want to accept it. T.J. Osbourne, big country music star in the US, only came out last year. Frank Ocean–'

'Footballers, totally,' Vanko cut in. 'Jake Daniels of Black-pool is still the only openly gay footballer in England's top four divisions. Justin Fashanu was the only other one, and he came out thirty years ago. I mean, how crazy is that?'

'It's exactly the same in the US,' said Russell. 'Carl Nassib came out last year. That's it.'

'To be fair, Frank Ocean came out a while ago,' Thelma said.

'And if they're not out, who's to know?' said Suzi.

'Is this something Jonni wants?' Francis asked, pressing on. 'Or is it Adam?'

More silence.

'Who even said Jonni was gay?' said Vanko.

'Ahem,' said Suzi.

'Jonni's a paradox,' Simon said, glaring at her. 'He's very open and public and hip in some ways – his cross-dressing and all that. But Russell's right, in other ways he's intensely private.'

'And why shouldn't he be?' said Vanko. 'Why do fans of his music need to know every last thing he gets up to?'

'You'd have to ask Adam,' said Russell, 'if it's an issue. He calls the shots with Jonni, really.'

'Does he?' said Francis. 'I thought he spent his time scurrying around trying to please Jonni. Satisfying his every backstage whim.'

'There is that,' said Suzi, laughing.

'He's clever, Adam,' said Vanko. 'He does that, at one level. You know, if Jonni suddenly wants a sea bream with hand-cut chips and bok choy on the side with kiwi fruit and pistachio ice cream to follow, Adam will send Charmaine out to get exactly that. But even as Jonni's scoffing it down, Adam will be working on him, telling him he doesn't like drugs, or it's great that he's so gender-fluid and undefined that nobody need know what his sexuality is – when, as we all know, Adam basically just doesn't want him to lose the devotion of the hordes of crazy female fans who secretly – or not so fucking secretly – want to marry him.'

'Oh, come on,' said Simon tetchily. 'That's ridiculous. And unfair.'

'It's a hundred per cent fair. I know what Adam's like. And I also know what the fans are like. Jesus, I've got a fan who's set up a whole website about our non-existent wedding.'

Simon staged a noisy fake yawn. 'For God's sake, Vanko. You're obsessed. You should be grateful you've *got* fans. And someone who wants to marry you,' he added with a chuckle.

'Just fuck right off, Simon,' said Vanko.

'Thanks for that,' said Francis smoothly, into another awkward silence. 'That's all very helpful. Amazingly, even though Nick and Adam called me in to try and work out what was going on, they didn't see fit to mention this fact about Jonni. Or that he was with Ricky. Or that Nils the crazy Dane was also a good friend of Ricky's. It kind of makes me wonder what else they didn't tell me.'

'Good question,' said Thelma quietly.

'OK,' Francis said. 'I'm going to share something else with you. And this must go no further.'

'You can trust us, dude,' said Russell. 'What goes on on tour…'

'…is going to have to be what stays in this room, I'm afraid.'

'I'm cool with that,' said Suzi.

'Go on then, mate,' said Vanko.

'When I was talking to Adam and Zak last night and they told me all this stuff, they also said that they hadn't even told Nick about Nils.'

'What d'you mean?' asked Suzi. 'Told him what?'

'That he was one of Ricky's lovers. And that what he said as he pushed Jonni off the stage was about Ricky.'

'That's no surprise to me,' said Vanko. 'Did he even know what was said?'

'He knew about *This is for Sandra*, apparently. But not what it meant.'

'He didn't know Ricky was Sandra.'

'No. Did you lot?' Francis looked round the room.

'I have no idea what you're talking about,' said Suzi.

'Me neither,' said Thelma. She did look convincingly curious.

Francis explained.

'I knew,' said Simon.

'So why didn't you tell me?'

Simon shrugged. 'Jonni asked me not to.'

'And what about the crew?' Francis asked. 'Did they know?'

'That I don't know,' said Simon.

'I think probably not,' said Vanko. 'Obviously they know that Ricky is Sandra. But if they'd known that Nils had said that, one of them would have told me about it. Mel for sure.'

'Vanko's little admirer,' teased Suzi.

'She's my guitar tech, Suzi. Bloody good at her job. And FYI, she's gay.'

'With a weird soft spot for an unreconstructed chauvinist,' Simon said.

'Fuck right off again,' said Vanko. He wasn't laughing.

'Don't the crew always know what you lot know?' Francis asked, before the pair came to fisticuffs. 'What goes on on tour, etc.'

'No,' said Thelma. 'Actually not. There are, like, band secrets and crew secrets. Aren't there, guys?'

'I guess,' said Suzi.

'So why hadn't Adam told Nick?' Francis asked.

'You know,' said Vanko, 'it's a funny thing about those two – those three, really. Despite everything that Nick is supposed to have done for him, Adam is much closer to Zak than–'

He stopped.

The door had pushed open and Bernie was there. 'Good afternoon, ladies and gentlemen. Just to inform you that the charming metropolis of Stuttgart is now merely one hour away. We will be going to the hotel first, so that we can dump

265

our bags and Jonni can have a nice shower in his own suite, and then we'll leave promptly for the venue. Where there will be food. So here's the routine. Disembark, check in, spend a maximum of thirty minutes in your room, doing your beauty routine, having a wank or whatever, then come back down to the foyer for departure to the lovely Hanns-Martin-Schleyer-Halle, capacity nine and a half thousand. For your information and interest, Hanns Martin Schleyer was a member of the Nazi SS in the Second World War and a big cheese in German industry afterwards. He was kidnapped by the far-left Red Army Faction in 1977 and murdered after the German government refused to negotiate with the terrorists – a tactic that was later adopted by our very own Margaret Thatcher.' Bernie bowed his little bow. 'History lesson over. I thank you.' And he was gone.

There was laughter, which dwindled into another silence, which was eventually broken by Suzi. 'I know the tour is going on and everything,' she said, 'and that's a good thing, in a way. But I still feel scared. As you pointed out, Francis, it's got to be one of us. So I'm looking round at everyone and I'm wondering, which of us would want to kill Topaz? And possibly Vanko too? It doesn't make any sense. At all.'

'It's not just us in this room, though, is it?' said Vanko.

'What d'you mean?'

'Well … Mitch and Omar … or someone higher up…'

'By which you mean…?'

'Who d'you think?'

'You really think Adam would want to bump off members of his own band?'

'Who else is there?'

'I nearly went to the airport yesterday,' Thelma said.

'Why?' asked Russell.

'Why d'you think?'

'To leave the tour?' asked Francis.

'Yes.' Her face was set and determined. She had clearly been thinking hard about this, even planning it.

'How would that work?' Francis asked. 'Aren't you contracted to stay till the end?'

'We are,' said Simon.

'How it would work,' said Thelma, 'is that I'd lose my *per diems*, wouldn't I, Russ?'

'You would.'

'More important, I'd lose my retainer and I'd never be employed by AZ Music again. My reputation as a reliable little backing singer who performs nicely and then goes to her room after the gig would be shot to shit. Chances are that Nick would make sure I was never employed by anyone else ever again. But at least I'd be safe. Here, I don't feel safe. Even with my hotel door locked. Whoever the murderer is, they've got access to a master key card. They can just slip in while you're sleeping and do their worst.'

'Even with the security guards in the corridor?' said Russell.

Thelma shrugged. 'Vanko's right. Who's to say it's not one of them? Or both? They have access. They're trained killers, as Suzi says.'

'But what would their motive be?' asked Russell.

'I've no idea. Maybe whoever is behind all this is paying them. Serious money.'

She was some way behind Francis in her understanding of what was going on, and he was tempted to put her straight. Ricky had overdosed himself and Jonni, possibly with Adam's encouragement, hadn't stopped him. Nils had pushed Jonni off the stage in a spiteful and pointless act of revenge. The issues were Vanko and Topaz.

Chapter Twenty-Five

The band were into a new routine already, it seemed. A new rhythm, post-Topaz. Halfway through the Stuttgart gig Jonni – still in black, though tonight it was a long backless velvet dress and a double string of pearls – broke off again to do his moving valedictory speech, then the whole stadium sang 'The Love That Tells Me', their eyes gleaming, lit from above by the myriad waving lights of the wristbands and mobiles.

There was a new development now, as the crowd called for Vanko during this song. 'Vanko! Vanko! Vanko!' came the chant, until Jonni gave way and waved for his reincarnated guitarist to do a solo. As Vanko obliged, taking centre stage, Jonni's face was a picture – and not a pretty one. And when at the end Vanko took to the microphone and sang a couple of lines of the famous song himself, you could see, despite his fixed, shit-eating grin, that the star wasn't happy.

As Jonni danced down to the front to carry on with 'Sometimes the Moon', he was lit by a single follow-spot. Kylie had dimmed all the other lights to allow him to take charge again. Even as Francis was wondering whether this was because she loved Jonni or hated Vanko, he followed the lone beam up through the smoky haze to the trusses high above. His eye settled on the guy in the yellow vest who was operating the spot. It was Steve 'Dolly' Parton, he realised, his regular bus driver. How hard they worked, these guys: driving the buses all day and all night, then doing this scary high-wire routine with the follow-spots as well. Well, three of them did anyway, while the other two seemed to make their extra cash with a bit of judicious online gambling, although that could presumably go either way. And then, in that moment of random, idle watching, Francis had a sudden revelation. Of course! How could he have been so stupid? One thought led rapidly to another, and finally raised the key question: when it came to what you wore – unless you were Jonni, of course, with a new audience to please every performance – why would you change what you were comfortable with, unless you needed to?

The band were quiet in the bus home afterwards, and Francis was too. He was late to the post-gig supper. Up in his room he put through a call to Polizeihauptkommissar Fischer. He was impressed by how quickly he got through to the Frankfurt detective, to hear again his measured and reassuring voice. With an apology, Francis outlined his latest suspicions; he could hardly believe it when Fischer confirmed what he had imagined. Yes, a specific item had been found on the floor of Room 539 of the Schlupfwinkel. It had helped narrow down the suspects, but hadn't yet incriminated one person. Francis's input was very interesting, Fischer said, and would hopefully help move things forward, though it didn't provide proof. Excited, Francis clicked off. He didn't need proof. He understood now why the two detectives had given him the weird once-over of his face and neck before they'd taken his witness statement. More to the point, he knew who had killed Topaz. What he needed to work out now was why.

'Fancy a nightcap?' Vanko asked Francis when they were alone at the end of the most muted supper of the tour so far. Francis was relieved that Vanko didn't require him to visit a flash VIP lounge in a Stuttgart nightclub to hear what he had to say.

'Nice little solo tonight,' Francis said as they headed up the corridor towards his room.

Vanko grinned. 'I'm not complaining. That was brave of you,' he continued when they were seated opposite each other in two shiny black leather armchairs, whiskies on the table in front of them. 'To open it all up like that, on the bus this morning, with the gang. Sorry if I was flippant.'

'No worries. I needed to know what you all thought. Adam and Zak gave me their story. How true is it? And there was Simon saying Jonni told him about *This is for Sandra*. Did he?'

'Major bullshitter, Simon. Hates to be left out. Especially if it involves me.'

Francis studied him. Was that true? 'So why didn't you give me the other piece of the jigsaw?' he asked. 'That Ricky was Sandra?'

'I didn't actually know. Seriously. At that point. That nickname. No.'

'But you did know that Jonni was gay? And in a relationship with Ricky. Which is another fairly important element.'

'Yeah, well.' Vanko looked down for a few seconds, clearly troubled. 'We're not exactly encouraged to gossip about Jonni. I've got a good job here, Francis, a job most musicians would kill for. I get to tour with one of the top pop stars in the world. I get a great big fat retainer, which continues when I'm at home doing my own stuff. I'm basically being paid – a lot – for doing what I love doing, staying up there, getting experience and exposure, and still having down time to build my own career. You don't imagine I want to be a sidekick forever, do you?'

'I don't know, Vanko. You tell me.'

'I'm ambitious, man, haven't you got that yet? That's why I don't particularly want to be electrocuted halfway through a gig.' Vanko flashed his smile. You could see why the women went for him. He was sweet, as well as fulfilling the sexy and wild side of the equation. Plus he was tall, and had not an ounce of fat on his lean, honed body. His upper arms were powerfully muscled. His legs fitted jeans where the inside leg was a much higher number than the waist. Francis almost fancied him himself.

'I want to be that person,' Vanko went on. 'Jonni the star. And it's within my grasp, man. Seriously. Between ourselves, I'm in talks with some very interesting people at the moment.'

'About what? A solo career?'

'I'm twenty-eight, man – that's young for a writer, but it's old for a musician who's still stupid enough to think he can live the dream. I've probably got a window of another five years. Max.'

'But there are plenty of older acts. It's hardly an ageist business. Look at the Rolling Stones.'

Vanko's laugh was one of pure disdain. 'Yes, look at them. They should change their name to the Rolling Zimmer Frames. But that's not the point. They're legends, obviously. If you're a legend you can go on performing till you drop. Though there are plenty of performers who were right up there and have vanished without trace – or worse, are still around, going nowhere. What about all those famous eighties acts? Not just Zak's Tainted Idols, but Madness, Duran Duran, the Pet Shop Boys, Eurythmics, Tears for Fears, Culture Club, Simply Red, Tender Plastique, Guitarmageddon, you name them. Where are they now? Eating bull's penis and being bombarded by live crabs in the Australian jungle if they're lucky. If I don't get there soon, I might as well give up and become a fat, happy session musician, married with two kids and living in Pinner. Which is probably what I will be, let's face it. But at least I'm still trying to give it a chance. So yeah, forgive me for not wanting to rock the boat. Quite apart from anything else, I need to keep in with these guys if I want to get on.'

There was an almost insane gleam in Vanko's eyes now. He was deadly serious, and Francis realised in that moment that the guitarist would do almost anything to achieve his ends.

'Adam and Nick?' he asked mildly.

'Yeah,' Vanko replied. 'I'm not saying they're going to manage me; they're not, obviously. But when I go, I need to go with their blessing. And Jonni's. Stitching him up and telling some random fake reporter detective person the full story would be shooting myself in the foot. Big time.'

'So why did you even tell me about *This is for Sandra* in the first place? And Jonni being "special friends" – your words, I think – with Ricky?'

'I told you before. You needed a heads-up. Someone was – still is, maybe – trying to kill me. You're supposed to be this great Sherlock Holmes type unraveller of mystery. I thought I should discreetly offer you something of what I knew. Without sending the balloon up.'

'So what are you saying? There's more.'

Vanko returned his gaze, levelly. 'There's always more,' he said.

'Are you going to share? For Topaz, if nothing else.'

'Poor fucking Topaz,' Vanko said. 'Look, I don't have any answers. I'm as puzzled as you. I kind of buy the story that Adam and Zak let Ricky kill himself, and that the Danish guy was a jealous lover of Ricky's. That's all possible. I also totally buy your take that Topaz was murdered because she knew something – too much, in fact. But me, that's what I'm puzzled about. Why would anyone want to kill me? Unless they thought I was unreliable, and I might tell you the real truth.'

Francis took a slow sip of his malt. He was wonderfully brazen, this guy, and Francis knew now exactly who had electrocuted him, and why he'd managed to survive that brilliant yellow flash, whether or not he was in rubber-soled boots. He met Vanko's gaze as sympathetically as he could.

'Why would anyone want to kill you?' he repeated slowly.

'I don't know,' said Vanko.

'Don't you? Really?'

'No.'

Vanko held Francis's gaze for a moment, and then he looked down. There was a nervousness there that told him all he needed to know. But more important than all that was suddenly this – *the real truth*. There was an even bigger fish in this pond, and Francis wasn't going to let it get away.

'So what's the real truth?' he asked. 'That might be serious enough to get you murdered...'

Vanko looked even less at ease, if that was possible. 'There's some unspoken stuff here, man, that none of us can really talk about. It's kind of a big deal, and then again, in my frank and personal opinion, it isn't. In some ways it's laughable, considering the history of all that's happened in rock and roll.'

What was he talking about? Francis stayed with it, nodding as supportively as he could in his state of suppressed excitement. If it took a ramble to get there, he would tolerate the ramble.

'You know the last time we did this nightcap thing?' Vanko said, after a silence of several long seconds. 'In Amsterdam, you were joking about the young girls up at the front, with their crazy outfits and signs and stuff, and we were laughing about me being a paedo and all that...'

Francis hadn't been joking, and Vanko hadn't been laughing, but now wasn't the time to say that.

'It was an interesting observation from an outsider, which is what you are, because we're in our own bubble, man, and as they always say, it's only the people in the bubble who can't see the bubble. But this young girl stuff is like a part of it all, for sure, going right back. You know, Elvis hooked up with Priscilla Beaulieu at the end of the 1950s, when she was fourteen and he twenty-four. In the early seventies, in California, there were the baby groupies, like Lori Lightning and her friend Sable Starr, who hung around the famous English disco in LA when they were young teenagers. Lori claimed that she was deflowered by Bowie when she was fifteen, and then she had a threesome with him the same night with Sable, who was the same age. Lori met Jimmy Page when she was thirteen and later had a relationship with him while she was still underage. Iggy Pop wrote about sleeping with Sable when she was thirteen in his song "Look Away". Bill Wyman met Mandy Smith when she was thirteen and he was forty-seven; whatever happened, they were going out publicly when she was sixteen, and she was only eighteen when they married. Jerry Lee Lewis married his cousin Myra Gale Brown when she was thirteen. Michael Jackson had Neverland. On it goes, with other big stars we don't even need to talk about. You know, when they came for the DJs, the Jonathan Kings and the Rolf Harrises and the Jimmy Saviles and all those other sleazy guys, they never went after the artists. Apart from Gary Glitter.' Vanko laughed. 'Perhaps he was too shit not to be punished, or perhaps he'd just gone too far. But that stuff was around from the start, and it stayed around. I suppose the thing is, it was consensual, even if some of the stars weren't that young. If the girls wanted them, so what?' He nodded meaningfully in Francis's direction.

'So what are you saying?' Francis asked. 'That the big dark secret about Jonni is that he likes very young girls? That he's not gay at all?'

'I could be killed for this,' Vanko began.

'You almost were,' said Francis.

'You're right.' Vanko flashed him his killer smile. 'So here's the thing, for your ears only, and you didn't hear it from me. If anyone asks about tonight, we were talking about my past or Topaz or something. OK?'

'OK.'

'Jonni does like them young, that's the thing. But it's boys he likes, not girls.'

Chapter Twenty-Six

Jonni's traditional Bavarian outfit was quite something, with its flouncy white sleeves, tight, beautifully embroidered black dirndl bodice and skirt, fetching pale blue apron, tight white stockings and black clogs. Costume mistress Laurent had once again excelled herself and when the fireworks finished and the star emerged from the smoke, there was an arena-wide gasp. Jonni had recovered his mojo. The young ladies of Munich, dressed to impress as always, could hardly match that.

One flushed female in the middle of the front row, whose glowing pink cheeks gave her a mumsy look even though she could have been no older than fourteen, was wearing a top cut so low that her breasts were continually on the verge of heaving free. A pinch-faced girl, with incongruous Edna Everage specs, was waving a placard saying *FUCK ME!*, almost as if it was an angry slogan on a political march. It was a wicked irony that for all his saucy teasing, none of this provocation would be tempting to Jonni at all – if, of course, this latest revelation of Vanko's was true. Or was Francis, after all, just the victim of another massive wind-up?

276

It was a question that had been with him all day, as they travelled down from Stuttgart on the crowded autobahn. After their confessional conversation last night, Vanko, weirdly – or perhaps not so weirdly – had avoided him. He had stayed downstairs with Russell, doggedly watching a movie for the entire two-and-half-hour road trip. Then he had hurried out of the bus ahead of the others and through the glass doors beneath the four colourful flags that hung above the balcony of the gleaming white stucco wedge of cheese that was the Munich Mandarin Oriental. There had been no smiles either on the minibus out to the Olympiahalle, set in pristine green lawns by a gleaming blue lake alongside its equally stylish sisters, the Olympiastadium and Olympiaschwimmhalle. Bernie had joked that its funky silver-grey canopy roof looked exactly like a couple of Madonna's bras, but nobody had laughed, so edgy was the atmosphere. Was the ambitious guitarist regretting what he'd said last night? Francis wondered. If anything, that made it more likely to be true.

The paradox was that Francis had spent last night worrying about Vanko himself. Would it turn out that walls did, as Topaz had said, have ears? Would Vanko be the next in line, and would the next attempt at silencing him be successful? And what about him? Francis had slept badly, one ear open for the click of his door. Would that be it: the stealthy operative of choice, master key card in one hand and neat silver gun with silencer in the other? Or a knife or a silk scarf or even just a bent thumb, poised to take him out, now that Francis knew the terrible secret? That Jonni was not fashionably G or B or T or Q or I or A or P or even K. He was another kind of P, the P that dare not breathe its name – not publicly, at any rate.

Vanko, Vanko, Vanko. He was one of the keys to the whole puzzle, Francis knew that. And now he had had time to talk to Mel and check out his intuition about the electrocution, which he'd done that afternoon just before sound check, things were

starting to fall into place. Perhaps the man himself had slept
better than he had, because now he was giving the performance of his life, throwing his guitar around like a man
without fear – certainly without the fear that someone had
tinkered with the electrics and he was about to go sprawling
across the stage, this time not to get up.

Meanwhile, as promised, Nick had rejoined the tour. From
his usual vantage point at the right-hand side of the stage,
Francis could see him, standing alongside Adam and Zak and
Charmaine in their regular spot on the other side. While Charmaine boogied and Adam shifted funkily from foot to foot,
Nick didn't move. They were loose to the music, he was tight; a
businessman surveying his investment, not a loved-up fan.

Two songs before the end of the show, Francis felt his
phone buzz. It was a message from Nick:

> Could we catch up afterwards please? Meet
> me in Catering and I'll give you a lift to the
> hotel.

That 'please' was mere courtesy, Francis was aware of that.
He held up his hand and was rewarded with an identical
gesture from the other side of the stage. As the show ended, he
made a quick call of his own. And when Francis found the
manager, talking into his mobile at one of the gingham-clothed
tables in the now empty restaurant, he was friendlier than he'd
been for a while. The tense Nick of Frankfurt had been
replaced by an altogether more relaxed version. Perhaps it was
just because the tour was back on the road, the money was
rolling in again.

'What a show!' he remarked, as he walked Francis down to
the car park. Despite everything, he went on, the band had
made an amazing recovery.

Despite everything, Francis thought bitterly. Is that it? RIP
Topaz.

They strolled past the two waiting silver band coaches and on across the marked tarmac to a black Mercedes.

'Just us?' asked Francis, as Nick nodded him into the back and got in beside him. A thickset driver waited at the wheel. In the sudden warmth of the car, Francis could smell his cheap deodorant, the flimsy chemical blanket over the tense sweat of a gym-honed muscleman.

'Adam and Zak are going with Jonni on his bus. I thought it would be good for us to have a little catch-up.'

So was Francis finally going to get Nick's side of the story? The truth about what Adam and Zak had told him? It would be more than just interesting to hear what he had to say. When it came to the conversation he planned to have with the three of them, later, back in the hotel, he needed to have all the information he could at his disposal.

'So, between ourselves, where are we?' Nick asked, as they slid out onto the side road that led away from the Olympiahalle complex.

'You're happy, presumably, that the tour is back on track?' Francis replied.

'Of course. But we're no nearer to solving our case. Or are we?'

Francis didn't want to say too much. 'What are the Frankfurt police saying about Topaz?' he asked.

'We're still awaiting the post-mortem results. They're not looking for anyone else, as far as I'm aware.'

'They're still thinking it's an accident?'

'Yes.'

'And you're happy with that?'

'We're guided by them, Francis. They have the evidence in front of them. They are the professionals.'

'Do they know about Ricky? That other tragic "accident"?'

'Not as far as I'm aware, no.'

'Don't you think they should know? To get the full picture?'

'I'm not sure it's relevant. Ricky's overdose was a matter for the Danish police. They were satisfied. The UK coroner has been informed.'

There was silence in the car. Francis looked ahead, at the driver's thick neck, as he sped along past the anonymous apartment blocks, a late tram suddenly rattling by on the tracks to their right, lit up inside and almost empty. This wasn't the moment to challenge his boss. Better by far to wait until they were safely back in the Mandarin Oriental.

'And what about Hamburg?' he asked.

'That was all sorted out satisfactorily. Didn't Adam tell you?'

'He did. They also told me, he and Zak, that Nils, the assailant, had been involved with Ricky.'

'A-ha.'

'Did you know that?'

There was a five-second pause. 'Of course,' Nick said.

'They told me you didn't. That they hadn't told you.'

'They didn't need to tell me.'

'You already knew?' Francis paused.

'I always know. That's one of the reasons I employed you.'

'To spy on them?'

'Shall we say: to give me another perspective.'

'So did you know about *This is for Sandra*?'

'Of course.'

'And you knew Ricky was Sandra?'

'I did.'

'So why didn't you tell your tame detective all that?'

'You didn't need to know. If you found out, as you have done, that's all to the good. Shows me you've been working hard, that you know what you're doing. Not that you've been entirely straight with me all along, have you, Francis?'

What was he to say? Stuck in this car with this fragrant beefcake of a driver who was Nick's man. Anything could happen, couldn't it? No, don't be silly, this wasn't *The Sopranos*. They were heading back to the plush foyer of the lovely Mandarin Oriental, of course they were. A late glass of champagne, some tasty cold meats and then a measured showdown in a place where Francis would be safe and in control.

'It's been a tricky one,' Francis replied. 'Keeping everyone's trust. They don't all want you to know everything.'

'I appreciate that. Paranoia and Paranoia, eh?' Nick chuckled. 'No, the thing about the rock and roll business is that for all their vaunted unconventionality, the staff are generally pretty loyal. What goes on on tour stays on tour, and all that. It protects everyone. If they keep quiet about what Jonni gets up to, then no one's going to tell the third lampy's wife exactly what he did with the Brazilian transsexual at the party in Rotterdam. But with Ricky, we'd got into very difficult territory. He felt aggrieved. We should have just got rid, but there were all these threats about going public, and the trouble with Ricky was that he had evidence. So we thought we had to keep him close. And see what happened.'

'Evidence ... of what?'

'You don't need to know. Let's just say it wouldn't have been helpful to Jonni's career.' He wasn't going to volunteer more.

'So what happened,' Francis said, 'was that you engineered an overdose?'

Nick shrugged, but he didn't deny the charge. 'When that sad event happened, and then our friend Nils mounted his bizarre attack, I thought things were possibly getting a little out of hand. I needed to know who might talk and who wouldn't. That's why I employed you, Francis. If X or Y knew the truth, and felt strongly that it should come out, they would tell the visiting journalist. Wouldn't they? And if they found out that the journalist was in fact a detective, so much the better. So we put you with the band, and we put you with the crew, and they all passed the test with flying colours. Not a brown M&M in sight. So I reckoned the worst was over, that Jonni's brand – to use a phrase I despise – was going to be OK after all.'

'But then, suddenly, Vanko,' said Francis. 'That must have been a shock to you.'

'A shock, very good. It was.'

'At the time, it seemed as if you really didn't know what had happened.'

'We didn't.'

'So suddenly I acquired an extra value?'

'Had you found out what had happened, you would have done.'

'Who's to say I didn't?'

'If you did, you didn't share with me. Or Adam and Zak. For what it's worth, Adam was convinced you were as stumped by the incident as we were.'

'I was. Initially. But that was my lead – when I realised Adam really had no idea about what had happened. Before that, I'd been thinking the electrocution had been set up as a warning. To Vanko. Because he'd spilt the beans to me about *This is for Sandra*.'

'A warning from Adam?'

'I'm afraid so,' Francis said. 'Or both – all three of you. I wasn't sure.'

'You're including Zak in this?'

'I was.'

'I'm not sure you quite understand how our little triangle works.'

'I'm not sure I do. Or need to, to be honest. No. Because I soon realised my mistake. This wasn't a sequence, with one murderous mind at the back of it. These were all separate incidents.'

'I see. So who was behind the incident involving Vanko?'

Francis paused before he replied. He turned to look at

Nick, beside him on the plush cream leather of the Mercedes. Did the manager know? Was he just testing Francis again? Looking into his nervy, curious eyes, he got the feeling he didn't. Well, that was one thing he had over him; one little success he could chalk up to his credit.

'That was the one thing I couldn't work out,' he said. 'Who had the motive – and the means? Who was close enough to Vanko to do that, yet get away with it? Was it a botched attempt at a murder, or just what it felt like, a warning? And if it wasn't you three, who on earth? And why? It wasn't until I was talking to the man himself last night that I suddenly realised. That the electrocution wasn't a warning – from you guys or anyone else. Nor the crazed effort of one of his disgruntled fans, as he'd so often suggested. It was simply this: here was a highly ambitious performer, who realised that there were international headlines for this ongoing *verhext* tour story, and that rather than be a bit part, he could be at the centre of it. He could give himself the exposure he needed to advance his burning ambition to be a star himself.'

'What are you saying? That … Vanko … did it himself?' said Nick slowly.

Francis nodded. 'I was stupid not to see it sooner. All the techies were baffled, as I told you at the time. It seemed as if a foot pedal had been compromised, but how would that have happened, with all the checks they do? Unless one of them was party to it. But then, thinking about it, and after watching a few videos myself, I realised this: there was this loud crack of a shock and an impressive yellow flash, but a real shock would have been silent and without a flash. If there had been one, it would have been blue. Vanko acted out the whole thing.'

Nick was silent, nodding slowly, clearly impressed. 'So what was the bang?' he asked.

'Firecracker. The crew use them with the other stage fire-works at the start of the show.'

'But there's always loads of smoke. Jonni is hidden by it.'

'Not from the firecrackers. They're smokeless.'

'So what – he organised this all by himself? How did he let off the cracker?'

'His guitar tech helped him. Mel. She's a big admirer of his, and it so happens she's in charge of the fireworks. You know who she is?'

'I'm not up with all the crew, I'm afraid. But Vanko's always been a hit with the ladies. So you're saying she let off the cracker and then he threw himself across the floor.'

'I knew he'd studied the videos of other stars being electrocuted, because he told me as much himself. I just hadn't realised that he'd watched them before the incident, rather than after. So yes, when Mel's cracker went off, he crumpled down, just as you can see on the footage. But everyone was so shocked they didn't realise.'

'The only one who wasn't shocked was him.'

'Exactly.'

Nick laughed. 'Brilliant. I knew that crazy guy had an ego, but that is something else. And what proof do you have of this?'

'I spoke to Mel. This afternoon. Before sound check. She's been feeling guilty about it all. Especially after Topaz.'

'Okay,' Nick said slowly, 'that's three incidents sorted. Where does that leave us with poor Topaz? Do you have an explanation for that?'

'I thought you were of the same mind as the Frankfurt Kripo. That she'd drunk too much and drowned.'

'I am, yes. But you're not, I don't think. According to Adam.'

'I have my … suspicions,' Francis replied, a catch in his voice. Sitting next to Nick like this, he realised he was trembling. This was not how he'd planned it. 'But I'd rather share them with Adam and Zak as well, if you don't mind. Back at the hotel.'

'Why do they need to be involved?'

'Because the three of you work so closely together. Because, I suppose,' he lied, 'I'd like to convince all of you.'

'You already told me you were surprised when they told you there were things they weren't planning to share with me,' Nick said, the old competitive edge back in his voice. 'The truth is, we don't really work that closely together. And even though you don't fully understand the ins and outs of our arrangements, you know that, don't you?' He leant forward abruptly to the driver and gave him an instruction in German. It ended with 'Englisher Garten', it sounded like.

Francis was suddenly scared. What had he been thinking, sharing the Vanko stuff before they got back to the safety of the hotel? Because if he was right about Vanko, and he was, why wouldn't he be right about Topaz? Now, ahead of them, at the end of the wide street they were travelling along, set high above the leafless trees, was a golden angel atop a tall illuminated column.

'The Friedensengel,' said Nick. 'The Angel of Peace. Lovely, isn't she? And that dark space in front of her is the river Isar.'

The car turned sharp left. Now there were apartments on the left-hand side of the road, and trees and parked cars on the right. Then they were slowing and turning left again, into a residential area. In the rear-view mirror Francis could see the headlights of another car right behind them. For one excited, relieved moment, he thought it might be a police car following them. But it was an identical black Mercedes.

Soon they had pulled up on a quiet street. Houses with tall metal fences on one side, trees on the other, darkness beyond.

'The Englischer Garten,' said Nick. 'One of Europe's largest parks. Created by an Englishman whose name I've forgotten for the Elector of Bavaria at the end of the eighteenth century. It's bigger than Hampstead Heath, your old stomping ground, Francis.'

'Well remembered,' Francis replied. Nick's tone had changed from affable to quietly scary. Francis thought he should do his best to keep things as normal as possible between them.

'You know,' Nick continued, as the engine died and the beefy driver got out to open the back doors, 'rock and roll tours can be hard work. Sometimes you need to find places to unwind on a day off. Sadly, we don't have a full day off in Munich this time, but we have done in the past. There's a lovely beer garden here, though I hardly think it would be open in February.'

'No,' Francis agreed. The second car had pulled up a few yards behind them.

'Shall we continue on foot?' Nick asked, though it was not a question, with the driver hovering menacingly nearby. 'A little walk in the park, and then once you've told me all you know about Topaz, for real this time, we might head back to the hotel for supper and a nightcap with the others.'

Francis didn't like the sound of that 'might', but he had no option but to follow Nick as he opened his door and stepped outside into the chilly night. He couldn't continue with what he'd planned to say back in the hotel in the presence of the others, could he? That would be downright dangerous now.

Outside, Francis peered at the second Mercedes. There was a slim driver at the wheel, but he didn't look any more sympathetic than Meat Loaf. Next to him, in the front, was security man Omar. There was another surprise. Omar got out and held open the back door, and Russell got out.

The accountant smiled sheepishly. 'Dude,' he said, but it didn't sound quite so cheery or confident as usual.

'OK,' said Nick. 'Shall we get going, guys?' He brought out

a small silver torch and clicked it on. 'Stay close to me,' he continued. 'There's no moon tonight. We don't want anyone falling in the river, do we?' He turned to the accountant. 'Francis was just debriefing me, Russ, on what he's found out about the various unfortunate incidents that have dogged the tour.'

'OK.'

'He's done well.'

As the three of them left the little side street and turned, past a parked camper van, onto a narrow pathway between low bushes and tall, leafless trees, Francis was tempted to scream. If he yelled at the top of his voice, might he be able to make enough noise to awaken the inhabitants of the van, if they were in there, or people in the neat flats opposite, where a light still burned in one of the upper windows? Or would he just be wasting his time?

The impulse passed. Francis stayed cool, listening politely as Nick summarised what Francis had told him earlier.

'Vanko, what a shit!' said Russell. 'Of course, of course. We should have worked that one out.'

'Russell has been working with me,' said Nick, 'in his capacity of PR for the American record company. As you know, Jonni is huge in America.'

'I started out as a tour accountant,' Russell explained. 'Managing the *per diems* is hardly rocket science.'

As the narrow path opened onto a wider one, with Narnia-style Victorian carriage lamps to each side, the torch became unnecessary. They came to a bridge over a straight, canal-like river. Omar was right behind them. An ex-mercenary, who would presumably do whatever he was paid to do, as Suzi had suggested.

Nick stopped in the middle. 'I assume you have your phone with you,' he said to Francis.

'Yes.'

'Hand it over, would you?'

There was no point resisting. It was all too clear what would happen if he tried. Francis reached into his pocket, reluctantly removed his iPhone and gave it to the manager.

Nick walked the five yards to the railings and dropped it in the river. There was a small splash as Francis's entire life vanished under water: his contacts, his emails, his messages, his WhatsApp groups, his music, his Audible books, his everything. Would it even matter? Very soon he might have no need for contacts. There might be no more messages. Or music. Or anything.

'Sorry about that,' Nick said. 'Erring on the side of caution. You never know who might be tracking you. So,' he continued as they walked on, up the wide metalled path ahead of them, 'Francis was about to tell me what he thought about poor Topaz. He's not convinced that the Kripo have got it right.'

'Is that so?' said Russell.

Francis's original plan had been carefully thought through. In a suite back at the hotel, with Adam and Zak present, it would have been straightforward to confront Nick with what he had worked out about Topaz's murder. But he could hardly share all that now, could he? In the middle of nowhere, without even his phone.

'Francis,' prompted Nick.

'So what I was explaining to Nick,' Francis replied, trying to keep his voice as natural and level as he could, 'was that my mistake for quite a while was thinking that the two deaths and the two other incidents were the product of one murderous mind. But they weren't. Poor Ricky's suicide. Nils's revenge. Vanko's bid for international fame. All very different motives. And finally Topaz. Who was behind that? I'm still puzzled, to be honest.'

'Nice try,' said Nick. 'I think you know perfectly well who killed Topaz.'

They walked on in silence, their faces lighting up as they approached a streetlamp, then falling into shadow again. The low wooden fence on each side of the path petered out, the tree trunks thickened, then the park opened out again. On the right, there was a steep little hill. Just visible at the top a white building loomed out of the darkness like a mirage: a Greek temple with a domed roof and columns.

'The Monopteros,' Nick said. He gestured upwards. 'Shall we?'

He led the way off the path and onto the damp grass. With Omar right behind them, there was nothing Francis could do except follow. If he tried to shout or scream now, out here, no one would hear him. Stupidly nervous of creating a scene earlier, he had missed his chance.

Chapter Twenty-Seven

The four of them walked silently up the slope. From beyond the park came the distant sounds of the city – a faint car horn, a distant plane. But otherwise it was quiet.

Close up, the Monopteros was quite something, with ten thick columns reaching to a dome perhaps fifty feet above them. Francis wondered idly what they were: Ionic? Corinthian? He couldn't remember the difference, not that it mattered now. *He went to his death without his phone and having forgotten the different styles of classical column.* Having said that, he thought, wasn't there a third type?

Nick approached the chunky whitewashed stone steps that ran round the circular base of the building. He sat down. Russell followed suit. Then Francis, a little way off. Omar stood to one side, ever the professional. His pistol was visible, slung next to his waist. This display of power over life and death had never bothered Francis before; it did now.

'OK,' Nick said, 'so tell us what you think happened to Topaz after your little night of passion. The truth, please, this time.'

Francis had run out of road. There was no point trying to

make something up, even if he'd felt able to. These two would see straight through even the most plausible fiction and then he'd be in worse trouble.

'I knew she couldn't have drowned,' he replied. 'She was pretty much sober by the time I left her. Sober and ready for a snooze. Why would she get up at four thirty in the morning and have a bath? So it was clear to me that someone had come into the room, made her get up and get into the bath, and then held her under. This person was clearly strong, and probably a man. Or else they had a gun, otherwise Topaz would have resisted or screamed the place down. Why didn't she, anyway? Perhaps, like me now, she thought that she was in a very serious situation, but that if she played her cards right she would be OK. Or perhaps she thought she could outwit her murderer. An apparently harmless bus driver called Ray, known as Jolly to the crew. Sadly, she didn't know that his nickname was not just a jokey reference to his surname, Rogerson, but also referred to his past in the Royal Marines. Ex-military, ex-mercenary, this kind of operation was routine for him.'

'What on earth made you think it was Ray? Of all people?' Nick asked with a nervous laugh.

Surely he wasn't going to bother to try and deny it now?

'Process of elimination,' Francis said. 'Because the crew were already on their way to Nuremberg on the night Topaz died, it had to be one of the band party. As you know, for a while I was convinced it was Adam, with possibly a little help from either Bernie or the security detail. But then I had a late-night chat with him and Zak, a confrontation really, and it became clear to me that (a) they really did think Ricky had topped himself, albeit not discouraged by Jonni; (b) they had no clue who had attacked Vanko, were still baffled by that incident; and (c) they didn't know about Topaz, still genuinely thought it might have been a horrible accident.

'So if it wasn't them, or the band, or Bernie, or Security,

who was it? It was only while I was watching Dolly, our band bus driver, doubling up as a follow-spot operator during the Stuttgart gig that two things dawned on me. First, that two bus drivers were also present in Frankfurt on the night Topaz died, even though they weren't staying in the hotel; and second, that though Dolly always drove the band bus, Jonni's bus was driven alternately by Ray and Gideon. And when one of them was driving Jonni's, the other was driving the lampies', the very bus Ricky had overdosed on. Was it possible, I wondered, that one of these guys was the link between the two murders? If so, it would have had to be Ray, because he had been driving Jonni's bus the morning after Topaz's murder, while Gideon was in Nuremberg with the crew.

'Now I'd noticed when I first met him that Ray wore a stud in his right ear, as some old-school gay men like to do. It was a gold anchor, tying in with his regular outfit of captain's cap and matelot top. But on the morning after Topaz was killed, he wasn't wearing an earring. Fair enough – perhaps he didn't wear it all the time. Perhaps he didn't want Jonni or the managers to realise he was gay. But then, when we left Stuttgart a day later, it had been replaced, in the same lobe, by a gold ring. Ray never changed the rest of his outfit, so why would he change his earring? Could he have lost it in a struggle? A phone call to Polizeihauptkommissar Fischer of the Frankfurt Kripo gave me my answer. The forensics people had found a tiny gold ear stud on the carpet by Topaz's bed. It was in the shape of an anchor. The police had checked the earlobes of all the suspects, but with no joy. Some, like me, didn't even have pierced ears. None of those who did wore a lone anchor. That didn't bother me. I knew what Ray had worn before the gold ring. It was he who killed Topaz.'

'I hardly think that would stand up in a court of law,' said Nick. 'Who's to say you didn't find this earring on his bus and plant it in the room?'

'No one. Except that (a) how could I, when it was permanently in his ear? And (b) why would I want to incriminate him anyway? I've got no skin in this game. My next question, obviously, was who was behind the Jolly Mariner? Because it seemed fairly clear that Ray wasn't doing it for himself. He was a compulsive gambler who presumably needed the money, and he'd found a better way of getting it than risking his life up on the trusses with follow-spots like the other drivers. But who would employ a remote killer? Someone who was well away from the area. Who had, as a result, a cast-iron alibi.' Francis looked significantly at Nick. 'At that point, I must admit, I didn't factor in your involvement, Russell.'

'For clarity, dude, not that it matters much now, I was never *involved*. "Aware" might be a better word. And believe me, I had no hand in what happened to Topaz.'

'You knew what the bottom line was,' said Nick sharply.

'I didn't know it would be actioned like that. For God's sake! There was another way of doing this.'

'Hard decisions sometimes have to be made, Russell. You knew that.'

This little spat didn't help Francis, though it had conveniently confirmed his suspicions. But even if he believed Russell about Topaz – and why should he? – the American was in too deep now. Both he and Nick needed Francis dead, and were ready to make that happen, otherwise why would the accountant have come along on this little excursion? Doubtless they both had their alibis ready. They would swear to the police that they had returned to the hotel, and the discovery of the Englishman's corpse on the floor of the Monopteros would be yet another thing for the Kripo to puzzle over.

Except, of course, that it wouldn't.

Francis stayed cool. If he was going to save himself, he needed to spin them out. Neither of them knew about the ace up his sleeve. That he had stayed in close touch with the Frankfurt Kripo from the moment he had phoned Fischer after the Stuttgart gig about Ray's earring; that he knew that their assertion about Topaz having drowned accidentally was just a smokescreen; that they were actively looking for the killer and, in pursuit of that objective, had been following the whole entourage ever since; that the neat individuals in hotel lobbies that Francis had been suspicious of were indeed police personnel; and that though in theory the state police forces worked separately, on big cases like this they co-operated. It wasn't just Hesse that was involved now, but Hamburg, Baden-Württemberg and, critically, Bavaria, the state they were in now.

The phone call Francis had made as he'd left the Olympiahalle this evening had been to a number Fischer had given him for the Bavarian Kripo. He had told the detective he'd spoken to that he was going in a car with Nick back to the Mandarin Oriental, and that if they didn't arrive within half an hour, the police should be concerned enough to send out a rescue team, following his mobile signal. He had obviously had no idea where Nick was planning to take him, and now his phone was in the river. Did that make it – and him – untraceable, or could the Kripo track it to there? Even if they couldn't, they could surely track Nick's phone. It was just a shame they didn't know about Russell too. Or perhaps they did? In any case, what Francis needed to do now was play for time.

'Involved or not,' Francis replied, 'you managed to fool me, Russell. I'd put the blame for Topaz's death fairly and squarely with Nick. As I had for Ray's first murder.'

'What do you mean?' asked Nick.

'You don't imagine I bought all that guff about Ricky overdosing, did you? Or even the story that he did it himself because Jonni was breaking up with him?'

'Adam did.'

'You made a bad man feel needlessly guilty. And Zak?'

'What about Zak?' Nick asked.

'Did he know?'

'Certainly not.'

Francis nodded slowly. 'I had an idea that you and Zak might be in cahoots, with dear Adam a befuddled innocent outsider.'

'No, Adam and Zak go too far back for that. Zak likes to think he's in control. But he isn't.'

'Does that make you feel better? Outwitting him?'

Nick shrugged.

'You've never liked him, have you?' Francis went on. 'For a while you needed his money to survive, but you've always resented him. And his hold over Adam.'

'Zak is a remarkable character,' Nick said. 'A lead singer of note, a famous actor, and a highly successful and ethical businessman, who makes cheeses that the French love and whiskies that the Japanese apparently die for.'

Despite everything, Francis couldn't help but laugh. 'An ethical businessman who got started with money he'd pinched from those closest to him, the fellow band members of the Tainted Idols. Zak is a dyed-in-the-wool hypocrite, as well you know. That's why you can't stand him. I'll give you credit for that.'

'Nice of you,' said Nick. 'Not that it matters much now.' He stood looking out into the darkness, nostrils twitching like an old tiger, as if double-checking that they really were alone up here on this hill. 'Shame you can't check out the view,' he added. 'It's just city lights at this time of night. But come up here on a summer's day, and you can see right across Munich.'

Francis got to his feet. He too was looking out and down the grassy slope to the dark bushes at the bottom, hoping against hope that he would detect some movement there. Masked Bavarian Kripo with guns and searchlights. Hadn't that bloody cop taken him seriously? Where was the blinking cavalry? He was running out of time.

'No,' Francis continued, 'it was clear to me that Ricky had gone too far. Even the suggestion that he might break the *omertà* and tell the world the truth about Jonni was too much. You had to make absolutely sure he was gone.'

'We did, I'm afraid,' said Nick.

'It was a shame that Nils came out of the woodwork. You hadn't bargained on that, had you? But letting him off his assault charge in return for an NDA meant you had him where you wanted him.'

'This is true,' Russell agreed.

'Vanko was a wild card. Nobody could have predicted that act of self-aggrandising madness – or the effect it would have on the press. But in other ways it was a distraction. If the jinxed tour was the story, it stopped people asking questions about Jonni. It was just a shame that Topaz knew what had happened to Ricky. And why.'

'So you've told Fischer all your little theories, have you?' Nick said.

'Yes,' Francis replied.

The manager turned to Russell. 'It looks like plan B will have to kick in.'

'I'm afraid so.' Russell pulled a mobile from his pocket and pressed a key. 'Plan B,' he said and clicked off.

'There we go, Francis,' said Nick. 'Congratulations. I never thought we'd have to use it. By the way, that phone of Russell's isn't his phone. That's back at the hotel, with mine. Because that's where we technically are at the moment. No, I'm afraid that nobody is going to believe that Ray has anything to do with us. Whatever you've told them, there isn't a shred of evidence to make a link. We always throw our SIM cards away – not that there's been much need for mobile calls with Russell on site.

We've always had our doubts about Jolly, haven't we, Russell?'

'We have.'

'I'm afraid the story will have to be that Jolly was a nasty little paedo who had been involved with Ricky in some fairly sordid activities. When Ricky threatened to dob him in, there was only one way out. Ricky had to go, otherwise Jolly would have gone down for a very long time. Then Topaz knew, as we now know, so he had to do away with her. Jolly had form. A criminal record, all that. Enlightened people like you, Francis, like to think that there's redemption for those kinds of people, but sadly that's a bit of a naïve illusion. A leopard rarely changes his spots. And I've got a horrid feeling that this particular leopard will have to be involved with your demise too. As you've already told Fischer, you realised about Ray as well.'

'D'you really think Fischer is going to believe your story?' Francis said. 'Given everything I've told him.'

'Why wouldn't he?' said Nick. 'Mitch is bringing Ray here as we speak. He will be discovered right next to you, on the floor of the Monopteros.'

'Dead, presumably. By his own hand. With the gun that killed me.'

'Exactly. Anyone would think you wrote crime fiction, Francis. As they say, dead men don't tell lies. And even better, you can blame any number of murders on them.'

'May I ask one question?' Francis said. 'If you already have Mitch and Omar on side to do your dirty work, why on earth did you need Ray?'

'Very simple. He's expendable. And as you've just made all too clear, sometimes you need expendable people. Mitch and Omar will do anything for the right price, but they are not expendable. More to the point, they would not allow themselves to be expendable. Now we really need to go.'

'You haven't got long,' Francis said, deciding to go for it

and play his trump card. 'I phoned one of Fischer's people as we left the Olympiahalle. He knew I was going back to the hotel in a car with you.'

'Did you now?' Nick looked alarmed, despite himself. 'You forget that I'm already at the hotel. A quick, very public drink with my co-manager and my star and I'm on my way to the airport. Come on, Russell.'

'OK,' said the accountant. 'He's all yours, Omar.' But as he turned away from the security guard, he wasn't looking at Nick, he was looking at Francis. There was a slight, mocking smile on his face. In that moment, everything that Francis disliked about the shiny-faced sleazebag rose to the surface. For a moment, he was all set to throw himself on him and damn the consequences. If Omar shot him, so be it.

But then Russell winked.

It wasn't a stagey wink. It was a tiny gesture, barely discernible. But it was there. Unless, in his rising panic, Francis was hallucinating. What did it mean? Was Russell teasing him in his final moments? Was this another ploy to save his own skin? Or was there, in this moment of seeming despair, hope?

'Jonni's image is pretty important to us,' the American was saying. 'I'm sure you get that, Francis. You know he's the biggest artist in the US since the Beatles?'

'Come on, Russ,' said Nick. 'You heard what Francis said about Fischer.'

'Huge,' the accountant went on, regardless. 'Absolutely huge. They love him, those dollar-rich American high school girls. It's funny, isn't it? What makes a British artist big in the States? Why Elton but not Cliff? Why Rod Stewart but not Marc Bolan? Why George Michael but not Robbie Williams? It's a puzzle. But one thing we do know is that a penchant for small boys wouldn't go down well on either side of the Atlantic.'

'I'm sure it wouldn't,' Francis said.

'There was a nasty moment when we had to sue a couple of the British rags a year or so ago, wasn't there, Nick?'

'Russ, we really need to go.'

'For daring to hint at the heinous thing they hinted at when they had no proof. But all was well. They accepted their stories were untrue and paid hefty damages without further publicity. The point being, there's never been any evidence. And unfortunately, that's what Ricky had.'

'In what form?' asked Francis.

'A video,' said Russell.

'OK,' said Francis. Of course there had been something concrete. Hearsay and rumour were never going to be enough. 'So that was it. Of what exactly?'

'What do you think? Bad stuff, I'm afraid. From one of the Cambodian getaways Ricky liked to organise from time to time. The man had no scruples. He had set Jonni up and he had us over a barrel. The story would have been huge – no getting away from it. The end of Jonni.'

'"Cambodian Girl",' said Francis. How stupid he had been not to clock that giveaway

'Exactly,' said Russell.

'Russell,' Nick said. 'We really need to go.'

'And Topaz knew about this video, presumably?' Francis asked.

'Worse than that,' Russell replied, ignoring Nick's waving hands. 'She had a copy. When Ray searched her room, he found it on a memory stick.'

'Why did she even have it?'

'She got it from Ricky. She had some mad plan to blackmail Zak into changing his mind about Frankie Freak's royalties. It was ridiculous; that's such an old bugbear. Frankie settled last year. He was happy enough with the result, even if it wasn't entirely fair. It was Topaz's private obsession that he get total justice. She was a feisty lady and I'm afraid Bobby

Fairhurst told her too many stories when she was growing up.'

'Stories that were true,' Francis said. 'So Adam and Zak were involved in her murder too, were they?'

'No,' Nick cut in. 'They knew about the sex tape, but despite the seriousness of the situation, they were never going to do what needed to be done. I'm sorry to say they were dithering stupidly. Things could have got way out of control.'

'But they knew what you were planning?'

'Sometimes it's easier just to act. Committees are never very effective at making difficult calls. I learned that during my national service back home. We had a few adventures in Zimbabwe that taught me a useful lesson or two – one in particular, up a lonely little *kopje*, a bit like this, actually, though without the temple, where I almost lost my life. Until I decided to act for myself.' With this sudden mention of home his South African accent had strengthened and got harsher, as if his vocal cords were remembering his past too.

And what about Seamus? Francis thought. Had this sex tape been what he and Topaz had been watching on the lampies' bus? It must have been. Surely, as Ricky's great friend, Seamus had been involved? Nick must know about that. So was he, too, about to meet a nasty accident? Certainly, Francis couldn't save him now. Perhaps Nick didn't know. Neither he nor Russell had said anything about him, had they? In this case, as Zak would have said, discretion was the better part of valour.

'So what's going to happen now?' Francis asked. He looked back at Russell, hoping, praying for a second indication that he hadn't imagined that wink, that there was something else going on, that all this extra info was the accountant, PR man or whatever he really was playing for time. Because if he and Nick – and Omar, presumably – had left their phones at the hotel, and his own phone was at the bottom of the river, maybe Francis's call to the Kripo wasn't going to save him after all.

'What's going to happen,' Nick replied, 'is that Russell and I are going to walk at a rapid pace back down the hill and then out of the park and into our car. We will leave Omar here to do his job, and he will follow us in due course in the second car. Mitch will be here soon, with Ray. The scene will be set. Good-bye.' He walked towards Francis and held out his hand.

Francis didn't take it. 'Is this ... really ... worth it?' he asked. He was trying to stay level-headed, but he could hear the desperation in his own voice. A horrid shiver of fear ran down his back. His legs felt as weak as jelly. 'You must be rich enough already, Nick,' he managed, breathless. 'You have ... other acts. How can it be worth ... getting rid of one, two, three people ... for the sake of a secret that is bound to come out one day anyway?'

'That's my call, isn't it?' Nick replied brusquely. 'In any case, it's a bit late to change our plans now.'

'And you think you're going to get away with this? That the Kripo won't work out what's really happened?'

Nick didn't reply. He and Russell turned and, as they did so, Omar turned too. Francis could see the tension in his eyes. He looked slowly and carefully from left and right, a younger and more highly trained feline than his boss, then advanced to the edge of the Monopteros.

'I'll lie to Fischer if you like,' Francis shouted after them, hopelessly. 'We can all gang up on Ray.'

But Nick and Russell were halfway down the slope now, as Omar scoured the bushes at the back of the temple then down the other way into the darkness of the park. Seemingly satis-fied, he turned towards Francis. He took his gun from the holster by his belt. Francis had no idea what type it was, but it was small and neat and silver. Omar reached into his bag and took out a longer black tube that Francis assumed was a silencer. This he screwed to the barrel of the gun, slowly and efficiently.

'Turn around, please, sir,' he said. 'On your knees, if you would.'

Sir! Was he really about to be murdered by a man who addressed him as sir? And what about Ray? Wasn't Omar going to wait? Force the disgraced Jolly to do the deed? Or was that more of Nick's nonsense?

Francis dropped down, as instructed, to the rough stone floor. As his eyes became accustomed to the darkness, he saw that the inside of the dome was a pretty pattern of squares, pale pink and blue. Was this really the last thing he was going to see in his life? Why had he even accepted this stupid commission? Curiosity killed the cat, and he was the cat. Where were the freaking Kripo? They had promised they would keep a close eye on him, that he would remain safe. And what about that wink? Had the bogus accountant just been teasing him? The bastard, he had never trusted him. He stayed as still as possible, staring at the column ahead of him, waiting.

Doric! That was the third style. As if he needed to remember that now. He wondered if Omar was going to keep him like this on the cold concrete until Mitch and Ray appeared, or whether it would all be over sooner. When would the shot come, and what would he feel when it did? Nothing, he imagined. Or would everything slow right down? Would he see his life in slo-mo flashback even as it was taken from him? He was trying to stay calm, but his body had gone into spasms. He was shaking uncontrollably. *For Christ's sake, man, if you're going to do it, get on with it!*

There was a brilliant flash of light, and it was all over.

Or was it?

Because now came an amplified German-accented voice, as if through, God help him, a police megaphone.

'Stay exactly where you are. Drop your weapon, please.'

There was a clang as the gun, presumably, hit the floor. Omar was nothing if not professional.

'Turn around, please, Mr Abdelrahman.'

Francis stayed on his knees, trembling. He didn't, he thought, need to pray any longer. If they knew the name of the security guard, that was good enough for him.

Chapter Twenty-Eight

Francis sat across the table from Russell and clinked glasses. He had decided to take the American to one of his favourite London haunts, the Martini Bar of Green's Hotel in St James's. This was not one of those cocktail bars that was heaving with fashionable humanity; indeed, this weekend evening at 6.30 p.m. there was just one other table occupied in the plush and elegant space, by an attractive blonde and her incongruously meaty, shaven-headed partner. Quite apart from being low-key and discreet, with the sensible injunction that customers switch off their phones before taking a seat, the place had, in Francis's opinion, the best martinis in town. They were not mixed by some funky young gunslinger who might ask your date for a date when your back was turned, but by impeccably dressed gentlemen of a certain age with indefinable European accents. Were they Italian, Montenegran, Albanian? Even if they looked as if they could do away with you with their bare hands in any number of insidious ways, they knew what they were doing with the gin and French.

'Thanks for this, dude,' said the American, grinning as he raised his glass. 'It's good to see you again.'

It was just twelve days after Munich, when Nick had been arrested by an impressive team of armed Kripo officers on the grassy slope below the Monopteros. As Francis had watched Russell running back up to find and comfort him, he had realised that he hadn't imagined that wink: that the dude-meister was not some murderous PR man who was working for the American record company. Or rather, that he was, but he wasn't murderous; he just had a brief to manage the sanctity of Jonni's brand while the star was on tour. Initially, Russell had explained when they had got back to the Mandarin Oriental later that night, he'd gone along with the clean-up plan, but not when he'd realised what had actually happened. From the moment he'd understood that Ricky's death had not been an accident, he'd been quietly on the case. He had worked out Nick's involvement long before Francis had, but had decided to stick close to him, even when the manager had continued to act on his own initiative and have Topaz killed. At that point, deeply shocked, Russell had also got in touch with the Kripo, all the while pretending to Nick that he was continuing to work with him, even if under protest about the murder of the beautiful guitarist.

In order to convince Nick that he was on side, he'd had to get involved with the manager's plan to 'liquidate' Francis. As he'd gone along with Nick's Englischer Garten idea, he had kept the Kripo carefully briefed. Francis's call to Fischer had been unnecessary; the elite police forces of three German states were already primed and ready to go. Omar and Mitch likewise. Nick's statement that they would do anything for the right money had been way off. They were as kosher as any ex-soldiers, and had been working closely with Russell. Francis had not been rescued in the nick of time; he had never been in any danger.

As they sipped their throat-burning cocktails, they discussed the many twists and turns of the case. As Francis had guessed,

Seamus had been involved with Ricky's Cambodian sex tape and Topaz's attempts to get justice for Frankie Freak, but neither Nick, Zak nor Adam had ever realised it: and to minimise collateral damage (as he put it), Russell had kept quiet about that. The press had got hold of a version of the story, but they were way off on the detail, as you'd expect. Nor had any of them worked out what Francis's involvement was, which was exactly as he wanted it to be.

Nor, Russell was glad to report now, had the media got any sniff of anything about Jonni and his deepest, most private inclinations. Now that Ricky was out of the picture, it looked, he said with a dry chuckle, as if Adam would be preaching the merits of celibacy as well as sobriety.

'Is that going to work?' Francis asked. 'Will Jonni really be able to give everything up?'

'We'll have to see. The boy's had a very big shock. And Adam's a fairly unforgiving mentor.'

'So what are you saying? That Jonni's going to get away with it?'

Russell looked mildly taken aback. 'How d'you mean, dude?'

'Whatever he's been up to. In Cambodia or wherever. The video. Is that all just going to be swept under the carpet?'

'Hey, no worries, dude,' the PR man replied. 'As I said, none of the bad stuff is going to be happening any more. He's off the booze, and' – his voice dropped to a whisper – 'he's off the boys. Ha, shame I can't use that, great strapline.'

'Going forward?' said Francis, with quiet amazement. 'Indefinitely?'

'Yeah, going forward. Indefinitely, of course.' Russell held Francis's eye measuredly for a good five seconds, then slowly winked.

'And you're OK with that?'

'I can't afford not to be.'

'And Adam. He's happy?'

'Of course he is. The star is back on track. Everything cleaned up and dealt with.'

'Shame about Nick.'

'Shame indeed about Nick. A wild card. That's a trial that's going to prove a PR challenge, for sure.'

'But won't he want to bring up Jonni … and what he's been up to … in his defence?'

'The ravings of a desperate man. There's no proof of anything. Anywhere. Our testimony will be that he went after Topaz because she was convinced that Jonni had been involved in Ricky's death.'

'Which is more or less true.'

Russell shrugged. 'Is it? There's no proof of that either.'

'So where's the incriminating tape? Eliminated as well?'

'No copies kept by anyone, even in a vault. Sometimes it's wisest just to delete every last pixel of this kind of thing. We have to thank our lucky stars it was never put online, even on the Dark Web.'

'And why was that?'

'Ricky wasn't stupid. He knew the value of what he had.'

'And what about Zak?'

'What about him?'

'I was happy to believe that Adam was truly in the dark about Topaz's murder, but Zak too? Really?'

'For sure. Nick acted on his own.'

'You don't think Zak had any idea what was going on? Even though he was actually out there on tour, and it was his dark secret that Topaz wanted justice for?'

'Here's the thing, dude: the Frankie Freak story is more about reputation than money, isn't it? I doubt "The Love That Tells Me" earns very much these days, even if Jonni does sing it at every gig.'

'So Zak would have been happy to let Topaz trash his reputation?'

'Her word against his. Frankie already had his day in court. Or rather, he didn't. But he had his chance. Silly girl, she was way off beam. On a total hiding to nothing, in my opinion. You know, the funny thing is about someone like Zak, people don't want to think badly of them. They love his songs, his films, his cheeses, his net-zero castle, his fucking tithe.' Russell laughed. 'I'm afraid the hoi polloi simply wouldn't want to believe the sorry truth.'

'And for all Nick said about committees, you really don't think that he would have spoken to Zak? At all? Before going ahead and killing her?'

Russell shrugged. 'If he did, I certainly didn't know about it.'

'But you didn't know about it anyway. Or so you said.'

'I didn't. Hand on heart, Francis. I absolutely didn't.'

'I believe you, Russell. I've told you that. As for Jonni,' Francis went on, 'what about the rest of his past? Other "bad stuff" that happened, videoed or not?'

'The past, don't they say, is another country. Probably another country in the Far East, if I was to hazard a guess.' The PR man chuckled. 'Loosen up, dude. I mean, I'm certainly not one to condone in any way what Jonni may or may not have got up to, under Ricky's terrible influence, of course, but this kind of behaviour isn't that far out of line, is it? In the wild world of rock 'n' roll.'

'Even in this day and age?'

'What can I say? When you get stars as talented and beautiful and popular as Jonni … you know, maybe there are different rules.'

'Should there be, though?'

'That's the million-dollar question. You don't often hear about the handsome guy being pursued for abuse, do you, even now? Especially not the handsome, talented guy. It's Harvey Weinstein, not David Bowie, isn't it? Jeffrey Epstein, not one of those fine old rockers that everyone knows about. And maybe that's right, dude, because maybe ultimately that's what it's all about. Consensuality. Isn't that it?'

'But how consensual is a thirteen-year-old?'

Russell was giving him the nod of one who got the point but who wasn't, in the end, going to make a big issue out of it. 'Personally speaking,' he replied, almost tetchily, 'I think if Jonni's learned his lesson and moved on, we can cut him a bit of slack.'

'Can we? By what right, exactly?'

'Francis! Chill, man. I thought we were having a friendly drink.'

'We are. I'm just interested to find out whether you think that you were guilty of a charge of conspiring. Covering up illicit acts against minors.'

'Dude.' Russell seemed genuinely baffled by the earnestness in Francis's tone.

'Because that's what this is, isn't it?'

'Loosen up, man. I thought this was one country where you understood this kind of thing. It's kind of normal behaviour in those private schools of yours, isn't it?'

'Not any more, no.'

'Boys will be boys. They know what they're doing, the ones that go in for this kind of stuff.'

'Do they?'

'Of course they do. It's one thing I've always actually thought…' The accountant leant forward and dropped his voice. 'Gay men. You know, it's not something they learn, is it? It's something they're born with. So, what's the problem if they start on what they want to do a bit earlier?'

'So, what are you saying? If they're underage, that's OK?'

'Age is just a number, dude.'

'And that number can be – what? Thirteen, twelve, eleven, seven? Where do you draw the line?'

The accountant shrugged, in worldly fashion. 'You've travelled, man. Bangkok, Cambodia, Morocco. I'm not trying to put the world to rights, but it's no big deal in these places. I mean, Christ, I've spent time in girly bars in Patpong. Some of those chicks are pretty young, let's face it. But when you're out there, it's a different vibe…'

Francis sat back and glanced at his watch. It was time. He looked across the bar and nodded at the couple sitting on the other side. DCI Peter Cummings and Superintendent Karyn Reed got to their feet as one and came over to Francis and Russell's table.

'Russell Miller,' the DCI intoned, 'I am arresting you on suspicion of conspiracy to cover up one act of statutory rape and three acts of child sexual abuse in the United Kingdom and abroad. You do not have to say anything, but it may harm your defence if you do not mention when questioned something which you later rely on in court–'

'For fuck's sake!' the American cut in, looking aghast at Francis. 'What kind of a stitch-up is this?'

'It's the kind of stitch-up that requires these,' said the superintendent, producing a pair of handcuffs.

After they had restrained the outraged PR man, and got him to his feet and led him out of the bar to the waiting police van, Francis sat back and switched off the hidden tape machine that had been recording their conversation through a tiny microphone on his lapel. Then he took a long, slow swig of his martini. On one level, he felt bad. In Munich, the American had saved him, and how had he returned the favour? But there was no way Francis could go along with the cover-up that Russell and Adam and Zak seemed to think was acceptable for a star like Jonni. After Nick's arrest, once Francis had told Erster Polizeihauptkommissar Fischer and his team exactly why Topaz had been killed, the plan had quickly been hatched to pull in, not just Jonni, but the members of his entourage who had thought that pop stars were somehow above the law. But with the tour moving rapidly from state to state and jurisdiction to jurisdiction, and with the incredibly high profile of the main offender, it had seemed wisest to wait for everyone to be back home in the UK before any arrests were made. These would obviously be simultaneous.

Francis pulled out his mobile. There was nothing yet on his Apple News app. But how quickly the informal citizen's journalism moved these days. #Jonni K arrest was already up there on X/Twitter, if it wasn't yet trending. A glance at the relevant feed showed a string of photos of the shocked star being led away from his lovely mansion in Highgate. Ditto Adam in Holland Park, and Zak at picturesque Glenveray Castle near Inverness.

By the end of the day, the takedown would have started. Long before any legal process, the self-appointed arbiters of justice and decency on social media would have started to scream their outrage. The agents and publishers and record companies and charities would have begun their disassociation with the assumed guilty ones. The pundits would be shocked, of course, hands over their mouths as they smirked and gossiped away from the camera. Some of them, doubtless, would always have known. Or suspected. Other prejudices would kick in. Jonni's brave and pioneering work with gender-fluidity would be trashed. The heinous trope that gay men were one step away from paedos would be repeated, then angrily refuted. The world would allow itself a long, satisfying gloat at the disgrace of these latest tainted idols, reassured that they themselves were not of that celebrated ilk, merely nameless and nondescript individuals who were allowed to worship stars if they wished, but were immune from any retribution themselves when those glorious celestial bodies crashed to earth. For who could cancel a nonentity?

So Francis mused, as for a confused, post-martini minute or two he wondered if he had made the right call. Of course he had! Humans wanted their gods, naturally: they always had, but that didn't mean those gods could behave like Zeus, did it? Come on, let's face it, those who live by the media die by the media.

Francis got to his feet and followed the police and their charge out of the bar into the strobe lights of the press flashbulbs.

And who on earth had arranged those?

THE END

The Band

Jonni K — The Performer

Simon Boles — Musical Director/Keyboards
Vanko Angelov — Guitar
Topaz Brown — Bass guitar
Steve 'Scally' Gouldson — Drums
Susannah 'Suzi' Chalfont — Backing vocals
Thelma James — Backing vocals

Nick Fourie — Manager
Adam Ainslie — Manager
Charmaine Cassidy — Management

Bernard 'Bernie' Beamish — Tour Manager
Russell Miller — Tour Accountant

Gary 'Mitch' Mitchison — Security
Omar Abdelrahman — Security

Selected Crew

Bruce 'Pants' Pantlin — Production Manager
Laurent Bisset — Wardrobe
Seamus O'Sullivan — Stage Manager
Kylie Anderson — Creative Director/Lighting Designer
Mel Dogood — Guitar tech
Ted Stewart — Drum tech
Ricky Fisher — Keyboard tech
Garry Phipps — Lighting crew chief (aka the Gaffer)
Darius Darke — Head chef
Jemima Blundell — Caterer
Flo Silverbird — Caterer
Ray 'Jolly' Rogerson — Band/crew bus driver
Gideon 'OJ' Owusu — Band/crew bus driver
Steve 'Dolly' Parton — Band bus driver
Bryn 'Taff' Thomas — Crew bus driver
George 'Ronnie' Barker — Crew bus driver
Edmund 'Dead Ed' Cheeseacre — Security

Plus assorted riggers, sound engineers, carpenters, projectionists and merchandise salesmen.

Also by Mark McCrum

Fiction
The Francis Meadowes Mysteries

The Festival Murders

Cruising to Murder

Murder Your Darlings

Ghosted

Non-fiction

Happy Sad Land

No Worries

The Craic

Castaway

Robbie Williams: Somebody Someday

Going Dutch In Beijing

Walking With The Wounded

Author's note

Vanko's spiel about pop stars and underage groupies at the end of Chapter 25 is based on many previously published and broadcast accounts. Priscilla Presley (née Beaulieu) met Elvis at a party in Germany on 13 September 1959, when she was fourteen and he twenty-four. In 1985, Priscilla wrote for *People* magazine about their parting six months later, when he returned to the US in March 1960: 'We were lying on his bed, our arms around each other. I was in a state of complete despair. Would I ever see him again, be in his arms the way I had been nearly every night for the past six months?' (She had begged him, she said, to consummate their relationship that night, but he had refused.) Lori Mattix (aka Maddox, aka Lightning) gave an interview to the magazine *Thrillist* in 2015 in which she made allegations of being involved in underage sexual relations with David Bowie and Jimmy Page, among others. Features in the *Guardian* in 2018 and *Rolling Stone* in 2019 repeated Mattix's story, and Lori's association with Page as a young teenager is detailed at length in *Hammer of the Gods* by Steven Davis and briefly mentioned in *I'm With the Band: Confessions of a Groupie*, by Pamela des Barres. Page has never denied these stories, though he expressed irritation that they had been raised, in a piece in *Uncut* in 2015. Fellow band member Robert Plant's song 'Sick Again' includes lines about a young girl in what he calls 'the city of lies' who has yet to reach sixteen, which Led Zeppelin biographers have related to Lori, though Plant insisted the description was general.

Bill Wyman met Mandy Smith at the BPI Awards in 1984, when she was thirteen and he forty-seven. She later alleged, in the Danish national newspaper *Berlingske* and elsewhere, that they had slept together when she was fourteen, but there was no public mention of any relationship until she was sixteen, the legal age of consent in the UK. The couple married in 1989 when she was eighteen, and divorced a couple of years later. In 2013, Wyman revealed that he had volunteered to be interviewed by police about his relationship with Smith, but the police chose not to pursue it. In 2010, Smith called for the age of consent in the UK to be raised from sixteen to eighteen, saying: 'People will find that odd coming from me. But I think I do know what I'm talking about here. You are still a child – even at sixteen. You can never get that part of your life, your childhood, back. I never could.'

Iggy Pop allegedly slept with Sable Starr when she was thirteen, as described in the first line of the original lyrics of his song 'Look Away': though, as Lucy Mangan pointed out in a piece in the *Guardian* in 2021, reviewing *Look Away*, the Sky documentary on the issue of teenage 'baby groupies', 'words are not deeds, of course'.

Acknowledgements

Though this novel is a work of pure fantasy, I remain grateful to all those musicians and others in the industry who made me welcome and shared their stories with me on various writing assignments over the years.

Thanks also to all those who read and commented on my early drafts and answered questions for me: Alice Thompson, ex Woodentops and novelist of note, who gave me the perspective of a genuine pop star; Dylan Rippon, for his wide knowledge of the music scene and some great band names; and Nigel Hoyle, for coming up with 'Guitarmaggedon'. Toni Harvey encouraged me and had some useful crits, as did seasoned tourer Liam Lever, particularly about brown M&Ms on the rider. Former BBC sound engineer Richard Cobourne went beyond the call of duty with his detailed explanations of how foot pedals, guitars and microphones might be sabotaged, quite apart from his more general take on touring. Sally Bevan put me straight on the difference between recording and publishing royalties. Michelle Rey corrected my German and went out of her way to video the Englischer Garten for me, while giving me the perspective of a young fan and a German simultaneously.

Ben Craib, Katrin MacGibbon, Stephanie Cross, Duncan Minshull, Linda Hughes and Jackie Nelson added the helpful insights of general readers.

My agents Jamie Maclean and Lisa Moylett encouraged me and did the deals, while Bloodhound Books have been superb in getting the Francis Meadowes series up and running, in particular my subtle but beady editor Abbie Rutherford.

Finally, thanks to my wife, Jo, who offered other constructive crits and insights, quite apart from sustaining me while I was writing.

A note from the publisher

Thank you for reading this book. If you enjoyed it please do consider leaving a review on Amazon to help others find it too.

We hate typos. All of our books have been rigorously edited and proofread, but sometimes mistakes do slip through. If you have spotted a typo, please do let us know and we can get it amended within hours.

info@bloodhoundbooks.com

Milton Keynes UK
Ingram Content Group UK Ltd.
UKHW040919020224
437147UK00004B/175